THE AVO

Kathleen E. Woodiwiss, Johanna Lindsey, Laurie McBain, Shirlee Busbee...these are just a few of the romance superstars that Avon Books has been proud to present in the past.

Since 1982, Avon has been continuing a different sort of romance tradition—a program that has been launching new writers of exceptional promise. Called "The Avon Romance," these books are distinguished by a ribbon motif on the front cover—in fact, you readers quickly discovered them and dubbed them "the ribbon books"!

Month after month, "The Avon Romance" has continued to deliver the best in historical romance, offering sensual, exciting stories by new writers (and some favorite repeats!) *without* the predictable characters and plots of formula romances.

"The Avon Romance." Our promise of superior, unforgettable historical romance...month after dazzling month!

LINDA LANG BARTELL

BRIANNA

AVON
PUBLISHERS OF BARD, CAMELOT, DISCUS AND FLARE BOOKS

AVON BOOKS
A division of
The Hearst Corporation
1790 Broadway
New York, New York 10019

First Avon Printing, May 1986

AVON TRADEMARK REG. U. S. PAT. OFF. AND IN
OTHER COUNTRIES, MARCA REGISTRADA, HECHO EN
U. S. A.

Printed in the U. S. A.

K-R 10 9 8 7 6 5 4 3 2 1

To Jennifer Blake,
whose writing has been an inspiration;
and to Julia Grice,
who taught me to rise to the challenge

I wish to extend my heartfelt thanks to the members of the Greater Detroit Chapter of Romance Writers of America for their support and belief in *Brianna* from the very first—and especially Debby Chrisman for all her help and guidance. Also, my family and friends for their encouragement and faith in me; my agent, Ellen Levine, for her efforts on my behalf; and my editor, Carin Cohen, who is as skilled in her editorial ability as she is warm and caring.

And my special love and gratitude to my husband, Bob, for his support from day one.

PROLOGUE

October, A.D. 1049

"Your word—I beseech you, Robert. *Give me your word!*"
came the weak but fierce whisper.

A storm raged outside the well-appointed wooden sleeping
bower; rain slashed against the walls and lightning streaked
the sky, piercing the stygian darkness with startling clarity at
erratic intervals.

And a storm raged within the breast of the tall man standing
over the bed illuminated by several brightly burning braziers
that revealed the small figure of his wife swathed in blankets.
Even now, after a long and difficult birth, with much loss of
blood and hemorrhaging that the midwife could not stop, her
haunting loveliness could not be denied. Her sunken eyes clung
to his with an unbelievable tenacity as she waited for him to
answer her desperate plea.

His dark eyes met hers, and she could read the cold fury in
them. *He knows,* she thought in growing fear, *and he will not
promise now.*

But the eyes that held hers also revealed a flicker of something Alicia vaguely recognized. Could it be the faint stirrings
of love in the cold ashes of his passion for her; love for the
beautiful, vivacious girl she had been when she had first captured his heart?

Then maybe there was hope.

She could sense something in his attitude as he stared down at her. His movements were tense, almost jerky, as he tore his gaze from her pale countenance and strode over to the cradle. He regarded the tiny human being sleeping so peacefully as its mother's lifeblood ebbed, and his stiff posture made it perfectly clear to Alicia that he had known all along that she had been carrying another man's child.

Alicia sighed resignedly. He had thought her a fool—gullible, he had said, and naïve where love was concerned. Surely she knew that it was a man's prerogative to take his pleasures where they were offered? Despite the bonds of matrimony. His inconstancy had nothing to do with her. It was just that no one woman could keep a man satisfied. Or so he had said.

He had shrugged off her disillusionment, telling her she could not have all his attention—all of *him*. So Alicia, finding in her marriage no resemblance whatsoever to the devotion and fidelity practiced by her own loving parents, had found love elsewhere, among the wealthy and titled men who surrounded Edward the Confessor.

Oh, yes, she thought tiredly. She had attracted the attention of many an all-too-eager swain, innocently and unwittingly. And many times she had been at court alone while Robert was away on official business for his lord, the powerful Godwin, Earl of Wessex.

With an effort she turned her head slightly to look at him again. His fists were clenched. Was he resisting an urge to strangle the precious life from the babe? Her mind recoiled with horror at her suspicion, and she forced herself to continue her train of thought.

Surely he had noticed her quiet withdrawal from him when she had discovered his infidelities. He did nothing to prevent her love from being extinguished slowly like the last flickerings of a worn-down candle. She could vividly remember her lack of spirit, her wistfulness.

And she could also remember with startling clarity the moment her spirit began to return—her cheeks blooming with color from warm blushes, her steps light and buoyant, as if a great burden had been lifted from her. And Robert had commented on it when he had returned to court one time from an extended absence. Did he guess? He must have, for he was no fool.

God, help me, she prayed fervently. *Let him believe that all babes have hair and eyes of a different hue at birth than that which comes later.* For if he took the raven fuzz on the fragile head to be the legacy from someone else, all was lost. Alicia noticed the child's eyes held a hint of the blue-green of her own, which, long ago, Robert had said was the exact shade of the ever-changing sea. But the hair was most certainly not the soft honey color of hers or the chestnut hue of Robert's.

She stirred softly in the richly adorned bed and thought of the child's father. Guillaume. The handsome and gentle Norman had won her heart in a way Robert never had. He had been so respectful of her married state, even as his warm topaz eyes had spoken of a burgeoning love. As Robert's behavior drove her further into the depths of despair, she found herself drawn more and more to Guillaume. He was one of the many Normans with whom the King surrounded himself, and as he listened to her disillusionment with Robert, their love began to take form. Slowly, so fragile, so unintentional at first—at least on her part—for she could not face the fact that she was beginning to follow the very course of action that had alienated her from her husband.

And now she knew she was dying, her strength draining away like the receding tide of the sea. She had to obtain Robert's promise to raise the child as his own. For a girl had no protection other than her family. A boy—even an illegitimate one—could always fend for himself. It was of the utmost importance that Robert accept the child. Guillaume did not know, for she had kept away from Edward's court when she suspected she carried the Norman's babe. She was afraid that Guillaume would insist she go to Normandy with him—even though wed to another. And that was impossible. She would not have been able to hold her head up. She had to exact a promise from Robert—while she was physically able. She had to—

Guillaume! Guillaume! her heart cried in silent anguish. What will happen to our child? What will—

Her eyes refused to open and she felt as if she were weighted down to the soft bed. Her senses began to betray her, for not only did her eyelids fail to obey the command to open, but the hiss and crackle of the fire receded until an unnatural quiet washed over her. Her pale lips formed the name *Guillaume*, but no sound issued forth.

And then she knew no more.

CHAPTER 1

"Brianna, wake up! Reverend Mother wishes to see you. *Brianna!*" came the urgent whisper of Wilfreda, one of the postulants.

Brianna sat up in the semidarkness, rubbing her sleep-laden eyes. "Wha-what? Oh, Wilfreda." She yawned in protest. "Reverend Mother wishes to see me?"

"Aye, Brianna. Hurry!"

She stumbled out of her nest of warm covers on the hard pallet in her cell and hurriedly performed her ablutions in the icy cold water in the small washbasin. Moments later she stood in the presence of the Abbess, wondering what the good woman could want.

"Good morningtide, Reverend Mother," Brianna greeted softly.

"Good morningtide to you, child. Please sit." She motioned to a plain, straight-backed chair near her desk. "I have a matter to discuss with you that concerns your future."

Her smooth, pale brow creased in puzzlement as Brianna did as she was bidden. The Abbess noticed for the hundredth time the unconscious grace that characterized the girl's every movement. With her long ebony tresses, alabaster skin and large aquamarine eyes, she was quite a beauty.

"Do you remember your father, Brianna?" the Abbess asked gently as she came to stand before her.

"Nay, Reverend Mother. Only a shadow of a face and a name—Robert." She had never revealed her curiosity con-

5

cerning her real family, having somehow sensed that it was not a subject easily broached. If the Reverend Mother had wished her to know more, she most certainly would have enlightened her.

The older woman sighed and then spoke once more. "Your father, Thane Robert, took you from the home of Sven and Gytha and gave you into my care when you were no more than five years of age. He, for reasons known only to him, found your presence . . . painful. I suspect 'twas because you reminded him too much of the wife he had loved and lost." *God forgive me,* she prayed silently, *for the lie that has crossed my lips.* "Thane Robert entrusted me with the decision of whether to keep you here and allow you to become one of us or to permit you to marry."

Brianna's head snapped up and her blue-green eyes were wide with shock. "You surely will bid me stay and join the order," she said in a low, strained voice.

The Abbess gently patted her on the shoulder—a gesture that went all but unnoticed, so keen was Brianna's desire to hear the answer she sought.

"My child, you were made to be a wife and mother. It is written in your every gesture, your deep capacity to love those around you—"

"But, Reverend Mother," she interrupted in her sudden panic, "to *marry?* I know naught of men!"

The gentle Abbess smiled and, overlooking her interruption with loving tolerance and understanding, reassured her. "They are but God's creatures, Brianna, as are we, and what you do not know you will learn."

Brianna's shoulders sagged. She looked down at her hands once more and in her misery barely noticed that the Abbess was speaking again.

" . . . that you would be a blessing to any man, for you can read and write and cipher. Who am I to make the decision for you when you have known naught but a cloistered life here?"

A hot tear splashed onto the back of one of Brianna's tightly clasped hands, and the good nun placed her fingers under the delicate chin and lifted it to gaze down into the pain-filled eyes. "And you can always return to us, my child, should you decide that it is not to be.

"Now." She began pacing the floor of the modest chamber, a thoughtful look on her features. "I have a nephew—the only son of my late brother—in a small village just half a day's ride south of here. He is a good and kind lad, only a little older than yourself. His father left him a homestead and a good-sized parcel of land on the road passing out of the village on the east side. He has agreed to take you to wife, my dear, and rest assured that I have spoken to him and have every confidence that he will make you a good and loving husband."

Brianna could only stammer, "When . . . when will I . . ."

"On the morrow you will turn seventeen. In a sennight you will leave for Derford, where you and Gilbert will live. 'Tis a lovely little village not too far from the sea and about a day's ride west of Hastings." She returned to stand before Brianna and once again sought to reassure her gently. " 'Tis best for you, Brianna, believe me, and you will learn to love Gilbert. I feel certain that 'tis God's will, my daughter, and all will turn out for the best. You must have faith in my judgment."

Faith in my judgment, faith in my judgment . . .

The Abbess' words echoed over and over in Brianna's mind—a litany of doom to her numb emotions. She felt betrayed, thrown to the capricious whims of fate. God's will, indeed! she thought bitterly, and then was instantly contrite. Had not the Reverend Mother been like a real mother to her all this time? Had she not shown Brianna love and kindness?

But her thoughts did little to boost her flagging spirits or calm her tense nerves as she clutched the sides of the swaying cart that steadily carried her ever closer to her destination. She tried to make her mind a blank to hold her fears at bay, and when that failed she began to make hesitant conversation with the wizened old man who drove the vehicle.

" 'Tis . . . 'tis a beautiful day, would you not agree, er—?"

The man threw her a lopsided grin, revealing several missing teeth. But his eyes sparkled beneath the bushy brows. "Kerwick," he supplied readily, "and indeed it is."

"And I am called Brianna," she told him shyly. Her reservations about speaking with a strange man were quickly overridden by her interest in his next words.

"Perhaps 'tis God's blessing on King Harold's victory at Stamford Bridge a fortnight past."

"Yes, we all knew—at the abbey, that is—that King Harold defeated Hardrada of Norway." She suddenly felt an inexplicable curiosity to discover more about what was happening in the outside world of which she had suddenly become a part.

"Harold can be proud of the way the fyrd rallied round him in time of such need. 'Twas no small thing, I can tell you, to have won the love and allegiance of so many of his subjects in the short time he has been king."

Brianna nodded in agreement, moved by the way the English rallied around the man who many felt had no real claim to the throne except the wish of a dying Edward the Confessor.

"God be praised for giving us Harold!" he continued, breaking into her thoughts. "Now that Hardrada is dead and William of Normandy never even showed his face to challenge Harold's right to the English throne, mayhap we can settle down for a peaceful winter."

Brianna chewed her lower lip thoughtfully. She was rapidly discovering an insatiable desire to know more of the dispute between William, Duke of Normandy, and Harold Godwinson, the new King of England. And so as they lurched and jolted their way to Derford, Brianna almost completely forgot her reason for the short journey as she plied the surprisingly knowledgeable Kerwick with a barrage of questions.

* * *

As they rode through Derford, Brianna could not help but notice Kerwick's growing uneasiness.

"Is aught amiss?" she questioned gently.

"Aye, but I cannot fathom what it be. Stamford Bridge is over, yet there is excitement and . . . tension in the air. But why? It bodes ill."

As they approached the last homestead on the far side of the village, Brianna's fears began to prick at her once more; her curiosity and her feeling of foreboding were equally strong.

Two figures waited in front of the hall, talking and gesturing toward men, young and old, who were walking or riding shaggy English ponies on the very road that had brought Brianna and Kerwick into the village.

"If I didn't know better, I would say 'tis a calling up of the fyrd once more," Kerwick mused aloud. "And that can only mean one thing."

Brianna said nothing, for she knew what it meant after talking to the man for so many hours about the threat from across the Channel. And her thoughts were very much on the two men still waiting before what she assumed was Gilbert's home. One of them wore the robes of a priest, and the other in all probability was Gilbert himself.

He was tall and sturdily built, with a shock of unruly brown hair. From her vantage point he was not unpleasant to look upon, and Brianna could only hope that Abbess Marie had been correct when she had said goodness and kindness were among the traits possessed by her brother's son. The nun had said nothing about his physical looks, and Brianna felt an enormous flood of relief wash over her at this added boon.

But as the cart came to a halt close to the two men, the last of her fears concerning Gilbert's disposition were put to rest. For, upon recognizing Kerwick, Gilbert left the priest and strode up to the wagon, kind brown eyes on Brianna, a warm smile lighting up his attractive features.

"My thanks, Kerwick," he said sincerely to the man, his eyes still on Brianna. "And you must be Brianna."

Brianna slowly relaxed the death grip she had on the side of the cart and gave him a hesitant smile. "I am. And you are Gilbert?" she ascertained shyly.

"Aye. My aunt did not exaggerate your beauty, if I may be so forward as to say so."

A slow blush crept up her cheeks at the unexpected compliment. She had never had reason, in the simple, unaffected life at the abbey, to dwell upon or even take much interest in her looks. She could only look down at her hands as her embarrassment left her tongue-tied.

Kerwick gave a warning frown to Gilbert, as if to remind him of where the girl had come from, and the younger man began to apologize at once. "Forgive me, Brianna, for my boldness. I—"

"Ahem." The priest had silently come up behind Gilbert. "My son, I am aware of the importance of the young woman's arrival, but other serious matters are afoot as well." All three people turned to him, and a shadow suddenly passed over Gilbert's face, for the priest had brought him back to reality and the immediate problem.

Brianna noted the intense look in the priest's eyes, the sudden grimness on Gilbert's face and the expectancy written across Kerwick's.

"William of Normandy has landed at Pevensey and burned and looted his way around the harbor to Hastings."

"Nay!" the old man breathed as Brianna stifled a cry of dismay.

"Aye. For three months King Harold waited for him fully prepared, and nothing came to pass. Now, after Stamford Bridge, he is come."

"The Norman has the devil's own luck," growled Kerwick. "He can have known naught of the fighting up north."

"And even if he had, how could he have controlled the Channel winds to aid him at the precise time when the fyrd of the northern shires was licking its wounds?'' added a suddenly angry Gilbert.

"There is no way he could have known. 'Twas pure luck, for he cannot have had God's blessing on this devil-spawned mission to seize the English throne,'' Father Simon answered vehemently. ''The fyrd in the south has been called up once more and every man between the ages of twelve and sixty is to meet at Caldbec Hill, just northwest of Hastings, with all haste.''

Gilbert's eyes suddenly were drawn back to Brianna, who was waiting silently during this exchange. "Let me help you down, Brianna. You must be stiff as a plank,'' he said with concern. His hand was warm and strong as he held hers. ''This is Father Simon, Brianna, and he is to wed us this day before I depart.''

Brianna nodded politely to the priest and tried to hide her confusion over Gilbert's words. But the observant Father Simon kindly explained, ''Gilbert is needed to fight, child, and he can only remain here in Derford long enough to wed you. You can understand, I trust, the unusual circumstances. Gilbert did not want to leave you alone and unwed.''

"Aye, Brianna. 'Twould be unseemly if you were to stay in my home without benefit of marriage, and I saw no reason for you to do so. I regret—''

"Do not speak of regret, Gilbert,'' Brianna intervened firmly. "Harold and England need you. I can wait as long as need be.'' She flashed him a shy but gracious smile that almost made him wish he did not have to leave, despite the urgency of the situation. He felt lost in the blue-green depths of her eyes, and his hand involuntarily tightened on hers.

"Why don't you take Brianna inside and acquaint her with her new home?'' interrupted Father Simon. "Then you can meet me at the church for the ceremony before you leave.''

Kerwick politely took his leave, Father Simon departed for the church and Gilbert and Brianna went inside the main hall of the homestead to get acquainted as best they could in the fragment of time left to them.

Brianna slept fitfully, tossing restlessly as her dreams became haunted by imagined battle scenes: men fighting and killing one another, grunting with exertion, bellowing in anger, screaming in pain. The clang of metal against metal, the thud of weapon against bone, the sight of razor-sharp edges cutting into unresisting flesh—

She sat up abruptly, her hands over her ears, shutting out the horribly realistic sounds, the gruesome images. "Nay," she whispered, "nay! He lives, I know he lives! He must! Am I wed only to be widowed before knowing aught of my husband?" She uncovered her ears and opened her eyes. In the semigloom of her sleeping bower, she perceived it was early morning. She dressed hurriedly in the penetrating chill and made her way from the sleeping house, a smaller, separate structure, to the main building that served as kitchen, eating hall and general living quarters.

After lighting a small fire in the hearth, she fixed a simple breakfast of milk, bread and cheese. She ate quickly and went to milk the cow, thankful for the numerous tasks she had to perform which, to some small degree, helped occupy her thoughts. For Gilbert was a villein—a cut above the peasant, or cottar—and he owed much to Wulfric, the thane who allowed him to farm his twenty acres. Gilbert's parents had only recently died and, with no brothers or sisters to help out, the entire load of caring for the homestead and fulfilling his obligations to his thane was now upon Gilbert's shoulders. Brianna marveled at her husband's strength as she dreamed of his return.

Muffled shouting from a distance broke into her reverie, and she bolted from the milking stool and rushed outside, pulling her mantle closer about her in the absence of the warmth from the cow's body. She reached the road and stood in the weak, late-morning sun, appalled at the sight she beheld.

Small groups of men and lone figures here and there were limping and staggering along the dirt road coming into town from the east. Many wore ragged, makeshift bandages, caked with dirt and dried blood, and some were helped along and even carried on crude litters by their comrades, or draped across an occasional pony.

Brianna's fists clenched as her eyes sought Gilbert. She could only stand frozen, searching the faces until her head ached from the effort and the terror that swept through her each time he was not among the figures rounding the bend in the road.

And then she spotted a lone, familiar form limping toward her. Kerwick!

"Kerwick!" she cried, closing the distance between them in seconds. "Kerwick!" She put an arm under his elbow in support. His face was pale and she could see fresh blood on a bandage above his knee.

"Come inside, Kerwick, and I will tend you—"

"Nay, girl. My sons"—he motioned to the two young men following close behind—"can get me home to my wife. Gilbert?" he questioned in a tired but concerned voice. "Has he returned, Brianna?"

"N-nay! But surely you know where he is? Surely—"

"I have not seen him since we were well into battle. I thought mayhap he escaped with his life and returned to you." His voice faded with his words, and he shook his head dispiritedly. "He must be—"

"Nay, Kerwick! Do not say it or 'twill be so. I must go—" Her eyes went to the stragglers, whose numbers had dwindled. "I fear the thought of not knowing more than I fear the truth, whatever it may be."

"Brianna!" He grasped her by the shoulders and gave her a light shake as if to dispel the sudden look of determination in her eyes. "Brianna, hear me! 'Tis folly to even *think* of searching for him. If he lives, he will return. The Bastard took no prisoners, but rather allowed the survivors to flee. These are rough men, the devil's men! You cannot go *there!* The battlefield is strewn with corpses and the earth red with blood! 'Tis no place for any Anglo-Saxon now—and especially a woman!''

She eyed his blood-soaked bandage and then the injuries of his two older sons. ''Let us waste no more time with useless talk. Go quickly to your wife before you bleed to death, Kerwick.''

''You must promise that you will not—''

''I give you no promises, Kerwick. Gilbert may lie dying somewhere for want of attention, and 'tis my duty to try to find and help him.''

''And what if you cannot?''

But Brianna had already turned and was heading for the main hall with purposeful steps.

''Father, you cannot mean to let her go!'' exclaimed Edwin, Kerwick's eldest.

''What can I truly do, my son?'' he asked wearily, his eyes still on her retreating form. He could only pray that she would not end up fair game for the Normans.

CHAPTER 2

The shaggy pony continued eastward, its head drooping wearily as it struggled to maintain the slow but steady pace. The girl who sat numbly on its back huddled into her thick woolen mantle and gazed up at the stars twinkling in the velvet black sky. It was such a peaceful time—the darkest hour just before the dawn—and Brianna tried to think of pleasant things, lest her fears creep up on her and sap her determination.

Brianna could almost feel Gilbert's warm, firm hand over hers as they stood side by side in the small village church repeating their vows. She could easily envision having Gilbert's children, learning to love him, working side by side with him. Reverend Mother had been right, for the prospect of being the wife of a good man and eventually a mother appealed to her more than the cloistered life of a nun.

Brianna had often wandered freely about the fields and forests around the abbey, and now she knew why the Reverend Mother had given her such license. The nun must have known from the start that Brianna would one day need more than what life at the abbey could offer. Though she had tried to curb her temper and maintain a modest and calm demeanor, Brianna had always been plagued by a persistent and embarrassing stubborn streak, a flash of temper that appeared in the striking blue-green eyes all too frequently. She possessed an undeniable determination to take things into her own hands rather than merely allow them to be shaped by divine will.

And so she had come here. If only she could find Gilbert! If only he were still—

Of course he is still alive! There were men returning along this very road, so it was possible she could meet Gilbert thusly, before she reached— Her mind shied away from even the name of where the battle had taken place. It was evident from the faces and attitudes of the men she saw that the victory had gone to the Normans. Brianna suddenly felt a sense of grim foreboding close in on her. Up till now she had been so concerned with Gilbert's fate that she hadn't given much thought to that of England's. If the Normans overran England—if no one could succeed in halting their invasion—what then?

The frosty dew melted slowly under the weak October sun. Brianna scarcely felt its meager warmth as she neared the site where Harold of England had faced the Bastard from Normandy.

She passed over Caldbec Hill and under the boughs of the gnarled, ancient apple tree that had been the meeting point for Harold's ill-fated army. Farther on she halted and stared at the scene before her, so shocked that at first she did not even notice several mounted men riding toward her.

William had camped on the far side of the ridge Harold had defended in the marshy valley. The stench was unbelievable and death seemed to reach out everywhere; she could only stare in horror at the heaps of English corpses stripped of everything of value. And unburied. Their weapons, chain mail and clothing were nowhere in evidence. Only naked dead men, eyes staring blankly heavenward, and dismembered limbs, heads and—

Brianna closed her eyes as she swayed on the pony's back, darkness threatening to engulf her as she clung to its shaggy mane.

A rough masculine voice brought her out of the clutches of shock. "Well, what have we here?" the man asked in French. "So this miserable place does have some comely wenches."

A hand reached out and roughly pulled the covering off her head, exposing her dark, lustrous tresses.

She turned narrowed eyes to the one who had snatched her headpiece. "Do not touch me, you—you Norman filth!" she spat.

He looked as if he would strike her for a moment as his features turned dark with annoyance. One of his companions chuckled. "So you have finally met a woman who does not cower at the sight of your ugly face, Hugh!"

Ignoring him, the Breton continued. "Spare me your insults, English vixen, for I am no Norman but a Breton. However"—he leaned toward her conspiratorially as he gestured at the others—"these unfortunates *are* Normans—although not necessarily deserving of the title you so readily bestow upon them."

Their amusement spurred Brianna's ire. How could they laugh while surrounded by such carnage?

". . . some diversion, *chérie?*" the Breton was asking in a cajoling tone.

Innocent though she was, she could not mistake the tone of his voice or the leer on his face. His companions moved in closer, and in her panic Brianna could only think irrelevantly that she had never seen such large horses. Huge and fierce-looking, they towered over her own mount.

In one fleeting moment she found herself surrounded; the Breton loomed over her, staring at her chest as if trying to visualize what lay beneath the mantle she clutched convulsively.

"Since we are only Norman 'filth,' my fine lady, mayhap yon Breton can convince you to show what delicacies you hide beneath all those garments," said a voice to her left, and coarse laughter once more assaulted her ears.

"And mayhap you should show the lady that we Normans do not deserve to be thusly named."

A rich, deep voice cut through the dying laughter like a

sword edge through a blade of straw. It was a confident, authoritative voice, and all heads turned toward its owner.

His face was impossible to make out because the sun was behind him, but he was in full armor like the others, except for his helm. His destrier, white as newly fallen snow, obediently moved forward at the slight nudge of his knees, and the others fell back to make room.

"Now, de Beaufort, do not prevent us from taking our pleasure where we find it. I've not seen so tempting a morsel since Edith Swan Neck honored us with a visit. Will you not join us?"

"Edith Swan Neck?" Brianna asked, unmindful of how precarious her position was.

"Aye, little dove. Only a lover could identify what was left of Harold."

More sniggering. Brianna's stomach lurched. Her face turned ashen at the thought of what they must have done to Harold Godwinson. And then to call in the mistress who had loved him faithfully to see their grisly handiwork!

"That is enough, Hugh. Your manners are sadly lacking. Why not return the piece of clothing you evidently took without the lady's permission?" came the deceptively soft command.

Brianna could now see his short, dark blond hair as the breeze ruffled through it, but her anger was beginning to bubble over like a steaming cauldron at the audacity of these men—the newcomer included.

"Before you came to our land, a woman was safe—even unescorted—for the length and breadth of England. And now—"

" 'Tis war, my lady, and many things change with war," answered the one called de Beaufort.

She derived a twisted sense of satisfaction in contradicting him. "My title is not 'lady'; I am but the wife of a villein. Now, if you will move aside, most noble Normans—or whatever else you claim to be—I would seek my husband's body."

Her aquamarine eyes sparked with ill-concealed anger, and this was not lost upon de Beaufort, although his features were as yet indiscernible to Brianna.

"You cannot search the field of battle without my lord William's permission," growled Hugh of Brittany, impatient with the intruder's interruption and eager to get on with his sport. The four Normans around Brianna, however, were silent. "But I would be happy to take you to him," he added, eyes suddenly aglow with nefarious intent.

In one quick, unexpected motion, de Beaufort unsheathed his sword and with its tip picked up Brianna's headpiece, which had been lying across Hugh's saddle, and extended it to her. "My apologies for my companions' lack of courtesy, *madame*. If you would see Duke William, I will be happy to escort you to his tent." He was suddenly at Brianna's side, and she noticed the anger in Hugh of Brittany's face.

His former good humor disappeared and he sneered. "So, de Beaufort, you will use the love William bears your father to have your way, as usual! We are five to your one—and yet you defy us." He glared at his companions in the ensuing silence, but none was apparently eager to challenge the knight on the white destrier.

"I do not think our Duke will take kindly to the mauling of an innocent woman—especially when she comes in peace to speak with him." De Beaufort moved his mount alongside Brianna's. "Come with me, *madame*. I will see to it that you have an audience with William."

But Hugh grabbed the slackened reins from Brianna's hands, causing her pony to start. "You are cocky for one who has only his sire's reputation to precede him, Norman." He turned to the other silent men. "Did you know that he has named his mount after the good Bishop Odo? I wonder how this keeps him in good stead with William, who is half brother to the Bishop."

"The Bishop and the stallion are both arrogant and also show a similar thirst for blood. What I name my horse is no

one else's concern. Now, if you will release the reins . . ."
De Beaufort's tone was smooth but it brooked no refusal. At
his imperceptible signal, the stallion suddenly slashed at the
Breton's unsuspecting mount with its forelegs. Hugh's surprised destrier jerked back, almost unseating Brianna as her
own animal shied away from the great war-horse.

In a lightninglike movement, de Beaufort caught up her
fallen reins and urged his well-trained steed forward, Brianna
and her bewildered pony close behind him. As they headed
toward a group of tents, an angry voice from behind them
shouted, "You'll pay for that little trick, de Beaufort! I'll not
soon forget it!"

Brianna glanced up at the tall, forbidding-looking knight
astride the fierce war-horse, but she detected no fear or even
anger on the well-defined profile exposed to her now. Against
her will, she was curious about the nature of this Norman who
had rescued her from his cohorts.

His hair was short, in the Norman style, with a tendency
to curl. It was a sandy color shot through with lighter streaks
from the sun, and several errant locks fell across his high
forehead in the cool breeze.

Brianna abruptly turned her head away, angry with herself
for even wondering about him. After all, she would have
eventually thought of *something* to extricate herself from her
predicament. He was merely amusing himself, no doubt, by
angering the Breton. She was here to find Gilbert—or what
was left of him. Guilt assailed her as de Beaufort's strong,
well-chiseled profile pushed at her memory, all but blotting
out the face of her new husband.

As if in sudden penance, she glanced to her other side and
let the ugly scene burn itself into her mind. *He* was responsible for this slaughter. The man beside her and others like
him. They had brought Bretons, and heaven knew who else,
to subjugate the English. Her mouth turned hard and her back
stiffened. *Were I but a man,* she thought fiercely, and turned
her gaze to the tents ahead.

"This is no place for a woman, *madame,*" said the man beside her as he turned to look at the pale, exquisite features silhouetted against her ebony hair.

Without looking at him, she answered stiffly, "My business is with Duke William, not you."

He studied her profile for a moment longer, hoping for a glimpse of her face once more. "As you wish, my—*madame.* William has allowed kinfolk and clergy to claim some of the fallen, though 'tis a grisly task for a woman."

Brianna was only half listening to his words, for she had caught sight of rows of shrouded bodies, naked and putrefying, lined up before shallow pits, awaiting burial, while wolves, wild dogs and ravens scavenged relentlessly. Nearby, the Norman dead were being blessed and buried.

This proved too much for Brianna's taut nerves, and despite her previous determination to ignore the knight beside her, she turned blazing eyes upon him, allowing free rein to her temper. "I do not suppose there are any Englishmen before yon burial pits," she hurled at him bitterly.

At his steady, probing look, Brianna had all she could do not to look down again. For she was not accustomed to mouthing such audacious sarcasm—and never to a male. She held his eyes with her own, using all her willpower to conjure up the image of Gilbert's kind brown eyes in defense against his. They were stormy gray, with a thick dusting of tawny lashes under straight brows of the same shade, set above a straight chiseled nose and high cheekbones. He started to speak, and she felt helpless to prevent herself from noticing the movement of his sensual mouth and the burnished tan of his skin.

What was wrong with her?

"Surely, unless you have led the most sheltered of lives, you must know that any army has all it can do to see to its own dead. The sheer numbers alone would make it—"

"Would nonetheless make it the Christian thing to do. 'Tis obvious you are not so far removed from your brutish Viking ancestors!" She clamped her mouth shut, appalled at her outburst. Tears formed in her eyes and, to her embarrassment, one spilled over and ran down her cheek. She quickly dashed it away with a slim hand.

De Beaufort sighed and held his tongue as they approached William's pavilion. The girl obviously was very ignorant of the ways of war—a far cry from Norman women. But then one never knew with these rustic Saxons.

Brianna concentrated on the large tent they were approaching, and through a blur of tears she noticed several colorful standards waving in the breeze. She thought of the contrast between the brightly colored banners and the grim scene around them.

And then one of the pennants caught her attention. Having been raised in an abbey, she recognized it at once. It was the papal banner.

Stunned, she began to think about the enormous implications of this; strong hands around her waist lifted her down before she could voice a protest, and then she was inside the tent, where metal braziers burned to ward off the chill.

The man she took to be William was engaged in conversation with several other knights and did not appear to notice their entrance. De Beaufort stood silently beside Brianna, waiting for a break in the conversation; one of the knights finally looked over at them, and this distraction caused William to turn toward them.

"Roland!" he greeted cordially. His eyes fell upon Brianna. "Who is this you have with you? My humble tent is a poor setting for such beauty." Even as he spoke Brianna felt him calmly assessing her beneath the jovial pleasantries. His voice was friendly enough, but his words did nothing to soften his demeanor. His dark eyes were stern, penetrating, unrelenting, and as he walked toward them, tall and broad-shouldered, he appeared very much in command.

"Greetings, my lord. I bring you someone who would have a word with you."

William of Normandy's eyes flicked to Roland, and then

he said to Brianna, "Come here, child, and tell me your name. And, Roland, you join the others and afford us a moment of privacy."

Roland joined the other men behind his lord, but Brianna could not move. The enormity of her action—venturing forth to the site of the great battle between her countrymen and the invading Normans—overwhelmed her as she stood face to face with the man responsible for the death of King Harold and the defeat of his army.

"How are you called, young woman?" repeated the Duke.

Brianna was finally moved to action and she hesitantly stepped forward. She took a deep breath to steady herself. "I am called Brianna, my lord," was all she could manage.

"Well then, Brianna, what do you wish to say to me? You may speak freely, for no harm shall befall you."

"I . . . I have come to find my husband, Gilbert of Derford."

The Duke's mouth turned grim. "I thought as much. You may do what you feel you must, but be warned—there are only dead men upon yon field of battle."

Roland de Beaufort was not listening to his companions. His full attention was on the girl. She had the most arresting face he had ever seen, and he could not fathom her unusual combination of docility and defiance. It was as if something inside her yearned to lash out, but some rigid training or strict self-discipline kept her defiance in check. She appeared innocent, yet her bravery was apparent by her solitary journey to a place where a woman's presence only stirred up the kind of trouble that could put her very life in jeopardy.

He strained to hear her words as William mentioned her name.

Brianna. Woman of strength. She had been wisely named, he thought.

She glanced his way once, as if feeling his intense gaze, and gave him another glimpse of her intriguing eyes. Roland had never seen such a shade of blue-green before. They were framed by slim brows and fringed by thick, long lashes—both the same hue as her glorious midnight tresses. Her slightly uptilted nose and determined chin hinted at a spirit that longed to be set free. The high, delicate cheekbones and soft, ripe lips had lost their pallor now that she was inside the tent and away from the horrors outside. Her skin was smooth and pale as alabaster, but he could see nothing beyond the slender neck, for her woolen mantle concealed everything but the fact that she was slim and of slightly more than average height.

But perhaps the most puzzling thing about her was that the clothing she wore—even the trappings of her horse—bespoke poverty. Not the poverty of a serf or peasant, but certainly not the social and economic position she seemed to have been born and bred for. It belied her poise and regal bearing, her sweet, mellifluous voice and flawless French.

Intrigued, Roland was hard pressed to keep his eyes from wandering back to Brianna and the changing expressions on her face as he tried to give some semblance of attention to the other knights.

"Mayhap she is a spy, de Beaufort," said one in a bantering tone.

"Aye, and even if she is not, you will never win over a stubborn Saxon," another added. He was Bishop Odo, half brother to William.

Roland grinned good-naturedly, despite his dislike of the Bishop. "Never fear, good Bishop. She is wed—and even if her husband were dead, when I enter that most exalted state of bondage, 'twill be with a woman of my own kind."

Their muffled laughter at his reply caught Brianna's attention, and she had the distinct impression that she was the object of their humor. Her cheeks turned pink and she suddenly wanted desperately to get away—even though it meant searching through piles of cadavers to find Gilbert.

William saw her discomfiture. "I cannot apologize for something I felt in my heart was my due—and for which I obtained papal approval. But I do hope, child, that your husband is alive and perhaps already home. I also pray that you may grow to accept what God has ordained and that I may one day soon have your love and loyalty.''

Brianna stared at him, unable to say another word for fear of the impact of the retaliatory words she fought to hold back.

''Roland!'' The Duke turned his head to summon de Beaufort.

''Aye, my lord.''

''Please escort Brianna in her search and then see her safely on her way.''

''As you wish, sire.'' He nodded his well-shaped head in obeisance.

''But I can—'' Brianna began to protest, for the thought of being in the company of this confident, high-handed knight for a moment longer was not at all to her liking.

''God be with you, child,'' said William of Normandy before he turned away, indicating the interview had ended.

Anger flared in her striking eyes at the abrupt dismissal, but she told herself she was in no position to protest anything; the main thing was to have this gruesome deed done with.

With a sigh she straightened proudly and proceeded toward the tent flap, heedless of the man who followed close behind.

Despite all her resolve to ignore Roland de Beaufort, she was unnerved by his nearness. When she surveyed the scene before her as they stood poised at the edge of the battlefield, Brianna felt the urge to strike out at him because he was Norman and she was appalled by what the Normans had done.

''Brianna,'' he began gently, ''are you truly desirous of—''

''I am not 'Brianna' to *you*, Norman!'' she said through gritted teeth. ''And if you do not care for my lack of congeniality, you are welcome to take your leave.''

A darkening of his gray eyes hinted at Roland's own anger,

but he merely said, "I would not leave a woman alone here—not even you, *madame*."

Brianna was surprised at this first sign that his imperturbability could give way to other emotions. She was secretly glad to have disturbed him at last. She prodded her pony forward. Even the beast was skittish at the stench of death that permeated the air, and it balked several times.

When she began specifically examining faces, her tears spilled over onto suddenly pallid cheeks. "Oh, England!" she cried softly and with deep anguish in her own language, forgetting for a moment the French Norman beside her. "What have they done to you? What have they done to all of us? To spill English blood on English soil—to murder and then mutilate our King Harold, and then to hide behind the papal banner!" She raised her tear-streaked face to the sky. "As God is my witness, I do not believe this papal blessing was obtained honorably! Never shall I believe that!" she swore fiercely.

So distorted was her vision by tears that she could not focus clearly on the blank, staring faces as she searched them. They all blended together into one grotesque death mask. Angrily she wiped away the offending wetness, and Roland missed none of it.

"You know 'tis treason to gainsay the Duke, *madame*," Roland said quietly, startlingly.

Brianna's head jerked up to him. "You understand English?" she demanded, as though he had deliberately withheld it from her.

He said nothing, but the answer was in his eyes. If she hadn't wished to think only the worst of him, she would have read compassion in their depths.

"An Englishman—or woman—cannot commit treason against a Norman—duke or no!" she retorted fiercely. And before he could protest, she slid off her mount and began walking among the dead.

"Look, Norman, what your brave companions have

wrought! This is victory? I see old men here as well as . . . as mere boys!'' Her voice broke and she began to stagger, so keenly did she feel the loss of life on the blood-soaked ground.

Roland dismounted in a flash and swiftly caught up with her. "Brianna," he said sternly, "you must not do this! You know naught of that which you speak. We also suffered many losses—''

She whirled around and struck him across the cheek with her open palm, her anger completely out of control. "I care not for your losses, Norman!" she hissed savagely. "I would that the lot of you had sunk to the bottom of the sea before you ever set foot upon our shores!"

She stared with grim satisfaction at the white marks across his tanned cheek, feeling no guilt now. "I ask you once again to leave me, Norman. I must find my husband.''

Roland curbed his irritation with an effort. Under the circumstances, he could not blame her for her feelings. Were he in her place, he would have felt equally frustrated and enraged, especially since he had not necessarily agreed with this venture of William's. So in spite of his anger at her physical assault, his urge to shake her was tempered by his understanding of her need to lash out.

Brianna was ahead of him now, stumbling blindly among the heaped bodies, her traitorous tears making it all but impossible to see anything clearly. Roland kept his distance, realizing he could do nothing but obey his lord's command to accompany her in her search. He felt the most compelling urge to take her in his arms and soothe away her hurt and sorrow, and it baffled him.

"Gilbert, Gilbert!" came her soft cry, borne on the chill October breeze. He could not make out any more of her words, but he thought of how much she must love this Gilbert to have exposed herself to unknown danger and then the heart-wrenching task of searching among her dead countrymen. A pang of envy pierced him as he led their horses, following behind her.

Get her through this and then on her way. You owe her naught, and 'tis just as well you will never set eyes upon her again.

When Brianna reached the far side of the field, she suddenly doubled over, retching violently. She stumbled toward a patch of dying grass near several trees and sank to the ground, fighting to get hold of herself.

Several urges warred within Roland. He knew he should allow her to recover a semblance of dignity on her own, especially in view of her feelings toward him. But a part of him wanted to comfort her as best he could, even at the risk of arousing her anger once again.

He found himself on one knee beside her on the damp earth, a hand touching her trembling shoulder tentatively. "Brianna?"

She slowly shook her head without looking at him. "Please . . . please go away."

"I will not leave you like this. Here—" He produced a flask of water from his belt and put it to her lips. After she had drunk her fill, he poured a little of it into his hand and gently ran his fingers over her pale face.

At this tender gesture, Brianna reluctantly raised her eyes to meet his. This time she recognized the warmth and compassion in the gray-eyed gaze and wondered briefly how a man could have such beautiful, expressive eyes. "I . . . I am sorry that I struck you." A hint of color returned to her ashen cheeks at the thought of what she had done. " 'Tis not my wont to—"

And suddenly her voice was muffled in the solid wall of his chest as she felt his strong arms envelop her and his hand gently stroke her hair. She had never known such a secure feeling, and even in the middle of their unlikely surroundings, she felt all other emotions flee before the warmth of his embrace.

Then the wind shifted and the smell of death invaded her nostrils. It was like a slap in the face. Brianna pushed away from him and shakily stood up.

Roland followed suit, not wishing to do any more damage than he felt he had already done. "Brianna, I only meant to comfort you . . . 'twas not what it seemed," he began.

"Then I beg you, allow me to ride through once more, and then I will return home."

He could not refuse her, and as he lifted her onto her horse he could still feel the sensation of her body within the circle of his arms—soft and yielding. 'Tis God's punishment, he thought wryly, to send a witch with eyes the color of the ever-changing sea to haunt me in this accursed place.

When at last he led her back to the top of Caldbec Hill, he asked, "Where do you abide, lovely Brianna?"

The words sounded strange coming from the lips of her enemy on the crest of a ridge overlooking the massacre of the flower of England. Brianna shrugged indifferently. "It matters not, Norman. I did not find my husband here and he may yet be alive. In that case I am still a properly married woman. Even a victorious Norman cannot force me to forsake the holy vows of matrimony."

Roland winced inwardly at the bitterness of her words.

"And even if Gilbert is dead, it will not further your cause, if that is what you seek. For I live in the heart of Wessex, the earldom held by Harold Godwinson before he became king. You shall find naught but hatred and resistance there, Norman."

And with a flick of the reins she let the pony take her westward and out of his reach forever.

CHAPTER 3

The night was haunted with visions of a pair of expressive gray eyes. Silver-gray, except in anger, when they turned dark as storm clouds. And even though the warmth and security Brianna had experienced from that fleeting embrace threatened to linger uninvited in her memory, she determinedly pushed Roland de Beaufort from her mind. Gilbert was the one of whom she should have been thinking—Gilbert, who could still very well be lying upon the cold, unhallowed ground near Hastings, for she had not covered the entire area in her search. Her revulsion had been too great. And the constant, unwanted presence of the tawny-haired Norman had only added to her roiling emotions.

Torn asunder by the thought of what would become of her should Gilbert be dead and by the fear of chancing upon marauding Normans, Brianna had finally lapsed into silent prayer, the only way she knew to keep her mind free of the demons that threatened her from all sides.

An hour or two after sunrise, she approached the outskirts of the tiny village of Derford from the east. She first passed the estate of Thane Wulfric, which was separated from Gilbert's homestead by a small woods, and she studied it with interest. According to Gilbert, Wulfric was a very wealthy thane. His position was very prestigious because his immediate overlord was the Earl of Wessex, who had been crowned King of England. Undoubtedly Wulfric's jurisdiction reached out farther than Derford, but its fairly centralized location and its rusticity and tranquility surely must have added to its attraction for the King's thane.

A ditch and fence surrounded the central area of Wulfric's holdings. A rectangular aisled hall of timber with a shingled roof stood near the center, an entrance at either end, with smaller detached structures leading from both of its long sides. Brianna supposed these to be sleeping bowers for the family and guests, and the latrine building.

Various other small buildings were scattered about, including a mill, barn, stables, various storehouses and servants' accommodations, and the small stone church where she and Gilbert had been wed.

She wondered if the Normans would burn everything to the ground or simply move in and take over. She had no doubt that if they came as far as Derford, the village would have a new Norman overlord.

She caught sight of Gilbert's homestead in the distance, separated from Wulfric's lands only by the short stretch of forest between. She had thought it was fortunate the house was at the eastern end of the village, near enough to the thane's stronghold should trouble arise. When danger threatened, the people of Derford looked to their thane for protection. This was one of the services with which they were provided in exchange for labor and food.

But if a Norman laid claim to Derford and the surrounding area, she and Gilbert would be much too close for comfort. Brianna shivered at the thought. What did the Normans know of Anglo-Saxon ways? And even if they were acquainted with the customs of her people, would it matter? From what she had seen, many—such as Hugh of Brittany—were obviously mercenaries, seeking riches and lands of their own. How else could William have gathered so great an army to stand behind him in so risky an enterprise?

"Brianna!"

A voice startled her and broke her train of thought as Brand, Kerwick's youngest son, emerged from the woods to her right.

He was several years younger than Brianna, with a crop of unruly blond hair that he was forever brushing out of his eyes. But his usually cheerful countenance was uncharacteristically solemn.

"Brand! You gave me a fine fright!" She smiled tiredly, yet she was unspeakably grateful to see a familiar face.

"I am sorry, Brianna, but we all fear a Norman raid at any time, and I was on my way to keep watch just east of Wulfric's lands."

As Brand reached her side Brianna regarded him intently, steeling herself for the inevitable. But before she could ask the dreaded question, he rushed on. "We were all terribly worried, Brianna. But you have come back." He paused and drew a deep breath. "Gilbert lives. He returned only yestereve with some comrades who also fought at Hastings."

The color slowly drained from her face as the impact of his words hit her. Gilbert alive? *Alive?* Oh, God—he was home and alive! Her color returned as the shock receded in an overwhelming tide of relief. "How . . . how is he? Was he . . . injured?" Her voice sounded faraway to her own ears as her pleading gaze met the boy's.

Brand looked down for a moment as if searching for the right words. "Brand?" she questioned softly, insistently.

When at last his blue eyes met hers, she read pity in them. "He was badly wounded, Brianna. He took a mace in the back of the head." She bit her lip to stifle her outcry of horror. "And . . . and he does not have full use of his limbs."

Brianna absorbed this for a few moments. "But he . . . he is at least alive and—"

"Oh, aye!" came the suddenly bitter reply. "That he is. But he cannot speak, nor does he recognize any of us. He is—"

"He is what, Brand?" she whispered tensely, leaning down over the horse's shaggy mane.

Brand licked his lips nervously, his eyes avoiding hers.

"When he is conscious he is much like a child—nay, rather like an . . . an idiot."

Brianna barely caught his last words, but she knew them before they were spoken. Her world seemed to recede around her as she tried to envision Gilbert's thick-lashed brown eyes staring uncomprehendingly.

Abruptly she straightened and pulled herself together with an effort. Her eyes on the village in the distance, she said quietly, "Thank you for telling me everything, Brand. It would have been more difficult later had you tried to spare me now."

At a loss for words, he watched her urge the pony ahead and move westward toward Derford.

Idiot . . . idiot . . . idiot . . .

The word echoed in her mind until she thought she would scream. One part of her dreaded what awaited her, yet another part of her—that which was well trained and self-controlled as a result of twelve years of rigid discipline—wanted to see Gilbert and get it over with. Well, at least he was still alive, she thought. Perhaps he would regain some of his memory and his speech. Perhaps this was a temporary thing.

By the time she reached the main hall of the homestead, she had a grip on her emotions and she entered the structure prepared for the worst.

At first she thought no one was about as her eyes adjusted and scanned the dim interior. But then she noticed someone sitting to the side of the fireplace, staring into the flames. As Brianna neared she recognized Kerwick's wife, Nedra. "Nedra?"

The woman turned, startled, and with surprising swiftness was upon Brianna, clasping the girl tightly to her. "You have returned, child. Praise God! We were so worried!" She released Brianna and held her away to examine her closely. "So you are unharmed. You look like you could use a good meal and much rest." Her eyes were full of concern.

Brianna nodded. "But what of . . . what of Gilbert? Brand told me that he had returned but was badly injured."

Nedra sighed heavily. "Only God knows how things will turn out, but right now he is asleep. You can do naught, so let me give you something to put in your stomach. You can see him after you've eaten and cleaned up, child."

Brianna allowed the older woman to lead her to a chair and obediently sat down. As Nedra stirred up the fire and set herself to preparing something for Brianna to eat, she threw a sidelong glance at the exhausted girl. "How long do we have, Brianna?" she asked quietly.

Brianna's shoulders sagged. She needed no explanation regarding the question. "I think not long. They were clearing the battlefield of their dead when I arrived, and from their numbers and what William of Normandy said—"

"You spoke to the Bastard himself?" Kerwick's voice demanded from the doorway.

Both women turned toward him, but it was Brianna who spoke. "I did, Kerwick. He even allowed me to search for Gilbert among the dead." She shuddered at the thought and pushed the unwelcome image of Roland de Beaufort from her mind. "Was he not generous?" she asked, her voice tinged with sarcasm that was alien to her, which took both Kerwick and Nedra by surprise. "And then he said that he prayed he might one day soon have my love and loyalty!"

"Mother of God," breathed Nedra.

Kerwick was silent a moment, as if weighing her words. His piercing blue eyes unwaveringly held Brianna's. "So 'tis as we've feared—he means to be King of England." He walked over to Brianna, who had begun to feel that all she had witnessed in the past two days was a dream. "Did they harm you, child?" he asked in a voice gruff with concern.

Suddenly Brianna began to giggle uncontrollably. "Oh, Kerwick! They . . . they hurt me beyond all telling! But they did not have to lay a finger on me to do it. Do you not think them uncommonly clever?" Tears streamed down her face as her laughter continued hysterically.

Kerwick seized her by the shoulders firmly and gave her a

shake. "Brianna! Take hold of yourself, girl. We all need your help—the entire village."

Her laughter died as suddenly as it had begun as his words sank in, and she nodded as she raised her tear-streaked face to his. "But there is little I can do. I know nothing of their plans."

Kerwick turned away and began pacing slowly, a thoughtful frown on his face. "We have been hiding reserves of grain—burying it—for we knew they would come. But we can only conceal a certain number of livestock, for the animals must be fed and watered. If Derford is taken over, it will be difficult to care for them under the Normans' noses. But if they . . ." He hesitated, as if reluctant to go on. "If they gut the village, we will at least have something to eat."

His words died in the ensuing silence. But then Brianna rose and clutched his arm. "But what of the earls in the north? Cannot one of them lead an army against William?"

"I do not think so, Brianna. Edwin of Mercia and Morkere of Northumbria are not yet a score of years old. Waltheof of Huntingdon is little more, and I know not if they are yet alive."

"But the King's brothers—"

"Dead. Both of them. We must deal with the immediate threat to ourselves, child—and the lives of our own villagers. We are close enough to Hastings that even if they make straight for London, they could easily strike Derford for food and whatever else they may need. Winter will soon be upon us, and William must feed his army."

Nedra placed a steaming bowl of stew on the table and gently prodded Brianna. "You must eat and then rest, Brianna, or you will be no use to Gilbert—or anyone else."

At the mention of Gilbert's name, Brianna dropped Kerwick's arm and wearily moved to the table. As she stared at the simple meal before her, she found that she was hungry and began to eat.

Kerwick sat down across from her, an intense look on his

weathered features. "I will tell Brand to help you in whatever way he can while Gilbert is . . . mending. I will also send one of my daughters to tend him when you need to see to other things. You cannot carry on alone, even though the harvest is in and most of the heavy work finished."

Brianna gave him a grateful look. "You will not miss their help, Kerwick?"

"Nay, child. I still have two strapping lads. We'll not be found lacking, so do not fret. My concern now is for the steps you must take to ready yourself and Gilbert in the event the Normans take Derford. In truth 'twould be better for us all if one Norman noble took over as lord, for even though he might be cruel, he would not plunder and burn the town that could serve him—unless he were a fool."

Brianna said in a strange voice, suddenly pushing aside her bowl, "And I do not think William will give our lands to just any mercenary who will not submit to his control. He is far too clever for that."

Kerwick wondered just what had transpired between Brianna and the Norman duke. She was definitely not the girl he had brought from Walshire Abbey. There was a bitterness about her, a cynicism, which made her seem stronger and somehow more capable—yes, more able to handle anything that might come up. How many women—and fresh from a sheltered convent at that—would have traveled alone to Hastings to confront William of Normandy himself?

Brianna pushed back her chair unexpectedly and stood up. "It is time I saw Gilbert. He is my husband, ill or well, sleeping or otherwise, and I must go to him."

Nedra quickly procured a basin and poured warm water into it from a cauldron over the glowing embers at one end of the fire. She placed it and a towel before Brianna and then cleared the remains of her meal away. "At least freshen up, sweeting. Then you will feel better and more like resting after you've seen him."

As she washed her face and hands Brianna was struck by

the thought that Nedra was trying to forestall the inevitable. But Kerwick's look was closed when she glanced at him, and after a few more moments he took his leave.

Brianna sighed and then straightened determinedly before following Nedra outside to the sleeping bower that she was to have shared with Gilbert. Several small braziers warmed the room. Brianna approached the figure on the bed with trepidation. His head was swathed in snow-white strips of cloth that came partway down his forehead.

As she stood looking down at him Brianna's heart went out to him. Aside from a few bruises on his face, nothing appeared to be physically wrong. She turned to Nedra, who stood silently beside her. "Brand said he did not have full use of his limbs. What is amiss, Nedra?"

The older woman's eyes went from Brianna's face to Gilbert's. "He cannot move his left arm or leg. He has no severe cuts or injuries other than that from the mace on the back of his head. But the blow affected his limbs—and his mind." Her eyes returned to Brianna, sympathy evident in their depths. "But," she added at the look on the girl's face, "that is not to say he will not get better."

Brianna looked at her husband's face once more and slowly shook her head. "We learned something of healing at the abbey, and I once helped Sister Margaret treat a man who had been struck in the head from behind by a tree limb while searching for his son in a violent storm. He could not move his legs, and his mind was much like a child's. He never recovered."

Suddenly, as if he were aware—from somewhere in the depths of unconsciousness—of voices nearby, Gilbert stirred. Both women's eyes were instantly upon him, anxious, expectant. His head turned slowly from side to side and his lips moved. Brianna leaned closer in an effort to hear his words, but she could only make out unintelligible sounds.

Undaunted, she took his limp hand and spoke softly into

his ear. "Gilbert . . . Gilbert, 'tis Brianna. Can you understand me?"

That soft, mellifluous sound must have been soothing to the injured Gilbert's mind, for a faint smile seemed to touch his mouth for a fleeting instant and then was gone.

Brianna looked up at Nedra. "Did you see, Nedra? He seemed to recognize my voice—he smiled!"

The older woman nodded hopefully. "Aye, love. 'Tis the first time he has responded to anyone." The hope in Brianna's eyes was so obvious that Nedra had to smile herself, for she had spoken the truth to the anxious girl. No one else had been able to elicit a response from Gilbert.

Brianna turned back to him and knelt beside the low bed. "Gilbert, can you hear me? You are safe now—you are home with me." Her words trailed off as his eyelids fluttered and then slowly opened. For a moment they seemed inclined to remain half open, as if the effort were too great, but as Brianna murmured soothingly into his ear, his gaze met hers at last— fully. The heavily lashed eyes were still the color of dark brown velvet that she remembered with affection, but the blank look in them finally threatened her composure. She blinked the tears back valiantly and spoke quietly to him of their meeting, their long talk before his departure, the marriage ceremony—things that might possibly stir his memory—but to no avail. He kept his eyes on her, but rather like a tame beast regarding its mistress instead of a man struggling to recognize his bride. Now and then there was a flicker of intelligence, but just as quickly it was gone, leaving Brianna to wonder if her mind was playing tricks on her, so desperately did she want him to recognize her.

All too soon his eyelids slowly closed, and Brianna gave free rein to her frustration as she stood up and regarded Nedra. "Oh, he is so close to remembering who he is, who I am—I know it! Did you not see the way he looked at me, Nedra?"

Nedra reached out and smoothed back Brianna's hair in a motherly gesture and nodded reassuringly. "Surely he will do better when his strength returns and his body mends. Come and rest yourself, child. You will be better able to deal with . . . with everything after a good sleep.''

Later, alone in the smaller of the two sleeping houses on a clean, soft bed, Brianna tossed fitfully. She kept remembering the intelligence and warmth that shone out of those blank brown eyes the first time she had met him, and the contrast haunted her. 'Tis the handiwork of the Normans, she told herself in a burst of bitterness. And as a gilded-haired Norman appeared in her thoughts out of nowhere to chase away the image of her husband's face, she angrily envisioned him with a blood-drenched sword in his hand and dead Anglo-Saxons all around him. She would not have been surprised if someone told her it was de Beaufort's mace that had dealt the cruel blow. She tortured herself with visions of the knight on the huge war-horse striking out viciously at the decidedly disadvantaged Anglo-Saxons on foot. What chance did English infantry have against mounted knights?

Her thoughts became so agitated she almost got out of bed. She needed to work off her feelings, but then common sense told her she also desperately needed sleep. With a concerted effort she forced herself to think of constructive things she could do when she was more rested. At long last her mind gave in to her exhausted body's demands, and she slept straight through until the following morning.

CHAPTER 4

An ominous tension pervaded the normally placid atmosphere of Derford. The village was set up rather haphazardly, with the seven homesteads of Wulfric's villeins and the five dwellings belonging to the cottars—the humblest of free men— randomly strung out along either side of the road that led east to the coast. The village was a day's ride from Hastings, and so was a prime target for foraging parties of Normans.

Brianna had passionately begged Kerwick to advise the villagers to arm themselves, but the old man only shook his head in regret. "We have nary a sword in all of Derford, child. The men who fought at Hastings used clubs and stones— homemade, primitive weapons. They were no match against fine swords and lances and studded maces—and even less so against mounted men in chain mail."

"But what of Thomas the Blacksmith? Could he not make swords for the men?"

"It would take days, Brianna, and even if he had enough time to make a hundred swords, we are not skilled at using them. We are men of the soil, not warriors." He sighed heavily. "We have no choice, Brianna. Anyone foolish enough to oppose them will more than likely be cut down. Do you not see the wisdom in submitting and not arousing their anger any further so that we can at least escape with our lives? Where there is life there is hope. Mayhap we can pick up the pieces of our lives and rebuild—"

"Only to be destroyed again!" she interjected bitterly.

40

" 'Tis a chance we must take—a part of life, although an unpleasant one."

And so, with Brand's help, Brianna buried their valuables, including the gold that had been her dowry. While Aleen, Kerwick's younger daughter, tended Gilbert, they picked the choicest of pigs, hens and sheep and hid them in the forest along with the only cow Gilbert owned.

Gilbert's recovery was rapid, if only partial. He was soon able to sit up for nourishment, and then even take hesitant, awkward steps with his right leg, leaning on a sturdy walking stick Kerwick made for him and dragging his limp left member after him. With his left arm hanging uselessly at his side, he made a pathetic picture. But what truly tore at Brianna's heart was the vacant look in his eyes. It was at times replaced by a flicker of recognition, which invariably caused her hopes to soar, only to plummet when he showed no more interest in—or capability of—speaking or communicating on any higher level than that of a pet dog.

A week or so after Brianna's return, she and the villagers were prepared—as well as could be—for the worst.

At Nedra's bidding, Brianna altered a pair of ankle-length braies, or breeches, and a tunic to disguise her slight form, for she had no desire to be raped by foraging Normans. And in a final act of desperation—or defiance—she took a well-honed knife to her luxurious ebony tresses and hacked them off to chin length.

Nedra was horrified when she viewed the results.

"But would I not give myself away, despite my clothing, if my hair were so long?" Brianna asked sensibly. "It will grow back fast enough, I warrant you." She gave Nedra a sudden impish smile, as if to show her satisfaction at having thought of one more trick to fool the Normans.

Nedra could only shake her head in exasperation. "I fear you may be harming your cause more than furthering it, for even now your hair curls about your face and only emphasizes your fine features." A polished metal mirror, hastily procured, served to prove the truth of Nedra's observation.

In desperation, Brianna suddenly ran to the fire pit. Dipping her fingers in the ashes, she smeared soot all over her face; then she faced the older woman once more for her reaction.

"I suppose you'll do as long as you keep those telltale eyes downcast," Nedra grudgingly approved.

Just then Brand came running into the main hall, a concerned look on his youthful features. "It's Gilbert. I cannot find him. He was—"

Brianna's look changed to one of alarm as she interrupted him. "You cannot find him? But where can he have gone? He is still not recovered enough to wander off—at least not very far."

"You had better find him, Brand," Nedra interjected. "There is no telling where he is and if—"

But both Brianna and Brand were swiftly moving toward the door before she could even finish her warning.

"He shuns people, so mayhap he went toward Wulfric's lands, Brianna."

As they hurried east across the desolate fields, the forest that separated the homestead from the lands of the thane loomed ominously before them. "It is inconceivable that he can have come this far," Brianna panted. "But if he is in those woods, it could take hours to find him. We could cover more ground more quickly if we separated."

"Aye, but you do not know the forest, Brianna. What good would it do to have you both lost?"

Brianna had to concede to the wisdom of his words, despite her fear for Gilbert's safety. The forest had been used by Wulfric for hunting and was well stocked with game. Gilbert could not possibly have protected himself from wild animals even if his mind had been whole.

They entered the wooded area out of breath. "Here—look, Brianna. Something—or someone—has crashed through the undergrowth."

They followed the path of broken boughs and trampled leaves as best they could, hoping it was Gilbert who was responsible for the crushed foliage and not some wild beast. After what seemed an eternity to Brianna, they approached the edge of the woods on the west side of Wulfric's deserted estate. At that moment they heard the pounding of horses' hooves. They stared at one another in surprise and then with foreboding, for it could only mean one thing.

"Get down, Brianna!" Brand warned urgently.

"But . . . but what of Gilbert? We dare not leave him wandering about with—"

"We do not even know if he is in these woods. You said yourself he could not have come this far. Be sensible," he exhorted as he pulled her down on her knees beside him. "If he *is* hereabouts, he is safer than if he were in Derford when they—whoever they are—get there."

Before Brianna could answer, a party of mounted riders came into view around a slight turn in the road leading to Derford. Brianna recognized them by the very fact that they were mounted. They wore full chain mail and helms, conspicuously carrying shields and swords. Their intent was blatantly obvious.

"Normans!" Brand made it sound like a curse.

Brianna bit her lower lip to keep from crying out in vexation, for the sight of them brought back agonizing memories. She fought to gain control of herself. *You are not in a sheltered abbey now, Brianna! You must be strong—for 'twould appear that even God Himself has forsaken England.*

"There are only half a score." Brand's voice interrupted her silent battle. "But look at their horses!" His voice was tinged with awe as the last of the Normans thundered past.

"Their size is only the half of it," Brianna said bleakly. "They are trained to fight with their hooves—I saw one such beast start to attack another mounted man before his rider brought him under control.

"Come." She stood up and turned back toward Derford. "We must get back to the village."

"But . . . but what of Gilbert?" Brand's voice stopped her as the note of indecision in it caught her attention.

Their roles seemed to reverse, with Brianna suddenly in charge. "I think you were right, Brand, and Gilbert is not here. If he is, I pray God he remains here safe and unharmed, for there is no telling what will befall Derford."

Brand tried to persuade Brianna to remain hidden while he returned, but she would have none of it. When they reached the rear of the buildings that made up Gilbert's small homestead, Brianna insisted that he find his way to his own home to do what he could to aid his family. But he was adamant. "They are five to our two. My father would never forgive me if I left you."

Brianna was about to protest, but the stubborn set to his jaw made her see the futility of it, and she reached out to squeeze his hand in a quick gesture of gratitude.

They could hear shouts and screams as the Normans began to loot the village, and the two young people cautiously made their way to the rear entrance of the main hall.

"Brianna, 'tis not safe to be seen. What can you do against them?"

"This is my home, Brand. I will not stand by idly while they—"

"Ahhh—"

The startled cry of pain came from inside, and the voice sounded familiar to Brianna. She unthinkingly lunged forward toward the doorway; Brand's soft but fierce whisper barely reached her as she bolted through. "Have a care to act as a boy—"

She came to a dead halt, Brand almost slamming into her from behind. A huge knight, sword in hand, was rifling through a great wooden chest that had caught his eye. Before he noticed Brianna and Brand standing frozen before the portal, they recognized the limp form on the floor near the front of the hall as Gilbert.

A rush of conflicting thoughts raced through Brianna's mind at the sight of him. She guessed in an instant that the Norman must have struck some chord of memory in her husband and he had attempted to either stop the miscreant or attack him directly. She stared at his unmoving body, shouts and screams forming a nightmarish background for the scene before her. Suddenly something snapped inside of her and she unthinkingly shouted in French, "Get yourself from here, you Norman filth, before I kill you!"

Brand's face turned chalk white at the tone of her words, and the knight jerked his head up in surprise and squinted into the dim shadows, his sword raised menacingly. "Who dares to threaten me? Come forward so I may see you before I run you through!" he snarled.

Brianna came forward a few steps, her lips drawn back in hatred. "Since when do the brave men of Duke William's army attack unarmed cripples?" She indicated Gilbert's figure with an angry jerk of her small chin.

As he regarded the two calculatingly, the intruder suddenly burst into harsh laughter, letting down his guard momentarily at this seemingly inconsequential threat. "Two scrawny lads we have here! Well, well—and one even speaks the French tongue, although he could use a few lessons in the art of bathing." He laughed uproariously once more, while Brianna merely scowled, grateful for the protection her grimy face afforded her. "Are you so foolhardy as to actually think yourselves capable of stopping me?" he taunted.

Brand did not understand a word of what was being said, but he could guess much from Brianna's tone and the intruder's insulting laughter.

"If I were but possessed of a sword you would not be so bold, Norman."

He smiled maliciously. "Your army of farmers could not

stop us. Think you two bumbling lads in a backward Saxon village could do any better?''

A quick blur of motion at the door behind the Norman caught Brianna's attention, and suddenly the figure of a youth was inside the hall, pressed flat against the wall. Brianna thought it was Walter, Kerwick's second son, but the light was behind him. Not wanting to give him away, she shifted her eyes once more to the man before her. In an effort to distract his attention, she said in a scathing voice, ''You'll find little of value here, Norman, for we are but a humble village of tillers of the soil.''

He studied her for a moment, a sudden frown of puzzlement across what she could see of his face underneath the nosepiece of his helm. ''Your voice is uncommonly sweet, even for an upstart lad, and your features are so fine—I wonder what you hide behind those dirt streaks.''

For an instant Brianna thought his words would be her undoing, for not only was she worried about her sex being discovered, but she felt queasy with dread at what Walter was planning to do. He was the hothead of Kerwick's family, and in the split second she had recognized him Kerwick's words came back to her in dire warning: *Do you not see the wisdom in submitting and not arousing their anger any further so that we can at least escape with our lives?* What if Walter attacked the knight? There would be no contest.

''. . . and you will perhaps find more valuables to your liking in the sleeping bowers.'' Brand's words startled Brianna out of her brief reverie like a splash of cold water.

The soldier shifted the position of his upheld sword, as if contemplating this proposition, and the soft grinding of his mail sounded oddly out of place to Brianna. But he was not so easily put off. ''Why don't you come hither, boy, and let me see what lies beneath those garments.''

The air of expectancy was almost tangible, and then a low groan issued from Gilbert as he slowly stirred. It couldn't have been better timed. In the instant the knight shifted his attention to Gilbert, Walter attacked him from behind. Both went down only because the Norman's heavy mail hampered his agility, enabling Walter to unbalance him. Over they rolled once, twice, and then Brianna saw the flash of a dagger just as his helm skittered across the floor. In that moment Brand flung himself into the fray.

The knight threw off Brand with one sweep of his mighty sword arm and knelt to face a panting, weaponless Walter. The dagger was poised threateningly at his chest as the intruder hissed jeeringly, "So you wish to die young, you bumbling whelp, and at the hand of one to whom war and fighting are a way of life!"

"It matters not who or what you are, for you have no right to invade our land, you mangy cur! Kill me now and I'll see you in hell for your sins!" Walter swore fiercely.

From where he had been thrown in a corner, Brand made another move to come to his brother's aid, but the experienced soldier seemed to have eyes in the back of his head. "Stay your hand, or I'll slit his throat like a stuck pig's!"

Slowly, slowly, ever so cautiously, Brianna bent to lift an empty metal chamber pot almost at her feet. She offered a brief silent prayer of thanks that she had followed Brand so hastily in search of Gilbert that she had not returned it to the bower where it belonged.

Suddenly and without warning the knight lunged at Walter, his armor once more hindering his movements. But Walter was not skilled enough in the art of fighting with a deadly weapon to escape the knife, and he took a sizable gash in the shoulder. The sight of blood moved Brianna to action.

She raised the heavy chamber pot over her head and quickly stepped closer, words running through her head in a litany of warning: *Thou shalt not kill, thou shalt not kill, thou shalt—*

Down came the vessel on the Norman's head with a force she never dreamed she possessed. The coif over his head and neck was little protection from the shattering blow, and he paused for a split second and then slowly slumped to the floor.

Absolute silence reigned in the room. All three of the young people were stunned at the enormity of Brianna's action. And then, as the sounds from outside brought them one by one out of their shock, Walter crawled over to the unmoving knight and cautiously rolled him onto his back. "He is dead," he stated solemnly after putting his ear to the stranger's massive chest.

Brianna, even more appalled by his words, could only stare in growing disbelief and horror at the evidence of what she had done. Walter eyed her compassionately. "It was a brave thing you did, Brianna, and no one would ever blame you. He was our enemy and he meant to kill me—or anyone else who opposed him."

"We must hide the body," Brand said in an unnaturally strained voice. "If the others discover him, there is no telling what kind of retribution they will exact."

This practical statement helped bring Brianna out of her stupor, and she nodded numbly. "But where? If we hide him under a bed, we risk being seen dragging him from the hall to one of the bowers."

"We have little time to decide. At any moment one of his cohorts could come through that door." Walter's face looked suddenly pale, and Brianna realized the need for expediency so his shoulder could be attended to as well. And then, of course, there was Gilbert.

"Behind the great chest." She motioned toward the chest which the knight had been searching. They dragged the corpse across the floor; the scraping of his armor seemed to resound through the room. They stuffed him between the coffer and the wall, hastily pushing the heavy piece of furniture as close to the side of the building as possible.

With that accomplished, Brianna was torn between the urge to run to Gilbert, to see what harm the stranger had done him, and to bind up Walter's wound. Her better judgment told her that in all probability Gilbert had been merely knocked unconscious. Not only was Walter losing blood, but if his wound were seen by another marauding knight, it would arouse suspicion.

"Brand, see to Gilbert," she ordered briskly, and gently but firmly pushed Walter down onto a bench. Her deft fingers lifted his tunic and gently probed the wound.

"Brianna, please forgive me for causing this to happen here. If they discover him and blame you, I'll never be able to live with myself. But when I saw him threatening you and Brand—" His eyes searched her face earnestly, then he paled as she pulled tight on the strip of cloth she had torn from her mantle which she was using to bind his shoulder. As she worked against time she hoped that once his tunic was in place again, no one would question the blood on it.

"You need not explain your actions, Walter. And you need not fear for Gilbert and me." She finished her task and turned toward Brand, who was kneeling beside Gilbert. "How is he?"

"I think he was only knocked senseless. Nothing else seems amiss."

Just then the smell of burning wood assailed Brianna's nostrils, and she looked at Walter. "They've fired the village!" She ran to the door, Brand close behind her. Despite his wound, Walter was beside her in an instant, pulling her back from the door before she could glimpse very much.

"I'll not see you place yourself in danger again, Brianna, for our father bade me protect you and help you in any way I could. Now stay behind me!"

She managed nonetheless to peek over his shoulder and drew in her breath sharply when she saw several Normans motioning to a riderless destrier wandering toward a patch of green grass toward the side of the road. "Pray God they do not search here!" she breathed fervently.

"He must have left the animal loose in his greedy haste," said Brand.

"A stroke of luck for us," added Walter in a low voice. "Let us hope they will be content to have a valuable horse— with or without its rider."

One of the two Normans approached the beast cautiously. The great stallion, inured to the noise and confusion of battle, had calmly wandered off. With the reins now securely in his grip, the Norman tied the horse to his own and joined his companion once more.

Several homesteads were on fire and the owners could be seen frantically trying to douse the flames with buckets of water. Slaughtered cattle lay in the road along with pigs and chickens, but the mounted Normans were carrying less than Brianna would have expected. Only two ponies were laden down with what looked like sacks of seed corn, and tied to Norman mounts.

"They appear to be preparing to leave."

Brianna silently agreed with Walter's assessment of the situation. It seemed to her that the raid had been short-lived, and although she was grateful for it, she wondered at the reason.

"Look—over there!" Walter commanded sharply.

Brianna and Brand looked over to the left where two Normans sat poised upon their horses, as if waiting for the others to finish their work. With a quick gesture, one of them astride a dun-colored mount dispatched the other, who rode through the village shouting in French to the remaining nine or ten. One by one they gathered what they had taken and rode toward the knight waiting at the end of Derford. When they all had gathered around him, they began a leisurely withdrawal eastward, apparently unconcerned that they were less one man.

"Thank God they did not search for *him,*" Brand said with relief evident in his voice.

And then, as the knight who seemed to be their leader remained where he was for a few moments longer, Brianna felt her heart begin to hammer in her chest. There was something familiar about the mounted figure, but she could tell nothing from his helmeted head. And as if in answer to her silent question, he slipped his helm off and ran a forearm across his brow. Then he quickly replaced it and, guiding his destrier's head around, turned and cantered away, a cloud of dust rising to mingle with the insidiously spreading smoke from the fires.

Brianna turned and leaned back against the wall beside the door, shock, dismay and then rage all hurtling through her in rapid succession. She had recognized his features the moment the knight had removed his headgear to wipe his forehead. She would never forget that face as long as she lived. It had been seared into her memory as if with a white-hot poker.

For it was none other than Roland de Beaufort.

CHAPTER 5

All the inhabitants of Derford pitched in willingly—almost eagerly—to repair and rebuild the structures which had been damaged by the fires set by the Normans. They welcomed the extra work to keep their hands and minds occupied lest they dwell upon the fact that the new Norman lord might arrive at any time. The consensus was that this was the reason Wulfric's manor had remained untouched. The men who had been feeding and giving water to the animals hidden in the forest, and seeing to the most basic tasks on the thane's property, had reported that no one seemed to have set foot behind the palisade surrounding Wulfric's stronghold.

"They must have been reasonably sure that someone well known to them would be granted land in this part of Wessex— even Derford itself," Kerwick remarked one night several weeks later after the evening meal. It was the middle of November, and the icy winds from the north necessitated a roaring fire in the central hearth of the hall. Nedra had sent Brand to fetch Brianna and Gilbert to sup with them, and now they all sat listening to Kerwick and his three sons discussing what the future might bring.

Gilbert dozed in his chair, a very silent Brianna nearby. Aleen, her sister Edythe, and Nedra sat close to her, trying to engage her in conversation. Nedra glanced across the room at Kerwick, catching his troubled gaze on Brianna. Brand and his oldest brother, Edwin, were discussing the advantages of a mounted army, now that Edwin's back and leg injuries from

Hastings were almost completely healed. Walter's eyes were also on Brianna, his concern every bit as evident as that displayed by his father and mother.

The burden of guilt weighed heavily upon Brianna. The responsibility for the death of another human being was troublesome enough for anyone unused to violence. But for one raised in a religious house, it increased tenfold. As much as she detested the Normans and the other mercenaries who had subjugated her people, and as much as she had wanted to save Walter's life, Brianna still could not come to grips with the fact that she had taken a life. Everyone had tried to persuade her that she had not meant to kill him, but merely to stop his attack on Walter. But their comforting words could not change the fact that, no matter what her intentions, the man was dead by her hand.

She turned inward for strength and consolation, but to those around her it seemed as though she had withdrawn from everyone but Gilbert. Her acceptance of this dinner invitation was in fact her first sojourn into company since the Norman raid.

Just then something Edwin was saying to his father caught Brianna's attention. ". . . told me that the Bastard carried the papal banner. He even wore a pendant with holy relics inside around his neck—so 'tis said. Surely the rumor is absurd!"

Brianna's head snapped up, her eyes alight with interest for the first time in days. " 'Tis true, Edwin. I saw the banner myself when I was taken to William's tent."

Startled faces turned to her instantly. "Are you certain, child?" Kerwick demanded.

"He told me himself."

Walter gave a low whistle that pierced the uneasy atmosphere her words had created. "Then perhaps that is the reason for King Harold's unseemly haste to leave London before his remaining troops had rested properly and before he was even assured of enough new recruits to fill his depleted ranks."

"I do not understand, Walter."

He sighed and regarded his father resignedly. "If Harold knew of this papal support—and there is no doubt messages must have been exchanged between the two men—then he would not have wanted rumors of it to spread before he could meet and defeat William."

"Aye," agreed Edwin. "It could have been disastrous had there been rumors before he even left London."

Kerwick stroked his bearded chin thoughtfully. "After all, what Anglo-Saxon would risk excommunication by fighting against an army blessed by the Pope?"

Surprising bitterness tinged Brianna's answer. "Anglo-Saxons who did not believe it! What had King Harold or England done to deserve such dire punishment? I'll warrant you that England was not even represented because Harold was never informed when the Norman put his case before the Pontiff. The whole thing smacks of treachery!"

Her words echoed in the ensuing silence; the same thought was going through Kerwick's mind as well, which was borne out when he spoke.

"You are probably right, Brianna, to believe that papal approval was obtained by deception and no doubt much political maneuvering that is beyond our simple understanding. But no matter the method; if it is true, it will be devastating to what is left of the morale of the English people. They will not fight an edict from the Church of Rome."

"But if they are angry enough at the Church's decision they could also ignore the possibility of excommunication and fight the Normans at every turn. This entire travesty may turn many of them against Rome." Brianna's spirit of rebellion shocked even her and she clamped her mouth shut, wondering what was happening to her.

A calm voice spoke from the shadows, soothing her turbulent emotions. "You must try to heal your bitterness and guilt, my daughter." Father Simon had entered quietly while they were engaged in conversation. He moved forward into the firelight and, after politely declining refreshment, he pulled a chair over to where Brianna sat and handed her a sealed letter. At her puzzled expression, he said quietly, " 'Tis a letter from the Abbess at Walshire."

Brianna's eyes lit up. "For *me,* Father?"

"Aye, child. It arrived by messenger this eve."

"Thank . . . thank you, Father. I—" She gave an apologetic look to the others. "I will read it after Gilbert and I return home."

"As you wish, Brianna," said Nedra with understanding in her voice. In her excitement, Brianna did not see the look that passed between Kerwick and the priest, for it was at Kerwick's request that Father Simon had written and dispatched a letter to the nun, informing her of Gilbert's injuries.

The evening dragged interminably for Brianna. She longed to get home and read the precious missive, but courtesy made her stay and at least affect a minimal amount of interest in the conversation around her.

At last Father Simon stood up to take his leave, the signal that she could now also depart.

Once Gilbert was safely abed, Brianna returned to the main hall and, by the light of a dying fire in the hearth, broke the sealing wax and began to read what seemed to be a lifeline thrown to her unexpectedly as she foundered in a sea of unhappiness.

My Dearest Brianna,

How many times I have thought of you! Yet everything has happened so unexpectedly and swiftly, and we at Walshire have been overwhelmed with healing our brave people—spiritually as well as in body.

You must bear no ill feelings toward Father Simon, for he had your best interests at heart when he wrote to me.

It was with the greatest sorrow that I received the news of Gilbert. He is such a fine lad. I pray God he will recover more fully and you both may share a normal and happy life together. If he remains as Father Simon described him, you must not despair, Brianna. Your going to Derford was nothing less than a blessing, for who would have cared as well for my nephew as you? It is not for us to understand God's will, but merely to submit to it.

There is something else, Brianna, of which you should be apprised, for I am the only person—besides your father, should he be yet alive—who knows of your origins. And in these troubled times, we never know what the future holds. Your father, Robert of Wessex, was a very wealthy thane of King Harold's when he was Earl of Wessex. His wife, the lady Alicia, was your mother. She died in childbed and Thane Robert brought you here to live. I suspect you reminded him too painfully of his beautiful wife, so he entrusted you to our care, giving me the authority to either take you into the order or to give you in marriage to whomever I thought worthy. What I would have you know, dearest child, is that you are gently born. I cannot foresee if this knowledge will ever be of any use to you, but I felt that it was time for you to be told.

I must close now, my Brianna, for we are so desperately needed in the village and surrounding areas that my poor order gets little rest. We must help wherever we can.

God go with you and Gilbert and keep you both safe from further harm . . . .

The closing words blurred before her as Brianna closed her eyes and let the tears come. She buried her head in her arms as she leaned on the table and sobbed—great, racking sobs that shook her entire body. What of her father? she wondered miserably. Why had Robert of Wessex never contacted her during all these years? Surely, if he had been possessed of any compassion or love for the child of his late wife, the passing of time would only have served to assuage his grief as well as the pain he'd once felt at the very sight of his daughter. At the least he could have tried to get in touch with her—even if only to see her briefly. Unless he were dead. And while that possibility brought home an even deeper sense of loss, it also served to alleviate some of her disillusionment, for it could have well been the reason for his failure to come forth.

As the tears flowed, however, some of the pain and bitterness began to leave her. And when Brianna's tears were spent, she felt somewhat lightened of the burdens she had carried with her since her return to Derford from Hastings. Yet she knew with a wisdom beyond her years that although the Reverend Mother's advice was sound and well-directed, the good woman could not possibly rid Brianna of her sorrows from the haven of Walshire.

Still, the letter was uplifting, and the reconciliation that was essential for Brianna's conscience began from the moment she read it. Brianna knew that in time the wounds would heal, but she also knew that it would take more than a week or a month or even a year.

But time was a luxury she was not to be granted.

"Gilbert! Where are you?"

Brianna had searched every hiding place she could think of among the several small structures that made up the homestead, but to no avail. "Gilbert! Please come out!" she entreated. Since the incursion he seemed to have suffered a setback and had begun to wander off in genuine fear to cower in some dark corner or a quiet place in the forest. Brand or Brianna, or sometimes even Aleen, would have to discover his hiding place, in order to soothe him and bring him home again. Brianna never knew when he would amble off. But although she feared for his safety, she absolutely refused to confine him. She felt he had suffered enough without having to be penned up like some disobedient animal.

"Gilbert!" she cried in frustration as she came through the rear entrance of the hall. There he was, a lopsided grin on his face, standing near the door which led to the road, as if expecting her to give chase. *Well, at least he is only playing* and not terrified of something, she thought with relief as she mustered a smile for him.

In mock annoyance she put her hands on her hips, an unconvincing scowl on her lovely features. "So there you are! You gave me a fine fright, Gilbert! Now come here and I will fix you something to eat. Are you hungry?" She made a motion as if putting something into her mouth, and his smile widened. He started to hobble toward the table with the aid of his sturdy walking stick.

Brianna suddenly remembered she had not smeared any soot on her face. In her fervent desire to keep to her disguise of an unkempt youth, she had faithfully worn her altered braies, undertunic and tunic along with a pair of Gilbert's large, heavy shoes. But she occasionally forgot to dirty her face.

As she bent to withdraw cold ashes from the edge of the hearth, she did not catch the thunder of horses' hooves in the distance. Rubbing vigorously at her cheeks, she said, "Nedra sent over some freshly baked bread, Gilbert, and I . . ." Her voice faltered and trailed off as she heard the thump of the wooden cane hitting the floor at surprisingly quick, regular intervals. She looked up in annoyance at this unexpected and unwelcome continuation of his game and froze. Gilbert had disappeared, and the sound that greeted her ears raised the hair on the back of her neck. Horses. Gilbert had no doubt heard them too, and had fled in the direction that afforded the least amount of safety—the road.

Oh, dear God! she thought wildly as she raced toward the door in her panic, dismissing all thought save that of Gilbert's safety. She moved as if in a nightmare, her feet as heavy as lead, her progress seeming painfully slow as she crossed the room. By the time she reached the entrance, the thunderous pounding was much louder and there was no sign of Gilbert.

Outside, she ran toward the road through a light but steady drizzle. The overcast sky was nonetheless fairly bright and she could now faintly discern Gilbert's figure ahead of her, about to cross the road to the beckoning safety of the forest on the south side.

Casting aside all common sense and caution, Brianna made a desperate bid to gain enough ground on Gilbert to thwart him and drag him back to relative safety before the horsemen were upon them. This was no easy trick, as the ground was beginning to turn to slick mud.

As she reached the road, she heard someone call her name, but no power on earth could have moved her from her purpose. *"Gilbert!"* she cried in desperation. Then, halfway to the other side, a harsh curse in French met her ears as her foot, in its oversized male shoe, slipped in the mire and she lost her balance just as Gilbert cleared the road.

As she went down she heard the protesting scream of a horse and stared up dumbly at wildly flailing hooves. A mounted Norman was furiously sawing back on the beast's reins, causing it to rear and slide in the mud only inches from Brianna's unprotected head.

She wondered dazedly why a Norman would bother to avoid injuring a mere Saxon lad of no consequence as the other riders reined in around her and the knight who had skillfully avoided trampling her. The sight of the detested Normans brought on a torrent of unwelcome feelings, but this brush with death made her aware how much she wanted to live—at any cost. Therefore, it was of the utmost importance that she keep her wits about her, and her turbulent feelings to herself.

For the horse that now stood quietly over her was white as newly fallen snow, and the figure astride it could only belong to one man. Even with his battle helm, Brianna would have known him anywhere now. All the hatred she harbored for William and his hordes of mercenaries, and what they had done to her life and that of the man she had wed, was directed at the tall, forbidding-looking knight who sat so confidently above her. And she dared not give in to her desire to unsheath the Norman dagger at her waist underneath her clothing and fling it at him.

Her eyes blazed as she slowly picked herself up and backed away slightly from the fearsome war-horse.

"What the devil did you hope to accomplish by jumping into our path, boy?"

"And since when does a Norman care aught about one more English life?" she returned in a taut, hard voice, fighting for control.

"Since this is now part of my newly granted land from Duke William. And you are of as much concern to me as any of them." He gestured toward the villagers who had cautiously gathered to witness the disturbance.

Despite her resolve, Brianna's temper was gaining the upper hand. All the festering guilt and confusion that was still with her sought release, and the object of her hatred had said precisely the wrong thing.

"I will *never* be subject to your will, Norman," she growled in as deep a voice as she could muster.

He ignored the contemptuous comment and slowly removed his helm. "What is your name, lad?"

The sight of his well-chiseled features—the thin red scar along one side of his jaw that had not been there before, the alert silver-gray eyes, the short, tousled, sandy-colored hair that had escaped the mail coif covering his head—all combined to make her hate him even more for the conflicting emotions he aroused in her. Brianna was so furious with him and herself that she could only stammer, "Bri—er, Bryce."

"Bryce, is it? Well, Bryce, even though you have grievous need of a bath, I have never seen finer features on a young man." A corner of his mouth quirked, and several of the others closest to him laughed good-naturedly.

The longing to wipe the smirk off his splendid face gripped Brianna with such force that she had to clench her teeth together to keep from blurting out what she had done to the last Norman who had made such an observation. Instead, she threw him a look of pure loathing as she unexpectedly demanded,

"Why have you come back, Norman? Have you not done enough damage?"

He studied her with narrowed eyes now, the laughter dying; the silence was suddenly deafening.

"Aye," some little imp prompted her to continue, "you and your kind have been here before."

"Then Derford was raided?"

How did he know the name of their village? she wondered before she cried, "As if you did not know it! Would you add lying to your many other crimes, Norman?" Her voice was losing its lower pitch. "I saw you with my own eyes!"

He considered this a moment as he sat back in his saddle, a slight frown on his face.

Just then a moving figure on the periphery of Brianna's vision attracted her attention, and she turned her head to see Gilbert coming toward them. His face was twisted with anger as he made his way over the mud with that curious thump-hop, thump-hop as he placed his crude walking stick ahead of his good leg before hopping forward. "Bra-na! Bra-na!" he managed to call out as he steered himself toward Roland de Beaufort.

Brianna was momentarily rooted to the ground in fear as several men closest to Roland drew their swords.

"Nay, Gilbert!" she cried as she threw her arms around him just in time to prevent him from attacking the knight who seemed to be a threat to her.

She struggled with him, silently thanking God that his pronunciation of her name had been so garbled that the knight would not be likely to recognize it. Walter was suddenly beside her and together they calmed the distraught Gilbert, Walter restraining him as Brianna spoke in hushed, gentle tones to him.

Roland watched with an unreadable expression on his face. "What happened to this man?"

Walter hastily spoke up before Brianna could open her mouth, fearful that she would give herself away. "He was struck in the head at Hastings, my lord.'' There was resentment in his voice, but since he did not want to antagonize the leader of this new group of Normans, he addressed him with grudging respect.

In a flash, William of Normandy's words came back to Roland as he regarded the three young people before him: *The girl lives in the village of Derford, for she said her husband was Gilbert of Derford. It just so happens that I have need of a loyal man in that part of Wessex. Perhaps you would be interested in the holdings of a certain wealthy thane known as Wulfric . . . .*

Roland said nothing of his thoughts, even though he wanted to inquire about the girl whose face had haunted his dreams. Instead he merely asked, ''Are you this Gilbert's only kin?''

''Aye,'' was the sullen answer. ''We work this homestead—or we did until my hus—er, my brother was disabled by a Norman mace.''

He studied her intently, as if trying to see through the grime and baggy clothing. ''I regret what happened to your brother, lad, but war is no child's game. Perhaps we can find someone to help you keep up the lands and care for the animals.''

Brianna straightened proudly, her chin set determinedly; the gesture was perplexingly familiar to Roland. ''If you mean that you are now lord of these lands, there is naught any of us can do about that. But I will die before I accept help from a Norman.'' Her passionate words brought a suspicious wetness to her eyes, and for one mortifying instant she thought she would cry.

''You may one day soon regret your hasty refusal of my offer, *Bryce*,'' Roland replied softly, oddly emphasizing her hastily assumed name, and then he ordered all three of them back off the road toward the rest of the gathered villagers, and wheeled his huge stallion toward the small crowd. He surveyed them slowly, impervious to the drizzle that still fell. He was prepared to be fair with them—they were *his* people now.

But he knew he had a long way to go before they would give him their loyalty—to say nothing of their trust.

"We have just come from Wulfric's stronghold, and I will make it my home until another can be built for me.· I cannot answer for the behavior of my fellow Normans, and other mercenaries who have viewed this invasion as a holy crusade, since we ride under the papal banner. But I will swear to you that I am not here to plunder or destroy your village.

"Therefore I will require an oath of fealty from each and every one of you, which in turn will entitle you to my protection from any more incursions by anyone—Normans included."

His eyes fell upon Kerwick, standing in front eyeing Roland with keen, perceptive blue eyes. Brianna and Walter stood protectively nearby. "What are you called, old man?"

"Kerwick."

"What damage was done to you in lives and property during the attack on your village?"

"They burned a homestead, two cottages and half of our seed corn. There was some random slaughter of livestock, my lord, but not enough to seriously harm our reserves. The draft oxen were not harmed, although our harvest next year will only be about one-half the usual—that is, if no other misfortunes befall us." He paused, lowering his eyes for a moment. "No one from Derford was killed."

Roland glanced at Brianna and then addressed all the villagers once more. "Canterbury has surrendered and Edith, King Edward's widow and Harold's sister, has submitted Winchester to William of her own free will. And now London is surrounded and there has been little resistance to William. The Archbishop of Canterbury, Stigand, has already seen the wisdom of surrendering the crown to William, for he could only incur the Pope's displeasure by defying the man chosen as the instrument of God's vengeance for England's sins.

"Therefore, by Duke William's command, I lay claim to all that was Wulfric's. I will rule with a firm hand, and if you cooperate, very little will change. But I warn you that I will brook no disobedience or treachery.''

These last comments were not heard by all, for at the news of the defection of Archbishop Stigand and the fact that the Pope had been in support of the invasion, murmurs of surprise and fear spread angrily through the crowd.

Brianna too, as though explaining Roland's message, was speaking to Gilbert in hushed tones, her small arm comfortingly around his shoulders as he stared in fear at the mounted men before him. Roland watched the villagers as they digested his news.

The realization suddenly dawned on him with such startling clarity that for one shocking moment it almost destroyed his composure: This *Bryce* was not the crippled young man's brother. The face was too fair, the body too slim and graceful—the swaggering movements could not hide their utter femininity. And the eyes. Even if he had never seen her again, he would always remember those eyes.

Father Simon stepped forward. ''I would inquire as to the legitimacy of that claim, er—?''

''Roland.''

''Well then, my lord Roland, with all due respect, I believe we are entitled to clarification of your words concerning the Pope and using the Archbishop as an 'instrument of God's revenge.' Are we to understand that Duke William was—and still is—supported by His Holiness?''

Roland, his eyes returning to Brianna, was making some mental comparisons, contrasting the hatred he had seen in her eyes when she had looked at him, with the tenderness on her features every time she looked at the man who was evidently the husband she had sought at Hastings. He tore his gaze away from Brianna and Gilbert to address the priest.

Carefully choosing his words, he answered, ''I do not know the particulars of what went on between the Pontiff and the Duke's representatives, but I can tell you truly that my lord carries a papal bull and wears a pendant round his neck containing holy relics. I give you my word on this before God, as a man of honor.''

Murmurs rippled through the gathering crowd like small waves in a pond as this information was assimilated.

''Since when are Normans men of honor?'' gritted Brianna under her breath, and Walter quickly grabbed her arm in warning.

''Do not be a fool,'' he said through clenched teeth. ''If you anger them, there is no telling what they will do to you. And remember, they think you are a boy, so they will not spare you.''

''And I tell you I do not care,'' she retorted fiercely. ''If you believe one word he utters, you are a fool, for he is a liar!''

''How do you know?''

''He was here during the raid. He was one of the leaders—*I saw him!*''

Walter stared at her in disbelief. ''How can you be so sure?''

''Because I also saw him at Hastings and I will never forget his face as long as I live.''

Walter had no immediate answer for this, but their low, intense exchange had riled Gilbert, who had been leaning upon his cane between them. The anger on his face was totally replaced once more by terror, and he strained to be free of Brianna's encircling arm, looking anxiously toward the main hall and safety.

''You may stay here and listen to his lies.'' She nodded her head toward Roland, who was patiently answering several more questions put to him by Father Simon. ''I must take him away from all this, or he will flee again.'' Brianna turned toward the hall, Gilbert in tow.

''Bryce!''

The voice was commanding, and in spite of herself Brianna halted, slowly turning to face him.

''I would speak to you privately concerning this matter of

my having been here before. On the morrow I will send one of my men for you at terce.''

Before she could answer, he signaled to the party around him, turned the white charger and made for the stronghold on his newly granted demesne.

CHAPTER 6

The cold, light rain stopped in the early evening and a clear sliver of a moon shone brilliantly in the brisk night air. All signs of activity on the estate of the late Wulfric came to a halt. A fire in the central hearth of the great hall glowed as most of Roland's men settled down on pallets for the night. Several men-at-arms manned the watch at various points along the wooden palisade; otherwise all was still.

In one of the sleeping houses, fires from several iron braziers cast an eerie luminescence over the bower. Roland had shed his mail and sat on a chair before one of the braziers, a thoughtful frown creasing his brow. A tall, dark-visaged man of imposing stature leaned casually against one wall regarding his companion as the shadows from the flickering flames played over both their faces.

"Well, Roland, are you content with your acquisition from our good Duke?"

Roland threw his man a look of both humor and annoyance. "You know as well as I, Dane, that 'twas my father who insisted I go with William in his stead. I had no quarrel with Harold Godwinson, despite William's accusations and his political manipulations to obtain Pope Alexander's backing."

"I see. Well, need I remind you that you speak treason?" Dane asked wryly.

"And will you betray my confidence, *mon ami?*"

Dane threw up his hands in mock repentance, a low growl of laughter escaping his lips. "You know me better than that,

Roland. We are sworn blood brothers. Or do you not honor our childhood vows?''

Roland stood up impatiently. ''Of course I do, but I cannot fathom why William granted me a fief in the heart of Harold Godwinson's former earldom!'' He unconsciously ran a thumb along the new scar that marked his jaw.

Dane pushed himself away from the wall and went to warm his hands over the brazier. ''William is shrewd and he knows he has less than your wholehearted support, so he has placed you where you are most needed—where your loyalty to him is needed for you to survive. He knows that as your father's son you can do naught but your utmost to uphold your family name, as well as your own reputation as a man of honor.''

Roland stopped his pacing and regarded Dane with unconcealed admiration. ''You are very clever, my good friend. I believe you have something there. So be it. But although I have accepted his reward for services rendered and will serve him loyally, I will never condone what was done to Harold and his people.''

''But you must never let them know, or *they* will rule *you.*''

Roland nodded in agreement and came to stand beside him. ''There is a mystery here, however, which I intend to solve—and quickly.''

Dane raised a dark eyebrow questioningly.

''The village has been raided before, and according to the lad Bryce, *I* was here at that time. It can only mean one thing.''

''Ranulf.''

''Aye.''

''But Ranulf loves you. Surely he would do nothing to jeopardize your position here.''

''No, he would not.'' He raised a hand to stroke the angry red line along his jaw, thinking of the one responsible for inflicting it. ''Hugh of Brittany would, though.''

''What do you mean?''

''The Breton was angry enough to come to blows with me over the girl I took from under his nose. If he got wind of where William was sending me, he might easily have come to Derford or the surrounding area to cause trouble.''

"But what has that got to do with Ranulf?"

"I am surprised that one so clever as you cannot see something so obvious." A glint of humor shone in the quicksilver eyes. "Ranulf managed to convince the Breton of his dislike and envy of me—or some such thing—and actually *joined* him in the raid. Being closer to William and higher in rank, Ranulf more than likely oversaw the raid and stopped it just short of being truly catastrophic for Derford.''

Dane's face betrayed genuine delight at this admirable piece of reasoning. "Of course! Ranulf could do no less. Why else would Derford have suffered so little compared to other Anglo-Saxon villages? 'Twould appear the joke is on Hugh of Brittany.''

"Aye, but I will deal with him when the time comes," Roland replied grimly.

"I would not want to be in his shoes." Dane's topaz eyes turned serious for a moment. "Nay, I fear the Breton's days are numbered. And on that note, I will bid you good night, *mon·ami.*''

Roland smiled good-naturedly at him. "Sleep well, for we have an unenviable task before us.''

"*You* have an unenviable task before you, Roland, for I shall remain only as long as you need me. Then I shall return to Normandy to help my father." And before Roland could object, Dane gave him a mocking salute and left.

As he made ready for bed Roland's thoughts returned to William's reasons for granting him lands right in the middle of Wessex. It occurred to him that the clever Duke of Normandy had made good use of Roland's ill-concealed interest in Brianna of Derford.

With a muttered oath he kicked off his boots and sat down on the large bed. Since when had anyone ever read him where a woman was concerned? I must be getting soft, he thought in disgust, to act like a besotted swain—and over an Anglo-

Saxon peasant girl. He thought of the dressing-down he would give Brianna in the morning for trying to foist off her ridiculous charade on him. He was probably the laughingstock of the entire village by now.

His thoughts were sour for a long while before he was finally able to relax and fall asleep.

Brianna slept very little that night. She alternated between fear of discovery and anger at the audacity of Roland de Beaufort. The very sight of him brought back memories she would rather have kept buried. It was almost as if he had been sent to remind her of the horror of Hastings, and her anguish and revulsion at having had to commit murder the day of the raid.

For the first time in her life, Brianna wanted to run away—as fast and as far as she could. If it weren't for Gilbert she could have gone back to the abbey at Walshire. To a safe haven— *Nay!* That would be cowardly.

She eventually succumbed to sleep, after assuring herself over and over of her ability to deal with Roland de Beaufort.

When she stood before him in the morning in the great hall, however, Brianna lost much of her hard-won self-confidence. She felt cornered—as if somehow she were walking into a trap set by Roland de Beaufort. She knew she was being ridiculous; he did not know who she was.

Or did he? Had his keen senses caught all the unintentional slips which could raise serious questions about her identity to someone who had seen her before and knew her name and the fact that she lived in Wessex?

She had taken great pains with her disguise today, but that did not guarantee it would deceive Roland when she finally confronted him. She scowled, much as she had seen Brand and Walter do, as he dismissed his men-at-arms and then stood conferring with another tall Norman. Both were wearing long, tight-sleeved undertunics, or chainses, with overtunics that came to midthigh and were belted at the waist. Braies covered their well-muscled legs and were tucked into finely spun chausses and cross-garters at the knee.

"We will not bite you, lad," said the dark-haired stranger. Impressive in face and form, he was the exact opposite in coloring of Roland de Beaufort. "I will leave you in privacy here, *mon ami,*" he said to Roland as Brianna frowned at his inference that she was afraid.

And then he was gone and she was left alone with the man whose very name was anathema to her.

"So," Roland began, stepping forward into the light of the wall torches in the dim hall to better inspect her, "you say you believe I was here before."

"Aye!" Brianna surreptitiously let out her pent-up breath. He meant only to question her about her accusation.

"And you saw me with your own eyes?"

"I did," she affirmed resolutely, more at ease because her identity was not in question.

"Was I riding Odo, perchance?"

A perplexed look momentarily crossed her dirt-stained features. "Well, er . . . no. But no doubt you have several such beasts at your disposal," she said in self-defense, her assurance crumbling a little at the way he was questioning her.

"Do you think I am such a black-hearted cur that I would attack an all-but-defenseless village?"

"You are a Norman. What more is there to be said?"

He sighed. "And to you, no doubt, every Norman, Breton, Fleming and the like is to be hated equally."

"How else am I to feel?"

"Would you believe me if I told you that I was not in favor of the invasion? That I owed Harold Godwinson my life?"

Momentarily nonplussed, she could only stare at him with wide eyes, wondering why he should even care that she know.

"When Harold was at Duke William's court two or three summers past, he accompanied my lord on a mission to relieve Dol Castle, which was besieged by Count Conan of Brittany."

"Near the monastery of Mont-Saint-Michel?"

"Aye." Roland continued as if there were nothing unusual about a country youth being familiar with Norman geography. "While crossing the estuary I unwittingly became trapped in quicksand, as did one other man. Harold valiantly rescued us both, putting his own life in peril, and carried me to safety on his back while he dragged the other man to shore."

Brianna was silent for a moment, thinking only of the bravery of the king who had been mercilessly cut down by perhaps the very men whose lives he had so generously saved. Her aquamarine eyes grew misty, and she turned her back to him for a moment. When she regarded him again, her face was a study in hatred. "Is *this* how you repay the favor?"

"There were obligations I had to fulfill—"

"Do not tell me of your 'obligations,' for I spit on them!" She was suddenly shaking, as much from the boldness of her outburst as from her anger. "Is plundering Anglo-Saxon villages also a way of showing your gratitude? If so, you cannot place a very high value on your life!"

"I did *not* raid your village!"

"You lie, de Beaufort, for I saw you!"

Roland ran his fingers through his hair distractedly, for he knew she would never believe the truth. And for some reason, he wanted her to believe him.

And then it occurred to him that he had not revealed his full name to the residents of Derford the day before. Frustrated at the way the conversation was going, Roland pounced on this. "How do you know my name, *Bryce?*"

Brianna was only caught off guard for a moment, for her mind was as quick as his. "I asked one of your men. And *I* wonder why you have summoned me here at all. What interest would you have in a simple Anglo-Saxon lad?"

Too late. Even as the words were spoken Brianna realized her mistake. She should have directed the dialogue toward anything but this.

"Lass," he corrected, and advanced on her like a beast

stalking its prey until he was inches from her, silver-gray eyes boring into hers as if he would see into her very soul. One lean, strong finger tilted her chin even higher as he inspected her face.

She held her breath, not daring to look away as she longed to do.

"No disguise on earth could keep you safe from me."

"Nor—Normans are wont to go after those weaker and more vulnerable than themselves," she whispered in sudden fear.

"That is not what I meant, and well you know it, Brianna of Derford."

The words mobilized her into action and she struck his hand away in panic. "I . . . my name is *Bryce,* Norman, and you"—she desperately looked around for a means of escape— "do me a grave injustice to call me a female." Her attempt to sound indignant failed miserably as her voice lost much of its unnatural gruffness.

Roland grabbed her shoulders firmly as he read her intention to flee. "You will not admit to what is obvious?"

"Naught is obvious! Especially the reason you had me brought here! May . . . may I go now?"

Ignoring her entreaty, he called over his shoulder to one of the servants, "A bath—a bath in my chamber with all haste!" And he picked her up and tossed her over his shoulder.

"Put me down, you devil! How . . . how dare you—" she sputtered, all traces of her affected masculine voice gone now.

As his long, easy strides took them toward one of the doors, he only asked, "Will you admit you are Brianna?"

"My name is Bryce—*Bryce!*" Brianna pummeled his broad back with clenched fists in frustration and rising terror, her obstinacy refusing to allow her to reveal what he already knew.

Roland cleared the door and began to make his way to the largest bower before he dimly heard an urgent voice behind him over the noise of his victim's decidedly feminine shrieks. He half turned, irritated at the interruption, and stared for a moment in surprise at an extremely agitated servant with two men right behind him—Father Simon and Kerwick.

"I beg your pardon, my lord, but—"

With an irritated wave of his hand, Roland cut him off and dismissed him, and then faced the two men expectantly. "This had better merit disrupting important and pressing private matters," he warned.

The two men looked at each other in bewilderment, and then Father Simon took the initiative. "It . . . er, does, my lord. It involves—"

"Unhand me, Norman dog, or I shall—"

A small squeal of mortification issued from the burden on his shoulder as he unexpectedly smacked its bottom; then it sputtered and was silent. "Where are your manners, girl?" he admonished. "You were saying, Father?"

Both men looked terribly affronted and Roland briefly wondered why, since he perceived himself to be the one who should be offended.

"It involves the girl you are . . . er, carrying," the priest finished rather lamely. "We humbly beg an audience with you concerning her."

Roland was surprised but did not show it. "Now?"

Both men nodded emphatically.

Suspecting the matter had to be of consequence for them to have risked their new lord's displeasure, Roland told them to wait in the great hall and he would join them shortly.

Roland quickly sought out Dane and found him in the other bower. He handed over Brianna with instructions to make certain she remained in his quarters—even if Dane had to bind her hands and feet to a chair—until he returned.

Dane ungently smacked the squirming, shrieking Brianna on the backside. *"Her?"*

"Aye, *mon ami.* Have a care, for he is a she," Roland cautioned, and left before the puzzled Dane could question him.

When Roland joined the plainly agitated men, he got right

to the point. "Now, what is it you wish to tell me concerning Brianna?"

Once again the two Anglo-Saxons looked at one another in astonishment and then at the somewhat irate Norman before them. "I . . . we believe you should know that Bryce—I mean Brianna—is not quite . . . ah, normal, my lord," began the priest uncertainly.

This proved too much for Kerwick—especially upon noting Roland's skeptically uplifted eyebrow at this inept statement. His temper took over. "Father means to say, Lord Roland, that Brianna has led a most sheltered life and was then unintentionally thrown into a frightful situation."

At Roland's apparent interest, he continued. "I was commissioned by the Abbess at Walshire to bring her here—to Derford—to wed the good nun's nephew, Gilbert. She had lived most of her life in the abbey, and she was as shy and sweet a lass as ever passed through our village."

Roland frowned, although not in irritation with the two men.

Kerwick perceived it that way, however, and the anger in his voice was very apparent as he began to speak. "But—"

"But God saw fit to take her new husband from her to serve in Harold's army," interjected the smooth voice of Father Simon, who by this time had recovered enough to step in and save Kerwick from his potentially dangerous course. "And when Gilbert did not return, Brianna went to Hastings herself to find his body."

"I know," Roland said quietly. "I took her to William's tent. That is how I knew her name."

Kerwick intervened once more. "She has been through much, my lord. More than any woman ought."

Roland nodded thoughtfully. "And why does she dress herself as a lad?"

"Fear of rape, my lord. She has never known a man, you see, and . . ." His words trailed off at the look on Roland's face. His eyes were glued to Kerwick's features in the brief, ensuing silence.

"But she is married—"

"Gilbert left immediately after the ceremony and—well, you saw him."

Roland slowly sank to a nearby bench, seeming unaware of his two visitors for a few moments. These revelations explained so many things . . . .

"We only wished to ask for leniency in your dealings with her, my lord," said Father Simon.

The fair-haired knight suddenly stood to his full height and faced them, an angry scowl darkening his face. "Do you take me for such a heartless, unfeeling lout, Father? Nay, 'tis too soon for you to know me, but that is not my way." He let out a heavy sigh. "No doubt you believe I was about to ravish the girl, but you are far off the mark. I am no user of women—at least unwilling women!" He paced a short distance and swiftly returned, hands behind his back, a slight frown creasing his strong, smooth brow as he stared absently ahead. "But I could not fathom that hint of meekness that was contradicted by flashes of unusual spirit. Now I can see how her training must constantly be at odds with her natural inclinations."

Assured for the most part that Roland intended Brianna no harm, Kerwick asked anxiously, "Do you think she saw us, my lord? She would not be pleased if she thought we had risked your wrath for her sake."

Roland assured him that Brianna had raised such a ruckus herself that not only had she not seen them, but she probably had not recognized their voices. "I think you are safe, Kerwick," he told the older man, a hint of a smile lurking on his chiseled lips. "I would have a word with her yet, but you are free to go."

The two men left the great hall vastly relieved that their new Norman overlord was perhaps human after all.

Roland returned immediately to the bower and flung open the door to find his best friend and his prisoner eyeing one another warily. Brianna was not in any way restrained, but Dane appeared ready to launch himself at her any moment.

At his unannounced entrance they both turned, and Brianna, having seen the two Saxons approach Roland, sensed intuitively they had revealed all in their desire to protect her.

Roland closed the door and leaned back against it, his face shadowed. "This, *mon ami,* is Brianna of Derford, of whom I spoke to you." He purposely made his voice expressionless to hide the fact that he was angry. Angry with himself. Angry at what had almost happened. He knew he would never have forced her, but because of her sheltered past and her extremely limited dealings with men, he could have done her irreparable harm.

"The game is over, Brianna," came Roland's implacable pronouncement. "I find there is too much coincidence in the fact that Gilbert of Derford has a 'brother' rather than a wife. That he was only wounded at Hastings and that is why a wife would not have found his body at the battle site. That this 'brother' would be so well educated as to be familiar with the exact location of Mont-Saint-Michel—even pronouncing the French name as if he—or she—had been speaking the language since birth."

Brianna paled in the face of all this, for she knew she could not convincingly refute his words. Roland moved into the firelight and, ignoring her for a moment, spoke in low tones to the dark-haired one.

Dane cast her one more dubious look before exiting.

There was a long, tense silence as the Norman knight and the Anglo-Saxon girl stared at one another. Only Brianna's ashen color gave away her inner anxiety. Roland's expression remained grim, expectant.

His rich, low voice broke the unnatural stillness as he suddenly asked in an oddly husky tone, "Brianna—Brianna, what have you done to yourself?"

His question startled her as much for its unexpectedness as for the underlying warmth of his voice, which was so at odds with his stern expression.

"I have changed, Norman; you once told me that many

things change with war." She turned her back to him to avoid the intense gray eyes, now almost black in the dim interior of the bower.

The naturally melodious voice brought back a flood of memories, and Roland felt his pulse quicken in response. "But to cut off your beautiful hair—"

Brianna whipped around to face him, her anxiety seeking some release in a stinging riposte. "Why not? Would you have some of your marauding countrymen use my body even as William's men now use England?" Her face turned hot with embarrassment. "Will you—please—grant me leave to return home?"

"This is your home, Brianna." The words came from deep within him, unbidden.

Puzzled, she could only stare at him, spellbound against her will by his splendid features. Time seemed suspended, and she felt his eyes roam over her face, clearly seeing what was beneath the grime. In an effort to break the hold he seemed to have on her, she said in a tight voice, "My home is with my husband."

If someone had doused him with a bucket of cold water, Roland could not have been more surprised. "So be it, Brianna. Your husband may live here as well."

Brianna gazed at him dumbly, unable to assimilate this.

"There will come a time when you will realize that you cannot possibly work that land alone. And as you will take no favors from a Norman, mayhap you would be more inclined to accept a mutually beneficial arrangement—a trading of services of sorts."

She silently acknowledged the soundness of his reasoning, but she did not trust him, even to the smallest degree. "What . . . what do you mean?" she asked suspiciously.

"Very simply this," he answered as he moved close enough to touch her. He gazed down at her, an undefinable look in the depths of his eyes. "In exchange for a position in my household—an honest one—I will see to it that Gilbert is properly cared for. You would not have to concern yourself with his whereabouts or his well-being. And, of course, you could be with him whenever you liked.''

Brianna bit her lower lip in indecision, almost tempted to take him up on his offer. But then the vision of this same man surveying the handiwork of his cohorts after they had burned and looted Derford rose up before her, and her stomach turned. She determinedly returned his unwavering gaze, her eyes cold and distant. "I think not, Norman. I would prefer to take Gilbert and live out our lives in the safety of the forest rather than under your roof.''

His eyes narrowed, but he merely said with a slight, mocking bow, "As you wish, urchin. But I do not ever want to behold you in this garb again. You will bathe yourself and dress as a woman should. That is my wish as your overlord. Do you understand?''

After he dismissed Brianna, Roland consoled himself that, stubborn and proud as she might be, in the end she would have no choice but to come to him.

Time was on his side, not hers.

CHAPTER 7

"I will never swear fealty to him!"

The vow she had made only hours before echoed dimly in her mind as Brianna watched the people of Derford assemble before the great hall of their new lord. The morning was beautiful. Many took the warm sun, cool breeze and azure skies to be a good omen, for it was as mild as a spring day.

Everyone had worn his or her best, but it was the Normans who were far and away the most magnificently garbed. She could not take her eyes off the new lord of Derford.

He wore a pure white linen chainse, the tight-fitting sleeves coming down to his wrists. His overtunic was scarlet with gold-embroidered edges, the wide, three-quarter-length sleeves a vivid contrast to the white undertunic. A wide leather belt circled his trim waist, an ornamental sheath for a dagger on one side and a scabbard for his dress sword on the other. Sheath, scabbard and belt buckle were encrusted with precious jewels that winked in the brilliant sunlight. A deep blue mantle, also edged with gold, fell from his shoulders down his back and was the perfect backdrop for the bright tunic. Because of the warmth of the day, the men only wore finely spun chausses and cross-garters tucked into soft leather shoes.

As Brianna helplessly took in every detail concerning Roland de Beaufort's appearance, she felt, for the first time in her life, that she wanted to look beautiful. She felt so inconsequential before their splendor—*his* splendor. Her hands went up to her hair, and she suddenly regretted her rash decision to cut it off.

She had donned her best garments—the ones in which she had been wed. Over a cream-colored undertunic she wore a fine linen bliaud in pale yellow with a bright green mantle falling gracefully over both shoulders to the ground, front and back; plain gold brooches held the double length of material at the shoulders in the Anglo-Saxon style. In spite of her feelings, Brianna still was by far the most richly dressed woman there.

Brianna could not know that Roland was admiring her as well. He was once more puzzled at the mystery surrounding her. Judging from the way she carried herself and a hundred other things about her, Brianna was no mere peasant. Even the meanest of garments could not detract in any way from her beauty. His eyes kept wandering to her throughout the ceremony, a glint of admiration in their quicksilver depths. He wondered at her acceptance of the inevitable, having expected a confrontation in which he would have either had to punish her as an example to the others, or take away her homestead. Both alternatives were abhorrent to him, and he had lost more than a little sleep over the problem the previous night. He suspected Nedra had had more than a little to do with her obvious turnabout, and he was thankful that the woman had so much common sense.

As Roland moved closer to her with Father Simon at his side, Brianna became aware of what he was doing. *Sweet Lord!* she thought in sudden panic. *He is kissing them! On both cheeks!*

The kiss was purely ritualistic, since it was between a liege lord and his vassals. However, some deep-seated instinct warned Brianna that any physical contact between her and Roland de Beaufort would be disastrous. But she could not refuse it.

And then *he* was before her, saying things to her that she could not even hear for the roaring in her ears. She felt icy cold and her face was like carved alabaster in the warm sunlight, her lips and cheeks bloodless. Her aquamarine eyes were enormous in the pale face as she stared into his eyes, feeling as if she were drowning in those warm, silvery pools. His sandy hair glinted like burnished gold in the sun—like a pagan god his Viking ancestors might have worshiped. She tilted her head slightly in preparation for his kiss, but unexpectedly his hand touched the side of her jaw. Startled, she raised her face to his, and he bent down to gently brush warm lips across hers. Her response was shattering and she felt literally helpless in its wake. Could men always do this to women if they so chose? she wondered dazedly as, after what seemed an eternity, he moved on. And did women always feel this helplessness, this desire to cling?

Her feelings were so unnerving she wanted desperately to be alone to examine them. But Kerwick sought her out to make certain that Brianna and Gilbert were within the circle of his family as they entered the hall at the behest of their new seigneur for refreshments. It had been cleaned and some changes made, according to Walter, who had worshiped the late Wulfric to the point of adoration. Fresh rushes had been laid on the stone floor, and several large, beautiful tapestries adorned the walls. From the rafters drying herbs and spices sweetened the air.

But what attracted Brianna's attention were the great hearths at either end of the hall. The raised central hearth had been removed and two huge stone fireplaces had been built into the two end walls, with great hoods suspended above them.

She wandered away from the table where the others were seating themselves, drawn to one of the new stone-walled hearths to more closely study the hood. She froze as she heard Roland's voice behind her. " 'Tis a chimney, Brianna. The smoke rises into the hood and then goes through a smoke chamber in the wall and up through the roof. We use them in our homes in Normandy, and not only do they heat several floors more efficiently, but they keep the smoke to a minimum.''

She slowly turned to look up at him but could think of nothing to say. Nothing at all. Her mouth went dry and her knees felt as if they would buckle.

Roland didn't seem to notice her discomfiture. ''You look lovely today, *ma chère*. I have never seen a Norman woman whose beauty can compare with yours.''

An aura of blatant sensuality seemed to emanate from his tall, smoothly muscled frame, and Brianna felt suffocated by his nearness. Her eyes went to his lips. The lips that had brushed her own so impersonally, yet somehow so warmly, only a short while ago. What was it about this man that turned her bones to water?

Confused, Brianna could only murmur, ''Surely you exaggerate, *chevalier;* how can you liken an ignorant country maid to a Norman woman—any woman—of noble birth and breeding?''

Had Roland not known of her past, he would have been amazed at her lack of awareness of her beauty. He smiled a beautiful smile that would undoubtedly have melted the hardest of female hearts, but Brianna's eyes were on the floor. ''I cannot help but think you more than equal to any woman of good breeding I have met, and I suspect your origins are very fine indeed.'' He tentatively reached out a hand and tilted her chin upward so that her eyes were forced to meet his.

As he drank in her loveliness Brianna suddenly surprised him by speaking. ''Are you not in demand among your new vassals, my lord? Surely they need to speak to you concerning any number of things.''

His eyes were dark with some emotion she could not yet read, his expression once more serious. ''I can always speak to them, *chérie*. 'Tis your company I crave; as a starving man seeks sustenance so do I seek you—''

Brianna jerked her head away, a scarlet hue staining her delicate cheeks. Never had she imagined hearing such an eloquent declaration of admiration—and from a man other than her husband. Surely he took too much for granted! "My oath to you does not entitle you to such liberties!"

But he was undaunted. "And how do I win your favor, lovely Brianna?" he asked gently.

"You do *not,* Norman! Do you forget I am a married woman? You are no better than any of *them*—William and his greedy lot! Going after whatever strikes your fancy!"

"Perhaps, but William felt the prize was worth risking all. And he won."

"I belong to Gilbert!" she cried passionately.

"And England once belonged to Harold."

Brianna's mouth dropped open in astonishment at this comparison. Surely he was addled. Only a Norman would say such audacious things! Her eyes blazed in fury, her confusion dispelled as a purging anger spread swiftly through her. "You are still my enemy and I shall never consider you otherwise," she retorted through clenched teeth. "I *saw* what your William did to England. Can you have forgotten that blood-soaked battle site so quickly? Think you that I can ever forget it so long as Gilbert is a living reminder? Nay, Roland de Beaufort, there is more between us than my husband, and nothing you do can ever change that."

Brianna turned to stalk away and almost collided with an angry Walter, who had decided it was time to come to her rescue, no matter what the consequences. She was too overwrought, however, to wonder why he should be angry, and she quickly returned to the table while Walter engaged Roland's attention on some pretext.

"Brianna! What is wrong?" asked an alarmed Aleen as she stared into the distraught girl's face.

"Everything is wrong!" she snapped and then turned to Nedra. "Please, Nedra, I need to be alone—away from here for a while. I must leave or I shall go mad! Will you or Aleen see to Gilbert?"

"Of course, child, but—"

Before Nedra could question her further, Brianna was gone, heading toward one of the huge doors almost at a run.

"Leave her," said Kerwick. "There is something between those two that festers. 'Tis her own private battle, and she must brave it alone."

In a burst of defiance Brianna returned home and exchanged her clothes for the garb Roland had forbidden her to wear. She derived a perverse satisfaction from replacing the feminine attire that *he* had complimented with masculine garments.

Still breathing hard from her initial flight, she nonetheless made for the forest behind the barren fields to the north at a run. The village was deserted and she was certain no one would ever seek her in the dense weald.

Refusing to think of possible danger from wild animals or scavengers—Norman or otherwise—she found a sheltered spot just inside the edge of the woods and sank down onto a log that had fallen conveniently near enough to a sapling so that she could comfortably lean back and relax. She closed her eyes and suddenly felt drained from her emotional upset and physical exertions.

As her anger cooled and her thudding heart slowed down to normal, she fell into a light sleep. But she found no peace in slumber, for gray eyes followed her everywhere and a deep voice echoed in the dim corridors of her unconscious: *No disguise on earth could keep you safe from me . . . starving man seeks sustenance . . . so do I seek you . . . you . . . you . . .*

Brianna woke with a start, the chill penetrating her woolen clothing as the sun began its descent in the west. She rubbed her eyes and yawned, but she could not rid herself of the feeling— She frowned and peered intently into the thick stand of trees to her left, but her eyes encountered nothing unusual. Why then did she feel as if she were being watched?

"Did you enjoy your nap, lad? 'Twould seem that you have

been remiss in not celebrating your new Norman overlord's good fortune.''

Brianna jumped to her feet in surprise, her eyes squinting into the forest once more. "Who . . . who is it?" she queried uncertainly in a gruff voice.

"You had better sit down again." There was a barely leashed threat underlying the words that indicated that he, whoever he was, was very much accustomed to being in command, and unthinkingly Brianna obeyed.

"That's better." A shadowy form emerged from its perfectly camouflaged position among the trees almost directly across from Brianna. He was tall and powerfully built, with silver-streaked chestnut hair down to his shoulders that was bound with a leather thong around his high forehead to keep it from falling into his face. His beard and mustache were also threaded lightly with silver, which did nothing to detract from his hard good looks. His dark eyes held hers for a long moment as they took one another's measure.

"What is your name, boy?"

"Bryce," she answered without hesitation.

"Well, Bryce, what do you here when all of Derford is— or was—paying homage to that Norman cur?"

"I . . . I could not remain in his presence any longer, for I *despise* him!" She was surprised at how easily the heated words came from her lips. "His arrogance knows no bounds—" She stopped in midsentence.

What if this man were a spy for the Norman, despite the fact that he looked very much like an Anglo-Saxon?

As if reading her thoughts, the stranger laughed humorlessly. "You need not fear he will ever hear what you say to me, for what is left of my life is dedicated to routing out William and his followers." His words were tinged with savagery, and Brianna realized he must be a displaced Anglo-Saxon lord, for his speech and mannerisms were those of someone accustomed to being in command—someone of noble birth.

"Who are you, my lord?"

"My lord?" He threw back his head in laughter, the bitterness very evident to Brianna. "I am no longer deserving of that title, as my domain consists of the forests and the wild beasts therein. Occasionally my scant following of men join me in my crusade to wreak havoc upon the Normans who seek to take over England, but their numbers vary, for our sport is very risky. We lose more men than we gain, it seems, and the Normans are a crafty lot."

"But . . . but who are you?" she repeated, her curiosity thoroughly aroused.

"They call me Rob."

"And you make trouble for the Normans?"

"I do my damnedest. As long as I live and breathe I will never accept the Bastard as King of England."

His voice was impassioned, and Brianna's eyes brightened with empathy. Her words tumbled forth before she knew what she was saying. "If you are willing to trust me, I would like nothing better than to help you."

As he raised a questioning eyebrow she added, "I have already killed one of *them*—when they raided our village."

"Well done, lad! Well done!" Rob's saturnine features lit up with pleasure as he grinned. "That makes one less for me to kill." He made a motion with his right hand, and another shadowy figure emerged from the trees behind him. "This is Ian, my right-hand man. If you are truly serious about helping us, you can keep Ian apprised of anything you may learn."

Ian was a brawny young man of about two and twenty. His expression was stony and he merely nodded as Rob said, "Ian, this is Bryce." He turned serious then. "Have you any kin?"

"Only my brother Gilbert. But he was struck from behind by a mace at Hastings and is disabled."

"Well then, can he at least play eyes and ears for you sometimes?"

"Nay," Brianna answered, a note of anguish threatening to

overset the gruffness in her voice. "His mind is not any more whole than his body."

Rob exchanged a knowing look with Ian. "Odo, undoubtedly."

"Odo?"

"Aye. The Bastard's half brother, Bishop Odo of Bayeux. He is more a killer of men than a spiritual leader. He fought at Hastings like a madman with a studded mace, for those who serve the Church are forbidden to spill blood. A mace crushes the skull without necessarily drawing blood."

"Oh." Brianna vaguely remembered Roland's comment to Hugh of Brittany concerning this Bishop Odo. Evidently Roland did not like him either, which struck her as odd since Odo was kin to William.

Lost in her thoughts for a moment, she did not notice Ian slip back into the forest. "Well, Bryce," said Rob, catching her full attention once more. "I believe you are trustworthy." He stood up to his impressive height and held her gaze. "Any information you could relay to me through Ian would be heartily appreciated, but know this." His face was suddenly grim, and Brianna shivered against her will as she read the threat in his eyes. "You may at any time decide to halt your efforts to further our cause, but should you ever make the mistake of betraying us, it will be the last one you make. Go with God." And he melted into the shadows as swiftly and silently as a wraith.

As the two men strode through the darkening weald, Ian spoke first. "She is the one?"

Rob smiled coldly. "Indeed. As a ripe piece of fruit, my faithful Ian, right into our hands."

Ian grunted. " 'Twas clever of you to make her whereabouts your business. You can use Derford's misfortune—and therefore hers—to your advantage."

And so I shall.

The shroud of approaching twilight hid the savage expression that tracked across the older man's usually well schooled features. *Blue-green eyes. Framed by thick, dark lashes. Beautiful eyes. Alicia's eyes. No, Brianna's eyes.*

The years had done little to mellow Robert of Wessex, and nothing had assuaged the feeling of betrayal he had suffered since Alicia's death. Now his patience was being rewarded, and the prospect of revenge dangled before him. He would be a fool to ignore it.

Brianna sat mulling over all that had happened. Whoever he was, he evidently was determined and would brook no betrayals. She stood up slowly and stretched, deciding she had better return.

She moved along the edge of the forest until she came to the stretch of woods that separated Gilbert's lands from Wulfric's—rather, de Beaufort's, she amended silently and with resentment. She then turned south and skirted the periphery of the trees, staying just out of sight of anyone who might be at the homestead.

As she made her way home she thought about Rob and Ian. She wondered who Rob really was—or had been before the Normans came. She remembered Edwin talking about rumors of an Anglo-Saxon lord whose followers continued to harass the invaders. Mayhap this Rob and the unknown leader were one and the same.

Cutting across the southeast corner of their lands, Brianna saw several figures moving purposefully about the structures that made up her home. Their clothing was brightly colored, indicating that they included Normans. One of them suddenly spotted Brianna and gave a low-pitched whistle. The others gathered about him, including one in a scarlet tunic leading a white horse she would have known anywhere. Her eyes widened in alarm as she recognized Roland. Her steps unconsciously slowed as the other men dispersed and Roland mounted his great horse and rode toward her.

Whatever can I do now? she thought in panic. Something

told her that Roland de Beaufort was a man capable of great anger. She was certain that beneath that cool, seemingly civilized exterior was a well-controlled but nonetheless real temper.

He stopped the enormous destrier directly before her and, unhampered by armor, slid off the animal with smooth, catlike grace. His features were grim, his gray eyes dark as storm clouds. Brianna could not tear her eyes away from the blood vessel that throbbed in his temple. He was furious.

"Where have you been, wench?" His words were clipped, tense.

"Surely you do not expect me—" Brianna began in an attempt to meet his rage head-on.

"I do expect, Brianna," he interrupted tersely. "Your well-being is of the greatest concern to me, as is that of every man, woman and child in Derford. Do you realize there are outcasts and deserters from both sides who would kill you in the wink of an eye for no more than the clothes on your back? And when they discovered you were a woman— Well, even a corpse holds attraction for a few sick—"

"Stop!" she cried softly and bit down on a bent knuckle to keep from retching at the mere thought of such an action.

"Need I say more?"

She shook her head mutely, wiping the tears that had spilled onto her cheeks, leaving pale tracks through the grime.

"You are fortunate that no one else heard me order you never to wear those garments again, for you would have had to be punished." Before she could protest, he lifted her onto Odo's back and vaulted up behind her. She sat ramrod straight, attempting to avoid contact with his chest, but that was impossible, even for the short ride across the remaining field.

Kerwick's entire family stood silently in the yard, deep concern for Brianna written across their faces. Even Gilbert was strangely subdued and wore a bleak expression as he watched Brianna being lifted down by the Norman.

Roland guided her firmly by the elbow into the hall, and

the others followed, partly out of fear of what he might do to her. They knew only too well how dangerous it was to wander away from the village alone. And they had also seen the exchange between Brianna and Roland, and her subsequent hasty departure from his hall. Kerwick was fearful she had gone too far in defying the knight. Walter was ready to spring to her defense even if it cost him his life.

"Bring me a basin of water and soap," Roland demanded curtly. Aleen hurried to do his bidding, and when they were procured, he commanded, "Wash your face, Brianna."

She reluctantly obeyed, not daring to upset him further.

"Now go to your chamber and change your clothes—and bring me back those which you are wearing."

With a small sigh Brianna resignedly left the hall to comply, lowering her eyes to hide the gleam of rebellion in them.

"Surely, my lord, you are too hard on her," began Walter, ignoring the warning look Kerwick shot him.

Roland accepted the cup of mead Nedra silently handed him and then turned to face the young man. "You are a fool, Walter, if you are unaware of the dangers lurking throughout the countryside."

"If they exist, 'tis because of you and your kind," he retorted angrily.

Nedra closed her eyes, a prayer on her lips at her son's reckless words.

"Aye," Roland said with a shrug of his broad shoulders, "perhaps you are right, but that does not alter the fact. She could have been murdered—even on my lands."

Nedra spoke up then, anticipating Brianna's embarrassment at having the entire family witness her humiliation when she returned with the offending garments. "Mayhap this business should be settled between Brianna and Lord Roland privately."

Kerwick took his cue and led them away without further ado.

Roland glanced over at Gilbert, who was sitting near the

fire. He was eyeing the Norman warily, as if ready to flee at any threatening sign. Poor devil, Roland thought as his eyes took in the lack of expression on Gilbert's features. But there was fear in the deep brown eyes. "You've naught to fear from me, friend," he said softly. "I will protect and provide for her as you could never do now."

Gilbert opened his mouth and struggled to speak, but whether he understood Roland was not apparent, for he could only stutter, "Bra-Bra-na."

"Aye, lad. Brianna." Roland turned and looked around him before moving closer to the hearth to regard the leaping flames. *I should most likely hate you for being her husband, but I cannot. In truth you have received no more from her than I. 'Tis her wish to keep you between us.*

A faint sound behind him put an end to his thoughts; he spun around abruptly. Brianna was in the doorway wearing a soft woolen bliaud, a bundle in her arms. She held her head up determinedly, but her pale face gave away her misgivings.

"Bring those here."

Roland took the bundle from her unresisting hands and tossed it into the fire. Instead of chastising her once again, he said, "I came here originally to ask your forgiveness, Brianna."

Her eyes shot from the burning garments to his face. The expression she saw there seemed sincere. "Forgiveness for what, *chevalier?* I disobeyed you."

"Aye, but my bold words caused you to flee in the first place. You will no doubt think my apology insincere, but before God I do not know what came over me. I spoke out of turn after the ceremony, and I ask your pardon."

Brianna could not believe her ears. A victorious Norman asking forgiveness of a mere Anglo-Saxon girl? But the look in his eyes was proof of his good intentions, and his intensity made her blush.

"I cannot refuse an apology given in good faith—even from you, Norman." She felt his sheer animal magnetism enveloping her and was once more powerless to pull her eyes from his. What *was* it about this man that affected her so?

He moved forward and took hold of her shoulders, his face so close to hers she could detect the not-unpleasant smell of mead on his warm breath. "You have bewitched me, *chérie—*"

"Gilbert . . ." she had the presence of mind to murmur in soft protest.

". . . is sleeping," he finished quietly.

She could not have moved a muscle. She was ensnared in his impassioned gaze, foundering, drowning in a vortex of conflicting emotions. And then his lips possessed hers, and a flash like white-hot lightning streaked through her body and settled in the core of her womanhood.

But that was only the beginning as the force of Roland's raging desire struggled for release. His lips were at first as gentle as a butterfly caressing a dew-kissed young leaf to drink of its moisture. Her lips parted of their own volition in response, moving against his in their own exploration. Then his tongue slid into the sweet honeycomb of her mouth, still ever so gently seeking.

She was shocked at this tender invasion of her mouth; her legs refused to support her, and only the fact that she was in Roland's iron-thewed embrace kept her from slowly sliding to the floor like a rag doll.

His hand moved through the opening at the side of her bliaud and caressed a firm young breast through the soft undertunic, sending shivers throughout her body as she clasped him more tightly to her in the age-old position of woman molded to man, thigh to thigh, chest to breast, mouth to mouth—

She was suddenly swept off her feet, and Roland moved with her toward the door leading to the sleeping houses. Somewhere in the back of her mind a warning went off, but his lips and hands were still doing things to her ripe, newly awakened body that threatened to drive her mad, and her weak protests were stifled by his urgent kisses.

He laid her on the bed in the bower she occupied alone and, afraid to even take the time to undress, he bent over her, murmuring words of love in French. Brianna was caught in a maelstrom of wondrous sensations that were slowly, inexorably crumbling her defenses. As his hand moved up her leg what little reason she possessed fled.

Her skirts were somehow around her waist then, yet the touch of the cool air upon her bare skin only heightened her delicious anticipation as Roland's hand between her thighs made her shudder with rising excitement. Her limbs languorously parted in response to his skilled exploration, and a wantonness seized her that delighted the man who had ached to possess her.

"Brianna," he whispered, his lips caressing her ear, his tongue flicking over the delicate contours.

And then he was sliding her skirts over her head and Brianna only yearned to be free of the hampering garments. Perhaps the cloak of darkness in the bower served to help dispel her inhibitions, for in the absence of a lit brazier, the brave but ineffective flickerings of a single lit taper only seemed to heighten the mood of warm, runaway desire, of driving need.

As his mouth gently attached itself to the soft mound that was her breast, she cried out and buried her hands in his sandy hair. She clung to him as one drowning, resenting the barrier of his clothing between them as her fingers moved to grip the sleek, hard planes of his back and shoulders, seeking access to skin she somehow knew would be warm and smooth and—

His face hovered over hers unexpectedly, and in the deep shadows she could barely make out his features. His breathing was ragged, and she could feel the strong, swift beating of his heart against her naked breasts. "Brianna, let me love you," he whispered, his voice steeped in desire, his breath fanning the wispy tendrils of hair around the oval of her face. Before she could think to reply or act, his lips captured hers in a burning kiss that seemed to sap the last vestiges of her determination.

He loomed over her, one leg moving to rest across hers, his need blatantly apparent as the hard length of his manhood throbbed insistently against her thigh. Without moving the gritty velvet of his open mouth and tongue from hers, he sought to loosen the cumbersome chausses at his waist. The movements of his fingers stimulated her rampaging passion and she unconsciously arched against him, inadvertently hampering his efforts. But not for long.

All too soon he was moving between her thighs, his tongue creating havoc with a nipple he had taken skillfully, urgently, between his teeth, and delicious sensations shot through her.

And then the pulsating, searing presence of his arousal positioned at the apex of her thighs dragged her reeling senses back to reality. She gripped his hair with both hands, fighting the fog of rapturous delirium that dulled her reason.

Pulling at him with the returning strength born of shame, she cried, "Roland, nay! *P-please!*"

He slowly raised his head as her use of his given name came through to him. His gray eyes were black with desire, his cheeks were flushed, his lips swollen and—

"This is sinful!" she panted.

"The only sin lies in your unearthly beauty, my Brianna. You would tempt a saint," he growled hoarsely.

She weakly pulled herself to a sitting position and hastily gathered her discarded clothing around her protectively. "Do not lay the blame at *my* feet, Norman!" she shot back. "The sin is in your wanting what belongs to another. 'Tis obviously a trait of your people!"

Roland sat straight up, his face very close to hers, his breathing still ragged. "Can you tell me you do not want me as much as I want you?"

She could not in all honesty deny this, and her artless reply shamed him. "I . . . I do not know how much you want me, my lord, so I cannot answer that. But yes, you have just done things to my body that . . . that made me ache for more. But I am wed, and no man but my husband has a right to do those things to me.'' Her face was burning, so acute was her embarrassment at her wanton behavior.

Once more Roland realized he had let his fascination—his intense desire for her—overtake his common sense and iron control. He knew he had to once more try to make amends, even as he desperately wanted to wipe her loyalty to her useless husband from her heart. ''I cannot seem to help myself when I am near you, wench. But you need not concern yourself further. I will allow you to keep your precious virtue for that husband of yours who sleeps before the fire, oblivious to your needs.''

That was unfair and he knew it, but his pride was smarting. He stood up abruptly. ''Sleep well in your chaste bower, Brianna.''

He turned on his heel and strode away.

CHAPTER 8

It seemed to Brianna that everywhere she went *he* was there. If she did not run into him while visiting or running errands, she would unexpectedly find him on her own doorstep, or in her own home, ostensibly with some question about local customs or to inquire of her needs. Whether she was scrubbing the hearth, milking the cow or baking for Gilbert—with flour smeared across her slim, lovely nose—Roland de Beaufort seemed to crop up without fail.

He was always accompanied by Dane or a man-at-arms. But Brianna noticed that no matter how busy he was scouting his lands for the eventual site of the castle he wanted to build, or preparing for the defense of Derford and his stronghold against any encroachment before he went to London for William's coronation at Christmas, he somehow found time to see her. And his behavior was without fault; there was not a hint of impropriety in his words or his actions.

At first Brianna's shame flared anew each time she saw him, for he was a reminder of the sensuous arousal of her body for which she had been totally unprepared and she feared his touch. But as the days went by she realized he meant to keep his word regarding her virtue and she began to relax in his presence.

Brianna discovered the exact day of his departure for London, and after several furtive visits to the place where she had first seen Rob, she chanced upon Ian and told him what she knew. At first she was glad to have been of some use to them, but as the time of Roland's leavetaking drew nigh, Brianna began to have second thoughts about putting his life in danger. She rationalized, however, that it was no secret that he was leaving soon and would be gone at least a fortnight. Anyone in Derford could have given the information to Ian or Rob. And besides, she thought bleakly, to whom did she truly owe her allegiance? An Anglo-Saxon lord or a usurping Norman?

Dane d'Avranches was to accompany Roland to London, and several lesser knights and a score of men-at-arms were to be left behind, to guard his possessions. Roland did not relish the idea of leaving his newly acquired estate and, more important, Brianna. He felt no one could perform the task as well as he, busy as he was, because his emotions were involved. More deeply than he cared to admit.

As the time drew near, his manner betrayed something of his turmoil to Dane. One evening after they had supped, Dane tried to rouse his friend from his preoccupation. "If it would set your mind at ease, I can remain here while you are in London, Roland."

Roland was idly toying with an empty goblet of wine. He eyed his friend with a deceptive grin. "You are certainly generous this night, *mon ami*. But"—his smile faded—"William will no doubt wonder at your absence. Nay, 'tis better you go with me."

"I have no lands here in England that I should show my gratitude by attending his coronation. If you remember, I am to return home as soon as you are safely ensconced in your new position."

Roland raised an eyebrow in mock indignation. " 'Safely ensconced'? Do you think me some lily-livered coward that I cannot hold my own?"

"You know as well as I that it is no laughing matter. William sent you straight into the middle of the most dangerous part of this island—into the heart of the late King's supporters."

Roland considered this briefly. "Perhaps you are right. I

can think of a score of reasons why I should not leave. Having you or Ranulf in my stead during my absence would put my mind at ease.'' His eyes went to the empty goblet as he frowned. ''You are willing to forgo the coronation?''

''I would much rather remain behind and guard the lovely Brianna.''

Roland scowled at his friend. The corner of d'Avranches' mouth quivered with suppressed merriment.

''Swine,'' he muttered. ''You are a swine to bait me so.''

''If you were not so besotted with the girl, you would not be such easy prey, *mon ami.*''

Roland's gaze rested on a servant stoking the fire in one hearth. As the lowering flames leaped to life he asked, ''You will not mind? She is a handful—God only knows! Impulsive, rash, easily angered—''

''Only by you, 'twould seem.''

Roland ignored this last comment. ''Will you watch over her? Without seeming to?''

Dane knew Roland better than anyone outside of his parents and brother. There was no mistaking the anxiety in the dark gray eyes now, even if the features were under rigid control.

''I will guard her with my life.''

The days dragged by interminably for Brianna. Christmas came and went, but she derived little joy from the celebration of her favorite religious holiday. Between her work about the homestead and caring for Gilbert, and despite help from Brand and Aleen, she was always exhausted by the end of the day, so that it was all she could do to clean herself up and crawl into bed.

Two days after Roland's departure she was returning home from tending Thomas the Blacksmith's little boy, who had come down with a fever, when a masculine voice interrupted her thoughts. ''Brianna.''

She looked up to see Dane d'Avranches approaching her on his great black horse. He stopped and looked down at her, his eyes smiling even as his mouth took on the sober lines of her own. "And how does the lovely Brianna fare today?"

"Well enough, my lord." She moved toward the entrance of the hall.

"I really came to ask for your help." Did his voice carry a touch of appeal? "I have need of your knowledge of medicine and healing. Several of Roland's men have contracted some sort of fever." He rubbed his hand over his face. "We need every man Roland left behind, for this Anglo-Saxon outlaw known as Rob has been harassing the men scouting sites for the new keep. I believe he is responsible for the broken fencing I have just come from inspecting. And we have also just found some of our cattle slain. Will you help me?"

Her heart unwittingly went out to this handsome, dark-haired Norman. Smiling faintly, she nodded. "Very well, Lord Dane." And then her smooth alabaster brow creased with worry. "But I fear 'tis the same fever Thomas the Blacksmith's child has, and he is deathly ill."

Aleen having agreed to care for Gilbert until she returned, Brianna rode with Dane to Roland's stronghold. She was startled at the additional changes that had taken place since she was there last, and men were still at work filling in the gaps between the crossbeams that had been added horizontally halfway up the walls to form a second floor. A completed stairway was at one end of the hall.

As Brianna stared in amazement Dane explained. "We use second floors often in Normandy. Many castles have even more because the chimneys running up the entire wall make it possible to have fireplaces on each floor. Roland would rather sleep in his own hall than a bower set apart from the main building. We do not use sleeping houses at home."

Dane took her by the arm and drew her toward several pallets in a dim corner of the hall, near one of the huge hooded fireplaces. Three men occupied them, two staring listlessly and a third tossing in fevered restlessness from side to side. Hilde, a comely young girl from Derford who served in Roland's household, stood nearby, uncomfortably licking her lips as her eyes went from the sick men to Brianna and Dane.

"How do they fare, Hilde?" asked Dane, his lack of confidence in her abilities implicit in the tone of his voice.

At Hilde's disinterested shrug, Brianna placed a reassuring hand on his arm. "We will see to them, my lord. Go now and see where else you are needed."

Several hours later, after having instructed Hilde to continue bathing the man who had been delirious, and also giving all three of them as much liquid as they would take, Brianna wearily stood up and set out to look for Dane.

One of Roland's men found him for her, and Brianna asked him to send another woman to help Hilde. She was tired and her face showed the strain she had been under. Dane suddenly regretted having put her through so much when she had such a heavy burden of work and responsibility at home.

"I thank you for caring for our sick," Dane said as he led Brianna out into the brisk winter night. "Since you've so graciously refused to sup with me, will you not at least allow me to accompany you home?"

She agreed to that, and as they rode toward the stretch of woods that bordered the estate, they fell into a companionable silence. "What made Lord Roland come with William of Normandy if he did not wish to fight King Harold?" Brianna asked unexpectedly, thinking this man might be able to give her some clue to understanding Roland.

"Roland's father, Lord Guy, has always been very loyal to William. He is said to have saved William's life as a child when the Duke was being protected and hidden from his enemies who did not believe Robert of Normandy's bastard should be heir to the duchy."

"Then he—Lord Roland's sire—is also here in England?"

"Nay. He was severely injured in a hunting accident and will never hunt or fight again. But he sent Roland and his brother in his stead, with all the backing the de Beaufort name could provide." They rode along the twilight-darkened road in silence for a few moments, and then Dane spoke once more. "Do not ever doubt this, Brianna of Derford. If Roland could have remained in Normandy without going against his father's wishes, he most certainly would never have set foot upon these shores."

Without warning, Brianna felt a soft, cool breath of relief waft over her heart—he had told her the truth. He might not have come and she might never have met Roland de Beaufort. She would have been sentenced to a calm, placid and mundane existence.

They rode the rest of the way, each immersed in his or her own thoughts.

The fever persisted throughout the unusually mild winter, striking Anglo-Saxon and Norman alike. And while Brianna and the other women of Derford battled the fever, every healthy man from the village was recruited to help mend the fences and repair other damage done to Roland's property. Dane wanted all put to right in time for Roland's return.

A fortnight came and went, and there was still no sign of Roland. Day by day Brianna became more and more fatigued, and her own resistance was sapped from the combination of work, lack of sleep and exposure to fever victims at every stage of the illness. She began to lose weight and grew pale and wan. Finally Dane insisted she stay in bed for at least a day, for she would be of no use to anyone if she herself succumbed.

Reluctantly Brianna agreed, for the contagion seemed to be on the wane. But first she retreated into the coolness of the tiny church near Roland's great hall for her daily prayers.

When she emerged, the yard was in an uproar. Dane had mounted up and was about to ride out when a grim-looking man-at-arms came crashing through the gate in the timber palisade, his mount foam-flecked from being ridden hard. He halted before Dane, and Brianna could only make out part of the exchange between the two Normans.

". . . party of riders . . . from the west . . ."

She stepped forward, a sinking feeling of dread forming in the pit of her stomach.

"How many are there?"

"Six."

" 'Tis a small enough group, thank God for that. Mount up!" Dane instructed Guy de Montrain and René de Falaise, two knights who were part of Roland's retinue. "And you, Vachel, Beorn—make haste!"

"There is no time, my lord. They were close behind me—"

And as if to confirm his words, the thunderous sound of fast-moving horses seemed to overwhelm them as the group of newcomers approached the gate and were brought to a screaming halt by lances braced butt end into the ground, their wicked points aimed directly at the destriers' massive chests.

They carried no identifying banner, but there was something familiar about the leader. Dane suddenly felt a growing knot of tension in his gut as he recognized the man. He fought the urge to curse aloud the fates that had brought this man into their midst at this moment. The leader was none other than Hugh of Brittany.

Dane's eyes flicked to Brianna, who was surreptitiously making her way toward her pony. "Bring her to me," he growled to Vachel, and the man grabbed the unsuspecting Brianna most ungently by the arm and practically dragged her to Dane. "Get into the hall and act like a servant," he said in a low, urgent voice. " 'Tis Hugh of Brittany, and I'll not have you riding about when some of his men may be hidden between here and Derford."

"Gilbert—"

"Do as I say! If you do not wish to be recognized, keep your head down and stay out of the way." The look on his face was like none she had seen before, and Brianna quickly realized the gravity of the situation. She disappeared quickly into the interior of the great hall.

Dane nudged the black war-horse forward, with Guy and René beside him on foot, hands on their sword hilts. "Who are you?" he barked commandingly in a bid to gain time.

"Hugh of Brittany. I seek Roland de Beaufort. Is he here?"

"Nay."

The Breton removed his helmet when he recognized Dane and eyed the two knights at his side and the men-at-arms behind him consideringly. "Well then, d'Avranches, I will speak to you in his stead if he is not here."

"Very well, Hugh of Brittany. But I warn you, I will tolerate no treachery. So if your intentions are not honorable, begone from here ere I give you cause to regret your actions." He signaled and the lances were lowered; the party proceeded into the compound, drawing many a curious stare.

Dane dismounted and waited for the others to do likewise. "We can speak inside the manor," he directed tersely, and gestured for the six men to enter the hall before him.

"By what right do you tear through Derford out of nowhere, unheralded, alarming my men and terrifying the villagers in your damnable haste?" he demanded when they were seated and had been served ale.

Hugh eyed him over the rim of his mug before he slammed it down unexpectedly, startling them all. "I have more reason to be wary than you, d'Avranches. I was attacked on the road and lost four good men! Could *you* perchance be the one who practices treachery by having such a clever system of warning? So clever that even after pouncing on my men you can cry 'foul play' to me because I arrive at your gates, less almost half my party, having neglected to properly identify myself and my purpose?"

Dane's dark brows rose at this, and Brianna, listening intently from the shadows, knew immediately who was responsible. "I can tell you truthfully that 'twas none of my doing, Breton."

Hugh of Brittany studied Dane for a long moment, weighing the truth of his words. "Then if you were not responsible for the deed, you should at least be apprised of the goings-on in the area. Surely de Beaufort left you well informed and had enough confidence in you that he could go to London, where I presume he is, without undue worry?''

The last words were said with heavy sarcasm, and Brianna could see Dane's features tense. "We have been troubled by an Anglo-Saxon who calls himself Rob, who no doubt has support from many English in the surrounding area. We have been hampered in our attempts to deal with him by the fact that Roland took a number of his retainers with him to London, and also by an outbreak of fever. I regret the loss of your men's lives, and we will see to it that they receive a proper Christian burial. Beyond that, however, I can do nothing.''

Hugh grunted and seemed placated for the moment. He glanced around the hall, taking in the changes being made, and then signaled for more ale. To Brianna, the five other men seemed rather quiet and ill at ease. She wondered if they were leery about being in the stronghold of a rich and powerful knight who had no liking for their leader.

Dane broke the uncomfortable silence. "You dare much by coming here, although 'tis undoubtedly safer than meeting Roland by chance in London. He has not forgiven you for disfiguring his face.'' His voice held a hint of challenge that was caught by Hugh of Brittany.

"That mere scratch? I owe him much more than a mark on his pretty face for what he took from me. If he had not weaseled into Duke William's favor through his family ties, the Anglo-Saxon girl would have been mine for the taking!''

"She was no one's for the taking. If it had been so simple a thing to take her for himself, why do you think Roland let the girl go back to her village?'' Dane asked mildly.

"De Beaufort fancies himself too noble to do such a thing. But I saw it in his eyes—he wanted the wench as much as I did. I tell you he had no right to interfere in my affairs—the arrogant swine! I would that the dagger had slit his throat instead of his jaw!''

Dane's grip on his cup tightened and every man in the hall tensed, the Norman guard ready to strike at the slightest sign from Dane. "You are a fool to speak thusly under Roland's roof, surrounded by his men."

"Bah! We can settle up when again we meet. I have come to inquire into the death of one of my men—another Breton, by the name of Alain. One of the other men here remembers seeing him enter a dwelling at this end of the village. He never came out."

Brianna muffled a gasp.

"If that is so, why did you wait so long to look into it? 'Tis a bit late by any standards, do you not agree?"

"My reasons are my own, d'Avranches. I intend to search that homestead from top to bottom until—"

"Admit it, Hugh of Brittany," Dane cut him off ruthlessly. "You do not care so much for the loss of a man as you do for seeing what Roland has been granted by the Duke—seeing what he has accomplished thus far and then causing trouble. You still itch for a fight, and you are a bigger fool than I thought."

"That idiot Ranulf was the cause of our hasty departure," Hugh rasped furiously. "He convinced me that a retreat was the wiser course when all along he meant to thwart my efforts!"

Brianna could just make out the low-spoken words, but in her growing alarm they made little sense to her.

"So you caught on to the game, eh, Hugh?" Dane laughed softly. "It took you long enough."

The silence was fraught with tension, and Hugh of Brittany was shaking in his terrible anger. But he could do nothing. "His part in that charade only adds to what I will collect from de Beaufort. First Roland takes what I claimed as my share of the spoils, and then Ranulf tricks me into believing he sided with me. I tell you I will leave here, d'Avranches, only when my men are decently buried and I *search that homestead!*"

His last words hit Brianna like a physical blow. What would

Dane do? she thought in a choking panic. And suddenly all thought save that of Gilbert left her mind and she knew she somehow had to prevent these men from searching her home and terrorizing Gilbert.

Her voice rang out in the deathly silence. "You need not search anywhere. I know what became of him."

The room stilled for a few stunned moments in the wake of her words, and then there were low murmurings among Hugh's men as all eyes turned to the small figure in the shadows.

Brianna stepped forward, her heart hammering against her ribs, and threw back her head in a defiant gesture that belied her inner fear. Despite her cropped hair, Hugh recognized the mellifluous voice and the proud gesture. He stared at her in growing disbelief, for this was the face he had dreamed of many a night. Her eyes calmly met his and then went to Dane.

For the first few charged moments Dane could only think, *By all the saints, where is Roland?* He was caught between admiration for Brianna's bold impulsiveness and frustration at her having placed herself in a potentially explosive situation. Years of decision making, however, enabled him to quickly pull his conflicting feelings together and take charge once more. "This is between Hugh of Brittany and myself, Brianna."

"With all due respect, my lord, you were not even here when Derford was raided. This matter is between the Breton and *myself.*" And before Dane could reply, she looked once more at Hugh of Brittany. "I went to Hastings to find Gilbert, my husband, and neither you nor Roland de Beaufort could have ever laid claim to me like some prize of war, for I would have taken my own life before submitting to either of you.

"As for your Alain of Brittany, he invaded my home—mine and my husband's. Not only did he do bodily harm to Gilbert, but he threatened the life of an unarmed friend, and *I killed him.*"

Her eyes were bright with tears of frustrated rage, but her steady voice continued as Hugh of Brittany and his men could only stare. "I did not mean to kill him, only to stop him, but what's done is done. I would do it again if the lives of my family or friends were threatened. 'Tis a small enough revenge to exact from so brutal an enemy."

The Breton took in her exquisite beauty, her fire and courage. Someone had cut off her glorious ebony mane, but that did nothing to detract from her striking features. She was, after all, the real reason for this visit. He would never admit it to anyone, but he had had a gut feeling that Roland de Beaufort had moved heaven and earth to find her. What man wouldn't? And so he had come in the hope of learning her whereabouts. And there she stood, magnificent in her blazing anger.

Dane spoke first, recovering from his surprise at her revelation and recognizing the look on the Breton's face. "Well, now you know. Are you satisfied?"

Hugh of Brittany tore his eyes from Brianna for a moment and regarded the Norman calculatingly. "What proof do I have except her word?"

Brianna took a dagger from beneath her mantle. It clattered on the table as she tossed it in the Breton's direction. "I took this from his body before it was buried."

The man sitting on the Breton's left said, " 'Tis Alain's dagger all right, Hugh."

But Hugh of Brittany, already having verified that in his own mind, was stalling—trying to gain more time now that he had the girl in his presence. "Then surely we can at least have his grave properly blessed?"

" 'Twas done by our village priest, Father Simon. There was nothing dishonorable about his burial." Brianna unexpectedly began to tremble and a curious buzzing began in her head.

"He could have lost it during the raid—"

"You are not making sense, Breton. This Alain is missing. Brianna said she killed him to protect a friend and crippled husband. There is his knife. Do you wish us to dig up the corpse as further proof?''

Brianna paled at Dane's suggestion and the bile rose in her throat.

''Very well. This is proof enough, I suppose. But perhaps we can work out some small recompense, Brianna—'' His voice grated on her raw nerves.

''Our business is finished, I believe,'' Dane answered coldly, and stood up in dismissal.

''Perhaps. But,'' the Breton added, turning to Brianna as he wiped his mouth on his tunic sleeve, ''if you ever need a *man,* little dove, rather than a useless husband or a mincing coxcomb like de Beaufort—''

''I can conceive of no situation so desperate that I would ever seek you out,'' she cut in tersely. ''I may be a woman, and one of a vanquished people, but I belong to no man but my husband.''

''You would be wise to let us see to the burial of your men and then leave immediately after—to never return.'' Dane was already moving toward the door.

The Breton and his men followed suit, but before exiting he turned once more to Brianna, who was clutching the table they had just vacated. She was physically exhausted, and beads of perspiration had gathered on her forehead and upper lip. ''You have not seen the last of me, my dove.'' His dark eyes moved to Dane. ''And you can tell de Beaufort my business with him is unfinished as well.''

CHAPTER 9

Two Norman knights in full armor rode south from London with a small armed escort. The two men were of an exact height and build, although a casual observer would not have found anything unusual in this, given the two huge destriers they were riding and the chain mail they wore.

The leaden skies promised a storm of some sort—whether rain or snow was hard to tell. It was cold enough for a freezing rain or possibly even a heavy, wet snow, and from time to time the knight on the white stallion uneasily studied the sky. Low, dark clouds were rolling in from the southeast, and he didn't like it.

"Surely you are not afraid of a little bad weather, Roland," his companion chided.

"I would much rather be safely in Derford when it hits, lest we rust right into our mail."

The knight on the dun-colored steed grinned, and Roland could just make out the curve of his mouth from beneath his helm. "Laugh if you like," he continued, "but all jesting aside, I have been gone overlong already. I told you of the trouble we have been encountering. I had not intended to remain in the city so long after the coronation."

Ranulf sobered. "Well, you could not be discourteous to William d'Avranches, could you? I wonder what made him come to England."

Roland's tawny brows drew together under his headpiece. "I cannot imagine, but according to William, he plans to re-

110

main for a while. Dane will be glad to see him without having to return to Normandy first. God's teeth, I owe him much! And especially after this!''

Ranulf nodded. ''He no doubt has handled everything as ably as you, brother, which must indeed be a relief in such times of uncertainty.''

''He has my eternal gratitude, although there is little need for words of such things between us. And speaking of gratitude, I never did thank you for the trick you played on Hugh of Brittany.''

Both men's eyes met, and they burst into hearty laughter.

''That strutting cock! Serves him right. Next time he dares toy with a de Beaufort he will think twice about it.''

Roland studied his brother. ''You know 'tis not quite the thing for a man to do when he seriously entertains thoughts of becoming a priest.''

Ranulf's mouth turned down at this remark. ''Do you mean 'tis not the duty of a man who serves God to prevent bloodshed? That was my intention, you know, and as far as I am aware, it worked—except for one man. And Alain of Brittany was a cruel and vicious man. No doubt he deserved what he got.''

''That is not a very priestly thing to say, Ranulf.''

Roland's tone was teasing, but his brother shot back, ''And I am not yet a man of the cloth, only a soldier of King William's.''

Roland nodded, his thoughts turning once more to the threatening weather. As far as he could tell they were within an hour's ride of Derford, and he prayed the storm would hold off.

Icy sleet began to rain down upon them. ''How much longer?'' asked Ranulf. His stomach was rumbling, and Roland had said they would stop no more to rest or for food.

''We should be there shortly—in time for the evening meal.''

* * *

Brianna had pulled herself together and ridden home on her pony after having waited to give the men plenty of time to retrieve the bodies Hugh of Brittany claimed lay in the dirt road.

Nedra met her at the door of Gilbert's bower. "Gilbert has the fever, child. It came on without warning." She shook her graying head and stood aside to allow Brianna to enter.

Sure enough, the chestnut-brown eyes were lightly glazed, the lids half closed in burgeoning delirium.

"Oh, Nedra," she sighed tiredly. "Has he not suffered enough?"

When the older woman insisted on sending Aleen or Edythe to care for him while she rested, Brianna adamantly refused. "He is my husband. I will tend him." And so, against her better judgment, Nedra left her alone.

Brianna alternated between sponging his flushed face as he stirred listlessly and slaking his burning thirst; her heart went out to him as she ignored her own body's warning signals.

As darkness descended, her eyelids began to droop sleepily, and her last thoughts were of Dane. Roland would no doubt be furious with her if he discovered what had happened, but Brianna didn't care. Just so Dane was not blamed . . . just so his silly honor would not make him feel obliged to protect her. Silly men. Ridiculous pride and honor—

Lightning tore through the dark, ominous-looking sky, rendering the deepening dusk bright as day. Thunder rumbled intermittently with ear-shattering force and the heavens opened, sending forth an icy cold sheet of rain.

Brianna's dreams were confused, fragmented; she was so cold, huddled in a little ball for warmth. And Gilbert kept calling for her: *Bra-na! Bra-na!* Why couldn't she see him? Where was he?

Brianna . . . Brianna . . .

A soothing voice over the roar of the storm. Gilbert?

Strong arms gently, tenderly lifted her and cradled her against a solid chest.

Warmth.

Someone was wrapping her in something soft and warm and she felt safe, secure. *Gilbert!* Her lips formed the word but only the faintest whisper emerged. Through her sleep-drugged mind she heard a deep, familiar voice say low into her ear, "Gilbert is safe, *ma chère.* Safe." And a warm cheek seemed to caress hers so fleetingly she must have imagined it.

And that voice—whose was it?

Roland's?

Nay, Roland was in London.

"Roland, listen to me—"

The tall figure pacing before the roaring hearth turned menacingly on his friend. "Your last words to me were that you would guard her with your life! Is this how you keep your promises, Dane?" Roland's face was white with fury.

"Will you not sit down and put something into your belly, Roland?" Ranulf urged. "You've had naught to eat since this morning, and a bit of wine can do you no harm."

Roland suddenly stopped pacing and ran his fingers distractedly through his hair. "Wine. A cup of wine, perhaps." He turned accusing eyes once more to Dane. "How could you let me down? I love you like a brother and I thought you loved me—"

"I do! By all the saints, you lay this at my head without giving me a chance to explain anything! Do you think I care so little for you—or Brianna—to have been deliberately careless? I have feelings for her too!"

Roland had been in the act of taking a goblet from a servant. His hand gripped the cup tightly and his eyes narrowed dangerously. "In what way, *mon ami?*"

"Do not put me on the defensive, Roland! She is like

the . . . the sister I never had. She is so kind, so loyal to those she cares for . . . . How could anyone not have feelings for her?''

"Roland does not believe in love without lust, Dane," interjected Ranulf dryly, "for he has never felt affection of that sort for anyone but family.''

Roland threw his brother a warning look and then continued to regard Dane with hostile suspicion over the rim of his goblet. After a moment he said, "And no doubt her beauty has no bearing on it? The way she moves—the sound of her voice—''

"You are in love with her, Roland. You have been for some time, and there is a great deal of difference between caring for someone and being in love with her.'' His look turned anxious. "Now will you let me tell you what happened?''

Roland hesitated and then shook his head wearily. "Nay, my good friend. I was wrong to condemn you unjustly.''

"My lord, the woman Nedra is come," Beorn announced from nearby. Roland looked up, grateful for the speed with which the man-at-arms had fetched her.

"Where is she?" Nedra's face was somber, only for a moment registering surprise at the sight of Ranulf. Roland led her to his own bower where he had laid Brianna upon the great bed.

Ranulf looked at Dane, and compassion swept over him. "You must forgive him, Dane. He is tired and obviously quite taken with the girl.''

"He is my friend, and nothing could destroy the bond between us, Ranulf. It is only that I do feel responsible for what happened. I sent her home late this morn to rest. But Hugh of Brittany dared to show his face on some ridiculous pretext of seeking one of his men—''

"Alain of Brittany?''

"Aye. But of course you would know. I had almost forgotten that you were here as well. He wanted to search the homestead where Alain was last seen. It was Brianna and her husband's home, you see, and she overheard his threat.''

At Ranulf's understanding nod, he continued. "She was standing in the shadows to avoid being seen. But she stepped forward, fearful of the effect his presence would have on her husband, and revealed that she had killed Hugh's man.''

"So now he knows where she is,'' Ranulf mused aloud, "and it obviously would do Roland no good to learn of this now. Perhaps in a few days' time . . . But you must finish your story, for I am puzzled about a few things. Why would her husband be so overwrought at the sight of Hugh of Brittany?''

Dane briefly explained Brianna's situation and the encounter with Alain of Brittany.

"So the girl has her hands full, 'twould seem,'' he said thoughtfully. "Well, I am eager to meet any female who can have such an effect upon my brother—and a d'Avranches as well. She must be something to behold.'' He smiled.

Dane met his smile with one of his own. "She will be fine, Ranulf, and *you* will fall under her spell as well.''

"Did you know your father is in London, Dane?'' Ranulf asked, purposely changing the subject.

"Father? In England? Are you certain?'' Incredulity replaced some of the tension on his features.

"Aye. That is what kept Roland away for longer than he intended. Lord William insisted on hearing about the Channel crossing, the battle itself and, of course, you and your exploits up until now.''

"Wine!'' ordered Dane to a servant within earshot. Temporarily distracted, he placed an arm around Ranulf's shoulders and drew him toward a table. "You must tell me more about this, Ranulf . . .''

"Good morningtide, *ma chère*. How do you feel?''

Brianna opened heavy-lidded eyes with an effort, and there above her was the masculine visage of Roland de Beaufort.

That was the voice she had heard in her dreams. Two spots of color appeared on her wan cheeks. Oh, why could it not have been Walter? Or even Dane?

She was as powerless as ever to tear her gaze away from his, and she noticed the drawn look about his beautifully carved features despite his smile.

"I . . . I am better, thank you," she murmured. And then she remembered Gilbert. "Gilbert?" she asked with a pleat of worry marring her brow.

"Gilbert has only a mild case of fever. He fares well." He paused. "You gave us quite a scare."

"Indeed?" She finally pulled her eyes away from his, only to realize she was in *his* bed. "I did not think a Norman feared aught." Afraid to look up again, she toyed distractedly with the blanket.

Roland studied her closely. Some color was returning to her face, and the contrast of her thick, dark lashes fanned out over alabaster skin as she kept her gaze downcast was striking. He had missed her so! He longed to plant a kiss atop the slim, pert nose—

As gently as the touch of a butterfly's wing, his hand reached out and pushed aside the raven curls covering her temple. Still she refused to meet his gaze. "Have I upset you, Brianna?" he asked.

She sighed softly. "Nay, my lord. 'Tis my own reaction to you that disturbs me," she admitted with disarming honesty, her gaze meeting his.

"I am not your enemy, Brianna," he said quietly. "I cannot undo what has been done. I told you—"

"Ahem."

Roland turned toward the door.

"May I come in for a moment, Roland?"

Brianna watched the tall figure move into the room, and confusion chased across her fine features as he neared. Roland introduced him, but Brianna only heard "my brother" as her thoughts whirled chaotically.

The two men were identical twins.

I did not raid your village. Roland's words came back to her in a flash.

"Brianna?" The voice so like Roland's yet somehow gentler summoned her, seemingly aware that she had not heard Roland's introduction. "I am Ranulf de Beaufort, Roland's brother. I pray I did not do the wrong thing by coming here when you are still abed."

Her cheeks were bathed with color as she turned her head toward Roland and met his silver-gray eyes. She could read nothing of perfidy in them. He had told her the truth, knowing she would never believe him. Knowing that in her righteous anger she would have thought he was telling tales to cover up his guilt—to make himself look less the villain.

Roland's hand covered hers, its strength and warmth imparting some sense of understanding and forgiveness to the mortified girl." 'Twas only natural, Brianna," he said quietly. "We are mistaken for one another often."

Brianna stared at the hand resting upon hers, and her words lodged in her throat. She did not notice Ranulf quietly slip out to leave them alone. Tears of frustration, augmented by an overwhelming tiredness, slid down her cheeks.

"Will you trust me now, Brianna?" His voice seemed to surround her—lulling her, caressing her tired spirit, her exhausted body. "Will you believe me when I say I only want what is best for you—and Gilbert—when I ask you to give up that homestead?"

With an effort she kept from succumbing to his soothing charm, the sincere tone of his rich-timbred voice. *You could better aid Rob and, therefore, England, were you to agree.* The errant thought came out of nowhere, a reminder she mustn't let herself give in to the enemy.

"I have need of someone to help me keep my ledgers while my men are so occupied with clearing and building my castle," Roland continued. "Also, until I can effectively deal with this Anglo-Saxon marauder called Rob, I will need every man I have to protect my lands." He smiled. "You *do* read and write?"

"I do. And I can cipher as well."

He nodded, well satisfied. "In addition, in the absence of a lady of the manor, I shall need someone well versed in the art of medicine. You can do me a double service in return for your keep and Gilbert's."

She hesitated still.

"If you become unhappy with your position here, you should remember it is only temporary. Eventually I will wed and my wife will see to the sick. As for the keeping of my accounts . . ."

Brianna didn't hear the rest. For some strange reason, the thought of Roland de Beaufort married to some wellborn Norman female caused a sickening feeling in the pit of her stomach. Why did he have to mention it now?

She looked up at him, irritation shading her finely molded features. "As long as Gilbert is well tended, there is no need for you to fear I will consider leaving. He is the most important person in my life."

Well done, my lovely, Roland thought wryly. He had sought to elicit some reaction to his reference to a future marriage. If his words had touched her, it could not compare to the way her words had affected him. But would he have expected less of her? Her capacity for love and loyalty had been evident from the first time he had met her.

Incredible aquamarine eyes met those of fathomless gray. "Will you accept my offer?" he pressed.

"I accept." But Brianna felt as if she had walked directly into a well-baited trap.

Only a visit from Dane, explaining Ranulf's part in the raid on Derford, succeeded in raising her spirits—until he told her he had to leave.

"Leaving? For London?" Brianna had grown fond of him in spite of herself and had felt an odd kinship with him.

"My father, for some reason, has finally come to England and is in London. I only remained long enough to make certain of your recovery."

Brianna smiled at his concern, secretly relieved that he would be gone, for her conscience was giving her enough trouble because of her decision to spy for Rob. Dane could not be harmed if he were not here.

"But I believe Ranulf will be the perfect buffer—someone to keep the peace between you and Roland. He feels called to God and is contemplating taking up the cloth." He smiled gently at the look of surprise on her face. "You really should get to know him, Brianna, for I think you would like him very much."

"He dared to show his face here?" Roland asked in disbelief.

"Aye. And he lost four of his men on the road into Derford for his efforts."

Roland stared into his goblet thoughtfully. "So that pest of an Englishman for once has done me a service."

Brianna's spine stiffened at his derogatory reference to Rob.

It was after the evening meal, and Roland, Dane, Ranulf, Gilbert and she were still at table. Roland had insisted Brianna and Gilbert eat with him, and Brianna felt self-conscious every time a servant looked their way. It had occurred to her that some among them might think she was giving her favors to Roland in exchange for their keep, and the thought rankled.

"So what excuse did the Breton use for coming here?"

"Well, he *said* he wanted to know what befell Alain of Brittany, but I believe his true purpose was to see if you had found Brianna."

Brianna felt Roland's eyes on her even as she shook her head disbelievingly at Dane's words. Surely the man was not searching for her—one hound on the scent had been bad enough! Her eyes met Roland's, and he seemed to have similar thoughts. "Do you see what madness your beauty has wrought among William's men, *chérie?*" he chided.

Unthinkingly she answered, " 'Tis a pity I could not bewitch them all," and colored at the boldness of her words.

"Aye. I am sure you feel it is. I only wish William had you on his side, Brianna." And his eyes lingered caressingly on her countenance until he remembered himself and looked at Dane in expectation. "Of course the Breton did not learn anything?"

Brianna drew a quick breath, determined to confess before Dane tried to shield her. "Unfortunately, my lord, he did," she said in a rush, her cheeks still pink from her previous words and Roland's intense perusal.

"Brianna, this is between Roland and myself," Dane warned, with an uncharacteristic edge in his voice.

She knew he was angry at her attempt to involve herself, but she could not let Dane take the blame for her precipitate action. She suspected Roland could be fierce when provoked, and something told her this news would wear heavily on his control.

"Lord Roland, it was totally my doing—"

"Brianna, *do not!*"

Roland, whose eyes had been going from one to the other, interrupted with a stern "Enough!" Brianna started at the sudden command and Dane compressed his lips in frustration. "Now, exactly what happened?" He addressed Dane, his voice deceptively calm.

Brianna grew annoyed at his dismissal of her words, although she was well aware that she was in his home, where he was lord and master, and she was only a woman. He had also addressed Dane initially and not her.

"Hugh of Brittany and his men came into the hall at my bidding, and Brianna was here. She had been to see Father Simon and—"

"I do not question her presence here, *mon ami.*"

"Well—damn it, Roland! You have acquired a habit of

putting me on the defensive!'' the dark-haired knight exclaimed.

''You should be very much on the defensive, Dane, if you
have allowed that swine from Brittany to discover Brianna's
whereabouts. Have you?''

''He did not! 'Twas *my* doing!'' Brianna cried angrily,
standing up and facing Roland. ''Dane has naught to be defensive about! *I* made my presence known by confronting him
before Dane even knew what I was about, and I will not let
you blame him!''

She knew that she was overstepping her bounds, but she
was not prepared for the black look that crossed Roland's
features. ''You confronted him?''

''Aye. He made it clear that he intended to search the entire
homestead to find his man's body, and I could not allow that.''
At Roland's frown, she added in a burst of bravado, ''You
see, I gave him more than a simple trouncing on the head,
Norman. I *killed* him. I did what I had to—Gilbert had already
been abused by this man, and God knows how he would have
reacted to this new threat.''

''I should have reacted sooner and let it be known that I
would not have countenanced such a thing—before Brianna
had a chance to expose herself,'' Dane said almost apologetically, ''but—''

''It seems to me, Roland, that these two are bound to
protect each other at any cost. I would think the fault lies
with neither of them in view of the unexpected turn of
events,'' Ranulf interjected. ''Why blame either of them?''

''Because Dane has let me down once already when I entrusted Brianna and my lands to him—''

''You *entrusted* me to him?'' Brianna asked in amazement.
''Your audacity has no limit, Norman, does it? How dare you
treat me as your—your property?''

Gilbert reacted uneasily to the tension in the air. ''Bra-na,
Bra-na,'' he mumbled until Ranulf, who was seated to
the other side of him, reassured him patiently.

Roland looked over at Dane. "I think we should talk in my chamber." At Dane's nod, he turned to Ranulf. "Will you see Brianna to her room? Hilde"—he gave the girl a meaningful glance—"can see to Gilbert."

Hilde, whose task it was now to tend Gilbert, immediately turned sullen and reluctantly left off vying for Dane's attention. She went to Gilbert's side in response to the cold look in Roland's eyes, and the group abruptly broke up.

"Perhaps it is just as well that Dane will be going to London," Ranulf said as he guided Brianna toward the stairs. She had anxiously glanced back only once to see both men standing silently, their eyes on her. "They seem to have been at odds with one another since Roland's return," he continued reflectively.

Brianna turned her attention to Ranulf. It was like looking at Roland, and yet it wasn't. Against her better judgment, she felt herself warming toward him. He seemed to have a way with Gilbert—much more so than Hilde, who obviously wasn't happy with her new chore. "You are very good with Gilbert, my lord. He took to you immediately, and that is unusual."

Ranulf led her along the upper floor to her room and they paused before the door. "I would like to have known him before his injury," he said gently.

Tears welled up suddenly in Brianna's eyes at the thought of what Gilbert was once like. "He was kind and so . . . alive. He would have made a good husband," she added bitterly. "Now I am reduced to *this*."

"You are not reduced to anything that you were not before, Brianna. You are virtually free to do as you please. Roland is no harsh taskmaster where you are concerned."

"He set out to get me here from the moment he came to Derford. At last he has succeeded." Her expression was troubled.

"It is not my place to lecture you, but Roland is my brother and I know he will do his best to rule wisely and justly. As far as you are concerned, I can only suggest you try to follow your own conscience. No one can force you to do anything that is absolutely against your principles. And the key here is to always look into your heart, for that is the ultimate truth for each of us, Brianna.''

She looked into his face and saw compassion and honesty there, as well as warmth and sincerity. ''I will try to remember your words, Lord Ranulf. Thank you for seeing to me.''

When he had gone, Brianna walked into the center of the room and looked around. She still could not believe she was here. The upper floor consisted of several bedchambers for Roland, Gilbert, herself and any guests Roland might entertain. Ranulf and Dane had just moved into two of the newly finished rooms.

Sounds from Gilbert's adjoining room caught her attention, and she carefully made her way to the door that separated the chambers and opened it.

Hilde was standing over Gilbert, who cowered near the bed. Hands on her ample hips, the girl was taunting him in an irate voice. ''You helpless idiot! Look, *look* what you have done now!'' She pointed a finger at an overturned basin of water on the floor, slowly spreading its contents in an ever-widening puddle. ''You have come a long way from the strapping man I once knew, Gilbert!''

''He is not to blame for what happened at Hastings, Hilde,'' Brianna said, fighting to remain calm. The girl whirled around in surprise. ''If you will be so kind as to clean up the water, I will put him to bed.''

''And no doubt you will go running to Lord Roland with damning words about what you have just heard!'' she sneered.

''Nay, Hilde. I am not so unforgiving as that.''

''Oh, come now, Brianna! I will wager you cannot wait to run to his bedchamber the moment I am gone. This arrangement is very cozy.''

Brianna colored at the implication. "Will you do as I ask and then leave?"

Without answering, Hilde proceeded to clean up the mess. Brianna went to Gilbert and carefully knelt down beside him. Taking his face between her hands, she looked into the fear-filled dark eyes and whispered soothing reassurances to him.

"I have finished. May I go now?" Brianna looked up and nodded. "And you will say nothing to my lord?"

Something about the haughty look on Hilde's fair features prompted her to say, "I will not have to, Hilde. For if you are given enough rope, I believe you will hang yourself."

"I think it is best I leave on the morrow for London." Dane was studying Roland, as if gauging what reaction his words would bring. "Of late I can do nothing right in your eyes."

Roland stared out of the newly cut, unshuttered window into the yard below. He remained silent.

"It is one thing to love a woman, but completely another to allow that love to distort your judgment to the point where you accuse falsely," Dane added quietly.

Roland continued to look unseeingly out the small window; the cold night air coming through it helped him to keep his anger leashed. "I do not think I accuse falsely. Perhaps you had little control over her abusing her health." He abruptly turned cold gray eyes on his friend. "But to allow her to reveal herself to Hugh of Brittany! You know how treacherous he is! Do you forget so soon how I got this scar, *mon ami?* He is perhaps not the most clever of men to ever number among William's ranks, but he is crafty, and when he wants something he will go after it no matter the consequences. And now that he knows of Ranulf's deception, he poses more of a threat than ever to Brianna." He began pacing before the fireplace. "Now that he has discovered Brianna dwells within my jurisdiction, he will take up the challenge with even more determination." He stopped his pacing and went to stand before Dane. "Do you still believe I accuse falsely?"

"Indeed. You never asked for a complete explanation, which would only be fair. But even worse, you doubted and denounced my capability as a man—as a Norman knight—as your closest and most trusted friend." Now Dane's dark eyes turned cold. "I can only hope that you will have come to your senses by the next time we meet."

In the morning he was gone.

CHAPTER 10

"Brianna! What would Lord Roland say if he discovered these?" exclaimed Nedra in unconcealed dismay.

Brianna knew what the woman was talking about before she even turned around to see. Her eyes rested on the altered garments of Gilbert's which she had made in a burst of defiance after Roland had thrown the others into the fire.

The two of them were packing Gilbert's and Brianna's belongings into the bound chest that stood in the great hall. Outside, a wagon waited with several men ready to load it at Brianna's bidding.

"I do not intend to let him discover them, Nedra," she answered simply. The implication was there, plain as day.

"You need not worry about me, child. Although I doubt the wisdom of your actions, I would never betray you. But the Norman made it plain that he objected—"

Brianna's look was annoyed as she took the offending articles from Nedra and placed them at the bottom of the trunk along with the pouch of gold she had retrieved and the letter from the Abbess.

"He does not own me, Nedra, nor anyone else. I work for our keep, and if I wish I can leave freely. An oath of fealty does not reduce one to the status of a thrall." She was silent awhile and then, "Nedra, what do they say in Derford now? I . . . I mean about *me?*"

Nedra smiled gently. "They think you did the wise thing, Brianna. Your love of England, your loyalty to her—no one questions them. And it was an honest trade—at least on your part—was it not?''

"But I . . . I live in his household! Surely there must be those who condemn that.''

"There will always be those who condemn what they envy or are too thickheaded to understand, child. But where else could you have dwelt? Gilbert needs constant watching and attention, and he could only get them under the Norman's own roof. So then, where would *you* stay?''

Brianna closed the trunk and sat down thoughtfully. "Indeed, where else could I have gone and remained near Gilbert?''

That evening Roland returned to the hall after the others had eaten. Ranulf, Guy and René were with him, and they were all tired and hungry and frustrated. Ranulf told Brianna briefly of their unexpected encounter with the ever-elusive Rob and their failure to apprehend him. Brianna had never known Roland to be so withdrawn, his expression closed.

Some of the tension began communicating itself to Gilbert, and Hilde reluctantly made ready to take him upstairs.

"Nay, Hilde. Not just yet. I know a way to calm him,'' Brianna appealed to the sullen girl. She ran lightly up the stairs and returned in a few moments with a lute she had been given by Abbess Marie.

She approached Roland hesitantly, afraid of his strange mood. "Begging my lord's pardon, may I play for you?'' As she spoke she noticed for the first time that he was pale, his lips in a tight line of anger—or pain. Was he hurt? His eyes were dark as charcoal, but that could be from any number of things.

Roland's expression immediately softened at her words. "Of course, *chérie*. How can I deny you so simple a request?'' His eyes cleared somewhat and the corners of his mouth gave her a hint of a smile.

"Thank you, my lord,'' she returned with downcast eyes.

It seemed to be increasingly difficult of late for her to meet those intense silver-gray eyes. Thinking of him as the enemy was proving to be no easy task either.

Brianna chose several soft and soothing ballads, carefully avoiding love songs, and sang to them all, her clear, sweet voice drifting across the hall like a caress. As her eyes studiously avoided Roland's they rested more and more often upon her husband, who sat enthralled, and her expression became wistful.

Roland watched her with a curious mixture of admiration and frustration. She was so near and yet so far . . . . He wondered just what she truly felt for the man who was her husband in the short time they had known one another. Surely it could not have been love. One did not fall in love in the space of a few short hours—or could one?

While his eyes remained riveted to the girl before him, his mind went back to the gruesome aftermath of a great battle and a young woman with long, glossy black hair that tumbled about her striking face, and blue-green eyes full of vitality and determination.

Had she not captured his love in those moments? Had she not unwittingly branded him as indelibly as a white-hot iron, searing for eternity her image, her essence, upon his mind and heart?

Now, as Roland consumed more wine than was his wont, he still saw those same qualities in the girl before him. The intense loyalty and sense of duty that had brought her to Hastings and into his life were as strong as ever. And directed toward the mindless shell of a man who sat mesmerized as the empty dark eyes remained on her face.

Roland de Beaufort found himself resenting whatever feelings Brianna had for her husband with a desperation totally foreign to him. A desperation born of unfulfilled love. He signaled for more wine as Ranulf gave him a look that conveyed concern. Roland ignored it; not even Ranulf's sympathy could banish his pain. But wine could dull it—and he could forget for a while.

No one knew of his pain—neither the fiery agony in his shoulder nor the anguish in his heart. Brianna would never betray a husband, even a mindless cripple.

How could he ever win?

The vision of her began to blur before Roland's eyes, for he had touched next to nothing on his trencher. Only the wine—soothing wine.

Brianna, his heart cried out to her as he sat there, barely able to focus on the dark tendrils softly brushing her flushed cheeks, the sparkling eyes that only rested on the man who was her husband.

Brianna, Brianna, Brianna—

Then, as if in answer to his unspoken plea, her face turned toward him and her eyes met his. Her beautiful, expressive blue eyes with a hint of green, like the ever-changing sea, soothing him, beckoning him—

"Roland?" Ranulf whispered with alarm in his ear as he began to slump on the bench. The slow seepage from his shoulder was staining his tunic bright red at last. Ranulf could not believe his brother had been hurt and no one had even noticed.

"Roland!"

But Roland had already slipped into unconsciousness.

Halfway to the stairway he came to, and insisted Ranulf and Guy allow him to stand on his own two feet. He was slightly unsteady, but he protested he was still capable of mounting the stairs to his room. "Brianna," he ordered, "I wish Brianna to see to my shoulder."

But Brianna had already anticipated she would be needed and, having gathered up a tray of potions and salves and clean strips of linen, was following close behind.

"Is there aught we can do, Ranulf?" inquired Beorn soberly as Roland sank down on the great bed in his chamber.

It was obvious that all the men felt badly at never even guessing their leader had been hurt.

"Nay, Beorn. Not right now, I think. I will call if we do need help." He smiled reassuringly and waved them out of the room. "Get some sleep now. We will need our wits about us in the morn."

Meanwhile, Roland was taking great pleasure in watching Brianna stoke the fire in the hearth and put on a small cauldron of water and herbs to boil. When Ranulf began to undress him, he said, "I am wounded seriously enough to require the ministrations of one skilled in the art of healing, not some *chevalier* who fancies himself a physician because of what he claims he learned in a monastery."

Ranulf finished his task with a good-natured smile on his face. "I concede the lady is much more pleasant to look upon, brother."

Brianna barely heard the exchange, for her thoughts were awhirl. Roland had been attacked by Rob and his men. What if he had died? Could she have lived with that after accepting his shelter and protection? He had been only kind and generous to her and Gilbert thus far, and he had made no improper advances. *But that is why you accepted his offer, Brianna,* said a small voice, *to better enable you to aid Rob.*

She pushed aside her disturbing thoughts and joined Ranulf at the side of the bed. Her eyes widened as she viewed the male form on the bed. She had seen men almost totally undressed when she had treated those with fever, and in the process had lost some of her shyness, although not her modesty. But none of them had the smooth-muscled perfection of Roland's magnificent frame.

His chest was covered with a light furring of dark blond hair which became a narrow line as it approached his slim hips and disappeared under the loincloth Ranulf had discreetly left to cover his midsection. His legs were well shaped and straight, not bowed or thin and gangly or even too heavily muscled. And his skin was burnished from the flattering firelight, with only a long, pale scar along one side of his rib cage and another on a sleek, steel-tempered thigh to mar its perfect symmetry.

Her eyes traveled back to his chest and iron-thewed arms of whose strength she was only too aware. There was a small, jagged hole in his left shoulder from which only a trickle of blood now flowed.

"It appears," said Ranulf as he, too, eyed the wound, "that you were pierced by an arrow with such force that it went clean through."

"But why did you not tell anyone you had been struck?" Brianna asked as she gently examined the small hole, carefully probing around it with her fingertips. "Why would you attempt to hide it?" Her voice trembled with some emotion she refused to attempt to identify.

"If you must know, I did not want to risk any of you riding off into the forest in pursuit of our attackers. They are very skilled at striking and retreating, and they are also more familiar with the woodlands around here. They cannot be beaten at their own game. They must be lured out to fight in the open."

"But . . . but you had no need to keep it to yourself when you were returning home," Brianna continued, puzzled and also angry for some strange reason. "Would you bring the water, please?" she added to Ranulf as she began to carefully clean the wound.

When he had complied, he answered for Roland with a gesture of resignation. "Obviously he did not think it serious enough to warrant immediate attention." At Brianna's angry shake of her head, he added, "And, of course, he was more than likely too enchanted with your skillful performance this eve to wish to disrupt or end it." He smiled at her, but Brianna's eyes were on Roland, who was listening with exaggerated interest to this exchange. Flushing, she dipped a clean cloth in the basin of water.

"Do you need more wine for the pain?" Ranulf asked as

Roland flinched when Brianna's light touch increased in pressure.

"He has had quite enough, I should think," Brianna interjected curtly.

"A man can never have too much wine—or love," murmured Roland.

Ranulf chuckled. "He will survive to torment us both, Brianna, and for a long time to come."

Roland's lightly bloodshot eyes went to Ranulf's face. "If the arrow had been a hand's breadth to the right, I would never have tormented anyone again, my loving brother. But we will have our revenge, do not worry. This English hero's days are numbered."

Brianna's face burned with a mixture of anger and guilt at his words.

"If you have no further need of my services, Brianna, I will leave you now," said Ranulf, and with one last assessing look at his brother he left.

Roland's gaze went to Brianna's face as she began binding the wound. He had not been so close to her since she had been the one abed, and the touch of her hands on his naked skin, intensified by the effect of the wine, was like fire. He struggled to control his desire, suddenly very aware that any telltale indication of his arousal would be all too obvious with only a light blanket covering him. He studied her leisurely at close range, thoroughly enchanted, despite the bothersome ache in his shoulder. "If this is my reward for stopping an arrow, I will have to do it more often," he said lightly.

Brianna frowned as she applied a healing ointment to the cleaned wound. "Do not jest. An injury such as this is no laughing matter."

"You hair is growing, *ma chère*. But I have decided it makes no difference to me. You are just as lovely with it thusly."

Flushing becomingly, she ventured, " 'Twould seem your

only interest in a woman is pretty hair and a handsome face, my lord.''

Too late Brianna realized she had played right into his hands, for pain had inhibited the effects of the wine somewhat and his wits were very much intact. "A comely form helps.''

She could not prevent the hint of amusement that shone in her eyes, but then she deliberately pulled the last strip of linen tighter with a jerk that caused him to wince. "I would not know of such things.'' She picked up the basin of blood-tinged water and emptied it into the chamber pot, then returned for the bloodied rags. "But then,'' she added, "I would imagine you are most experienced at judging what is comely in a female form.''

Roland lifted an eyebrow in mock surprise. "Surely a man does not reach the age of eight and twenty without some knowledge in these matters, my little innocent.'' His smile was pure deviltry.

"Will that be all, Norman?'' she asked, gaining control of her wayward tongue at last and suddenly eager to quit his presence.

"I am sorely in need of a bath, *chérie*, and the other servants are undoubtedly abed by now.''

"You are in no condition to bathe,'' she replied with a hint of alarm.

"But I am not in the habit of sleeping with a hard day's accumulation of sweat and dust still clinging to me. Could you not at least help me with the task by fetching clean water and a cloth?'' he asked innocently.

Torn between the strain on his face from pain that was very real and the instinctive knowledge that she would be courting disaster if she complied, Brianna hesitated.

He wickedly took advantage of her uncertainty. "I will not be overlong, as it is only my upper torso that needs cleansing.''

With reluctance, she proceeded to refill the basin with warm water, her back to him. "And how is it that the rest of you escaped becoming soiled, my lord Norman?'' she threw over her shoulder.

Roland smiled as he took in her shapely back and almost forgot the discomfort of his shoulder at the prospect of being in her company awhile longer.

When she stood beside the great bed with the water, cloth and towel, he made a move to take the cloth from her.

''I will do it, Norman,'' she said with a sigh, but her look was wary. She laved his face carefully, and his eyes closed so she was free to inspect every well-carved contour of the face that disturbed her so. Then she washed the arm closest to her and then his chest. His eyes were suddenly open again and on her, but she was engrossed in the crisp feel of the dark-gilt hair that formed a light tangle over the smoothly muscled expanse. Touching smooth, bronzed skin under the soft, springy tendrils of his body hair felt infinitely sensual and she felt a sudden lassitude begin to slip over her and settle in her loins. She ached for . . . for what?

She stopped unexpectedly, trying to get hold of herself. Her head turned slightly and her gaze met Roland's. There was an unfathomable look in the now smoky gray eyes, and it brought back her determination to finish quickly and take her leave.

She finished his upper torso with alacrity and reached over to his right arm. That was a mistake. His warm breath fanned over her cheek as she fought to keep herself from leaning against him and tried to concentrate on her task. Her cheeks burned self-consciously as she felt his eyes on her; his face was mere inches away.

As if compelled by some unseen force, she turned to him. Unbidden, the picture of Rob aiming a razor-sharp arrow at him flashed vividly in her mind's eye, and instead of squelching the inexplicable compulsion that drew her toward him, the vision buttressed the unknown force as guilt welled up inside her. Sweet and invisible as gossamer, the mysterious thread of emotion proved unexpectedly strong and resilient, leaving her powerless to resist its attraction.

Blue-green eyes locked with gray, and all else faded into insignificance. His wet arm went around her and drew her to him, warm, wine-kissed lips moving to possess hers with infinite gentleness. A tear slipped down the glossy black lashes that feathered his cheek and regret surged through her as she remembered the look of anguish in the gray eyes when she deliberately ignored him earlier in the evening.

"Brianna." His rich voice caressed her name in a husky whisper as he pulled his lips from hers. "Why do you weep, *mon ange?*"

She would not—could not—answer him. Never could she allow him to suspect her duplicity.

And then his mouth was upon hers again, gently moving over her sweet lips, tasting, savoring, and Brianna drank of his unique and intoxicating taste as her tongue encountered his. A tremor of delight shook her as he lazily explored the silky inner lining of her mouth.

With a will of its own, her hand stroked his powerful chest, and then Roland covered it with his own, guiding it downward, meeting only token resistance. Lower and lower it slid, as naturally as a bee drawn to nectar. The smooth, taut belly under her questing fingers tensed with delicious anticipation as she paused before the heat of his manhood, a heartbeat away. And all the while she could not even think of pulling away, for this seemed as natural as breathing. A warm, melting sensation settled in the center of her being and she wanted— Oh, God forgive her, she ached for more.

Her breasts, crushed against him as his embrace tightened, tingled until a low moan of pure pleasure issued from deep in her throat. His lips became more demanding, his tongue plundering the honeyed inner sanctum of her mouth with increasing boldness. Liquid fire flooded through the core of her and a mystical weakness seized her in its sweet grip as his right hand slid her skirts up along a sleek, quivering limb in response to her hesitant yet eager exploration.

She never knew what it cost him to reach over with his

right arm and ease her body over his, for he tested every ounce of willpower he possessed to keep from tensing or flinching at the shooting pain that jolted through his shoulder with the effort of the movement. He did not dare break the enchantment that had settled over them both, lulling the girl in his arms to complacency and then overt desire.

He slowly rolled to one side, slipping her slim, acquiescent form beneath his, all the while continuing the tender marauding of his tongue in her mouth until he knew she was helpless to resist the raging tides of mindless desire that gripped them both. With her skirts drawn over her hips, the contact of his pulsing masculinity with the sensitive, throbbing area between her thighs was shocking, yet at the same time enough to cut through the sensual euphoria that held her ripe body captive. She jerked back as one singed by a flame.

Totally relaxed and unprepared for her unexpectedly sharp movement, Roland flinched and caught his breath. The look on her face at the pain she had inflicted gave Roland the needed impetus to take advantage of her confusion and work his magic upon her once more. He deftly released the narrow girdle encircling her waist and slid her skirts up even farther until, unhampered by clothing, the powerful expanse of his chest met the soft mounds of her breasts.

"Roland, nay—"

But Roland's mouth had closed over a rosy-crested peak, and even as he gently suckled the throbbing bud, his fingers stroked and caressed the soft, smooth flesh of her inner thighs.

She writhed in an agony of excitement, uninhibitedly arching against his hand when it tenderly cupped the apex of her thighs and then stroked the satiny folds within. "Nay, Roland, please," she protested softly even as her body begged for more. His mouth moved from one breast to the other and then silenced her murmured pleas as he positioned himself between her quaking limbs.

Slowly entering her virginal sheath, he paused when Brianna stiffened at the sharp stab of pain. "The pain does not last, my love,'' he whispered into her mouth, their breaths mingling as one. Yet she began to shake her head in vigorous denial when he thrust easily through the barrier of her maidenhead and began a slow, steady rhythm deep within her.

After a few moments indescribable waves of pleasure began to radiate through her. The last vestiges of discomfort melted beneath Roland's tender onslaught and at last Brianna knew what her eager, frustrated body had so yearned for as the man above her took her to heretofore undreamed-of heights.

Several hours later, Brianna awoke to the sound of Roland's steady heartbeat under her ear as his chest pillowed her head. Her eyes flew open and it all came back to her in a rush.

Cheeks burning in mortification, she eased her leg from its position entwined with his and stole a glance at his face. She could only see its outline in the fading glow from the dying embers, but his breath softly brushed her upturned face with each exhalation as he continued to sleep.

Carefully she sat up and eased herself off the feather-stuffed mattress, turning to cover Roland's nude form with a blanket before quitting the room.

Once she was in her own chamber, shame and regret washed over her with the force of a tidal wave. What had happened to her? In a moment of physical weakness she had given in to the base, wanton responses Roland de Beaufort seemed to elicit from her like a practiced sorcerer.

God in heaven, she moaned, throwing herself onto her bed in despair. She buried her head in her folded arms while her tortured conscience berated her over and over again for her loss of control, and her weak and unexpected feelings of compassion and protectiveness for the man to whom she had given her virtue without a qualm.

The contact with the bed aroused her still-sensitive breasts as her impudent nipples sprang to life and desire flared through her like a fanned fire.

''Nay!'' she cried and pushed herself off the offending mattress to pace her room like a caged tigress. Anger helped clear her traitorous body of the last vestiges of sexual languor. "How can I go on like this?" she asked the empty room in a voice of genuine distress. "He is a Norman—my enemy—despite my wanton behavior! And I am Gilbert's wife!" But for once the thought of Gilbert did nothing to shore up her disintegrating resolve or ease her overwhelming regret. He could not provide her with what she desperately needed—what she had found in the arms of the lord of the manor.

CHAPTER 11

Brianna breakfasted early and retired to a corner of the great hall to attempt to immerse herself in her scrolls and ledgers. Vellum, inkpots and freshly sharpened quills stood ready to aid her in the task of keeping the accounts of Roland's fairly large estate and the village of Derford. But she was hard pressed to find something to do, for everything was in good order.

She was frustrated by the image of a man and woman intimately entwined on the great bed upstairs that came between her eyes and the figures before her.

"Brianna?"

She started at that familiar voice, and then quickly realized it was Ranulf who stood before her. Roland had not come down for the morning meal.

"I did not mean to startle you, Brianna." He regarded her with serious gray eyes. "I wonder if I did the wise thing by leaving you alone with Roland last eve. I thought that surely he was too weary to cause you any mischief."

Brianna felt the blood rush to her cheeks. Surely he couldn't know! She managed a weak smile. "You are kind to be so concerned about my feelings, Lord Ranulf, but . . . well, nothing is amiss." Her face flamed again and belied her words.

"Roland means you no harm, Brianna, you must believe me. He would rather give up his own life than hurt you."

"Well, things between us are not in so sorry a state as to merit the look on your face, Lord Ranulf."

"Please call me Ranulf, Brianna."

His voice was so soothing, his expression so . . . so sincere and without guile. "You must want something of me, Lord—er, Ranulf. I can feel it coming!" she teased, her earlier anxiety gone.

He broke into that beautiful smile that was obviously a distinct trait of the de Beauforts. "Well, I must concede, you are right. But I swore to my brother that I would personally challenge him if he offended you."

Brianna's smile faded and for a moment she saw a look in his eyes—tender and sweet, much like Roland's when his gaze rested upon her. "I am grateful for your taking up my cause, Ranulf de Beaufort, but I wonder if I am so deserving of such gallantry."

"A man whose heart was not already taken could do little else but care for you, Brianna. Surely you are deserving of much—and for many reasons. But I am rambling," he added as her eyes became downcast at his compliment. "Roland has asked specifically for you. One of the other servants has taken up his meal, but he asked if you could spare some time for him."

"Well, I am quite occupied here . . ." Guilt flooded through her at the lie, with embarrassment hard on its heels. How could she face him?

"Just for today, Brianna. Tomorrow he will want to be up and about, for Roland and sickbeds do not agree. And you have only to leave his company in anger or humiliation and I will personally see to it that he does not take advantage of you again."

She idly fingered an unused quill and sighed softly. How could she refuse Ranulf? "Very well. I will spend some time with him—for you."

As Brianna reluctantly climbed the stairs she wondered at Roland's request for her company after what had happened. Did he wish to gloat? To show her how easily he could further ensnare her within his aura of magnetism? Or did he wish to make amends?

Roland was sitting propped up in bed, trying to shave without making a mess. At the sound of the door opening, he turned and smiled hesitantly—questioningly. A new look of tenderness softened the sculpted features. "So you have allowed Ranulf to persuade you to keep me company." His voice lowered soberly. "I do apologize, Brianna, although in truth, *chérie,* naught I could ever do with you would cause me regret for its own sake. Yet I do not relish the thought of having caused you unhappiness."

"You are so . . . eloquent. I do not wonder that men and women alike make haste to do your bidding. But I never meant for—" Her words died in a fresh wave of shame.

"I will treasure the memory until I cease to be."

His soft, heartfelt declaration unexpectedly sent her heart tumbling about her rib cage, and in an effort to change the subject she asked, "Would you care to play a game of chess, Lord Roland?"

"I would indeed. I am curious as to your skills in anything you may do." As always, Roland was enchanted with her sweet, soothing voice, and at last the mouth he ached to kiss had pronounced the name Roland, and in beautiful French.

"Why did you come to England with William if you owed Harold your life?" Brianna asked a while later between games.

Roland's face hardened for a moment and he studied a smoothly carved pawn carefully as he considered his words. "I swore fealty to William at six and ten. I knew he might release a man from his obligations for unusual circumstances, but my father told me I would be a fool to think I would be one of those men." His mouth tightened as he reached back in his memory for the exact words. "Father said I was too 'valuable' to William in his quest—'too good a fighter' to ever nurture hope of release from so important a campaign." He began to set up the board once again, and his next words sounded bitter. "And, of course, Father wished Ranulf and me to go in his stead, you see. He was seriously injured in a hunting accident two years past and cannot use his legs. Ranulf agreed to take his place, but Father always insisted we go everywhere together.''

Brianna listened with interest, seeing a new side of Roland in his differences with his father. ''So you allowed your sire to coerce you into coming here?''

He laughed, cynicism edging the sound. ''Almost, my wise Brianna. And now your barbs pierce me to the quick when I merely attempt to satisfy your curiosity.''

She flushed guiltily and was about to apologize when his eyes met hers above the readied board. ''Ranulf, ever the peacemaker, interceded on my father's behalf. Between him and Mother, I had little choice in the matter.''

Brianna looked puzzled. ''Well, then why did you accept William's grant of land? Land stolen from an Anglo-Saxon?''

''How can you steal from a dead man? I knew Wulfric was dead—''

''But *Harold!* You took land from the man who saved your life! Dead or no, you repaid him with treachery!'' she reminded him angrily.

Roland's eyes darkened suddenly in annoyance. ''Treachery is a strong word, Brianna. The deed was done—William took the battle and was intent on having England. I could not have taken my leave honorably immediately after Hastings—''

''That depends upon where you owed your honor.''

His face flushed a shade darker and a blood vessel throbbed in his temple. Brianna knew she had dared too much.

Then, without warning, as if drawing on some inner reserve of self-control, Roland's expression changed to one of mild irritation. ''You can know little of life and death, honor and dishonor, having lived within a convent for most of your life, sweet. My obligation was to my liege lord and I was expected to help him hold England. I could not merely fight the first battle and then run back to Normandy.

"But I will tell you this, Brianna. I would not have raised a hand against Harold Godwinson if I had come face to face with him. No one knew—not my father, nor Ranulf, nor William—that I vowed to let him slay me before I would move against him to defend myself."

"It was a noble thing to have decided—"

Roland interrupted her grudging words of admiration with a burst of warm, resonant laughter. "I did not tell you of my vow to ennoble myself or my actions to you, *chérie.*" He turned serious again. "However, you had better keep me in good spirits if you do not wish to . . . ah, entertain me on the morrow as well, for they say laughter is the best medicine."

He could not quite extinguish the glimmer of merriment in the warm gray eyes, and Brianna caught it. But, in spite of the jest, Brianna took him at his word and, not believing she could tolerate another morning of his presence without being totally won over, followed his suggestion most readily.

So the morning passed quickly for them, and every now and then low strains of laughter drifted through the partly open door into the corridor beyond.

It was April and the weather was warming, despite an uncharacteristically mild winter. Roland had chosen a site for his keep and the men were starting to clear the forest. Also, Ranulf, Guy, René and himself were teaching any interested men of Derford the art of mounted fighting on the backs of their small English ponies.

Roland could feel the villagers' slow acceptance and was not surprised by their acquiescence, for he realized that the lives of the English lower classes would not change much. The Anglo-Saxon nobility had been largely killed off or—according to what he had heard in London—imprisoned if they did not go along with William's assumption of the crown. Therefore, if a Norman lord treated the people of his newly acquired lands reasonably, he did not have much reason to expect resistance.

Brianna saw all three of Kerwick's sons several times as they trained in a section of the huge yard. Brand and Edwin were affable, but Walter was sullen and cold to her. She feared she knew why, but it was not a certainty until they came face to face one day after the lesson and practice were over for the morning.

Brianna was walking with Gilbert on a mild, sunny day when Walter stepped into their path to deliberately block them. He was dirty and his clothing sweat-stained from physical exertion under the Normans' strict tutelage. His brown hair was tousled, his hazel eyes blazing. He was anything but sullen now.

"Hello, Walter—" she began uncertainly.

"So you have finally given in to that charming, glib-tongued Norman. What is it like to warm his bed at night?"

Unthinkingly Brianna slapped him across his cheek.

"I do not regret my words," he continued through clenched teeth. "You do not deserve respect from me or anyone else—"

"Walter!" Her face turned as white as the marks on his tanned cheek.

"Walter!" he mimicked in a falsetto voice. "Do you forget what *he* did? That he raided Derford and was indirectly the cause of your taking a man's life?"

"You were the cause, Walter," she said quietly.

"I? Now you even begrudge me the saving of my life? When I only interfered to help you? Because I loved you?"

"It was not Roland that day. I was mistaken—"

Gilbert suddenly bolted in the direction of the gate and Brianna made to stop him, but Walter grabbed her arm. "The guards will stop him. We have not finished our talk."

"Oh, but we have, Walter. I will not stand here and listen to any more of this!" And with a determined jerk of her arm, she turned and hurried to the gate, ignoring the guilt she felt for contributing to Walter's bitter hostility.

Ranulf was there beside the guard, engrossed in a conversation with Vachel. The slight, quick-moving form caught his attention and he looked up. Seeing the look on Brianna's face, his own glance went to the road and beyond, a flash of movement among the trees telling all.

"What is amiss here?" Roland unexpectedly queried from behind them.

Brianna clenched her fists in vexation, for now Roland would press her for an explanation and she had no desire to draw his anger down upon Walter.

"You can explain, Brianna. I'll fetch him."

Both of them followed Ranulf's quick, sure movements to the road and then Roland's keen gaze was upon her, noting the hectic color splashed across her cheekbones. " 'Tis not like you to allow Gilbert to get so far away from you—if he is already in yon forest. I wonder what happened between you and Kerwickson, *chérie*," he mused aloud.

She bit her lip and avoided his gaze, pretending to be absorbed in Ranulf's progress.

"Come, we can wait inside, Brianna. The sun is warm but the breeze is chill." He took her arm, and as she reluctantly went with him they passed Walter. He directed a cold look at Brianna while ignoring the Norman beside her.

Roland sat her down, once inside, and brought her a cup of wine. "Now, what happened?"

"Naught, my lord," she denied, hating herself for lying.

Strong but gentle fingers lifted her chin so she was forced to meet his gaze. His touch caused a liquid warmth to course through her and settle in her loins.

"You are a poor liar, Brianna. Did Walter frighten Gilbert?"

Her aquamarine eyes, misty with tears as she regarded him, told him what her lips would not, and Roland felt his heart melt like a drop of butter on a warm trencher.

"I tried to go after him but could not . . ." Her words trailed off into silence, but she knew it was too late.

"Because Walter prevented you? Did he hurt you, Brianna?'' His voice was taut with sudden anger and he stood up before she could reply. ''I'll throttle him!''

''Nay! Please, my lord, do not! I beg you, think what it will do to Kerwick and Nedra if he is punished—and for such a slight offense,'' Brianna pleaded.

''No offense is slight when it involves you. Surely the boy dared much!''

''I pray you, do not do this—for my sake if for nothing else.'' Her eyes met his and he suddenly felt helpless before the supplication in their blue-green depths. Her lips were moist and parted, pearly, even teeth visible. He remembered the taste of her mouth, wonderfully soft and—

''Very well.'' He wrenched his thoughts from such dangerous ground. ''The lad is in love with you, Brianna, and a man in love does foolish things in jealousy or anger. But that is still no excuse to have accosted you thusly.''

''He is bitter, my lord. He believes that we . . . er, you and I—'' She stumbled in embarrassed confusion.

''He thought I had made you my mistress? He does not know the woman he loves if he believes that. No doubt he had hoped the same for himself!''

''Oh! That is an unfair thing to say! He is pure and clean—and honorable!'' she defended him in a rush.

Roland threw back his head and laughed in genuine amusement. ''No man can harbor only pure and clean thoughts, as you so aptly put it, about a woman he desires. You are surely an innocent, my sweet.''

''And what would you know about true and decent love, Norman, when you act like a rutting stag whenever a comely maid crosses your path—married or not?''

His eyes darkened, his face suddenly tight with irritation. ''So I am a rutting stag, am I? And I have never known true and decent love?'' He brought his face very close to hers. ''Let me tell you that love and desire go hand in hand, my righteous Brianna. I do not desire every 'comely maid' I see, and I have loved—*do* love—with an intensity that would frighten you. So do not speak of my so-called ignorance in the matter when you know naught of me!''

A noise at the door caught their attention abruptly, and Brianna was relieved at the interruption. Ranulf was leading Gilbert toward the stairs where Hilde had appeared, and Brianna saw an opportunity to escape Roland's presence.

"I trust this incident will not cause you to forbid our outings, *chevalier*, for both Gilbert and I benefit greatly from them.''

He regarded her with a softer expression, already regretting his angry words. "This is not a prison, Brianna, but your home. You may come and go as you please—as long as you are back before nightfall and as long as you do not go wandering into the forest.''

"Thank you, sire. I must go now.'' Her voice told him she was eager to get away, so he merely nodded, keeping his reluctance to part company to himself.

Brianna turned and almost ran across the great room, lightly ascending the stairs until she caught up with Hilde and her charge.

After she was assured that Gilbert was unharmed, she thanked Ranulf for his efforts and went into her own chamber. It bothered her much more than she cared to admit that Roland was evidently in love with someone. Her eyes filled with unexpected tears and she dashed them away angrily. What concern is it of mine? she thought as she unsuccessfully fought her distress.

And you are a married woman, said a small voice in the back of her mind. *Or does that make no difference now that you have lain with him?*

She had to plan her meeting with Rob. She had to meet Ian—tomorrow if possible. All her work was caught up and her time was free. Roland would have said nothing even if she were to fall behind in her accounts. He allowed her every freedom, every courtesy . . . .

* * *

The day was overcast but dry, and Brianna felt a sense of freedom overwhelm her as she made her way to the edge of the forest, pushing aside her trepidation at an eventual meeting with Rob. The thought of the man made her slightly uneasy— almost as if there were much more to him than met the eye. Obviously it took an intelligent, complicated man to outwit the flood of Normans that had washed over their land, but it was more than that, although she couldn't quite put a name to it.

Brianna was disappointed after prowling around the periphery of the area where she had first encountered Rob and Ian to find no sign of anyone. It was too chilly to sit and wait for long, and she debated returning after half an hour or so.

"So you have returned, Bryce."

Startled, Brianna spun around to marvel at how easily Ian had appeared from nowhere. Even though she had hoped to see him, she couldn't shake the fact that he had taken her off guard.

"Aye," she managed to respond. "I wish to see Rob. I would like to tell him of my true identity and—well, things have changed since last we met, Ian."

His expression remained unreadable. "We have been aware of your movements."

Brianna's mouth opened in surprise. Rob must have others in Derford working with him as well. For some strange reason this unnerved her.

"Well, may I speak with him, then?"

There was a long moment of silence before he answered. Brianna thought she heard a twig snap behind her but did not want to let him know she was uneasy by glancing over her shoulder.

"That would be dangerous. Very few know where Rob dwells, and we do not know how trustworthy you really are— or if, under duress, you could be depended upon to reveal naught."

Brianna chewed her lower lip nervously. "Could you not blindfold me? It is very important that I speak with him."

Another deep silence.

"You are very sure this is what you want? And you will not be missed?"

Brianna nodded vigorously, her dark curls bouncing. "I will say nothing, believe me. No one questions my absence, either, and—"

Suddenly a blinding white **flash** of pain tore through the back of her head and everything blurred. Darkness descended and she melted into unconsciousness.

CHAPTER 12

Brianna awoke to a pounding in the back of her head, and she moaned softly in pain. The low voices in the background ceased and a door opened and closed. And then there was only the hiss of the fire.

She felt a hard pallet under her, and for a moment she could not remember what happened before all went black. As she slowly opened her eyes to the dim interior of a small cottage, she saw a tall man standing over her, arms folded and a shuttered look on his face.

She managed to sit up, swinging her legs over the side of the low cot and placing her feet upon the floor. The contact jarred her throbbing head, and she involuntarily winced.

"I must apologize for Ian's exuberance in his desire to guard my secrecy, Brianna. Here, drink this. It will ease the ache in your head."

Brianna gratefully accepted the bitter-tasting brew and emptied the contents of the cup. She handed it back and leaned forward on her arms, braced on the edge of the pallet on either side of her thighs. She finally managed to raise her sea-blue gaze to his.

"I hope you do not deem it necessary to mete out such treatment the next time I return," she said with a trace of irony in her voice.

He smiled, a chilling smile which Brianna noticed did not reach his dark eyes. "You need not worry about that."

Brianna glanced around the drab, sparsely furnished room. "How . . . how did you know my name?"

He sat down before her, his chair facing backward, his hands resting on bent knees. "I make it my business to learn as much as possible about those who profess to serve me."

The tone of his voice made it clear that he was in doubt as to her loyalty.

"Profess?"

"Aye. We heard nothing from you for several months, and then you come seeking an audience with me. Your behavior is contradictory."

Brianna dropped her gaze for a moment, feeling like a reprimanded child. Then she looked up once more, the ache in her head having subsided somewhat. "Surely you must know, if your sources are so reliable, that there was an outbreak of fever in the village and then I took up residence in Roland de Beaufort's household. It is no simple task to meet with anyone under his watchful eyes."

"It would seem he has a soft spot for you." She felt the color creep up her neck to her face and once again could not meet his look. "And how did you manage to escape him this time?"

"He will be told that I tended an injured child in the village and then visited Kerwick of Derford's family."

He appeared to ponder this for a moment. "Let us hope you have covered your tracks well, or you will have much to explain when you return."

It seemed to Brianna that he was cold and distant compared to the first time they had spoken. Was it because she had disappointed him? There could be no other reason. "I will tell you here and now that I meant no harm by staying away so long. I can only hope that by living under the Norman's roof I can provide you with even more valuable information regarding his activities. Is that not important?"

He nodded slowly, stroking his bearded chin with one hand. "It is. But are you prepared to send him to his death?"

There was a moment of heavy silence, and Robert of Wessex detected a flicker of doubt in the bewitching eyes of the child born of his late wife. He watched her like a hawk, his eyes missing nothing.

"Aye."

"Very well. There will come a time when you will be called upon to play an instrumental part in his destruction, and there will be no room for any sentiment other than the determination to serve England. Do you understand, Brianna?"

She swallowed past a lump that constricted her throat. "Yes, I understand," she whispered.

"Good. How is your head?"

"Much better, thank you."

"Can I get you something to drink? Wine or mead perhaps?"

She shook her head. "May I have a little water?"

He stood up and turned away to pour her drink. How beautiful she was! The eyes, the pert nose and beautifully molded mouth, the creamy, flawless skin, the melodious voice— His heart constricted in painful remembrance, and then anger quickly replaced the pain. She was not his, and he would use her against her own kind. Perhaps this de Beaufort was some kin to her. What a coincidence that would be. To bring about the demise of one's own half brother or cousin. Who knew?

He turned back to her, silently handing her a cup of water. "How does he treat you?"

"He treats both Gilbert and myself well—as well as can be expected," she amended. "He has kept to his part of the bargain. I keep his accounts and treat any illnesses or injuries that occur in Derford or among his men. In turn he provides a home for us and sees that Gilbert is well tended."

"I see. Do you service him as well?" he asked crudely.

Brianna's face flamed, for she was learning much in an almost all-male household. "Of course not!" The words spewed forth in a burst of indignation at the insult, temporarily oversetting her awe of him. "I am no loose wench, I assure you, my lord!" Her blue eyes flashed, and his heart wrenched as he was unexpectedly reminded of Alicia.

He sought refuge in mockery. "You are a beautiful woman with a useless husband. The Norman would be a fool not to have at least attempted to have you, my girl. Or are you unaware of your attributes?"

"Lord Roland knows I would never consort with another man—let alone a Norman!" she retorted heatedly, but her eyes could not hold his.

"I think, Brianna, that you are not unaffected by this man," he said thoughtfully, his eyes narrowed on her. "The man you claim to hate has mayhap captured your heart?"

She was stunned to hear those words spoken out loud and by the man to whom, above all others, she desired to prove her loyalty. The question caused her conscience to writhe in an agony of guilt.

"He has done no such thing, Rob! Do not doubt my love for England and my hatred of the men who have subjugated her. I was at Hastings and I *saw* what they did!"

"Ah, yes—I had forgotten that you saw the aftermath." She looked at him sharply. "That was a courageous thing you did, Brianna. We could have used more men with your determination."

"You knew of that?"

"Aye. I know all about you—for my own protection. And did the Bastard of Normandy treat you well?"

The underlying bitterness and sarcasm in his words struck a chord in Brianna. "Well enough for a dangerous and determined usurper. Tell me, Rob, how he managed to obtain a papal bull." The grimness of her voice and the bleak set of her features made him aware, for the first time, of the sincerity in her animosity and also alerted him to an intelligence and perception he would have been loath to attribute to a woman.

"It was obtained through secret bargaining. My lord Harold never even suspected. And now it seems the attitude is that this was a judgment in William's favor, despite the will of the English people, and therefore the burden of guilt must lie upon all of England. Many perceive it as something to be accepted—a punishment from God."

Brianna said nothing as she absorbed this. Then wrath flared in her eyes. "Then England is ruled by a foreigner through fear and a belief in the intervention of God on behalf of the Normans? Because of some imagined guilt of all Englishmen? It is absurd!"

"Aye, lass, but it worked because it is so potent a weapon—stronger than an army of all the mercenaries in Europe," Rob said quietly. The girl was astonishingly intelligent and quick to assess a situation. How many others in her place would care to understand the way of things even if they could manage it?

"Well," she said with a dejected sigh, "I only thought to apprise you of my position now. You have only to ask it and I will do what you wish."

Were her words said with less than enthusiasm?

"I am considering killing de Beaufort—and his brother as well—either as he travels to oversee part of his lands or within his own stronghold. If I choose the latter, your help will be invaluable in helping me gain access to the area behind the palisade. I will be in contact with you, so you need not try to meet Ian anymore. I think you may find yourself in trouble with the Norman, as it will be dusk before you return. He will wonder at your long absence."

"He can do naught to ever make me regret my actions this day."

But Brianna was dead wrong.

It was twilight by the time Ian and another man returned

her to within a half mile of where she had met them and removed her blindfold. "The Norman searches for you even now. We dare not venture closer. Have a care."

The ground was soggy from a rainy winter, and Gilbert's shoes impeded her clumsy progress even more. The now deeply shadowed weald made it all but impossible to tell in what direction she was headed, and imperceptibly she veered off course to begin a gradual circle well before the edge of the wooded area. Panic began to set in. She had no weapon and nothing with which to make a fire.

She stopped and leaned against a giant beech to catch her breath and try to get her bearings. Which way was south? she wondered in growing frustration.

And then she heard it. An ominous, predatory growl that raised the hackles on the back of her neck. It seemed to surround her, reverberating from everywhere at once, low-pitched and eerie. It came from no one spot and filled her with dread because she could not pinpoint it.

She pushed away from the beech and made her way through the clinging undergrowth. The frightful way she crashed clumsily through the vines and dead leaves made her an easy target for any predator. Was she going in the right direction? She stopped again in confusion and growing terror. A rustling sound came from one side and then abruptly subsided.

It was following her.

Dear God, what was it? A bear? A wolf? If only she had a weapon. Her eyes quickly scanned the forest floor and in the growing darkness she spied a short branch the thickness of her wrist. She hastily stooped to pick it up when she heard another rustling sound behind her. She whirled, the branch clutched above her head ready to swing downward at the slightest provocation. As she strained to see more clearly, the glow of a pair of feral yellow eyes appeared before her.

It was a wolf.

Brianna's palms began to sweat and she stood rooted to the ground in horror.

The low, rumbling growl issued forth once more and then turned into a vicious bark as the beast emerged from the trees before her, large and evil-looking, its yellow-gray fur blending in with the shadows. Even in the deepening gloom Brianna could make out a dark splotch on its hindquarters that was obviously blood. The animal was wounded and half crazed with pain. From the sound of its savage snarl through bared teeth, the strange, pain-glazed light from its eyes and the half-crouched position of tensely coiled sinew and muscle, Brianna knew it was moving in for the kill.

Suddenly it leaped into the air, its sleek, coarse-haired body melding into one graceful line, the wide head with its exposed fangs hurtling toward her and freezing the very blood in her veins.

And then, as a small, ineffectual cry escaped her lips, the beast veered off to one side with a startled yelp of pain and fell heavily to the ground, the long shaft of a lance protruding from its throat.

Brianna turned toward the noise of feet trampling through the underbrush and recognized the emerging male figure as Roland. She staggered toward him, her entire body limp with relief, her cheeks wet with her tears.

"Brianna," he murmured softly as his iron-thewed arms went around her to crush her to him.

And for once she reveled in the feel of his strong, warm body against hers, and his lips in her hair. She never wanted him to release her, for in the space of those few moments she felt as if she belonged in his protective embrace.

And then he held her away from him, squinting against the encroaching dusk. "Are you unharmed?"

"Aye, only shaken."

He released her and went to retrieve his lance, wiping it with a handful of dead leaves after wrenching it from the dead animal's neck. He returned to her side and took her hand to lead her out of the forest.

The evening meal brought a radical change in Roland's behavior. He was quiet and withdrawn. Ranulf had softly warned Brianna to "have a care with Roland," for he was angry with her. But as the meal progressed Brianna began to realize just how angry he was as he either shot her brooding glances from time to time or completely ignored her.

Once in her bedchamber, Brianna tried to occupy herself with tidying the already neat room. She was still too overwrought from her harrowing experience to go to sleep. Time lay heavily upon her.

Mayhap a goblet of wine would lull me to sleep, she thought distractedly. Instead, she decided to seek out Roland and thank him, despite his anger.

Gathering her courage around her like a mantle, Brianna walked to the door, a lighted candle in her hand. The thought of going to his room did nothing to bolster her courage, especially in light of what had happened there another night, but her resolve was steady. She could wait no longer.

The door to his chamber was partly open; she lifted her hand to knock and paused, peeking through the narrow opening. She froze at the sight before her.

Roland was seated on a chair before the hearth, a wine goblet in one hand and Hilde standing behind him while she massaged his shoulders.

The candle went clattering to the floor, spewing hot wax over her bare feet. She hardly noticed in her desire to get away, to get back to her room before he—

Too late. The door swung wide as Brianna reached the portal of her own chamber, and Roland stood looking from her to the extinguished candle on the floor. "Do you make a habit of prowling the hall and peering into bedchambers at night, *madame?*"

Hilde giggled from behind him, and Roland said something to her over his shoulder which Brianna could not distinguish. It served only to incite her further and gave her the courage to speak up as Hilde left his room and, hips swaying suggestively, walked past her to Gilbert's.

"I but meant to speak with you; the door was open," she retorted with an attempt at dignity, noting in the dim torchlight that the usual gleam of tender amusement in his eyes was gone.

She dropped her gaze before his cold one. "I would think that you would close your door when you are . . . occupied," she added almost inaudibly.

"Why did you come to my room? Perhaps to force my hand? To see what punishment I had in mind for you?"

Her face paled visibly at his words, but she lifted her chin a notch higher, her beautiful mouth set mutinously. "I came to thank you for . . . for saving my life." Her wide-eyed gaze met that of stormy gray—almost black.

"Then come with me, lovely witch, and we can speak of this matter more privately." His fingers closed about her wrist and he literally dragged her back to his chamber.

When the door was closed and bolted securely behind them, Brianna jerked her arm from his grasp. "I am no serving wench that you can imprison me within this room at your whim. You forget my place, Norman," she said through clenched teeth.

"And *you* forget it as well, wench," he growled, his hands coming up to grip her shoulders. "I am your liege lord, and therefore when I forbid you an action that endangers your life it behooves you to obey me!"

"I am not your *thrall!*"

"Surely you are not so ignorant of the bond between a man—or woman—and his lord that you find it so easy to ignore. Do you not realize how close to death you came this day, Brianna?" His face was set in angry lines, a barely controlled fury in his eyes. "I was frantic with worry—to discover that you were gone and long overdue to return—and then that you had gone into the forest alone! Good God, woman, how did you expect me to react?"

"Your concern is truly touching, my lord, and I am grateful—"

"I do not want your gratitude, Brianna!" he cut her off sharply. "I would have done as much for anyone under the circumstances, to say nothing of the woman I—" He stopped abruptly, the look in his storm-dark eyes taking on a new light. "You will be punished, wench, for giving me such a scare." And his mouth swooped down to take hers.

It was meant to be a cold, punishing kiss, and Brianna balked under the unrelenting pressure of his lips. Her strength, however, was no match for his, and she felt overwhelmed and engulfed as his mouth worked over hers, tasting, teasing, the nature of the action imperceptibly changing from punitive as love and desire took over.

Roland could not hurt her, even with a kiss.

This was to be her "punishment"? she thought as her reserve began to crumble away under his heated assault.

He was clad only in undertunic and braies, she in a shift. Their bodies melted into one tightly molded form as pent-up passion began to mount with dizzying speed. She felt her knees buckle as the familiar lassitude stole through her, warming her from within, while Roland held her to him in strong but gentle support. His lips caressed her mouth, her cheeks, her eyelids, as he murmured her name over and over.

Then abruptly his arm swept under the back of her legs and he effortlessly swept her off her feet, while still keeping her tightly pressed to his body. He moved to the bed and carefully laid her down, his own body covering hers. The insistent pressure of his manhood singed her thigh through their clothing, and she suddenly felt the need to have his body pressed to hers, skin to skin, with no hampering garments between them.

He blazed a searing path of kisses from the sensitive spot under her delicately shaped ear down her throat and over the leaping pulse at the base of her neck. He lingered over her smooth shoulders until his mouth sought a pink-crested breast. As he took the nipple gently between his teeth, she arched against him in pleasure, eyes closed, lost in pure sensation.

With his free hand he slipped her shift up her body and over her head, never once letting up in his arousal of her. Before she knew what had happened, she felt him naked, warm and solid against her. Her eyes opened in momentary surprise to meet his smoky gray gaze, a gleam of tenderness, desire and much more in its depths.

"Let me love you, Brianna, my sweet. Let me love you." And suddenly his eyes were moist with emotion.

She did not demur as one of his hands caressed her silken thighs, moving inexorably toward the center of her femininity. His mouth sought hers once more and he whispered love words in French against her lips as she tasted the last vestiges of wine that still lingered there. He played her body as one plays a finely tuned instrument until she ached for him, her slender arms going around him, her nails digging with insistent, wild need into his back.

She needed no urging to part her thighs as she felt his throbbing shaft nestle between them. And then he was slowly penetrating the velvet softness of her.

"Roland," she whispered huskily, and he rejoiced to hear his name on her sweet lips as he rested a moment inside her, his eyes devouring her face.

He began a slow, steady rhythm at first, wanting only to give as he was being given. And as the tension built within him, Brianna's body answered with a rising need of its own—a buildup of heightened awareness and pleasure that threatened to pull her under in a vortex of exquisite sensation. Under the increased rhythm of his lovemaking, she suddenly felt an explosion of ecstasy sweep through her that made her aware of nothing but this man who could take her out of herself and send her soaring to the height of sensual fulfillment.

Roland felt her tense violently and only then did he allow himself to come to a shattering climax, spilling his seed deep within her.

They lay side by side afterward, the fine sheen of perspiration covering their bodies, burnished by the firelight. Brianna's hair was like a dark cloud about her head, the now almost shoulder-length tresses curling around her fine-featured face.

Roland propped himself up on one elbow and tenderly smoothed the errant curls back from her brow and cheeks. Her eyes opened and met his. "I love you, my sweet Brianna," he said simply.

She smiled faintly, a troubled look clouding her aquamarine eyes. "What we did was not right, Roland."

"Do you feel sullied in any way from my loving you?" She moved her head from side to side in silent denial. "It is as it should be, then. What I feel for you is beautiful and pure. What we shared was beautiful, even more wondrous than the first time. There was naught to tarnish you. We belong together. I knew it from the moment I held you in my arms at Hastings."

A tear slipped down a flawless cheek as her eyes closed once more. "I am Gilbert's wife."

"But Gilbert does not—*can* not—satisfy your needs." He leaned down and gently kissed away the tear. "Your marriage was not consummated, therefore he is no true husband to you."

"You make it sound so simple." She regarded him with misty eyes. "But there is nothing beautiful about betraying your husband."

"Gilbert is no longer the man he was when you met him,

Brianna! He is a mindless shell of what he once was, and he would not begrudge you happiness if he could reason.'' He had leaned over her, his face very close to hers, his breath fanning stray tendrils about her cheeks as he spoke passionately. ''I love you and I believe you love me. There cannot be a question of your being married to what Gilbert has become. You are *mine.*'' And his lips took hers in heated possession, sending shivers through her body as the devastating wildfire raced through her veins at his touch once again.

Brianna was lost.

CHAPTER 13

The next morning Brianna found herself back in her own bed, her feelings very mixed. She condemned herself for having allowed Roland to make love to her. For even though she was ready to admit there was a strong physical attraction between them, she did not believe it was possible to be in love with one man while she was wed to another.

She did not believe that he loved her either. A man such as Roland could not love one woman any more than he ''loved'' a dozen others whose hearts he must have captured.

And yet she bloomed under Roland's loving glances, and his searing yet tender gaze whenever they were alone caused her senses to take charge of her mind. He managed to be around her as often as his duties would allow, like a bee drawn to the sweet lure of a flower.

But she still had dark dreams of the people of Derford deriding her, led by the contemptuous Walter and a Gilbert miraculously whole again, his brown eyes filled with pain and anger: *How could you consort with a mortal enemy? How could you? How—?* And she would wake up trembling and sweat-soaked, with no idea how to reconcile her feelings with her conscience.

As the weather turned mild she began taking Gilbert for long walks, often visiting the site of the new keep. For some reason the activity there fascinated him and held his attention for hours. Sometimes Roland or Ranulf would take time out to acquaint them with what was happening, and Brianna was grateful for their tact.

Late one balmy spring morning Brianna and Gilbert returned from a visit to the site to find the mule train of a traveling merchant before the hall. Brianna took it upon herself to procure a fresh supply of wine, seasonings and spices from the shrewd but honest Rolfe of Dover and assured him she would inform Roland that he would remain in Derford until the next day should the lord of the manor desire anything else.

"Silver dishes from the Mediterranean? Ivory from the purest of tusks? Why did you not send a message to me, sweet?" Roland asked at the evening meal, his eyes resting on her warmly as he ate.

"Well, I . . . I had no idea you were interested in silver or ivory."

"Ah, my sweetest Brianna. Do you forget so soon that I will one day have a wife? I would have the best my gold can buy for her. I will send someone after him."

"He . . . he will be in Derford until the morn."

"Then that can be easily accomplished." He looked at her seriously for a moment. "Is aught amiss, *ma chère?*" Ranulf, too, was watching her, and Father Simon, who regularly dined with them, was openly eyeing her untouched trencher of hard bread. Then he glanced at her face, puzzled.

"Nay, my lord. I am only tired. May I have your leave to retire?"

"We will miss you sorely, for I had hoped you would play the lute and sing for us this night. If you are fatigued, however, we will contain our disappointment."

Brianna readied a bath with the help of Hilde and allowed the warmth of the water to relax her tense body. She closed her eyes and suddenly felt the sting of tears behind her lids. So he wished to purchase silver and ivory for this bride-to-be of his! How like him, with his smooth-tongued lies! He had said he loved her. She was right not to truly believe him! she thought grimly. At least she had learned enough of men not to take them seriously in matters of the heart. Let him store up a veritable treasure for the woman unfortunate enough to become his wife. She would need something to comfort her while he was bedding every comely wench and serving girl in sight. Never again would she succumb to his devilish charms. Never again would she allow him to—

"Brianna, love," came a husky whisper in her ear, startling her and scattering her thoughts like so many leaves in the wind. A warm kiss was planted on the exposed nape of her neck, and she mentally rebuked herself for having pinned her hair up.

"What . . . what are you doing here when I sought the privacy of my bath, Norman?"

"So it is 'Norman,' is it? The lady must be angry with me, for in truth she has not called me such for several weeks."

"You are vile," she hissed furiously. "In one breath you speak of your bride-to-be, while in the next you remind me of our lust for one another. It must not happen again!" Her arms were protectively crossed over her breasts, providing very little in the way of a shield, and her chest heaved indignantly. The cloudy water hid nothing from his penetrating gaze as his eyes hungrily devoured her fair form.

"So 'tis the mention of my bride that stirs your ire. Perhaps you should look beyond your lovely nose to discover who I have in mind." The glint of amusement was unmistakable in his now smoky gray eyes and did nothing to appease her.

"I do not care what Norman woman you are betrothed to! I only hope she can tolerate your philanderings with those unfortunate enough to serve you. I can keep my silence, but Hilde is another matter entirely."

Now his humor began to fade. "Do not ever put yourself in the same class with the fuller's daughter. There was naught between us that would give her any reason to tell tales to any wife of mine."

"And how will you explain *our* relationship, *chevalier?*" she snapped.

"She will understand—she will indulge me." He smiled again suddenly, his boyish charm lost upon the now totally infuriated Brianna.

"Oh, you!" She started to rise and then remembered herself. "Give me a towel, you—you insensitive—" Her words were cut off abruptly as his lips clamped down over hers.

His mouth was sweet and warm, and Brianna felt her anger giving way to a burning hunger in her loins. Mother of God, not this! Anything but *this!* Her head was trapped against the back of the tub by the inexorable pressure of his insistent lips and tongue, and the treacherous languor washed through her to settle in her belly.

"Roland, please! I—"

Her protests were ineffective under his gentle yet determined assault. "I have been denied too long that which I crave above all else. I need you, my love." His hands were everywhere and she could not pull away from his lips, cover herself with her arms and keep his searching hands at bay all at one time. And then his mouth left hers to trace her fragile jawline, lingering under a dainty ear. As she turned her head away he continued to worship the slender column of her throat down to her collarbone and toward the gentle swell of her half-submerged breasts.

In desperation she swatted water into his face, which was perilously close to the waterline in the tub.

"Ahh!" he snorted and choked back an oath as he grabbed her arms and pulled her dripping-wet body from the tub. He crushed her against him, heedless of the water streaming onto his clothing. "So, my vixen, you will make your own rules to this game." He turned aside his head and coughed.

Brianna stole a glance at his wet face. Shimmering droplets of water clung to the long, sandy lashes and thick brows, glistening crystalline in the muted torchlight. Laughter bubbled unexpectedly in her throat. "No fierce Norman knight are you now, Roland de Beaufort!"

Without answering or releasing her, he managed to wrap the towel around her slippery form and carried her to the bed. He set her down with a soft jolt and stood looking at the impish smile that still lit her expressive face. His well-chiseled lips split into a grin. "So you have won the battle, but the war is far from over, my lovely nymph." And before she could collect her wits to retort, he stripped off his garments and joined her on the bed.

"Nay!" she shrieked in angry frustration.

"Hush, wench! Or do you want Hilde to discover our secret?"

Her sudden silence was all the answer he needed.

When they were sated, weak from the release of days of pent-up longing, dizzy from the heights of delight to which they had soared, Roland drew her to him, pressing his cheek against the silky curtain of her hair. Soon his steady even breathing indicated that he slept, and only then did Brianna allow the tears to slip silently down her cheeks.

Roland was not next to her when she awoke and, from the absence of warmth where he had lain, she surmised he had been gone for some time. As she tossed aside the warm pelts she noticed a small piece of vellum near the foot of the bed. Holding a light woolen blanket around her for some warmth, Brianna picked it up and unfolded it, her curiosity piqued. She read, *Gilbert's life is in danger.*

A tremor passed through her. Who sent the warning? Not many people besides herself could read or write—Roland, Ranulf, Father Simon. But there was no reason for any of those three people to warn her in writing. Then who? Rob! It *had* to be Rob! But who could be a threat to Gilbert and why? Good God, *why?* Gilbert was of no real importance to anyone but herself. Why would anyone wish to harm him? She quickly dressed and descended the stairs to the great hall. She was relieved to see Gilbert seated between Ranulf and Father Simon, with the former feeding him patiently so that Hilde could aid the other serving girl. How kind Ranulf was!

She said nothing of the brief, mysterious missive and greeted everyone, although her eyes shied away from Roland's ardent gaze. The meal seemed to drag and she could not wait until Roland and his men left for the castle site.

An hour had not passed after Roland's departure when the sound of heavy hoofbeats caught Brianna's attention. She quickly put aside her ledgers and threw open the great door at one end of the hall. Roland, Ranulf and several others rode back through the stockade, their faces taut with anger.

Just then Father Simon appeared at the church door; seeing the extra horse with two bodies slung over it, he motioned to Brianna and they ran over to the pack animal and examined the injured men. One was dead of a crushed skull, while the other moaned softly in pain from burns over his arms and chest.

It was Walter Kerwickson.

"Walter!" she cried softly as Ranulf swiftly dismounted to help Beorn lower the youth gently to the ground.

"My lord Ranulf pulled him to safety," Beorn mumbled at the stricken look on Brianna's face.

" 'Tis of no import who performed the deed, Beorn," Ranulf replied gravely as they settled Walter on the ground beside Brianna.

"What happened?" she asked softly, looking from one to the other.

"They—someone—fired the palisade and the timber that was to be used for the keep," Roland answered in a voice that was calm but deadly. "It had to be him—that bastard

Rob. I'll see him in hell for this!'' He gently lifted Walter while Father Simon and Guy saw to the body of the dead Norman.

Brianna directed him to place Walter on a pallet near one of the hearths and she hurriedly fetched her small chest of medicinals. While she cleaned the burns and spread a salve of goose grease and honey over them, she listened to the men talk.

''Two men guarding the site are obviously not enough to ensure no interference from this English swine who fancies himself a savior,'' Roland growled. ''Now he would kill Anglo-Saxons as well in his fanatical zeal.''

''But . . . but why did you choose *Walter* to stand watch?'' Brianna queried in genuine puzzlement. ''He—he—'' Her words died in her throat.

''He bears me even less love than the others?'' Roland finished for her, the look in his eyes telling her he was well aware of Walter's animosity toward him. Brianna averted her gaze before the intensity of his. ''What better way to win his loyalty than by placing my trust in him? And 'twould seem this Rob has unwittingly aided me in obtaining my objective.''

''Kerwick believes he was one of the late King Harold's most powerful thanes,'' Ranulf interjected.

''One of Godwinson's right-hand men, eh? Well then, his loyalty is to be commended, but surely he will come to realize his efforts are for naught. What can he hope to achieve?''

Once more Brianna's gaze met Roland's, naked frustration and then anger lighting her eyes and communicating very effectively to the Norman what she dared not say before his men.

''Walter is one of your own, *chérie,*'' he admonished. ''He needs your attention more than does our conversation.''

Brianna felt he had put her in her place. Tears sprang into her eyes and spilled over onto her cheeks, but she kept her gaze down.

"There is also talk that he is the same one who led the last stand for Harold at Malfosse."

Roland regarded his twin thoughtfully. "Then he is indeed a man to be reckoned with if he is the man who made William retreat. His actions say much for his courage and tenacity, but he is on the wrong side.

"We will increase our guard at the site and then we must rout this devil out. Now we will have to begin the cutting and hauling of timber all over again. Luckily a fire could not undo the work done on the moat and the mound inside of it."

"Things will move more slowly, I fear, Roland, for 'tis plowing and planting time. The men from Derford cannot give you much more than their allotted time," reasoned Ranulf.

"If we had built with stone this would not have happened," interjected Vachel with some rancor, for he was an architect and would have preferred a solid, beautiful stone wall and keep.

"We have neither the time nor the stone," Roland snapped. "We are right in the middle of Wessex—Godwinson lands and Godwinson sympathizers. We are troubled by someone who was possibly one of Harold's strongest and most loyal supporters. Even if we had the biggest quarry in all of England, we could not afford the time it would take to build a great stone keep."

There was a moment of silence, and then, "We should search for this Rob as soon as possible, Roland." Ranulf's tawny brows were drawn together.

"Aye. We will leave at first light on the morrow."

CHAPTER 14

The day dawned warm and wet. The dull leaden-gray skies cast a pall over Brianna's spirits. As she stared out through a small uncovered window in the hall at the steady drizzle, she found her thoughts more on Gilbert and his well-being than on the outcome of the search for Rob. Rob could take care of himself, Gilbert could not.

The only person who could benefit from Gilbert's death was Roland. Roland believed Gilbert was an obstacle to her affection—to *her*. And it was partly true. She could never consider any serious alliance with the Norman while she was wed to Gilbert.

But was Roland capable of doing away with Gilbert? He could be as fierce as any—and more—when aroused, and his temper and determination were things to be reckoned with. But murder? He was not devious—at least he did not seem to be.

Why had Rob warned her?

At sunset the party returned and supper was served. Roland was preoccupied, for they had not had any success and he was irked by the actions of a clever foe. In conflict, one's enemy came out and faced one. He did not skulk about the woodlands, strike when the back was turned, and then retreat to the safety of the forest.

"If I may speak my mind, Roland," said René de Falaise, "you are mayhap too lenient in your dealings with the people of the village. There are no doubt those who are not above aiding this outlaw and his cause. After all, what do they owe you?''

Roland suddenly hit the table with his fist in frustration. ''They swore fealty to me!''

''There are those who would say that an oath taken under duress does not hold. It was either a pledge to you or slavery. What choice did they have?'' asked Ranulf quietly.

Roland shot him a bemused look. ''And on whose side are you, brother?''

''I merely suggest 'tis possible that René is right. It would seem this Rob has a spy in Derford.''

''How would you suggest I find out, Ranulf? Torture them to a man?''

Brianna drew in her breath sharply, but no one noticed.

''Some would suggest such a thing, but perhaps you need not use so drastic a means.''

''You plainly do not know the English yet. They are obstinate, and I doubt anything but the harshest measures would produce any results. I think I will wait a little while longer before I interrogate the men of Derford. I will search for him again. I cannot believe how cleverly he eludes me.''

''You never could do anything right without me.''

All heads turned toward the open door at the sound of that familiar voice. There stood Dane d'Avranches, leaning nonchalantly against the doorpost, arms and feet crossed.

Instant pandemonium broke loose, and, laughingly, Dane turned and beckoned to someone behind him. A tall, mailed figure, minus his helm, entered, and as the two men stood side by side Brianna saw that one was an older version of the other.

''Lord William! Dane!'' exclaimed Roland and Ranulf simultaneously above the din, and Roland, as lord of the manor, went forward first to greet them.

''You have forgiven my rash-tempered accusations?'' Roland said, low, for Dane's ears alone.

"A man in love says and does strange things until he is certain that love is returned in kind."

Roland laughed heartily and pounded him on the back, then turned to the older man. "Welcome to Derford, Lord William. Come and shed your armor and take some refreshment."

William d'Avranches smiled fondly. " 'Tis good to see another friendly face, Roland. You look well."

Ranulf and the other men crowded around the newcomers. Brianna remained at the table with Gilbert, taking in the jubilant scene.

When things had quieted down, Dane broke away from the others and came toward Brianna. She stood up to greet him.

"Dane, you have come back! I have missed you—and Roland has as well, although you would not know it the way he watches us."

"He knows by now, I think, that we are just friends. I would never allow myself to love the same woman as he."

Brianna laughed, a pleasant, tinkling sound in striking contrast to the deep voices of the men around her. "He thinks he feels love for me, but 'tis only because he cannot have me."

"Oh, but you are wrong . . ."

Brianna suddenly had the oddest feeling that someone was staring at her. Staring with an intensity that made her neglect Dane's words and look about for the source of the unwavering scrutiny.

She encountered the gaze of the Lord William. His eyes were riveted to her face, and for a moment she felt mesmerized.

Dane, finally sensing that he did not have her full attention, turned and saw William close behind him. "Father, come and meet Brianna."

"Father?" she asked inanely.

"Aye. Brianna, this is my sire, William d'Avranches. Father, Brianna of Derford."

"I . . . I am pleased, my lord—"

Recovering himself somewhat, Lord William interrupted

gently, "The pleasure is mine, Brianna. Dane has spoken most highly of you." He smiled, a charming smile like that of his son. "You are, in fact, part of the reason I have come to visit Roland here. I had to meet you, for Dane said you put all our Norman women to shame. I find he is right in his assessment, if I may be so bold as to say so."

A becoming hint of color rose up Brianna's graceful neck and swept across her cheekbones at his frank compliment. "You do a country lass great honor, my lord," she managed.

"So you have met the greatest prize in all of England," Roland said in his resonant voice, and Brianna bristled at the remark.

"I am no prize, *chevalier*, and least of all yours," she riposted heatedly.

"My apologies, my sweet. You have a way of making a man forget himself. Please forgive my unruly tongue."

William shot the fair-haired knight a disapproving look. "Your lack of respect is unbecoming to one of your father's house, Roland."

Roland replied easily, "I assure you, sire, that Brianna has every bit of my respect. Now, may I offer you a seat at my humble table?" he asked, wisely changing the subject.

After Dane and Lord William had eaten, Roland asked Brianna to play the lute and sing. She willingly complied, and as her clear, sweet voice floated through the hall, servants, men-at-arms and knights alike sat enthralled.

They stood before the charred ruins, surveying the damage: Lord William, Dane, Ranulf and Roland. The May sun shone brightly, and Brianna noticed the way it gently gilded Roland's tawny hair. How like a god of old he was! she could not help thinking. Perfectly formed in every way. If only he didn't have such a devastating effect upon her! If only she could resist him in body as well as mind! After all, he was her enemy—

She sighed and sat down on the grass, a short distance from

where they stood, Gilbert beside her, to contemplate the latest of Rob's efforts to impede Roland.

" 'Tis a pity," said William as he walked a ways and kicked at a pile of blackened timber. "If you have no quarry nearby and no masons at hand to erect a proper stone keep, you will have to begin anew with wood."

"We will stay to help you apprehend this criminal, Roland," added Dane soberly.

"That's just it. He is a criminal to us Normans, but to the English he is a hero more than anything else. I will eventually catch him, make no mistake about that, but now is not the time. You must get back home as soon as possible. We need Normans to rule in Normandy as well."

Ranulf commented, "If we catch and deal with this Rob too soon, we will only stir up sympathy for him and his cause."

"Yes," William came back, "but if you wait too long he will only cause mischief and loss of lives—more deeds to stir the people against you. You must not tarry overlong."

Roland turned his face from the charred ruins to Brianna sitting quietly with Gilbert. "Aye, Lord William, everything is in the timing." He could not allow himself to think of her reaction to putting the Anglo-Saxon to death. He could not allow her to affect his judgment and his decisions. They were of two different minds, although he had tried to be fair and just with her people.

William walked over to Brianna. "May I join you, Brianna?"

"Of course, my lord. What an unfortunate thing to witness on so fine a day."

"Roland will double the guard and under Vachel's direction they will rebuild. He is a very determined man, much like his father."

"You know Lord Guy?"

"Our families are quite close." He paused. "And what of yours, Brianna?"

Brianna looked momentarily surprised. "My family is at Walshire Abbey. I was raised there and they are all the family I know."

He stared at the men clearing debris. If she didn't know any more of her family, he would probably never discover her origins. "You may wonder why I ask, *ma petite*. Please forgive an old man's reminiscing, but you remind me so much of someone I once knew. An Anglo-Saxon girl. Alicia was her name."

Brianna's smile froze on her face. Alicia? That, according to the Abbess, had been her mother's name. Could it be the same? Her father had not wanted their identity revealed, for his own reasons. Therefore it behooved her to honor his wish, especially with a Norman stranger.

With an effort she brought herself back to William d'Avranches. " . . . offended you in some way?" he was asking concernedly.

"Offended me? Oh—no, my lord. I . . . I was just remembering a friend at the abbey whose name was Alicia, also." She hated herself for lying. "What a lovely name it is. I regret I can be of no help to you, for I do not know if my mother's name was the same."

"Was?"

"Aye, my lord. I was only told that she died in childbirth and my father was so stricken that he could not bear the sight of me."

His forehead creased and the topaz eyes were puzzled. "That is truly odd."

Now it was her turn to question. "Odd?"

"Yes, child. A man deeply in love would want to keep his wife's child, I would think, as some living part of her to cherish."

Brianna was silent at this moving observation.

"So it seems you have bewitched my guest, Brianna. I have never seen Lord William more interested in a female than in the construction of a keep," Roland chided. Both people looked up at him, and Brianna noted the damp spots where his tunic clung to his broad chest from his exertions. "Although, where you are concerned, a keep could never take precedence in my thoughts." His eyes held hers, and for a moment she felt giddy with the promise in their silver-gray depths. "Forgive me, sweet, but I need Lord William's advice. Will you excuse him for a moment?"

Brianna was rather relieved that Roland had come to her rescue, for she could feel Gilbert getting restless and she needed some time to deal with the conflicting emotions Lord William's questions had stirred within her.

That evening after supper, she sang and played the lute once more.

Roland and William d'Avranches had eyes for no one but Brianna, one anticipating the future and the other lost in memories of the past. The other men spoke to one another in hushed tones between songs, if at all, and afterward Dane managed to escort Brianna to her room. "How is Roland treating you, Brianna?" he asked with a grin.

Blushing, she could only manage guiltily, "Well enough for a Norman."

He sighed exaggeratedly. "Well, he cannot help that he is a Norman, and I fear you are stuck with us. Besides, you could never find better Normans in all of Normandy!"

She laughed at that and went into her room. As she readied herself for bed a short while later, she was startled by a loud crash from the adjoining chamber. She flung open the door separating her room from Gilbert's to find him huddled in a corner in terror, one arm flung protectively over his head. The washbasin and pitcher had been knocked from the table and lay in pieces on the floor. Evidently he had bumped it with either his bad leg or the walking stick. Hilde was not in the room.

With tears of frustration in her lovely eyes, Brianna comforted the frightened Gilbert. "There, there, love. It's all right now. Brianna is here with you,'' she soothed. Slowly he began to relax and finally allowed her to help him up and to sit on the bed. She began to pick up the pieces of the broken vessels. Where was Hilde? she wondered angrily. She didn't mind tending Gilbert, but Hilde should have told her of her intention to leave him alone. This incident could have been avoided.

"Oh!" she cried as a shard of pottery sliced into her palm, instantly drawing blood.

"What happened here?" demanded Roland from behind her. After taking in the enticing sight of her shapely bottom, he realized something was amiss—Gilbert looked wary and Hilde was nowhere to be seen.

Brianna jumped at the sound of his voice and succeeded in cutting her knee as well. Blood darkened her nightshift.

Roland was at her side in a trice. "Where is Hilde?" he asked tersely as he gently examined her upturned palm.

"I do not know. I came in here when I heard the noise and found this—" She gestured with her free hand. "Gilbert was in the corner, frightened out of his wits. He should not be left alone, Roland."

He guided her to her feet, his mouth in a tight line. "Stay with him until I find Hilde. I will not be long." And he strode from the room.

Where *was* the wench? he thought angrily. The answer came to him in a flash, and without bothering to knock he threw open the door to the guest chamber where Dane was sleeping.

The two figures on the bed sat up abruptly, one with a muffled expletive and the other with a shriek of surprise.

"For the love of God, Roland, must you barge in at night when a man is abed with a comely wench?"

"Only when the wench is shirking her duties elsewhere," Roland answered curtly.

Hilde, a guilty look on her face, quickly began pulling her shift over her head.

"What exactly is she neglecting?"

"Gilbert."

Dane quirked an eyebrow. "Oh?"

"The idiot can get into bed himself!" she said sullenly.

"No, he cannot. Brianna found him huddled in a corner after knocking over the table with the washbasin and pitcher. I discovered Brianna on her hands and knees, cleaning up the mess and injured for her efforts. You are walking a thin line, Hilde."

"Aye, my lord," she mumbled.

"I am truly sorry, Roland, but I had no idea . . ."

Roland shrugged and addressed Hilde once more. "If you neglect Gilbert one more time, you will be severely punished and put into the kitchen to work. Do you understand?"

"Aye," she whispered, and slid off the bed to move toward the door.

"My apologies for interrupting, *mon ami*," he said, and then closed the door and followed Hilde down the hall.

Brianna was awkwardly attempting to undress her husband without using her injured hand when the two entered the room. Roland took her by the elbow and steered her through the door into her own bedchamber.

"Sit here," he said, and pushed her down gently onto a chair. He poured clean water into a basin and expertly cleaned the cuts on her hand and knee.

"You need not bother, Roland," she said softly, "for I am well versed in the art of healing."

"So I have seen." He smiled at her brilliantly, and her heart skipped a beat. He tenderly kissed her palm over the linen bandage, and her pulses leapt.

"Do you wish to heal me or seduce me, *chevalier?*" she asked in a shaking voice.

"Both, my love." His grin was wicked.

"Then you must allow me to clean and wrap my knee myself, for I am of no mind to comply this night."

Roland's eyes pierced her own and he saw fear and suspicion where of late there had been warmth and desire. "What is amiss, sweet Brianna?"

"Naught," she lied. "I merely do not want to play the whore for you, Roland."

A flicker of annoyance lit the smoky gray eyes. "You never played the whore for me. Was that how I made you feel? Was that what our lovemaking meant to you?"

"You are a determined man. Are you not accustomed to getting whatever you wish?" she asked in a taut voice.

He looked at her oddly, a questioning frown drawing his brows together. "Aye. I go after that which I deem necessary to my well-being and happiness—as long as I do not harm others in the process."

Brianna studied his face through glistening blue-green pools. *Oh, how I wish I could believe you would not harm others who stand in your way!* Aloud, she asked, "And do you not want me? Do you not wish to be rid of my husband?"

Roland raised the hem of her shift and began tending the cut on her knee, thus giving Brianna no chance to read his expression. "There are ways to remove Gilbert as an obstacle without killing him. God's blood, woman! Do you believe me a cold-blooded killer?"

She winced as some of his tension made his hands less than gentle as he wrapped her knee. Why did he keep his eyes down? she wondered. Why did he not meet her gaze? Guilt? "What *did* you think to do to remove Gilbert from my life, Roland?" she asked tensely.

At last he looked up, his gray eyes dark with anger. "The marriage was never consummated. It could be annulled."

"Nothing would make me consent to deserting him like that."

"We shall see about that," he said with conviction, and suddenly she found herself in his arms, with his mouth pressed against hers.

An idea unexpectedly wormed its way into her mind. Something that had occurred to her before which she had always rejected as being abhorrent. Now, however, Gilbert was more important, and for him she was willing to sacrifice her honor.

She had to tell Roland before she was swept away on a dizzying current of passion.

She struggled against his chest and finally succeeded in breaking away. "Roland—Roland, listen to me! What if—what if I gave myself freely to you any time you wished? What if I were available for your needs—"

He gripped her by the shoulders and jerked her away sharply. "What are you saying? You would sink so low—to trade your body for Gilbert's assured safety? *Well?*" He shook her with such force she felt as if her neck would snap.

"Aye," she answered with a quaver of fear in her voice. "He means that much to me."

His eyes were like storm clouds. "What makes you think I would ever settle for *that?* I do not want your favors like a whore."

Color flooded her delicate features at his harsh rejection. "Well, I am sure you have had your share of . . . of women flinging themselves at you! What do you need as proof of my good faith? Did you have others who signed documents attesting to their good intentions?" she demanded, her own ire rising along with his. "There can never be aught between us but that of which I speak. I have nothing left to bargain with."

His eyes narrowed. "I have never heard of anything so ridiculous. You do not understand—you refuse to see what is before you!" He turned away from her, running a hand in agitation through his dark-gilt hair. When he swung back to her, his angry frustration had abated. "Have I not declared my love? I can offer you marriage and a good life. Would you give that up for some absurd sense of responsibility when the one who commands your loyalty is incapable of comprehending your admirable efforts? I fear your sacrifice is in vain, Brianna."

Her eyes sparked blue-green flame. "Do not dare to tell me anything I do where Gilbert is concerned is in vain! He was prepared to give me a home—to share his life with me—until you and your fellow Normans with your foreign mercenaries made him what he is," she ground out through gritted teeth. "And even were Gilbert dead you would never succeed in persuading me to take you seriously where marriage is concerned. I have learned many things since you came, and I will never believe you would ever honestly offer me marriage when you seem to delight in mentioning your real bride-to-be. How gullible do you think I am, Norman?"

Roland groaned inwardly at her last words. His little hints had worked against him. They had not caused her any jealousy or even to hope that he had meant her. Rather she had taken him at his word and now thought him insincere.

"I would return to Walshire and take my final vows before I would remain here without Gilbert."

"You would do no such thing!" he shouted in vexation. "You swore fealty to me."

"In Gilbert's stead. If he were dead I would owe you naught!"

Roland's face was very close to hers. "You deserve a good beating for your impertinence, wench. If Gilbert's presence can stir you to such anger and insolence, then perhaps you would be better off without him," was his final thrust before he stalked from the room.

He was to dearly regret those words.

CHAPTER 15

The next morning Roland seemed intent on speaking to Brianna alone—and was impeded at every turn by a phalanx of men and servants. Finally Ranulf and Dane good-naturedly pushed him out the door, and Brianna caught a look of resigned regret on his bronzed features.

She was vastly relieved when he had gone, however, for rather than go to the castle site with Gilbert this day, she had decided to visit Kerwick's family and look in on Walter.

As she and Gilbert walked to Derford, Brianna inwardly marveled at Roland's equanimity. Obviously he'd been eager to make amends. *Do not close me out*, his gray eyes had seemed to say, yet Brianna found herself caught in the throes of a growing doubt where before there had been the beginnings of contentment and even trust. Roland, in a moment of anger, had unwittingly set himself back in his quest to win her.

They arrived right after the noon meal; fortunately, Kerwick and his sons had not yet returned to the fields. Everyone was cordial and happy to see both Brianna and Gilbert, except for Walter. Although decidedly pale, he was up and around, the white bandages showing above the neck of his tunic and at the wrist of one arm. Sullen and uncommunicative, he allowed Nedra to answer Brianna's query about his injuries. "He is healing well, Brianna, thanks to your ministrations. He cannot do any work in the fields for a while."

Before Kerwick, Edwin and Brand returned to their work,

183

they lingered awhile to hear the news from the stronghold. Brianna talked of William d'Avranches but said nothing of his questions regarding her past.

" 'Tis a pity a man had to be killed and the site fired," commented Kerwick.

"Better a Norman than one of our own," Walter interjected. "As for the firing of the stockade, why should we not fight Norman subjugation?"

"Because, my son," replied Kerwick, "if Rob angers Lord Roland overmuch, I have a feeling we will all pay dearly. Thus far he has not accused any of the villagers of consorting with Rob, but it would be well within his rights to do so."

"He could prove nothing. Even were we all involved he could never make anyone talk."

Kerwick eyed his middle son speculatively. "You have never known torture, my son. Even the bravest soul can break under such a harsh measure."

"Bah! Do not think all of Derford is so spineless as not to be willing to go along with our brave Rob. Thank God there are those who refuse to kiss Norman backsides." His eyes turned to Brianna accusingly.

"Enough, Walter. You have every right to resent the Normans, but violence breeds violence, and we are not leaders or even fighters," Kerwick reproved.

Nedra was shaking her head slowly, her hazel eyes on the rash-tempered Walter. " 'Twould seem that you owe Brianna more than a cold shoulder and derision, my son. She did tend your wounds after the man you so heatedly defend nearly brought about your death."

Walter had the grace to redden under his tan, and his glance flicked to Brianna and then away again. "I am grateful for that, but never will I believe that Rob would have intentionally harmed an Anglo-Saxon forced to do his lord's bidding."

Brianna remembered Roland's words concerning winning Walter's loyalty. "Did Lord Roland actually *force* you to guard the keep?"

A fleeting look of guilt crossed Walter's face, but as he opened his mouth to speak Nedra intervened, "Enough of this rash talk when tomorrow you must work for Lord Roland. Now off with the rest of you, while I have a quiet visit with Brianna."

When they had gone and Walter had retired to his bed to rest, Nedra and her daughters spent a pleasant hour with Brianna.

"Hurry, love," Brianna called with just a hint of anxiety in her voice. Gilbert had fallen behind for some reason and she did not want to alarm him. Dark storm clouds were sweeping across the blue skies, blotting out all the brightness of a beautiful day as the wind picked up in warning. They were about halfway home and Brianna wanted to beat the rain and, more important, the thunder that could frighten Gilbert into bolting.

She stopped and waited for him to catch up. If she touched him reassuringly, perhaps he would move at a faster pace. But he seemed skittish already, his eyes wide in fearful expectation, his progress slower and slower. He knows, she thought in agitation. He senses a storm is brewing and already he is afraid.

"Come along, Gilbert. We are almost home now. Just a little farther and—"

Lightning rent the heavens and a tremendous peal of thunder split the air. Gilbert's eyes rolled back in abject terror. With surprising strength and speed he tore his arm from her grip and turned toward the northern forest.

"Gilbert, nay!" she cried out as another peal of thunder resounded through the heavy air, but there was nothing she could do to stop him short of flinging her arms around his good leg and tripping him—which she tried in desperation.

Her effort failed in the face of his superior strength and gained her a bloody chin as her face bumped the rutted hardness of the road as she fell. She scrambled up again and started running toward his limping form just as a sheet of rain swept across the open stretch of the road, taking her breath away with its unexpected fury. "Gilbert!" she cried shrilly as panic gripped her and she fought her way toward him in the blinding downpour. "Please come back! Please—"

He was at the edge of the road where the forest began, and Brianna knew that if he disappeared into the thick trees she would never find him alone. Tears of frustration filled her eyes and ran unheeded down her rain-spattered cheeks.

And then his wildly scrambling figure stopped abruptly in midmotion and slowly crumpled to the ground. From Brianna's position a short stone's throw behind, she could not tell what had made him fall, so distorted was her vision by the curtain of rain. She hoped, as she stumbled closer, that he had lost his footing and gone down. Anything, she prayed, to slow him enough to enable her to reach him.

Nothing prepared her, however, for what she found as she finally knelt beside his still form. A scream of horror rose to her lips and was lost in the roar of the wind and rain. An arrow had penetrated his throat deeply enough to protrude from the other side of his neck. Blood mixed with rainwater streamed downward toward his chest, staining the top of his overtunic crimson. His gasps for air were audible above the din of the deluge, and Brianna looked helplessly at the blood bubbling from the two wounds.

"Gilbert!" Her lips formed his name but no sound came forth as his glazed eyes locked with hers.

She tried to cradle his head and shoulders in the small circle of her arms without causing him further pain, but he was so much larger and heavier than she was that it was impossible.

"Gilbert, Gilbert," she cried over and over as she clutched him to her as best she could, knowing it was useless to attempt to dislodge the arrow. As Gilbert's life drained away from his body, his lips moved, forming the word "Bra-na." She put her forehead to his in an exquisitely tender gesture.

"Do not leave me, my husband," she whispered as the

wind suddenly died down and the rain changed into a light drizzle.

The fact that his labored gasping had ceased penetrated her pain-racked thoughts, and she raised her head to look down upon his face; his features were still, the vacant eyes stared into nothingness.

"No, *no!*" she wept and sobs shook her slim body.

She lost all sense of time as she knelt in the muddy road, supporting Gilbert's upper torso with arms numb from the weight. She wept long and hard, from a wellspring of sorrow deep within her. She mourned the fall of her country, the severe injuries sustained by Gilbert at Hastings, the death she had caused by her own hand, and her surrender to Roland de Beaufort and his fellow Normans. She sobbed aloud until her throat ached and she was hoarse. A churning sickness began in the pit of her stomach that grew and grew until she vomited onto the road, partly in reaction to Gilbert's senseless death and partly in response to her sickening remorse and regret over her own actions in the past months. She had fallen under the spell of Roland de Beaufort, and had betrayed Gilbert as well as England in the process.

She did not hear the pony approach behind her, but Walter's hand on her shoulder brought her tear-streaked face up to meet his grim look. "Are you all right, Brianna?" At her slight nod, his eyes went to Gilbert's still features. "The Normans did this, by God! None of us in the village even own a bow. Hunting with such weapons is reserved for the rich and privileged. You know that, do you not, Brianna?"

"Aye," she whispered hoarsely. " 'Tis the work of those loathsome creatures who call themselves men."

"Let me help you, Brianna. I think we can manage to put him across my pony and take him home. Home to Derford where he belongs."

"Yes, home . . . to Derford," she said in a shaky voice. "I should never have taken him away from there." She looked at Gilbert's face once again and for a moment saw him as he had been the first time she had met him. Warm, thoughtful, eager. A great hatred welled up inside her for the man she knew to be responsible. Rob had warned her, but how could she ever have protected Gilbert from something like *this?*

"Nay, Walter," she repeated, her tone husky with emotion and strain. "I should never have taken him to live under the Norman's roof." Her tears fell freely again and she put her warm, damp cheek to her husband's lifeless one. "Only why?" she cried. *"Why?"*

The pounding of horses' hooves sounded close by; Walter heard them before they registered in Brianna's grief-stricken mind. "Mayhap you should ask your Norman, for he comes to see his handiwork close up," he said bitterly.

Roland sat astride Odo, Ranulf beside him, staring in ill-concealed disbelief at the scene before him. Brianna, rain-soaked and bloodied, was kneeling in the mud, clutching Gilbert's lifeless body to her own in an attitude that told the whole story at a glance. His words of the night before came back to him with startling clarity, only to cause his stomach to churn sickeningly. And he, who feared no man, remained pinned atop his destrier, dreading the accusation he knew he would encounter in the aquamarine gaze of the dark-haired girl huddled beside her dead husband.

Out of the corner of his eye he saw Ranulf moving to dismount. Taking hold of himself, he swung down to the wet road in one fluid motion. As his twin bent to examine Gilbert, he asked in a voice devoid of emotion, which thoroughly deceived Walter and Brianna, "What happened here?" His tawny hair was plastered to his head, and he looked evil to Brianna, who slowly brought up her head to meet his eyes.

"What happened here, O most noble Norman?" she said through stiff lips, a sudden trembling overtaking her body. "What happened here! As if you did not know, in all your false, righteous-seeming innocence!" Her eyes kindled with an intensity that shook him to the core.

Ranulf interjected, "An arrow through the throat, and from the looks of it his murderer was hidden in the north woods."

"Which one of your henchmen did it, de Beaufort?" sneered Walter. "No Anglo-Saxon in these parts even owns a bow, let alone is capable of such an accurate shot."

He had a good point, Roland had to concede to himself as his eyes briefly met Ranulf's. "As improbable as it may seem to you, this is not my doing. 'Tis not my wont to kill defenseless men, and from the safety of a forest." As Brianna's mouth opened to retort he added quietly, "I believe your gallant Rob uses such tactics."

"Rob had no reason to harm one of his own!" Brianna cried. "You would say *anything* to remove the blame from yourself, Norman. What a coward you are in actuality while you play the noble and valiant warrior-knight!"

The look in her eyes reminded him forcibly of the way she had looked at Hastings, heedless of her own safety, concerned only for the fallen Anglo-Saxons and the plight of England.

"You do me grave injustice, Brianna," he answered somberly. The look in his solemn gray eyes was so sincere that for an infinitesimal space of time she felt doubt sweep through her. But it was gone so quickly it might have never occurred. Then he stooped beside her to better see Gilbert. "Poor lad," he muttered softly, but Brianna caught his words and flung him a look of pure loathing. "We must get both of you home," he began.

"Our home is in Derford, Norman, and you will not defile his body by touching him!"

Roland's face paled under her scathing words, but his voice betrayed nothing of his emotions. "I will not touch him if it offends you so, but your home is with me, not in Derford. You gave that up when we struck our bargain."

"Bargain? Here is grisly evidence of how you keep your bargains!"

Roland's eyes narrowed slightly in anger. She looked like a wild creature of the forest, with her black hair damp and curling around her delicate features, her deep sea-blue eyes wide with shock and shimmering with tears. And Gilbert's body—the final outrage in the poor boy's life—cradled against her, and both of them obscenely bloodied. Roland held back his own angry retort.

Pulling his eyes from her face, he said with quiet authority, "Ranulf, put Gilbert's body across your own mount with Walter's help. You can ride with me, Brianna."

"You will have to lift me bodily, Norman, for I owe you no allegiance now."

"You are under oath to me, Brianna."

"In Gilbert's stead, and now you have murdered him. I am free to do as I please!"

Roland's mouth tightened at the word *murdered.* "Not according to Norman custom. You are the wife of my vassal. Now that he is dead, you are under my protection."

Brianna eased Gilbert's body down and, in a last tender gesture, smoothed his chestnut hair back from his pale face. She straightened slowly and turned to Roland, anger blazing out of her eyes. "Protection such as that you afforded my husband?"

"Brianna!"

She stood before him defiantly, small fists clenched, and then, without warning, her expression softened. Tears of frustration welled up in her lovely eyes once more and she looked puzzled. "What will Reverend Mother say?" she questioned softly. "What will she think of me now?" The look on her fragile features reminded Roland of the docility and naïveté she had displayed on the first day he had met her. "I . . . I must take him back to Reverend Mother, my lord Norman; she will know what to do," she ended in a whisper as the tears slid gently down her cheeks.

"Brianna—"

" 'Tis the shock of his death, Roland," said Ranulf soberly. "Can you not see? She is confused."

"You may well have been her undoing, de Beaufort," commented Walter acidly.

"Nay, Roland," Ranulf hastened to assure him. "This type of thing is only temporary. You would do well to go along with it while it lasts, for when she comes out of it she will be bitter and resentful once more."

Roland sighed in resignation and spoke to Brianna soothingly. "Will you not allow us to take you both to my home? We can send a message to the Reverend Mother if you wish."

She nodded mutely and allowed Roland to lift her to Odo's back while, at the Norman's signal, Ranulf and Walter quickly placed Gilbert's body upon the other charger. When Ranulf had mounted behind the corpse, Roland turned briefly to Walter, who stood watching them with no sign of getting up on his own pony.

"Can you make it home, Kerwickson?" At the youth's curt nod, he added quietly, "Summon your mother. Tell her Brianna needs her."

Roland urged his horse toward the manor, all thought of whether the rebellious Walter would obey him gone from his mind. The only thing that mattered at the moment was the slip of a girl he held tenderly before him. He dared not press her to lean upon him, for he did not know how long her oddly submissive mood would last.

He need not have worried, however; Brianna, exhausted from her ordeal, closed her eyes and sank wearily against his solid body. He cradled her gently as he slowed Odo to a walk, treasuring the feel of her slender form against his, and her soft hair caressing his chin. He longed to kiss away all her pain, her doubts, her fears.

But he merely narrowed his gaze upon the road ahead thoughtfully, and Ranulf followed silently close behind him.

CHAPTER 16

The somnolent midsummer breeze gently lifted curling wisps of Brianna's now shoulder-length raven hair. A persistent fly lazily buzzed around her head as she thoughtfully contemplated the patch of lush emerald grass on which she sat under a sheltering oak.

She absently brushed the bothersome insect away and raised her sea-blue eyes to study the great manor and then the lesser buildings before her. Outwardly the hall, the small stone church, the bowers where René de Falaise and Guy de Montrain now slept and the other smaller structures appeared as they had when she had first arrived at Derford.

How deceptive, she thought with a soft sigh, and waved away the tenacious fly once more with a hint of annoyance. She had refused to visit the castle site since Gilbert's death and spent her spare time under the ancient oak, daydreaming of happier times at Walshire and nursing her grudge against Roland de Beaufort.

She spoke to all the Normans but Roland, and, as if he anticipated her rebuff, he kept his distance. His eyes, however, were on her almost every moment she was in the same room, sometimes brooding, sometimes with a burning hunger in their depths, other times thoughtful. The expression on his sculpted features was more often than not unreadable.

She closed her eyes and leaned back against the solid tree trunk, allowing her thoughts to take her back a few weeks. She had refused to come out of her room for several days.

The one exception to her self-imposed isolation was when Gilbert was buried in the orchard beside his former homestead. But this almost proved more than she could bear, for the Breton she had killed had been laid to rest nearby, and along with her sorrow came a flood of guilt.

In her room, Brianna had thought of many things, but uppermost in her mind—beyond her grief over the loss of Gilbert's life—had been the disillusionment and hatred she felt toward Roland de Beaufort. So, locked in her chamber, with Hilde bringing her meals, she had pondered her future.

She could either try to get to Walshire—even though Roland would undoubtedly follow her and attempt to obtain her release—or she could go to Rob.

Both prospects seemed bleak indeed, but how could she remain under the same roof with the man who had murdered her husband?

In the end, she allowed Dane to persuade her to end her deliberate seclusion, but nothing else had changed. Not even Dane could convince her of Roland's innocence. Nor had Nedra been successful in persuading her that Roland was blameless.

Her thoughts came back to the present. She was no closer to a solution to her untenable situation than before. And she was finding it more and more difficult to ignore Roland. Despite her grievance against him, and her resentment and anger, she admitted grudgingly to herself that she was not yet unaffected by Roland de Beaufort.

The sound of pounding hooves brought her out of her reverie, and she opened her eyes to look toward the gate in the palisade nearby. Roland and the others usually did not return from the building site this early.

But it was none other than the object of her animosity who rode through the open gate with half a dozen men, including Ranulf, Lord William and Dane, behind him.

Brianna was about to glance away when a figure in the drab garb of a common peasant, trussed and astride a pony, caught her eye. Despite her natural inclination to turn her head so as not to look at Roland, she strained to better see who had been captured by the Normans who surrounded him in tight formation. And then she saw his face clearly.

It was Ian.

Outrage surged through her like quicksilver. God in heaven, they have managed to snatch Rob's right-hand man, she thought, bemused. Her eyes did not betray her, however, as she caught Dane's subtle nod of greeting. With studied care she busied herself with a piece of embroidery she had brought with her. There must be no hint of her association with Rob or any of his followers.

A light frisson rippled through her as once more she raised her eyes. The horsemen had reined in before the great door of the manor. Roland signaled for his men to dismount, and Ian was hauled from his pony by two of them. Once on his feet, he stood with his own kind of dignity, looking beyond his captors into the distance, his face devoid of expression.

Brianna's fingers moved automatically over the vibrantly colored silk threads while she hazarded a guess at Ian's fate. The party was moving into the hall. What can I do? she thought in agitation. How can I aid him without betraying myself to Roland? Her hands trembled at the knowledge of her own helplessness. Indeed, how could she aid Ian at all?

Unexpectedly, a shadow fell across her lap and the sunlight was partially blocked by a man's form. Brianna's hands stopped but her eyes remained downcast. She could feel *his* presence even as she stared unseeingly at her needlework. Her heart began to slam in her chest, partly in fear, partly in anger. How dare he approach her!

"Brianna?"

She bit her lower lip and attempted to calm herself before allowing her gaze to meet Roland's. She was silently eloquent as she allowed her face to mirror her outrage.

With seemingly dispassionate eyes, he studied her features, pausing at her mouth, and ending with his stormy gray gaze locked with hers. Even in her anger Brianna thought she saw a fleeting look of something akin to longing soften his carved features. His voice, rich and soft, gave away more than did his expression. "I regret that I am forced to intrude, but I would have you hear what this captive has to say."

Searing words rose to her lips, but she fought them back. As it was, her clipped pronouncement was more effective than any fierce retort. "This captive's words cannot restore Gilbert to me, Norman."

His eyes darkened momentarily. "I wish to clear myself of the crime of which you so readily accuse me, Brianna."

Brianna folded her embroidery methodically and ignored his outstretched hand as she gracefully rose to her feet. Looking past him toward the hall, she said, "You can persuade a man to say anything you wish if you administer the right torture. I am not so dull-witted as to believe the words of a man thusly treated." Her eyes met his then and accusation burned in them.

"And if I do not resort to such methods?"

"Then you are more of a fool than I thought, fierce knight, for nothing else would persuade a man such as he to utter a word more than he wishes." Her words hung heavy between them like an invisible barrier.

Roland did not question her assumption that the prisoner was one of Rob's men. He knew she was intelligent enough, and more, to surmise correctly. "Will you consent to be present when I question him?"

Even though he chose to make it a question, Brianna could see the determination in his eyes, hear it in the timbre of his voice. He would brook no refusal. "It seems I have little choice in the matter, Norman." With a quick shake of her skirts she moved toward the great portal.

Conscious of Roland's presence close behind her, she entered the cool interior of the hall, the blinding sunlight making it difficult to adjust immediately to the dimness. She hesitated for a moment, expecting Roland to pass her. But he paused beside her and waited. His fingers touched her elbow and she felt them burn through her light garment. So he would even guide her to the precise place of his choosing. What did he truly mean to do?

Brianna glanced up into Roland's features, but the brightness behind them cast his face into shadow and she could see nothing of his expression. She allowed the gentle but firm pressure of his hand under her arm to compel her to walk forward and to the right, toward a settle near the now cold hearth at the end of the hall.

Ian stood with his back to the hearth, flanked by Vachel and Beorn. The remaining men stood to one side, speaking in quiet tones. Roland joined them and, after a few words, went to stand before Ian. Brianna could see the Anglo-Saxon clearly from where she sat just off to the side.

Roland studied his captive briefly, but it was impossible for Brianna to see his face. Then he began slowly pacing back and forth before Ian, remaining silent awhile longer, as if giving careful thought to what he would say. The silence that ensued was deafening as he finally stopped just to Ian's left.

"How are you called?" His words were firm, authoritative, and his attitude that of one accustomed to obedience.

Brianna's heart skipped a beat as Ian remained silent.

Vachel elbowed the Anglo-Saxon viciously in the ribs, but Roland shook his head and the man's arm dropped.

"You would not perchance be this Rob in the flesh? The coward who makes war from behind trees and then retreats from the enemy and melts into the forest at his convenience?"

Ian's face flushed a dull red in the first indication of anger. His fists clenched, but he said nothing, his dark eyes fixed on the other end of the hall with renewed determination.

Roland stroked his chin thoughtfully as he watched Ian. He appeared perfectly at ease, but Brianna sensed it was otherwise.

"Are you the man who fires Norman keeps with no regard for Anglo-Saxons who might be injured or killed as a result? Who deliberately attacks and murders disabled men—men all but defenseless in mind as well as body? If you are he, surely you must be proud of the example you make for your countrymen!''

This was a new side of Roland Brianna had never encountered—deadly, provoking, softly incisive, as he stood before Ian, hands clasped behind his back. He began to pace slowly once more, ruminating, his eyes on the floor.

Brianna jumped, startled, as Ian spoke harshly into the stillness. ''How dare you call a man such as Rob a coward? Norman dog, you have much to learn about courage!''

Roland stopped again, fair eyebrows raised in feigned surprise. ''I have much to learn? If this man's actions are considered courageous, then perhaps I would do well to continue to muddle along in my own ignorant ways, for I have no desire to be compared to the likes of him.'' The last few words were clipped, emphasized.

Ian drew back his lips in a feral snarl and spat into Roland's face. Beorn growled and Vachel swung his fist toward Ian's midsection, but Roland was quicker. Clamping a hand on his man-at-arms' wrist, he stopped the move in midswing. ''Let him be,'' he ordered tersely as he wiped the spittle from his cheek. ''Why was Gilbert of Derford killed?''

Ian's look was murderous. ''You should know better than anyone else.''

Brianna drew in her breath sharply at the implication of his words.

''I had no reason to be rid of him, but perhaps your leader's perverse code of honor moved him to rid us of the unfortunate lad. What better way to turn the people of the village against me?''

Ian's angry scowl slowly dissolved into a humorless smile, followed by a burst of sardonic laughter that echoed throughout the hall. The laughter was coarsely mocking, and as Roland turned to look at Brianna she had the distinct feeling that he had maneuvered the exchange to his advantage—that Ian had fallen into a subtly baited trap while the captive man's laughter only served to make Roland's point.

Why did Ian not deny the Norman's last accusation? she thought uncomfortably.

Brianna met the clear, gray gaze head-on, but confusion mounted inside her as she wondered at this last exchange. His eyes still locked with Brianna's, Roland gave the command to remove the Anglo-Saxon. Brianna dropped her glance and bit her lip in an effort to gain control. She need not have worried, however, for when she glanced up again, Roland had joined the small group of knights standing to the side.

With one last look toward Ian's retreating form, Brianna gratefully took her leave and fled to her room, there to deal with the doubt that had insidiously crept into her belief that Gilbert's death was solely Roland de Beaufort's doing.

As Roland watched Brianna while they ate supper, he wondered how he would tell her of his decision. Dane, Ranulf and Lord William had been in total agreement with him when he declared his intention to execute the captive Anglo-Saxon if he would not tell what he knew. Brianna had been avoiding him, and he could not be certain his brief interrogation of Rob's man had planted any seeds of doubt in her mind. Would the death of this captive turn her even further against him? The thought ate at him until he became annoyed with himself. He could not worry about such things now; he had a keep to finish, a group of desperate men to capture, a village of resentful Anglo-Saxons to win over—

And her love, whispered a voice in the back of his mind.

He looked down into his wine goblet, a frown marring his handsome features. "You do not look happy with your decision, *mon ami.*" Dane's words ended his contemplation of the contents of his jeweled cup. Stormy gray eyes sought the face that had come to be so dear and encountered that incredibly beautiful blue-green gaze. Roland recognized ill-concealed doubt and uncertainty lingering there. His heart soared.

"Oh, but I am, Dane. I most assuredly am."

The change in expression was not lost on the dark-haired Norman. "Aye, there is Brianna to consider, along with half a score of other things. I do not envy you, Roland."

Dane moved away and joined his father, Ranulf and Brianna. As she greeted him Roland's eyes hungrily roamed over her. Her raven hair shone like black silk in the torchlight and set off her cameo skin. A sudden yearning to hold her in his arms overcame him and he longed for the taste of her lips under his. He suddenly felt a wild stirring in his loins. Why should the others enjoy her company while I must watch her from afar? he wondered with growing irritation. Enough time had passed since Gilbert's death. The doubt he had seen on her face only moments before served to bolster his confidence, and his hunger for her—if only to hear her voice—drove him unerringly in her direction.

But young Roger approached him unexpectedly. "My lord, there is a messenger from King William waiting to see you."

Roland's impatience was stilled for a moment. "Bring him to me, Roger."

Brianna had seen Roland's intent to approach and she observed Roger waylay him with much relief. She was enjoying herself more than she had in weeks, and the thought of Roland breaking his silence was upsetting. He could still arouse feelings within her, and the conflicting emotions of desire and mistrust pulled her heart to and fro as easily as a ship tossed about on a turbulent sea.

But Roland was not to be denied. A short while later, much to Brianna's chagrin, he moved toward them once again. Her heart began to pound and she looked about the hall in a panic. She could not break away from the three men who engaged her in conversation unless she actually turned and fled from the room. Her heart in her mouth, Brianna waited for Roland to intrude on the easy camaraderie of the small group.

"What is amiss, Brianna?" inquired Dane.

Her head came up. "Oh, I . . . well . . . naught, Dane," she stammered as Roland stopped beside her and looked directly down into her flushed face.

"Aye, sweet Brianna, what is amiss?" he inquired softly, his look disturbingly intense.

"So, the reason for her unease has become obvious," Dane said bluntly. "Your abrupt appearance has made the lady uncomfortable, *mon ami.*"

Roland ignored his friend's frown and addressed William. "The King sends this to you, Lord William." He handed a piece of sealed parchment to the older knight and then said to Ranulf, "I have been granted the neighboring village of Wexton, Ranulf. You must ride out and look it over soon, for if you decide against the religious life, I could easily be persuaded to let you oversee it in my place."

Ranulf raised a sandy eyebrow in surprise at his brother's generous offer. "My thanks, Roland. Perhaps Wexton holds a treasure tempting enough to entice me from my present course." His gray eyes went to Brianna, which made his meaning very clear.

Brianna looked down again in embarrassment, and Ranulf, suddenly aware of his poorly timed compliment, added quickly, "And what of your news, Lord William?"

"William summons Dane and myself once more to London." He sighed heavily in resignation. "I wonder if we will ever return to Normandy."

Dane laughed outright. "For someone who once spent so much time in England, you are very anxious to leave."

William frowned and seemed to withdraw.

It appeared to Brianna that everyone was trying to make light of the situation—and Roland's attempt to act as if all were well between them only served to make things worse.

"If you will excuse me—" she began.

"Of course they will excuse us while I walk you to your room," Roland interjected smoothly. Before she could protest, he placed his hand on the small of her back and guided her away from the others.

As they neared the stairs Brianna envisioned Roland cornering her in her bedchamber and then— "I . . . I need some . . . fresh air. I can see myself outside if you wish to return to the others."

She stopped abruptly and Roland looked down into her face, the amusement in his eyes hidden by the shadows. "But I much prefer your company, *chérie,* to that of any man."

His self-confidence irked her. How dare he act as if nothing were wrong? "Naught has changed, Norman," she said tartly, turning on her heel in dismissal.

But when she stepped into the balmy summer night, he was close behind her. "One so fair as you needs a protector, my lady, and I would be that one."

Too late, she realized the folly of her actions, for he could easily take advantage of their relative isolation outside the hall. She slowed her steps away from the building and finally swung to face him in anger over his last remark. "I need no protection such as the likes of you can offer! You—"

Warm fingers pressed against her lips and silenced her verbal attack. "Are you forgetting the actions of our captive, Brianna? Does his laughter not ring in your ears yet? Did his behavior not vindicate me as words could never do?"

Brianna brought her clenched fist to her mouth in renewed agitation. Ian's behavior *had* raised doubts in her mind that served only to complicate matters.

"Brianna!" he insisted softly. "I did not kill Gilbert. I had nothing to do with it, I swear before God!"

She shook her head in denial. "Nay, Norman, do not try to fool me!"

Roland took her by the shoulders. In the bright moonlight she could make out the well-defined planes and angles of his face. "Do not keep this between us, Brianna. You will drive me mad! Look at me and tell me that you believe I murdered Gilbert—that I wanted a harmless, crippled boy dead! What manner of man do you think me to be?'' His eyes burned into hers, their intensity effectively disrupting her thoughts. She could not sort things out with his hard, lean body almost touching hers, his determination obvious in his tone, his attitude, his facial expression.

''You . . . you said things the night before . . .'' She trailed off weakly as he gave her a light shake.

''I said things in anger and jealousy. That those things came to pass was purely coincidental. Why would I ever have dropped even the remotest hint if I wished to keep myself free of blame? *Why?*'' He pulled her firmly into his arms and buried his face in her fragrant hair. *''Mon Dieu,* Brianna, how I have longed for you!'' And his lips moved from the soft, smooth tresses to her mouth.

She did not even struggle. She felt unsteady from his very nearness, and even weaker from his kiss; at first tender and searching and then hard and possessive, he plundered her mouth with a thoroughness born of passion too long denied. The heat of his body seemed to melt through her defenses and she helplessly allowed herself to become one with him. Her blood sang in her veins, desire running rampant and leaving her breathless in its wake.

Roland's mouth moved to her eyes, her cheeks, her neck, his hands wreaking their own kind of devastation on her already reeling senses.

''Roland, no,'' she breathed.

''Oh, yes, love—yes!'' he whispered huskily before taking her lips with his own once more.

In a last, frantic bid for sanity, she tried to concentrate on something sobering. Ian's face flashed through her roiling thoughts without warning, and with it the sound of his harsh laughter rang in her ears. It seemed so real that she found herself trying to resist Roland. But it was when that mirthless sound turned to pain-racked cries that she realized it was not in her mind and she stiffened.

Roland responded immediately. He pulled away from her, cursing softly in French.

Brianna sought his eyes with hers. "What is that?" she asked in sharp contrast to her helpless entreaty moments before.

Roland's gaze went to an empty granary behind the two sleeping bowers, his eyes narrowed as if in thought. At Brianna's question, he looked at her without speaking for what seemed an eternity. All passion was wiped away from his grim countenance as he studied her consideringly. Then, "It seems the man we captured is human after all."

Brianna's breath caught in her throat. Ian! Dear God, they were torturing Ian!

Before she could speak, Roland's voice cut into her thoughts relentlessly. "What did you expect, Brianna? That we turn him loose to aid his leader in his fight against me?"

"I should have expected no more from a Norman."

The unfairness of her words hit Roland like a blow. His mouth tightened. "He is a ruthless, unprincipled enemy, and I would be a fool not to try to glean every bit of information possible from him."

"But torture?"

"There is no other way, you said as much yourself. If he does not speak, he will be put to death." His voice was flat. "I know you do not approve, so I ask only that you try to understand—"

"Understand?" she cut in. "I only understand that you will murder a man—one of my countrymen—because he has the courage to resist the Norman scourge."

"It is not so simple, Brianna. He and the others are rebelling against a king supported by your own governing witan." His scar gave him an almost sinister look as the moonlight played about his features.

"They were *deceived* into espousing his cause, so I have been told. William's empty promises caused many to regret that support." Bitterness tinged her words.

Roland felt her withdrawing and cursed the fates that had decreed they should be enemies. "You cannot continue to berate me for upholding Norman justice—"

"In *England!*"

"In an England now ruled by a Norman king!" he gritted. "You cannot go on this way—assuming me guilty of every conceivable atrocity when I only do my duty. Only a blind man—or woman—would fail to see that I try to be fair and just with all men, whether Norman or Anglo-Saxon."

"I only see that you will commit a second murder to achieve your own ends."

His gray eyes glinted in anger at her implication, and Brianna knew she had dared too much. Her words had a hollow ring to them, for deep down she now suspected that he might not be responsible for Gilbert's death, although she was loath to admit it.

Summoning all the dignity she could muster, she straightened and turned, unable to face him again. Over her shoulder she said coldly, "I wish to retire to my chamber, *chevalier,* for I find it most difficult to speak of Norman justice with a condemned Anglo-Saxon's cries echoing through the night." And with slightly shaky steps she moved toward the great door, praying that he would not attempt to stop her.

CHAPTER 17

"Brianna!"

The underlying threat in Roland's voice brought her up short. She slowly turned and faced him, all her instincts telling her to run.

"One step more and I will take you over my knee!"

He stood where she had left him, poised as if in readiness to spring. Brianna could almost feel the tension emanating from him, and a prickle of fear skimmed down her spine.

"Our conversation is not finished, *chérie. Come here.*"

The words were calm and sure, but underneath the smooth-sounding command Brianna caught a hint of menace. He expected her to comply.

It was the second time that he had given her an order that day, and everything inside her rebelled. Anger slowly began to replace fear. He was so confident she would obey! Never mind that at that moment he was evocative of a Viking god as he stood bathed in moonlight, with his gilded hair and well-chiseled features. Never mind that—

"Brianna?" called Dane from behind her.

The sudden sound of his voice gave her renewed courage. She deliberately turned her back to Roland and walked purposefully toward Dane and Lord William. Dane moved away from his father and Ranulf to meet her, and she breathed a sigh of relief, for Roland would never dare to carry out his threat—

The look on Dane's face should have alerted her. Without

warning an arm snaked out from behind her and she was pulled securely against the solid wall of Roland's chest. She was momentarily dazed by the suddenness with which it happened. "You have a habit of disobeying me, wench," he grated in her ear, his wrath unmistakable.

"Put me down, Norman," she hissed at him. If she hadn't feared to make a spectacle of herself she would have struggled. As it was, all eyes were on them, and humiliation washed over her in a hot wave.

"Aye, unhand her, Roland, or you will have *me* to contend with," Dane said in a tight voice, the grim look on his face in full accord with his threatening words.

Brianna felt Roland's body tense at his friend's words. "Are you telling me what to do, *mon ami?*" There was a deadly softness to his words, and Brianna felt her heart in her mouth as the two men faced each other like mortal enemies. She looked in silent appeal at Lord William, who had come to stand to one side of his son.

"I will not allow you to humiliate Brianna like this," Dane answered.

"Roland, for God's sake—"

"Keep out of this, Ranulf," Roland replied curtly, his eyes still on Dane.

Unconsciously his arm had tightened around Brianna until she began to feel faint. "Roland, please . . . I cannot breathe!" she protested softly.

"Release her, Roland."

"This is no concern of yours, Dane. Let us pass."

Dane's answer was to grab Roland's free arm and in a lightninglike movement twist it behind his back, forcing him to ease his hold on Brianna. She stumbled forward, and William steadied her before she turned around to face Roland. His features were rigid with fury as Dane loosened his hold.

"Someone must teach you a lesson, Roland," Dane said quietly, and he moved from behind his friend.

"You dare too much under my roof, Dane. Once again you

exhibit an unseemly amount of concern for Brianna. Can it be that you lust for her right under my nose?''

Dane shot a fist toward Roland's face, but Roland deflected the blow with his left arm. His right fist flew out to make solid contact with Dane's jaw.

Brianna stifled a cry as Dane stumbled to one knee, blood trickling from the side of his mouth. "You will regret that, *mon ami,*" he said softly, his topaz eyes glittering.

Lord William bent to help his son to his feet. "I think we will take our leave in the morning, Roland. I cannot blame my son for interfering on Brianna's behalf, nor do I believe I could stand by idly should you mistreat her again," he said coldly.

"You must not leave with bad feelings between Dane and Roland," Ranulf began.

"Let it be, Ranulf," Roland cut in. "Until both Dane and Lord William realize that they have no right to meddle in my affairs, it is better this way." His eyes lighted on Brianna, lips curving into a travesty of a smile. "You may retire, *chérie.* I will join you later, for there is unfinished business between us."

Brianna needed no urging, and with one last look at Dane she hurried toward the stairs, dignity forgotten.

She had been in her chamber only moments before there was a firm knock on the door.

"Brianna?"

Lord William. Of course. Roland would never knock. She opened the door to admit him, closed it swiftly and turned to lean against it in relief. "You risk Roland's wrath, I think, to come here, my lord."

He shrugged in dismissal. "Never have I seen him so unreasonable. You have wrought havoc with his common sense." A smile played about his lips.

Brianna's cheeks colored becomingly. "I have never sought to engage his attentions, my lord. You must believe me."

"I do, child. But yours is a beauty that ensnares even the

wariest of men.'' He motioned her to a chair and pulled up another for himself. "I feel almost a father to you, Brianna. That is why I said what I did to Roland. If your mother is dead, God rest her soul, and you have heard nothing of your sire, then you are truly alone."

Brianna stared down at her folded hands, pondering whether she should reveal what she knew. "Lord William, there is something I must tell you. I . . . I regret that I was not truthful with you when I first met you, but I was told my father did not wish anyone to be apprised of my identity." William raised a silvered eyebrow in expectation. "It does not matter now, because I trust you as much as I trust Kerwick or Father Simon. My mother's name *was* Alicia, and my father was Robert of Wessex. I was afraid to tell you before, but I know now that you would never do me any harm."

A strange look flitted across his features and then was gone. "I knew it. No one else could have been your mother but Alicia. And now a part of her lives on in you, Brianna. I thank you for telling me, and you can rest assured I will keep your secret." He touched her cheek gently, as if he wanted to be sure she was real. When he rose he offered her a helping hand. "Come to see us off at dawn. Dane will be loath to leave without bidding you farewell, you know."

"I value his friendship very much, my lord. I look upon him as a brother."

An odd look crossed William's face for the second time. "You have not seen the last of us, *ma petite*. We will meet again, one way or another."

Brianna nodded slowly. "And now you must leave before Roland discovers you here."

He shook his head, struck suddenly by another thought. "I made no secret of the fact that I was coming here. He cannot forbid me to say farewell. But I would have you know that Roland is fair and honest, Brianna. No matter how it looked, he was not responsible for Gilbert's murder."

Brianna's expression became troubled at the mention of Gilbert. "I almost wish I could believe that."

"Roland has always been like a son to me, and I know him almost as well as Lord Guy. He would never do anything to hurt you, in mind or body." He paused, searching for the right words. "He loves you, Brianna. He has never, as far as I know, been in love before, and his actions have been rash and out of character. I know of few women who ever resisted him, and therefore he must find it very difficult to be spurned by the woman who has finally won his affections. If, in his misguided attempts to woo you, he does you harm, however unintentionally, you must go to Ranulf. Or send this"—he removed his signet ring and placed it in her hand—"and we will come to you."

Brianna stared at the heavy gold ring. "Thank you, my lord. I will remember that."

He kissed her lightly on the top of her head. "God be with you, child, and remember what I said."

When he was gone, Brianna examined the ring. It was beautifully carved, with a hawk in flight worked in jewels. The garnet eyes winked at her in the dim light. She clutched it to her, her forehead against the cool wood of the closed door.

She was certain no one could help her now.

. . . fair and honest . . . Roland is fair and honest . . . not responsible for Gilbert's death . . .

Brianna dozed lightly as the candle next to her bed burned low and cast an eerie shadow in the otherwise dark room. She tossed fitfully as Lord William's words echoed in the corridors of her mind, interfering with restful, deep slumber.

. . . I did not kill Gilbert. I had nothing to do with it, I swear before God . . . nothing . . . nothing . . . Roland's denial floated through her sleep-drugged mind, and then Dane's: *Roland would never stoop to murder . . . never . . . never. . .*

Brianna sat up with a start. The room was empty and she glanced around, half expecting to see Roland standing in the shadows, ready to carry out his threat. She walked to the open shutter and gazed out into the inky blackness of the night. She was only vaguely aware of the beauty of the silvered moon and the myriad of distant stars dotting the heavens. The soothing sounds of night from the forest also failed to penetrate her beleaguered senses.

Was Roland innocent of Gilbert's murder? Dane and Lord William were certain of it, and she believed now that neither of them would lie to her. And why would Roland have insisted on her being present when Ian was questioned? If he were guilty, would he have done the same thing? Ian's sardonic laughter could have been an admission that Roland's reasoning was correct.

Brianna closed her eyes against the warring thoughts and images, but to no avail. Roland's face loomed before her, his quicksilver eyes beckoning her—willing her to believe him, to trust him—

She turned from the window and moved toward the door, clad only in her whisper-thin ivory-colored nightshift, her feet bare. Perhaps she could find a way to see Ian.

It was pitch black on the stairway and she failed to discern a sleeping hound before the bottom step in the deeply shadowed hall. She almost cried out in alarm as her bare foot made contact with the animal's warm body. The dog growled from deep within its throat, then was silent as it caught her scent.

The hall appeared to be empty and she had almost made it to the closest door when a resonant male voice came to her from the shadows. "What is this—a lovely nymph of the night seeking companionship?"

Roland.

Brianna was at a loss for words; her pulses raced at the unexpected sound of his voice. Oh, why did he have this effect on her? she thought in agitation. Why did she have to come across him now, when she was so unsure of everything?

"Come and join me, nymph," he invited cordially enough.

She strained to see in the dimness and perceived a man's form on the settle where she had sat this afternoon, his long legs stretched out before him.

"N-no," she managed, her voice sounding faraway to her. She felt trapped and tried to marshal her defenses. "What . . . what are you doing here at this hour?"

He rose and lit a candle from one of the sputtering torches, and set the holder down on a table nearby. It illuminated his face, its glow eerily playing about his granite features. There was something about him— And then he raised a goblet to his lips before reaching for a flask to refill it.

He must be drunk, and if he had been drinking since supper, he could not be unaffected.

"What am I doing here?" he repeated in a voice that sounded oddly surprised at her question. "Why, I'm thinking, wench. What else?"

Brianna stood rooted to the spot, neither wishing to approach him nor convinced she could retreat without stirring him to pursuit.

At her failure to respond, he continued. "I'm wondering why I ever came to this accursed island."

The words bubbled forth before she could squelch them. "Perhaps for our excellent mead—you seem to be enjoying more than your share, Norman."

Roland frowned thoughtfully and raised his foot to brace it on a bench before the table. He leaned one arm across his knee while he used the other to gesture in intoxicated eloquence. The contents of the goblet sloshed dangerously as he moved. "I was given this elegant hall"—a slight hiccup—"and all of Derford and its surrounding lands to oversee. And what do I get for my pains to rule fairly and with tolerance?" He was silent for a moment, and Brianna breathed easier. But his next words had an uncharacteristic and unexpected bite to them. "A self-made renegade hero who seeks to foil me at every turn. And"—he held her gaze with sudden, startling power, his behavior suddenly far from that of a sot—"a woman who not only spurns my affection, but denounces me as a murderer of innocents as well."

Brianna searched for the right words. "Mayhap . . . mayhap you spoke the truth—"

Too late she discovered she had only made matters worse, for rather than appeasing him, her words seemed to inflame his anger. Down came the goblet with a thud. He straightened and advanced toward her, his back to the table and candle, making it difficult to see his face.

"My dear Brianna, I *always* speak the truth. Did I not tell you that I was not party to the raid on Derford?" He stood directly before her, blocking out everything but his shadowed face.

"Aye," she whispered, taking a step backward.

"But you would not believe me until I presented you with unassailable proof. Will you hold me at bay for all my supposed misdeeds until I am driven mad with desire?"

"Nay . . . 'tis not my intention, Roland—" she began breathlessly, his nearness threatening to undo her.

"What *is* your intention, Brianna?" He made no move to touch her, yet she felt weak and giddy. She could smell the mead on his breath, but it did not offend her. Oddly, it served to stimulate her heightened awareness of him.

"I—" She managed to take another step back. "I will give more credence to your words in the future," she trailed off lamely. Why couldn't she get hold of herself? He had managed to gain the upper hand and was pressing her relentlessly, when she was not at all certain that he was blameless. How could he behave so if he were in his cups?

He muttered an expletive under his breath. "Give more credence to my words? You seek to throw me a bone—as you would yonder hound. But I need more than that, Brianna. Much more." He reached out and, in a motion at odds with his gruff tone, gently stroked her cheek. The heat from his hand seemed to burn her skin. She stood trembling, unable to move, but his next words alarmed her. "I believe I owe you a turn over my knee, wench," he murmured.

Her eyes widened and she pushed his hand away. "You . . . you wouldn't dare!"

"You think not? According to you, I am capable of all manner of brutalities." He turned and, reclaiming the goblet from the table, sprawled himself out again on the settle. He drank deeply and, draping one arm over the hard back of the bench, regarded her unwaveringly. "I wonder how you would fare if I returned to Normandy and let someone else claim what William granted me. Someone like Hugh of Brittany."

Brianna shuddered at the thought of someone like the Breton taking his place, and it did not escape his notice.

"Ah! Then you will concede that I am not so undesirable an overlord?"

She was awkwardly silent for a moment, then she remembered Ian. "Nay, *chevalier.* In all honesty you are not." She could only hope he would be contented with her words.

"At last we come to grips with the truth." He patted the seat beside him. "Come sit with me, *ma chère,* and we will drink to this most eagerly awaited change of heart."

What could she do? Perhaps, if she pretended to go along, he would consider her plea on Ian's behalf. She moved toward the sideboard and obtained a clean cup, filled it halfway and warily approached him.

He made no move to take down his arm as Brianna gingerly sat down, and his hand touched her shoulder caressingly. "I propose a toast, sweet Brianna. To us—to the beginning of trust and a promising future."

A warning went off in the back of her mind, but she ignored it. Her primary concern was getting him to agree to her request to see Ian—even to release him.

She raised the cup to his and took a drink of the fermented liquid. She could see his eyes more clearly now, and they were studying her over the rim of his goblet.

"I remember when first I saw you at Hastings as if it were

only yesterday: You were the most enchanting girl I had ever seen. Beautiful, spirited, docile—and all at the same time. A most intriguing combination.''

Brianna was thankful for the darkness of the hall as her cheeks flamed. ''Thank you,'' she murmured simply. She lowered her eyes, disturbed by the intensity of his look.

''You haunted my dreams until I knew I would move heaven and earth to find you again.''

Strangely enough, something inside her wanted to believe him, but she wondered fleetingly how many others had heard those same words.

''Brianna . . .'' Her name was a caress on his lips. ''We were meant to be together—do you know that?''

Somehow he had put down his goblet and his one arm dropped down from the back of the settle to encircle her shoulders; with his other hand he drew her head forward to meet his kiss, pulling her body up against his so that his iron-muscled chest crushed her soft breasts. From the center of her being, she felt wave after wave of growing pleasure radiate outward. ''Roland, nay—'' She feebly attempted to push him away.

To her surprise, he complied and held her from him. ''What is it, sweet?'' he asked in that beautifully rich voice, his eyes searching her passion-flushed features.

''I . . . I must speak to you, Roland . . .'' She drew a shaky breath and stared down at her hands, smoothing the material of her garment nervously. ''I ask you, in all sincerity, to . . . to spare the man you captured this afternoon.'' She felt him stiffen and she went on in a rush. ''He can do you no more harm—if he is indeed one of Rob's men—while he is your prisoner.'' She looked at him imploringly. ''I beg you, Roland—''

''Do not beg, Brianna. It does not suit you,'' he said harshly, and released her abruptly.

''Roland—''

''Roland? How easily you use my given name when you

feel it will further your purpose! If I even considered your wish—which I will not—how long would it be before I became 'Norman' or *chevalier* again?'' He rose quickly and strode to the table, lifting the entire flask of mead to his lips in a swift motion.

Brianna stood up, knowing she had failed miserably. He turned toward her, his body tense with anger. ''You play me for a fool, Brianna—attempting to lull me with your compliance while you scheme to have your own way.''

Brianna quickly realized that while he had been drinking, he was not drunk, and she knew she had done precisely the wrong thing. She opened her mouth to speak, but he cut her off tersely. ''Very well—go to your precious captive. I will not spare his life, but I will allow him the pleasure of your company. And''—he thrust the flask into her hands—''here is something to ease his misery. 'Tis obvious you would rather spend the night coddling him than keeping company with a Norman murderer like myself.''

The vitriolic tone of his words was so alien to his character that Brianna realized she had hurt him—and more than he ever would admit. Although for some strange reason she felt surprising regret, she didn't know what she could say to make amends, short of apologizing. And that she was not ready to do.

Roland raised his goblet in a mocking salute. ''To our mysterious prisoner—may your talk with him be most gratifying.'' He replaced the vessel on the table and was swallowed by the shadows as he strode in the direction of the stairs.

She should have known Roland would never leave a captive unguarded. As she approached the granary Beorn's form was revealed by the moonlight. He was dozing, seated with his back against the small hut.

The hissing flame of her torch wakened him. He bolted to his feet, squinting at her, one hand on his sword.

'' 'Tis I, Beorn, come to see the Anglo-Saxon.''

He frowned in bemusement. "Does Roland know of this?"

"Aye, but if you do not believe me, I will—"

"Oh, I do not doubt your word, my lady, but 'tis not a pretty sight." He eyed her consideringly. "You may see him if you wish. And do not be afraid, for even were he in any condition to do you harm, I am right here."

Brianna stepped into the small hut and held the torch up to better illuminate the dark interior. She dropped the flask and brought her hand to her mouth as a scream rose to her lips. Ian sat on the floor against the opposite wall, hands and feet bound. His head was propped against the wall behind him, his face totally unrecognizable. His clothing was torn and revealed bruised and beaten flesh in many places.

Brianna swallowed the bile that burned the back of her throat. "Ian?" she whispered incredulously, and received no response. She knelt before him and tried again. "Ian? 'Tis I, Brianna. Ian?"

Very slowly his eyes opened to slits in the mass of puffy, discolored flesh around them. Tears sprang into her eyes and she bit her lip in an effort to keep them at bay. "Ian? Oh, Ian! How did they ever capture you?"

"You can do naught. Leave me," he croaked, and his eyes closed.

"I . . . I cannot leave you like this—" Her words died in helpless frustration.

He looked at her tiredly. "You are the last person I want to see, so do not waste your pity. I only regret . . . that Rob thought you of enough consequence to . . . save from being drawn into league with de Beaufort. You are a traitress."

The words pierced Brianna to the quick and, realizing there was some truth in what he said, she hung her head and drew a ragged breath. "You are right, Ian," she whispered.

"I . . . never trusted you, Brianna of Derford. Not for a moment was I fooled into believing you were with us," he rasped. "But you had our leader convinced that you meant well—that you could be of some value." He coughed suddenly and blood dribbled from his mouth. "So when he . . . thought your loyalty was in peril he took steps to . . . convince you that de Beaufort was a cold-blooded murderer."

Brianna's expression turned puzzled. "Took steps to—?" And realization began to dawn.

"Aye. We knew the Norman was besotted with you and would . . . never do anything so drastic as to alienate you." He tried to smile, but his face was too badly beaten and the most he could manage was a grotesque-looking grimace. "Rob has never been so foolish where a female was concerned. I . . . do not know why he took the trouble, but I did as I was told." His slitted eyes held hers for long moments, glittering with derision, before he delivered the final blow. "Am I not skilled with the weapon of the wellborn?"

Brianna stared at the battered face in disbelief. *"You?"* The word was barely audible.

Ian made a sound that could have been a cynical laugh, but the blood seeped from the corner of his mouth once again and he ceased. "Aye, none other."

"Why . . . why did you not admit as much to . . . to Roland?" she asked dazedly.

His black eyes gleamed with hatred. "I would not give him the satisfaction."

"But . . . but then, why did you tell me now?"

"It does not matter now, for I know you will continue to crawl into his bed—whether you believe him guilty or no. Women such as you have no loyalty for anyone or anything except themselves. We know much about what goes on here, and 'tis no secret you used your unfortunate husband to hide your lust for de Beaufort." He gasped for air, but Brianna was too affected by his words to take heed or show concern.

"Roland is innocent of Gilbert's murder," she said slowly, wonderingly, as if savoring the sound of the words exonerating him.

"He is a murderer—just as every other Norman in England."

A desire to defend Roland took hold of her without warning. "And what of our men who fought and killed Normans? Are they not guilty of the same crimes of which you accuse William's followers?"

"That is not the same." He hawked and spat blood on the ground where she knelt.

Brianna began to tremble with anger. "Rob had no right to do away with Gilbert! I was willing enough to do his bidding, in spite of what you think. He gave the command to sacrifice an innocent man—one of his own—when it was not necessary! He never gave me a chance, so how could he possibly know?"

Ian turned his face aside. "Enough of your mewling, bitch. Get out."

CHAPTER 18

Dawn found Brianna huddled before the cold hearth in her room. Knees drawn up and chin resting thereupon, she opened her eyes at last, jarred out of her withdrawal from her surroundings by the noises of early-morning activity below.

Her desire to bid farewell to Dane roused her sufficiently to unbend her cramped limbs. She stood up gingerly and stretched, then stiffly made her way to the basin of water nearby. As she automatically performed her ablutions guilt and remorse crept back into her consciousness—the same feelings that had plagued her lonely vigil.

How could she have ever believed, in her heart of hearts, that Roland had ordered Gilbert slain? What a fool she was! Her sinful pride had refused to let her see him as anything but a marauding foreigner, even when she had shared his bed.

She frowned at her image in the polished metal mirror above the basin as she brushed her thick, shiny mane until her scalp tingled. Roland had never, as far as she knew, lied to her. She had assumed him guilty of the murder simply because he was a Norman.

She closed her eyes in mortification. Letting the brush drop from her lifeless fingers, she hung her head, her deep regret overwhelming her.

The sound of stamping horses outside brought her back to the moment. She must not miss saying farewell to Dane. Resolutely wiping away the tears with the back of her hand, she changed her wrinkled shift for a fresh undergown and overtunic she took from a wooden chest at the foot of the bed, and fairly flew down the steps and across the cavernous room below.

The sun was rising, splashing the sky with a glorious orange-pink as she emerged into the yard. Her eyes sought Dane among the men-at-arms and servants milling about. Lord William stood nearby, deep in discussion with— Her heart skipped a beat. And then she realized it was Ranulf and not Roland. Dane was nowhere to be seen.

"Are you looking for me?" asked the object of her thoughts from behind her. "Or is it the fair Roland you seek?"

She whirled around and impulsively threw her arms about his neck, grateful that with him she could be herself—he cared for her as a friend or even a sister. And he was leaving.

"Easy, my girl. You'll have Roland at my throat in a trice!" His voice held a trace of laughter even as he returned the embrace.

Brianna quickly withdrew her arms and met his amber gaze, her eyes suspiciously bright. "Do not jest, Dane. I have been the cause of ill feelings between you and Roland twice now, and it pains me."

He gently lifted her chin with a finger. "That is in the past now, *petite.*"

Brianna's eyes widened questioningly. "What do you mean? I don't understand . . ."

He grinned into her upturned face. "The jealous lout apologized to me. I only wish he could take back his blow as well as his words." He lightly fingered the swelling along his jawline.

"I am glad to hear that," she said, her face lighting up with relief.

"He is undoubtedly still abed, for he came in to me very late last eve, reeking like he'd fallen into a barrel of mead."

Brianna glanced at the stairway, half expecting Roland to appear. Then her gaze returned to the tall Norman before her. "I only wish that you did not have to leave—"

"The horses are ready, my lord," announced a young page from behind Brianna.

Her smile disappeared and she touched his arm anxiously. "I have a terrible feeling that I will never see you or Lord William again—"

"Nonsense, little one." He guided her through the door toward where his great destrier snorted impatiently. William was mounting as Ranulf watched their approach.

She stopped suddenly, forcing Dane to turn his back to the other two men, so that his broad-shouldered form blocked them from view. "I . . . I know now that Roland was not in any way responsible for Gilbert's death, Dane." Her eyes clouded with uncertainty. "But how can I hope he will forgive my unfair accusation? Do you . . . do you think he will find it in his heart to—?"

Dane's expression turned sober. "I know he will forgive you anything, Brianna. If ever you looked at another man, he might not be so willing to welcome you with open arms, but otherwise you have no need to worry. Trust me." He kissed her lightly on the cheek before turning to join his father.

Brianna looked up at him as he swung into the saddle. "Godspeed." Her lips formed the word silently as a tear slipped down her pale cheek.

"We will meet again, child," said William reassuringly. "Do not doubt it."

She stared blindly at their retreating forms and raised her arm in an answering salute as father and son turned to wave before riding through the gate. And then they were gone.

"Come now, Brianna," Ranulf chided softly, his arm going around her slim shoulders. "They will come back before returning to Normandy, you can be sure of it."

"Aye." She straightened with sudden determination and gave Ranulf a watery smile. "I cannot doubt the word of two honorable knights."

He laughed as they made their way to the hall.

* * *

After breaking her fast Brianna tried to work on the ledgers. Her thoughts kept wandering, however, to the still-sleeping Roland upstairs. He might not have behaved like a man besotted the night before, she reasoned, but he must be suffering from the effects of his overindulgence.

Even as she fought to keep her mind on her accounts, Brianna realized she would have no real peace of mind until she spoke to Roland. Until she admitted to him that she had been wrong. Until she asked for, and was granted, his forgiveness.

Now? she asked herself as she ascended the stairs with leaden feet. *Now,* answered a voice in the back of her mind. *Before your courage flees altogether.*

Before she could further ponder the wisdom of confronting Roland alone in his bedchamber, Brianna pushed at the heavy oak door until it protestingly opened with a squeak of its hinges. Standing poised on the threshold, she was greeted by the sight of Roland's prone figure on the bed in the center of the room. Naked.

Some unseen force propelled her forward until she stood beside the bed.

The window on the opposite wall was unshuttered and the soft light from the scintillating early-morning sun bathed that part of the room in muted tones. The lord of the manor lay on his side, one leg thrust out while his outstretched arm held a rumpled bedcover in a slumber-induced embrace.

Brianna knew suddenly that she had overstepped the bounds of decency by boldly entering his chamber, yet the sight of his magnificent unclothed body caused her no more than a hint of embarrassment.

His limbs were covered with a light furring of dark blond hair, and the sculpted lines of muscle and sinew were very much in evidence. His broad shoulders gave way to a lean rib cage and then narrowed to a flat belly and slim waist. Firm, well-shaped buttocks tapered down to sleek flanks and long, smooth-muscled legs.

His face, half hidden in the bedclothes, was relaxed and

youthful-looking in repose, the fine lines splaying out from his eyes almost invisible. He looked younger than eight and twenty. An unruly lock of gently curling tawny hair fell over his high forehead.

"Do you like what you see, or have you come to ask another favor?" queried the object of her scrutiny.

Her eyes encountered those of silver-gray and she was momentarily speechless, her cheeks turning pink.

"I . . . I came to apologize . . . for . . ." Her voice trailed off as, in fascinated horror, she watched Roland attempt to sit up, with no show of apology whatsoever for his state of undress.

He emitted a low groan, his face changing from ruddy to pallid as he sat up. "The . . . pot—chamber pot—" he pleaded hoarsely. But it was too late; he suddenly lurched drunkenly toward the window. Brianna's hand went over her mouth to stifle a snicker. This was no proud Norman knight leaning out to spew his insides into the yard below.

When at last he turned back, Brianna modestly averted her gaze, her merriment finally under control. When she looked up, he was rinsing his mouth with rose water from a pitcher nearby. He spat it out the window before sinking down onto the bed with a sigh.

"And now 'tis only your head that pains you," Brianna guessed.

He raised a slightly jaundiced eye to her. "You display a surprising amount of wisdom for one raised in the shelter of an abbey."

Brianna asked sweetly, "What makes you think I could not have learned of such things after coming here, my lord? I most certainly have had many opportunities to witness the results of overimbibing under your roof."

He scowled, but it only served to aggravate his headache, and his expression swiftly turned bland. "Are you going to stand there all day and bait me, wench?"

Brianna walked to the window and gazed out at the activity

below. She looked toward the granary where Ian was imprisoned and afforded Roland an unobstructed view of her delightful profile. He surmised where her glance rested and said, "You said you came here to apologize. For trying to interfere in my affairs last night?"

She shook her head slowly and turned to face him. He had carelessly pulled a blanket over his lap, for which she was secretly grateful. "I am deeply sorry that I accused you of ordering Gilbert's death. I did you a grave injustice, and I have finally recognized the folly of my actions."

He gingerly raised a tawny eyebrow in surprise. "And when did this revelation come about? Surely you did not obtain such information from our recalcitrant Anglo-Saxon?"

"I did no such thing, Norman. I . . . I am not sorry for interfering on his behalf, although I concede that as lord of the manor you are free to deal with any threat to yourself or your holdings as you see fit." He was taking this with much more grace than she had ever expected, but hadn't Dane said he would forgive her almost anything?

"Look at me while you tell me how you came to such a decision, Brianna."

When she raised her eyes to his, he was sitting perfectly still, all trace of emotion absent from his features as he studied her face.

"Well . . . there is no one thing which made me change my mind," she lied, using all her self-discipline to keep from giving herself away. "I think it was partly because of Dane and Lord William. They tried to convince me you were not responsible. You have a friend in Dane that many men would envy."

"Are they gone yet?" he asked unexpectedly, skillfully changing the subject.

Her eyes grew misty, to her dismay. "Aye. They left at sunrise, and Ranulf and the others are gone as well."

His look seemed to pierce her to the quick, as if he could read her very soul. Then he turned the dialogue to an even more touchy subject than the first. "I would that you cared for me that way, *ma chère.*" He stood, barely keeping the blanket around his midsection, and walked toward her. "Do you love him?"

She drew a deep breath and expelled it before answering, her eyes riveted to his. "Aye," she murmured.

Something akin to pain flickered in the clear gray depths of his eyes, and it touched Brianna so deeply that she knew she could never mislead him—or hurt him—again. "As a brother," she finished.

He was very close to her when he stopped, and Brianna knew an irresistible urge to throw herself into his arms. Could it be, she wondered in sudden, wild elation, that she was in love with this man?

He lowered his head slowly, his eyes holding hers until she was lost in a vortex of quicksilver.

This man who epitomized everything she had ever dreamed of in a lover—?

Silver-gray eyes came closer, searing her heart indelibly with their intensity.

This man who could make her forget all but his touch, his embrace, his kiss—?

Warm, firm lips took hers in sweet rapture and ignited that spark deep within her that came to life only through him.

"Tell me, Brianna," he whispered raggedly, "that you regret your judgment because you know, in your heart of hearts, that I had nothing to do with it. Tell me you cannot truly believe that I, who love you beyond all things in this world, could ever be capable of such treachery."

His lips hovered a breath away from hers, waiting for her answer.

"Yes, Roland. Yes!" She was lost in the moment and unwittingly deepened the lie in whose ever-tightening web she was caught.

His mouth closed over hers in a fiercely possessive kiss that sent her pulses racing as a sweet ecstasy swept through her veins.

"Roland," she murmured as he let slip the cover and encircled her waist, pulling her against him to feel his overwhelming need for her.

His kiss was long and thorough, as if he could not get enough of her. "Brianna, Brianna," he murmured over and over again, his hands stroking the silken flesh of her arms, then her back, and finally pulling her even closer to him, until they were almost as one.

She felt at peace with herself for the first time since leaving Walshire. He was the man whom she knew now that she loved. Whom she needed. All those months she had allowed her pride to stand in the way, holding Gilbert as a shield against not only Roland but her own burgeoning love. How blind she had been!

Roland drew back, his eyes searching her lovely face questioningly as he sensed her preoccupation. "What is it, *chérie?* What is troubling you?"

She licked her lips, suddenly nervous now that she faced baring her soul to him, but her gaze did not waver. "Roland, I . . . I think I love you," she said, suddenly breathless with the heady excitement of her revelation.

He stared uncomprehendingly for a split second, and regret surged through Brianna at not having acknowledged it sooner. But then his splendid features lit up and her moment of self-flagellation was gone. He hugged her so tightly she was sure she would never be able to breathe again, and then he whirled her around as effortlessly as a rag doll until she protested laughingly, "Roland, please! You will make yourself sick again!"

But he didn't seem concerned. "Do you know, my sweet Brianna, that you have made me happier than any man has a right to be?" He took her face gently in his strong, callused swordsman's hands and absorbed the incredible beauty of her delicate features with suddenly serious gray eyes.

"Roland?" she queried softly, shyly.

"Aye, my love?"

"Do you . . . well, do you love me, too?"

He frowned, and Brianna's heart lurched in dreaded anticipation of his next words.

"I ought to take you over my knee as I threatened yestereve, wench!"

Her aquamarine eyes filled with tears of disappointment. She tried to pull away from him, but he would have none of it.

"You are a true innocent, Brianna, which sometimes tries my patience beyond endurance. Do I love you? *Do I love you?* Does the sun not rise in the east every morn? Does the eagerly awaited spring not come every year? Does the calm not follow the storm, no matter how fierce?"

Brianna could only continue to stare at him, her wide-eyed uncertainty still obvious.

"I *do, mon coeur!* I do beyond measure! Ever since I held you in my arms at Hastings. Why do you think I followed you to Wessex? Did I not tell you as much in besotted eloquence last night? Have you not read it in my looks, my words, my actions? In a thousand different ways? God in heaven, Brianna, how could you ever have doubted it?"

He crushed her to him once more, his face buried in the soft, fragrant cascade of her hair. "What of your Norman bride-to-be?" came her muffled words from the area of his shoulder.

"My what?" He held her away from him, a frown creasing his brow.

"The bride whose duties I was to temporarily assume when I moved in here. The one for whom you purchased silverware from Rolfe of Dover."

"Oh, that." A devilish gleam lit his eyes. "I merely wished to make you jealous, hoping to lure you into a display of temper—*anything* to indicate that you cared for me."

"Why, Roland de Beaufort—you—"

"Try 'Norman.' It has always suited your needs before," he prompted with a grin.

"That was unfair!" she accused.

"Unfair? When I had to look upon your fair countenance every day with a yearning that would make a sword wound pale in comparison? When you favored everyone—Gilbert, Ranulf, Dane—with your sweet smile and delightful charm while I had to fight for the smallest crumb? Nay, sweet, 'twas not so unfair as you would make it."

"Then there is no one back in Normandy you wish to wed?"

"The only woman I wish to wed has hair as black as a raven's wing and eyes the color of the sea on a calm, clear day. She has a sense of loyalty and courage that would put many a man to shame and"—his smile faded as his words turned sober—"I desire, above all things, to make her mine forever."

"Oh, Roland!" she breathed, her eyes alight with joy.

"You are so lovely—I cannot wait much longer," he said softly, his gray eyes darkening with desire.

And then the brilliant smile that lit her features faded, and Roland thought of the sun when a cloud passes over it. "Your *wife?*"

"Did you think I would have you any other way, Brianna?"

Color stained her cheeks at the implication of his words. She drew away from him and averted her gaze, for even the meager protection of the blanket was gone. "I cannot marry you."

"You cannot? Whatever can there be to prevent it?" he asked in perplexity, bending down in a swift, lithe motion to retrieve the fallen coverlet and wrap it securely about his trim waist. And then he loomed before her again.

"You . . . you are a Norman!" she said lamely.

Roland laughed softly and gathered her to him, despite her halfhearted attempt to resist. "Aye, that I am, as you seem to

delight in reminding me when you are angry. What has that
to do with our love?''

Her eyes met his and mirrored her confusion. "What will
the people of Derford think if I wed a Norman? Will they not
call me a traitress?''

"I think rather they will believe you wise in attempting to
live in harmony with your new liege lord. I am not so ill
thought of, *ma chère,* as you seem to think." His wounded
look at her inference was too much for Brianna and she gave
in, snuggling against him and relishing the warm, secure feeling that enveloped her whenever she was in his arms.

"Well, Aleen is half in love with you now, and Nedra
thinks you can do no wrong. Perhaps you have won over more
souls than I had thought," she conceded grudgingly.

"I will tell Father Simon and we can be wed in a sennight." He lifted her into his arms and carried her toward the
great bed.

"A . . . a sennight? Roland, I need more time!" she exclaimed, pushing her hands against his chest to better see him.

He playfully dropped her onto the bed in response. "So
you would act the complaining wife when we are not yet even
wed?''

A tinkling of laughter was his answer. " 'Tis no fault of
mine that in your eagerness you play the besotted swain.''

He sat down beside her, pinning her wrists on either side
of her head, a roguish grin playing about his lips. "If I act
the besotted swain, 'tis your doing, blue-eyed witch. You've
had me under your spell since the first time I looked into your
eyes. Now it is your turn to suffer my personally devised
torture.'' And he bent his head to kiss her.

But the word *torture* brought back a flood of unwelcome
memories from the night before, and Brianna turned her head
away.

Roland, caught up in the exhilaration of her love, was slow
to realize her reluctance was not a lover's ploy. When she
refused to turn her head back to him, he released her arms

and sat up. "What is it now, woman?" he demanded in exasperation.

"How can I pretend the man you captured does not exist? Has not been tortured—condemned to die on this day?"

Roland's eyes darkened in real irritation for the first time. "You said only moments ago that it is my right to deal with any threat to myself or my holdings as I see fit. This man— and others like him—is a menace not only to myself and my men, but to your people as well, Brianna. In their desperation, they do not care that they may kill Anglo-Saxons as well as Normans." He ran his fingers through his tousled hair in frustration, and Brianna was torn between the desire to soothe away the tension written across his features and press him further to be merciful toward Ian. "If you seek to use my love as a tool to manipulate me, the result will be disastrous. I must remain firm, Brianna. A weak, inconsistent leader cannot effectively manage his men, his people or his holdings. There is no other way in this man's case. If he had spoken I would have spared his life, but he will reveal naught."

Brianna closed her eyes, admitting to herself that he was right. If he were any less a leader, a man who would waver from his set course, a man beset by indecision and partiality, he would not have won her love. She turned her head to look at the features now so dear to her. "I *am* sorry, Roland. I have no right to try to use my influence unfairly." She was beginning to see just how much influence she could wield and realized it was wrong of her to put him in such a position— especially in an instance where she was biased. He had been fair to the people of Derford, and now she must learn to trust him, even if she didn't always understand or agree.

He smoothed back the soft strands of midnight-black hair that framed her face, as gently as a father with a child. "I know 'tis difficult for you to accept all that has happened. Were I in your place I would have reacted in the same manner, for I, too, am proud and stubborn. I, too, have principles for which I am prepared to die, Brianna," he said gravely. "But

what would you have me do? Return to my homeland only to
let someone like Hugh of Brittany or his kind take my place?
What's done is done, and my leaving would change nothing.
I would like to believe that no one could be a more concerned
or just overlord. If that is true, then Derford would probably
suffer at someone else's hands, and I would not want that,
would you?''

Brianna was touched by his words. She sat up, her eyes
shimmering with tears. "Please forgive me, Roland," she
asked humbly. "I have been too proud, and too determined
to think the worst of you. How could you have ever loved one
so blind?''

He gathered her into his arms and lifted her onto his lap.
"Nay, sweet. Yours is not the blame entirely. You were
pitched headlong into a world of chaos, for which you were
unprepared. I marvel at your determination, and your strength,
ma chère." His lips lightly brushed her temple as he rocked
her to and fro comfortingly.

"I am not so wonderful as that, Roland."

"Oh, but you are, my love, and more. You have been kind
to everyone around you, and even my men feel more at home
in this new land because of you."

"My lord?" Hilde's blond head appeared at the door, which
Brianna had inadvertently left ajar.

"What is it, Hilde?" Roland asked good-humoredly, despite the hint of a frown at the unwelcome interruption.

"I only wished to see if you might be wanting something
to eat. But I can see you are . . . er, occupied," she said
slyly, looking pointedly at Brianna seated on the lord of the
manor's knee, enfolded in his arms.

Brianna tensed instinctively, embarrassment coloring her
cheeks. Roland took one look at her face, and his tone lost its
humor in an instant. "You have not seen Brianna here, Hilde.
Do you understand? I am alone in my chamber and I do not
wish to be disturbed. That is all."

"Aye, my lord." She bobbed her head quickly and made a hasty exit, closing the door firmly behind her.

He looked ruefully at Brianna. "And now I must go hungry, wench," he growled in mock annoyance.

She was instantly contrite. "Oh, Roland, I forgot you've had nothing to eat yet."

"Oh, but I think I can find better fare than Hilde can offer without even moving from this bed." He grinned at her, all innocence. "There is nothing to prevent you from staying here and helping me celebrate our mutual discovery." And before she could protest, he lowered her back down on the bed, pinning her down with his upper torso. He nuzzled her gently and his lips found a small, shell-shaped ear, sending delightful sensations through her body.

"But what of your head?" she managed to ask, remembering how indisposed he had been earlier.

"You've cured me, *chérie*. And now I want to show you just how much I really love you," he murmured huskily into her ear.

"Oh, Roland—'tis midmorn!" she gasped in protest as his intentions became clear.

"You are astute as well as beautiful," he replied in mock solemnity as his lips tasted the sweet curve of her jaw and then her neck.

She felt the familiar languor sweep through her, and in a last, halfhearted attempt to stop his tender assault she whispered, "This is sinful—defying all decency and—"

"Hush, sweet," he commanded against the leaping pulse at the base of her throat, and she moved her hands to the tawny head below her chin, her fingers luxuriating in the thick crispness of his hair as she gave in to the thrill of desire that overcame her weak protestations.

Suddenly Roland was removing her skirts, and she eagerly helped him slide them over her shoulders and then her head.

A small sigh of pleasure escaped her lips as he settled the warmth of his solid chest against her sensitive breasts. "The time of day or night makes no difference, my love. The light can only enhance the pleasure.'' And before she could reply he bent his head to capture a rosy-crested peak in his mouth.

Relaxed, reveling in the knowledge of Roland's love, Brianna gave herself up to the delicious sensations his lips and tongue were creating and arched against him in growing urgency.

Her fingers caressed the smooth-muscled expanse of his back in exploration and then tightened convulsively as he shifted slightly to one side so his hand could move up the satiny length of her inner thigh, stroking lightly as a feather. She waited in bittersweet anticipation as his fingers hovered inches from that most secret of all places, the desire in her so acute that it was almost painful. But when at last he gently touched the silken folds, she unwittingly tensed with the last vestiges of shyness.

''Let me, *mon coeur*. Let me love you all over,'' he whispered, and then closed his lips over hers to silence any objection. His tongue moved within the warm lure of her mouth in an ancient rhythm that moved his fingers within her at the same time, until Brianna's limbs relaxed and parted in natural, uninhibited invitation. The searing heat of his turgid manhood along her limb emphasized that he, too, was swept up in the raging current of euphoria that threatened to engulf her with its intensity.

And then he was between her thighs, his lips at her ear whispering words of love in his native French as both hands reached up and buried themselves in her glorious ebony tresses. He poised himself before the core of her femininity, holding his own need rigidly in check until she grasped his lean hips and pulled them against her urgently.

''Roland,'' came her ragged plea. ''Now, my love—''

And he eased into the moist velvet sheath of her as unerringly as a sword into its scabbard, filling her, causing her to moan softly in ecstasy. He rested inside her a moment, his eyes, molten silver, worshiping her vivid, passion-flushed features. Instinctively she moved against him, and he answered with slow, steady thrusts of his own until together they strove for fulfillment, the sunlight from the unshuttered window bathing their sweat-sheened bodies with its golden glow.

When they lay sated, damp limbs entwined in an age-old position of rapture shared, Brianna raised her gaze to his. "Oh, Roland, Roland—you do love me."

His lips caressing her temple, he answered quietly, "I have from the first, my sweet Brianna, and I always shall."

CHAPTER 19

In retrospect, Brianna wondered why it had never occurred to her that Roland might love her. His every word, every gesture, every expression had told her so. And she walked on air, her heart and mind brimming with happiness. In Roland's arms she was able to forget Rob and Ian and even that he himself was a Norman.

Brianna pushed aside any lingering doubts, reasoning that she loved Roland, that as his wife she could do much more for Derford and its people. As for Gilbert, Brianna knew now that she had loved Gilbert in a different way than she loved Roland, and feeling guilty was unfair to herself. It was now time to put all that behind her—to continue her new life with the man she loved.

Secure in the knowledge that the keep was almost completed and in capable hands, Roland sought the luxury of spending more time with Brianna when she was not involved in preparations for the coming wedding. And because she had asked him to be discreet in their actions, Roland found himself regretting that he had not made her his wife immediately.

That first afternoon after they made their commitment to one another, they wandered outdoors, hand in hand, until they came to the ancient oak between the palisade gate and one end of the hall. They sat down beneath its leafy emerald canopy, the lush patch of springy grass beneath it forming a soft blanket to accommodate them.

"You grow more lovely every day," he said huskily.

"Thank you, my lord." Brianna flashed him a dazzling smile. "You will turn my head with your warm looks and honeyed phrases."

His eyes darkened with emotion. "Every word is sincere, Brianna." He put his arms around her and pulled her to him, his chin resting on top of her head as he gazed thoughtfully at the stretch of woods between his estate and the village. " 'Tis a crime that we cannot walk through the forest on my own holdings," he exclaimed suddenly, a dark frown momentarily replacing his look of contentment.

"Because of Rob?" Brianna asked in a guarded voice.

"I do not fear him, love. Only what would happen to you should he capture or kill me."

A heated flush crept up Brianna's neck to her cheeks as guilt surged through her. But along with the guilt came the realization that Rob would not spare her life if she should encounter him again. Now that she was to wed a Norman, she would be considered as much an enemy as any foreigner. Strangely, that did not worry her now.

"I know you are a fine swordsman, Roland, for I have watched you train with your men from my window, but if he is—was—a nobleman, he is undoubtedly highly skilled as well." She nibbled at her lower lip worriedly.

He looked down at her, a smile softening his features. "I am touched by your concern, *chérie,* but you must not dwell on such things. Fighting is a part of my life, as it is of every knight's. It has come to be second nature. Even now that I must settle down I am bound to defend what is mine against any threat. You must learn to accept the possibility that I might be killed, Brianna, and then try to forget about it. I am supported by skilled men when in battle, if that is any comfort, and"—he kissed the tip of her pert little nose—"I have no intention of getting killed now that I've attained my heart's desire."

"If you killed I—the captive," she amended hastily, "Rob—"

" 'Tis already done," he interrupted soberly.

"Oh." She pushed aside the feelings of sadness that threatened to end her new peace of mind. "But now that he's been put to death, will Rob not seek to destroy you with renewed purpose?"

Roland shrugged. "I do not know how valuable this man was to him. But if he was close to his leader, perhaps the Anglo-Saxon will seek retribution. I would welcome the challenge and wager he could easily become careless in his eagerness to avenge his man. Rob may seal his own doom."

Brianna hadn't thought of that, but hearing it from Roland made her even more apprehensive for his safety. As much as she had admired Rob and what he was doing, she had been appalled by what Ian had told her. Her loyalty to Rob had all but disappeared in light of that revelation, and her love for the man in whose arms she rested was now greater than anything else.

"But enough of this talk." He turned toward her face, his eyes locking with hers. "We have better things to do . . ."

Brianna took charge of the domestic tasks of Roland's household. Fresh rushes were laid on all the floors and sprinkled with rosemary. Tapestries were aired, and tables, benches, settles, chairs and other furniture were scrubbed and polished until they gleamed. Hearths were swept, bedding aired or washed and clothing mended or, in some instances, replaced.

Brianna made up the menu for the huge midday meal to be served the day of the wedding, for Roland had decided to invite all of Derford to share their joy. And, to Brianna's delight, Dane and Lord William were invited to attend if they could get away from London. "Do not pin your hopes on it," Roland had advised her, "for the King needs every spare man to quell the riots that are springing up north of Yorkshire." The thought was sobering, and a frisson of unease swept through Brianna at his words.

A message was also sent to the Abbess, and the joy of her presence was anticipated by both Brianna and Roland.

Two girls from the village came to help Hilde, along with the several servants Roland had brought from Normandy. Within three days all was close to readiness. Roland grumbled that Brianna had no time for him anymore and played the neglected lover to the hilt, much to Brianna's amusement. "But 'twas *your* wish that we be wed in seven days, and there is so much to be done!" she gently chided.

He presented her with several bolts of fine linen and silk. When she looked at him questioningly, he explained, "Rolfe of Dover had many treasures, sweet, and almost robbed me blind when I finally caught up with him. The cloth is for your wedding garments and anything else you may need."

Brianna was stunned by the generous gift, for silk was very costly. "Oh, Roland, you did not have to spend your gold on me like this!"

"All the gold I could ever amass means naught if you are not beside me to enjoy it, Brianna," he answered as she raised glowing eyes to his.

So, along with her new role of lady of the manor, Brianna was occupied with making a new undertunic and bliaud. She chose ivory silk for the undergarment, and the overtunic was to be a shimmering blue-green silk that matched her eyes. Nedra and Aleen came to help her one afternoon at Roland's request. Brianna was grateful for their help, to say nothing of being delighted to share her happiness with them.

"Oh, how I envy you, Brianna!" Aleen exclaimed, starry-eyed. "Lord Roland is the handsomest man in Christendom!"

Brianna smiled in complete accord. "He is also kind and generous, Aleen, or he would not have won my heart." She glanced up at Nedra questioningly. "Do . . . do the villagers think that I have betrayed them, Nedra?"

"Nay, child. Lord Roland has won their respect—however unwillingly. You are young and alone, they know, and most of them believe 'tis a good omen that Anglo-Saxon and Norman are willing to live in harmony.'' She smoothed the blue-green silk on which she was working with practiced fingers. '' 'Tis indeed a man in love who gives his bride-to-be so generous a gift.'' She looked at Brianna again, a knowing smile on her lips. ''He has loved you for a long time, Brianna, and I am happy his patience has been rewarded, for he is a good man.''

Brianna nodded thoughtfully. ''You know Gilbert's death was not his doing.''

''Did I not tell you that from the first? Your knight is too honorable a man to stoop to such barbarism.''

Brianna was relieved to hear Nedra reaffirm her belief in Roland's innocence. ''I will make him a good wife.''

''You will make him happy, Brianna, for you are so beautiful and kind,'' added Aleen with conviction. ''I wish that my brother would take an interest in someone like you.''

Nedra looked at her younger daughter with a frown.

''Edwin?'' Brianna asked in surprise.

''Nay, Walter.''

''Walter has been giving his attentions to Hilde, it seems, and we think he is heading for a broken heart,'' Nedra explained. ''That is, if he truly feels anything for her. I think rather that he is nursing a grievous hurt over you, Brianna.''

Brianna colored guiltily. ''I never intended for him—''

''Oh, I am not blaming you, child,'' the older woman hastily added. ''You have never encouraged him, but you could not prevent him from falling in love with you.''

''Well, 'tis good he realizes he cannot have Brianna,'' said Aleen. ''But I fear he has gone from the pot into the fire. If only he had chosen anyone else but *her.*''

''With Hilde's reputation for having bedded every man in Derford, I only hope he is toying with her as she is undoubtedly doing with him. She cannot be the kind of girl Walter would want for a wife.'' Nedra sighed and paused in her stitching. ''Hilde has always thought herself too grand to remain in Derford. Her father has forever doted upon her because of her beauty, and I fear she will break poor Walter's heart when someone more to her liking comes along. If he is sincere.''

''Mayhap they are only friends,'' Brianna began cautiously, trying to remember when she had seen them together. But she still felt a certain fondness for Walter, as she did for all of Kerwick's family. The next afternoon she took advantage of his presence in the compound as Roland instructed some of the young men of the village in the art of defense.

She approached him as the others were dispersing. ''Walter?'' she called hesitantly, not certain of her reception.

Walter was wiping an arm across his forehead in weariness, for it was a warm, sultry day, the kind that sapped a man's energy. He looked up at the sound of her voice, and an ugly expression crossed his features. ''Do you not have better things to do, my fine lady, in preparation for the *wedding?*''

Brianna suddenly wondered at the wisdom of confronting him. ''Hello, Walter. There is something I must tell you that . . . well, it concerns Hilde.''

An eyebrow raised in exaggerated surprise. ''Oh? Now you poke your nose into my dealings with other women? Are you jealous perhaps, Brianna?''

She felt her ire stir. ''I care not what you do with 'other women,' Walter, but Hilde plays you false.''

''Oh, she does, does she?'' He scratched his head in feigned disbelief. ''Now, how can that be, Brianna? We are just friends, so how can she play me false?''

Brianna unexpectedly felt foolish, but she was not finished. ''Well, your mother seems to think that you are involved with Hilde, and it would pain her to see you hurt, Walter. I would only tell you that Hilde has cast her eyes at Dane. In fact, she has . . .'' she trailed off, uncertain whether to tell him so much.

''Slept with him?'' he supplied. ''Oh, I do not doubt that she has coupled with every Anglo-Saxon—and Norman— within twenty leagues, Brianna, but then you have no cause to point a finger when you have been warming the bed of a certain Norman for several months now. Even when your husband was alive.''

Tears of rage blurred her vision for an instant, and Brianna wanted to slap his face. How could he have known what had happened between Roland and herself? "That is unfair, Walter,'' she began through stiff lips.

"Unfair? You have no idea of what is unfair, Brianna. Unfair is being head over heels in love with a beautiful, innocent young girl who is wed to someone else. Unfair is when that woman is freed from her vows through the death of her husband and in the next breath becomes betrothed to another man—and not only an enemy, but the murderer of her husband as well.''

"Walter, I never meant for you—''

"Spare me your weak excuses, Brianna, for in truth you are no better than Hilde.'' He looked at her then, his face flushed from anger and exertion. "I loved you more than any Norman could ever love you. When Derford was raided, I would have given my life for you—''

"But instead I killed a man to spare yours,'' she finished quietly.

He paused, the impact of her words hitting home. "So, you mean that I owe you something for saving my miserable life?''

"Nay, Walter. Only that you could be fairer to me instead of condemning me for things I have not done—or things that you do not understand.'' She stepped closer, a hand reaching out in a gesture of truce.

"Stay away from me, Brianna. You might soil your skirts.''

She stopped, her hand falling to her side in defeat. "Very well, Walter. I cannot talk to you when you are so bitter and unreasonable.'' She turned away, but his next words stopped her cold

"Rob is very disappointed in you," he said softly.

She whirled around, her face paling. "Rob?'' She glanced around hastily to ascertain if anyone else was within hearing distance. Roland was still engaged and no one else was close enough to hear what they were saying.

Walter laughed softly, and Brianna was reminded of Ian's sardonic laughter. "He seems to think that you could have done something for Ian—that you could have taken advantage of your relationship with de Beaufort to help our cause."

Her mouth dropped open. "*Our* cause? You mean you are—?"

"Don't change the subject," he jeered. "What shall I tell him, Brianna? Or would you like to tell him yourself?"

The hateful tone of his voice brought her reeling thoughts into focus. Without warning her eyes blazed. "You can tell the noble Rob that I want no part of him! That I know he had my husband slaughtered in cold blood!"

Walter frowned slightly. "What do you mean?"

"I spoke to Ian the night after he was captured, and he told me Rob had ordered him to kill Gilbert. He wanted to turn me against Roland."

He looked surprised and had no immediate response.

"But it was a waste of his efforts and a man's life as well, for I never betrayed him. I would have done anything he asked! But now I have no use for him or his methods. Do you hear me, Walter?" Her fists were clenched at her sides, her eyes narrowed in anger.

Walter recovered himself enough to say, "That is absurd. Ian could not use a bow with such skill."

"He could and he did." She straightened proudly and looked him in the eye. "So do not try to frighten me by using his name, for I am finished with Rob and his kind. I do not support a man who resorts to the murder of innocents to further his cause."

"Perhaps you *should* be frightened, Brianna."

Brianna stared at him with unconcealed scorn. "How is that, Walter?"

"He may decide to make you twice a widow."

* * *

"To Brianna—the fairest maiden in England *and* Normandy!"

Roland's resonant voice permeated every corner of the huge hall, followed by the roar of enthusiastic approbation from knight, man-at-arms and servant alike.

Brianna rose gracefully to acknowledge their homage with a brilliant smile that bedazzled all. She felt ready to burst with joy as she basked in the knowledge of Roland's love and the hearty approval of those around her.

But at the height of the din, Hilde's gray-green eyes, glittering coldly, caught her own sea-blue gaze and shattered her enveloping joy. All the fear and apprehension unleashed by Walter's warning that afternoon flooded over her again, effectively breaking the spell cast by the overwhelming response to Roland's tribute.

Hilde tossed her silky blond mane contemptuously and moved to refill the empty cups and goblets thrust toward her, leaving Brianna to deal with her trepidation.

Roland was looking at her, concern evident in his expression. "What is it, sweet?" he asked as they sat down.

Brianna let her eyes linger on the beautifully carved features that had come to mean everything to her. Nothing must happen to him—nothing! She pushed aside her anxiety with the greatest effort and conjured up a smile. "Naught, my lord Norman. Naught."

Not quite convinced, he placed a warm strong hand over the small one resting beside his empty trencher. "Two more days, my love. Two more days and we will be as one forever." His eyes darkened with desire, and Brianna felt a tingling sensation spread like wildfire from where his fingers touched hers to every part of her body.

"He doesn't know how easily I could steal your affections." Ranulf's voice jarred Brianna out of her sweet reverie.

She pulled her eyes from Roland's, laughing at his twin's bantering. "Well then, Ranulf, he had better toe the mark, or he will discover the bride has run off with another," she answered, playing along.

Ranulf looked over her dark head at his brother. "Do you hear that, Roland? There is still hope for me." He winked at Brianna over the rim of his goblet. "But there is is one thing I would know from the lovely lady."

Brianna raised a finely arched brow in expectation.

"How is it that you are always able to tell us apart? Often I have dreamed of your mistaking me for Roland, but in vain."

Brianna managed to look mildly surprised. "Surely you know the answer, having known him all these years, Ranulf."

Roland leaned to look around Brianna at his brother. "There's the answer, brother. Not only am I the better-looking but also the cleverer of the two of us for having already known it."

Ranulf shook his head in exasperation. "Come now, Brianna. Surely we look alike, do we not?"

"Of course you do, Ranulf, and you are every bit as handsome as your brother."

Ranulf's face lit up at the compliment, and Roland suddenly looked wary. "Then how can you tell us apart?" Ranulf persisted.

Her saucy reply bubbled forth before she could squelch it. "Why, 'tis Roland's arrogance that gives him away every time, Ranulf."

Ranulf threw back his head and gave a shout of laughter as Brianna innocently glanced at Roland. He took one look at the impish smile tugging at the corners of her mouth and the teasing light in her eyes, and joined in Ranulf's merriment.

" 'Tis a good thing that we go to Wexton on the morrow. Perhaps my being away for a day will make you appreciate me, wench."

The smile froze on Brianna's face.

"Do you see, Ranulf? My ruse works already . . ." His words trailed off in midsentence at Brianna's look of alarm.

"Must . . . must you go to Wexton, Roland? What if Rob is waiting for you? What if—"

"No one but Guy knows of this, *chérie*. There is no possible way Rob can accost us by design." He didn't add that returning was another matter.

"We will be back by nightfall, Brianna," Ranulf added reassuringly. "You must not worry."

But Brianna was thinking of her conversation with Walter. If he wasn't romantically involved with the sullen Hilde, was he somehow getting information from her concerning Roland's movements? Could that be the reason for their "friendship"? If it were, how could Brianna tell Roland that Walter was working for Rob? That she herself had seen and talked with him, even offering her services while under Roland's own roof? Dear God!

"Brianna?" Roland's voice brought her back. "I *forbid* you to worry yourself sick over this. I would not have told you had I known it would distress you so."

She shook her head in denial. "Nay, I am glad you told me, Roland. I must learn to have faith in your judgment and your ability to defend yourself." She gave him a bright smile. It would never do to have him preoccupied with concern for her when he would need his wits about him while traveling between Derford and Wexton.

"Roland is too 'arrogant' to allow someone like Rob to do him bodily harm," Ranulf quipped in an effort to coax Brianna out of her apprehension.

"True, brother. He must be titled and wealthy before I will let his blade touch me." He grinned at Brianna.

Later, as they stood outside her room, Roland turned Brianna toward him. He took her in his arms and kissed her lingeringly, reluctant to let her go. " 'Tis torture—a living hell, Brianna, to hold you in my arms—to taste the heady wine of your kiss, yet be unable to end it as such things were meant to end."

"I know, my love," she said breathlessly as his lips caressed her eyes, her hair, her neck, and then forced her head back to sear a path down to her breasts, the thin linen of her bliaud a poor shield before the onslaught of his burning hunger for her.

She felt the sweet, familiar languidness sweep through her until she was so weak she would not have stopped him if he chose to follow where his passion led.

His mouth sought hers once more, hovering a moment so he could murmur, "I love you, Brianna. *Mon Dieu*, how I love you! I am not whole without you, do you know that?"

Brianna began to tremble for want of him. "Yes, my Roland," she whispered in a shaky voice. "I know it now."

He suddenly clasped her to him so tightly her bones cracked. His breath was fast, labored, and she could feel his rigid staff pressed against her, vital, insistent. Her head was against his chest, and Brianna could feel the pounding of his heart as it matched the erratic beat of her own. She raised her mouth to his again, all control gone, as she sought his lips.

"Nay," he groaned, fighting his driving need. "I gave you my word—"

"It does not matter now, Roland." Her eyes, vivdly colored pools of aquamarine in the wavering torchlight, met his and communicated the urgency she no longer wished to control. "Make me yours tonight, Roland—please make me yours!"

He hesitated only a moment, searching her face for some sign that she might waver, but there was only yearning etched across her exquisitely wrought features. He swept her off her feet and carried her over the threshold, kicking the door shut behind him.

As twilight fell Ranulf strolled leisurely through the compound, enjoying the cool night breeze drifting over him like soothing fingers. He was immensely relieved that Roland and Brianna had finally come to terms with what had been obvious to him since he first came to Derford. He loved his brother very much and had always been concerned about Roland's happiness. Brianna, Ranulf thought, was everything a man could possibly want in a woman. Roland, for the first time, was deeply, irrevocably in love.

Which brought to mind another thought. He could not continue imposing on Roland indefinitely. Although Roland would have been annoyed to think his brother considered himself an imposition, Ranulf had to make his decision: a life dedicated to God or to a woman—like Brianna—and a family. Perhaps the trip to Wexton could help him decide—God knew he needed some sign, something to push him either way.

He found himself face to face with Guy de Montrain, who was leaning negligently against the doorframe of his sleeping bower, a flask of wine in one hand, a cup in the other.

"A perfect way to end the evening, Ranulf," the knight commented before raising the tumbler to his lips.

"I prefer to walk. Sometimes 'tis equally soothing as the wine," Ranulf replied, his smile all but indiscernible in the deep purple shadows.

Guy grunted. "But what else can equal a cup of good spirits and a woman to warm your bed? They are a fine ending for a full day, you must agree—or are you already practicing your vow of celibacy?" he asked half in jest.

Ranulf glanced up at Brianna's window, then back to his friend. "Nay, de Montrain. I have not taken any such vow as yet. I just have not found a woman to my liking here."

"Except Brianna," Guy added. "We are all smitten with her." His voice was wistful.

"Aye, and so we are. Roland will always have to contend with admirers of his wife-to-be, for she is an angel."

"Well, friend, I'll not be alone this night." He took another drink of wine and wiped his mouth on the back of his hand. "Then again, I do not have so danger-fraught a day before me as to need a full night's rest. Have a care, *mon ami.*"

Ranulf nodded his acknowledgment and then smiled as

Hilde appeared at the door of the hall, her pale hair flying as she stepped outside and hurried toward them. "She seems eager enough," he chuckled as she slowed to a more sedate pace upon seeing Ranulf.

"Good eventide, my lord," she said airily to him, not at all embarrassed by his presence.

" 'Tis indeed a good evening, Hilde. Sleep well, you two." And he moved toward the hall, a rueful smile on his chiseled lips.

CHAPTER 20

In the early-morning light, swirling tendrils of white mist reached over the road from the dense English forest. The ghostly vapors clung to the two mounted figures like a hazy shroud from some maleficent miasma. Roland shivered unconsciously. He raised his eyes to search for some break in the fog as the still-weak sun tried unsuccessfully to burn through the mantle of cloud.

"Damn this cursed land with its fog and dampness!" he muttered under his breath.

Ranulf looked over at his brother, a smile playing upon his lips. "What's this I hear? Have you had a change of heart since I took you from the sweet company of your betrothed? Did I hear you damn your new home?"

Roland's eyes strained to penetrate the clinging mists. "Aye, so you did. How can you fight that which you cannot see? I do not like this, Ranulf. That insidious coward would have the perfect cover were he to attack."

"Ah, but your mind must still be on the incomparable Brianna," Ranulf chided, "for you have not also considered the fact that since the visibility is poor, any would-be adversary would be foolish to make a move under the conditions."

Roland ceased his frowning contemplation of the dense curtain that obscured their surroundings. He glanced at his twin. "All right, Ranulf. But I would feel much better if we were wearing our mail."

"We would be soaked to the skin in this heat and humidity.

Come now, Roland, why would he be waiting in the woods now? If he did not know of our plans—''

"How do you know he didn't know of this?" Roland interrupted.

Ranulf frowned thoughtfully. "Well, Guy is your man. He would die before he would betray you. As for Brianna—'' He shook his head. "Rob could not possibly know. I believe we are safe as long as the fog holds.''

They rode in silence for a while.

"Anyone could have overheard me the night I offered Wexton to you," Roland said suddenly.

"Aye, but who would ever guess you would leave for there—or anywhere else—on the day before you are to be wed? And why this route? Why not north or west?''

"North or west does not lead to Wexton.''

Ranulf rolled his eyes heavenward. "Shall we turn back?''

Roland shot him a quelling look. "Do not be ridiculous. Skulk back to the manor within an hour of our departure? They'd laugh us back to Normandy.''

Ranulf coughed to hide a smile behind his hand.

"I am not afraid, Ranulf. You know me better than that.'' He glanced at his brother again. "And wipe that patronizing look from your face! Your problem is that you believe yourself protected from all harm by God. But remember, you are not a saint . . . yet.'' He rubbed the thin scar along the side of his jawbone, his expression suddenly intent. "It's just that—''

Odo tossed his head skittishly, fighting for a moment Roland's tight rein. "Easy, boy.'' He patted the great destrier's neck. "You see? Even Odo does not like this. My every instinct calls out in warning.''

Ranulf was about to comment when he had a disturbing thought. Guy de Montrain had spent at least part of the night in Hilde's company. Suppose that after drinking all the wine in that flask, his tongue had loosened enough to drop some hint, however unintentionally, to Hilde . . . No! He shook his head slightly, as if to rid himself of such a notion. Why would Hilde ever pick up on such a thing? Hilde working for Rob? Absurd. The girl was too preoccupied with herself and her pleasures to ever—

Roland's snow-white stallion abruptly brought up his head, eyes rolling in alarm. Roland spoke reassuringly to the agitated animal as it pranced sideways, and drew up the slackened reins. But the well-trained war-horse did not respond. He rose up onto his hind legs, front hooves frenziedly thrashing the air in front of him as Roland fought to gain control. Then Ranulf's own mount shied away from the side of the road as his brother's voice carried across the widening breach between them, "It seems you were wrong, Ranulf!"

In that instant an arrow shot through the mist, whizzing past the exact spot where Roland had been. It nipped one of the destrier's forelegs, the blood a startling contrast to the pristine color of the animal's hair. Another flew from Ranulf's side of the road but, because of the erratic movements of his dun-colored mount, failed to find its target.

Roland succeeded in curbing Odo, and the brothers moved closer spontaneously to mount their defense.

"Do we outrun them?" Ranulf shouted, knowing in advance what his brother's answer would be.

"And die of a broken neck in this godforsaken fog?" Roland demanded, drawing his sword.

Just in time, for at least a dozen faces appeared out of the mist, surrounding them. None were on horseback, but they brandished makeshift or stolen weapons menacingly.

The brothers met their attackers with skillful, unerring thrusts and parries that were no match for the men on foot. Their battle-toughened war-horses lashed out with bared teeth and lethal hooves, their excitement fanned by the smell of blood drawn by both sides alike. The minutes slipped by, only the grunt of a man, the whinny of a horse, the clang of a sword shattering the morning stillness with wrenching clarity.

Then Roland stopped an Anglo-Saxon sword with his left

leg and pain tore through him, threatening to engulf him in its red haze. He repaid the owner of the offending weapon with a downward stroke of his own, the resounding scream evidence of his deadly accuracy. Then out of the corner of his eye he saw a crude lance come up toward his right side and, arcing his blade over in that direction, he severed the arm from the shoulder of his attacker. The man's shrieks rent the air, but Roland was oblivious to them as his eyes shot to his brother just as a powerful-looking Anglo-Saxon buried his sword edge in Ranulf's horse's neck, effectively bringing the stunned animal to its knees, blood spurting everywhere, and leaving Ranulf open to the next sweep of the wicked-looking blade.

In an instant, Roland called into action all his skill and every reserve of strength as he leaned over to the right, his weapon slicing sideways to meet the Anglo-Saxon's in a shower of sparks. Their eyes met briefly, stormy gray knifing into deep chestnut, and Roland knew instinctively this was Rob himself.

Ranulf had leaped clear of the dying horse, only to be set upon by four more assailants. His grunt of pain penetrated Roland's intense concentration and he pulled back his sword from its macabre stalemate to go to his brother's aid.

Too late. Ranulf was lying on the ground, unconscious, blood staining his light-colored tunic in an obscene pattern. Roland went wild at the sight of his fallen sibling, driving Odo over the dead destrier, swinging indiscriminately at the remaining men around him, his strokes guided by instinct, finely honed senses and, finally, by blind fury.

The raiders were driven back into the mists from whence they came, and although Roland's mad grief threatened to cloud his reason and judgment, he did not pursue them, refusing to be drawn away from his injured brother. He waited until they had disappeared, fighting to bring the frenzied Odo under control. Bodies littered the road, and Roland estimated he and Ranulf had reduced their attackers' number by more than half. But it was little consolation as he slid down to the ground, oblivous to the heavy breathing of the still-agitated charger and the fierce pain in his leg. All else faded into insignificance as he knelt beside the pale, inert Ranulf.

"Ranulf?" he croaked softly, his throat raw from repeated renderings of his battle cry. He put his head to his brother's chest, bloodying the ends of his tawny hair as they touched the crimson puddle over Ranulf's right shoulder. A faint pulse greeted his ear. Thank God he was still alive!

All was quiet, unnaturally still. Roland wiped the sweat from his forehead with one arm and collected his thoughts as his eyes returned to Ranulf's face.

He quickly stripped off his clinging tunic and, folding it a few times, packed Ranulf's wound. Tearing the bottom of Ranulf's shirt into several strips, he secured a makeshift bandage in place, and prayed it would stanch the bleeding.

Just as he tied the last knot, Ranulf slowly opened his eyes, much to Roland's relief. His mouth moved but no sound came forth.

"Save it, *mon frère*. Let's get you home and out of harm's way, then you can regale me with your routing of the Anglo-Saxons." He managed a forced smile.

"You . . . you cannot fool me," Ranulf managed. "I fear I am mortally . . . wounded—"

"Nay!" Roland cut him off angrily. " 'Tis only a shoulder injury."

"A wound to the shoulder would not . . . feel like a blade twisting in the . . . chest every time I draw breath. It . . . seems you were right and Wexton will have to wait."

"We will get you to Wexton soon enough," Roland answered, but his eyes were moist. "Can you sit up?" He braced his brother from behind with a powerful right arm, but the effort made Ranulf grimace in pain.

"Leave me, Roland," he rasped. "I will never make it to Derford. I will only . . . slow you down and . . . what if they come after you again?"

"Be silent, Ranulf, and save your strength."

"You . . . you cannot defend yourself with me to burden you—" He broke off, exhausted from his exertions.

Roland ignored his last comment and looked around for Odo. The great destrier was standing ten paces away, his sides still heaving. Roland gave a low whistle, and the stallion moved toward them.

"Come, Ranulf, you must try to get up."

Ranulf's eyes opened and focused on the huge white horse. "Surely . . . surely you jest, Roland. I may be able to stand with your help, but I will never be able to climb up on his back."

"Damn you, Ranulf! You will mount him—you *must!*" And he applied all his remaining strength toward getting his brother to his feet, trying to ignore the stabbing pain in his own leg. Ranulf moaned and Roland feared he would faint. "Easy, brother. Just a little more . . ." And then they were up.

"Now, you must step on my knee—"

"I cannot," Ranulf whispered

"You can! You can pass out after you mount Odo, for I will keep you secure. But now you must use every bit of strength you can summon, or we will never get to Derford alive. Do you hear me?"

Ranulf's answer was to lift a leg to step onto Roland's good knee and, with another groan of pain, he gripped the saddle. His strength gave out as he swung himself onto the animal and, overwhelmed by the excruciating pain, he slumped forward against the destrier's neck.

"Good boy." Roland patted the horse. He toyed with the idea of mounting from the other side but quickly decided against it. Ranulf was balanced precariously against Odo's neck. If he startled the animal by mounting from its right side, Ranulf would topple off. So, teeth gritted, he put his left foot in the stirrup and swung up behind his unconscious twin.

The world spun dizzily for a moment as the gash in his leg screamed in protest. But Ranulf was still in place. Drawing deep gulps of air to steady himself, Roland glanced around once more.

The dun lay in its own pool of blood, flies swarming over its slashed throat. Eight bodies were visible in the dispersing haze over the dirt road, all very still. Ranulf's sword lay on the ground as well. Roland, however, knew it was not worth the risk to retrieve it. He carefully guided Odo around toward Derford, his left hand holding Ranulf steady. It was just as well he had passed out, Roland thought. The pain from being bounced and jolted on the ride back would have been unbearable. As it was, his own wound throbbed anew with every step of the horse. He felt incredibly weary now that the skirmish was over. His sword arm ached, and he soon discovered a host of other discomforts.

Not the least important thing on his mind was the fact that they were easy prey if Rob should decide to attack again. He could summon up enough strength to use his sword, but Ranulf's life would be sacrificed in the fray. Perhaps God *was* watching over Ranulf, he thought wearily as they painstakingly headed toward Derford, for it was nothing short of a miracle that they were so far unmolested.

Roland finally allowed his thoughts to drift elsewhere. Brianna. Woman of strength. *His* woman of strength. She would know what to do. She would help Ranulf. She had to— for Roland was as close to his brother as one man could be to another.

Brianna.

Holding her name before him like a talisman, he made his way home.

"Reverend Mother!" Brianna exclaimed joyously. She turned from her window and flew down the stairs and through the hall to emerge from the manor, one hand shading her eyes from the bright morning sun.

The Abbess, flanked by Roger and Beorn, paused just inside the gate. Then she saw Brianna running toward her, and her face lit up. She prodded her docile pony and moved forward to meet the girl. Beorn hurried to assist her as she dismounted.

"Reverend Mother, you came!" Brianna said happily, embracing the Abbess.

"Of course I did, Brianna. How could you ever have doubted?"

Brianna laughed from sheer jubilation and then sobered abruptly. "Why . . . why, I *did* have my doubts, Reverend Mother, that you would approve of my marriage so soon after Gilbert's death. And to a Norman."

The nun put her arm about Brianna's shoulders and started toward the manor. "Father Simon wrote of your grief and your belief that Lord Roland was responsible. The good priest believed that time would prove you wrong and hoped you would eventually discover the truth."

"I did, Reverend Mother. I know now that Roland would never have done such a thing. And I did—I still do—mourn my loss." A shadow of sadness passed over her exquisite features, but nothing could mar her newfound happiness for long.

"Gilbert would never have begrudged you happiness, child, and you were very good to him."

Brianna sighed softly and ushered the Abbess to Gilbert's former room. "Will you have some wine? The midday meal will be served soon, unless you would—"

"I am fine, Brianna, thank you. Stay with me while I wash the grit from my hands and face. There is no breeze, and every bit of dust and grime kicked up by my pony seemed to settle on me." She walked to the basin of water and rinsed her face and hands. As she dried them she turned to Brianna. "So, tell me, where is your Roland?"

Brianna's dark brows drew together. "He and Ranulf went to Wexton after breaking the fast. They should return this afternoon."

Abbess Marie studied Brianna thoughtfully. "What is bothering you, child?'' she asked gently as she sat down beside her, one warm hand covering hers.

Brianna bit her lip. "I cannot shake the feeling that something has befallen them. I—'' She was about to divulge her past dealings with Rob, but something held her back. Instead, she related Ian's capture and death, omitting her confrontation with him.

"So you believe this Rob will seek to avenge his man's death?''

Brianna nodded, her eyes straying to the gold crucifix the nun wore on a chain around her neck. "They wore no armor and went unescorted.''

"Surely you know God's protection is more effective than anything contrived by man, Brianna. You must have faith.''

"And what if God is protecting Rob?'' Brianna retorted before she could stop the impulsive words.

The older woman sighed. "You have learned cynicism, I see.''

"No, Reverend Mother. I am sorry, but loving a Norman makes me wonder about many things. I do not doubt that God is with him, but I am afraid that I may be unable to accept what He has decreed for Roland. Oh, I love him so! To lose him now would be more than I could bear.''

The nun put a comforting arm around Brianna. "Nothing will happen to him, child. He will return to you safely and all will be well, you must believe that.''

Brianna smiled, feeling better after the Abbess' reassuring words. "You must lie down until we eat, Reverend Mother. You are probably tired, and I have worn you out still further, chattering about Roland.''

"Nonsense. I am so glad to see you that I hardly feel the strain of the journey. And Walshire is not so far away.'' She changed the subject. "What of the wedding preparations? What will you wear?''

"Just wait till you see!'' Brianna jumped up and disappeared through the connecting door. The Abbess followed to find her kneeling before a wooden chest at the foot of her bed. "Roland gave me some lovely silk—look!" She held up the shimmering blue-green garment.

"It's lovely." Just as the Abbess reached out to touch the fine bliaud, the sound of a horse being ridden into the yard drifted through the unshuttered window.

Brianna froze, then dropped the overtunic and rushed over to the window. One of Roland's men was below, speaking agitatedly to Beorn and Roger. He glanced up just as she espied him. The look on his face told all.

"Vachel and René are bringing them home. They are both of them wounded—Ranulf is unconscious," the man called up to her.

Brianna's hand came up over her mouth. "No," she whispered, and her eyes went to the Abbess.

"We must be prepared when they arrive. Where are your medicines?" she asked with the brusqueness of one accustomed to taking command.

Brianna pointed to a small chest on a table. "If you need anything else, ask Hilde—"

The girl appeared at the door as if conjured up. "You have heard?" she asked in a tone that hinted at triumph.

"Aye. See that Reverend Mother gets whatever she needs, Hilde." And at last she was mobilized into action, hurrying from the room.

Roland! Ranulf! Hurt! Dear God, she had been right! Grisly images flashed through her mind as she raced through the hall and across the yard to the road. Beorn and Roger had just ridden away with the third man, the dust kicked up by their mounts lingering heavily in the sultry August air.

She stood indecisively in the road, feeling helplessly inadequate, and finally went back to the hall to help the Abbess.

Brianna was in a daze as she and Hilde heated water and tore strips of clean linen for bandages. She methodically went through the motions, aware of only the somber litany of doom—*They are wounded—wounded—wounded*—sounding over and over again in her mind.

A shout went up from outside, and Brianna heard her name being called. Before the guard could reach the door, she was on the threshold, her heart in her mouth. She stood rooted to the spot as Vachel came through the entrance first, his face grim. Behind him rode René de Falaise, abreast of Roland's snow-white stallion, its coat glistening with sweat and spattered with blood.

Brianna's stomach lurched as her eyes settled upon the two men atop the destrier, one slumped forward against the animal's neck. Roland's face was flushed, whether from the heat or his recent exertions it was impossible to tell. He, too, was covered with dirt and gore; his overtunic was gone and his lightweight chainse clung to his body.

As Brianna approached Odo she saw Roland's blood-soaked breeches. She swallowed hard, fighting the nausea that washed over her, leaving her light-headed.

"Steady, child." The Abbess' soothing voice penetrated her befogged mind. "You must be strong for them." And she moved forward with Brianna.

"Brianna—" Roland's hoarse word sounded like a plea. "Ranulf—We must help Ranulf—" He broke off, unable to continue as Brianna searched in vain for words of comfort.

He dismounted, staggering into Beorn, who caught and supported him. Ignoring his own injury, he limped to his brother's inert body, reaching to take him down.

"Leave him, Roland," said René. "We will do it." Vachel helped the knight ease the unconscious Ranulf from Odo's back.

Brianna felt the bile rise in the back of her throat once more as she took in the horse's crimson-streaked neck. She closed her eyes fleetingly, willing the giddiness to subside. "See to Lord Roland, Brianna," Abbess Marie instructed curtly, and she motioned for the two men holding Ranulf to follow her into the hall.

The nun's words moved her to action and she quickly followed Roland and Beorn to his room.

Once Roland was laid out on the bed, Brianna set to work. She cut away the leg of his breeches to see what damage had been done.

"The man had an ill-kept weapon, fortunately for me. The blade was dull, or it would have sliced through to the bone," Roland observed quietly.

"Then it may have been rusted," Brianna answered, a worried frown marring her smooth brow.

Roland sighed tiredly. "It bled freely enough to wash itself clean. Just be quick about it, Brianna. I must see Ranulf."

"But you need to rest, Roland. Let me wash the grime from you and—"

He impatiently waved her into silence. "That can wait, woman. Enough of your useless fussing! My brother may be dying!"

She nodded her acquiescence, the tears coursing down her cheek betraying her reaction to his terse command. Gentle fingers lifted her chin, forcing her eyes to meet his. "I'm sorry, my sweet Brianna." His gray eyes were infinitely tender for a lingering moment. "I love you more than life itself, but I love Ranulf deeply as well."

Brianna kissed him softly on the mouth, then reluctantly stood and moved to the hearth for hot water. She returned to the bed and wound a strip of linen around the top of his thigh, pulling it tight to halt the lazy trickle of blood still leaking from the wound. "How could Rob ever have known you were going to Wexton?"

"Obviously we have an informer in our midst."

Brianna felt so overwhelmed with remorse she had difficulty performing the task at hand. "What . . . happened to Ranulf?" she asked in a shaky voice.

Roland's fists clenched at his side. "Rob himself felled the dun before I could reach Ranulf." He raked fingers through curling, sandy hair in visible agitation. "He cannot die!"

Brianna's eyes met his, her distress dwarfed by the naked anguish in the smoky depths of his. "Reverend Mother is renowned for her skills," she reassured him. "You must have faith, Roland."

CHAPTER 21

"He has lost much blood and now he is weak. If he had been tended sooner . . ."

Roland's look turned bleak and he slammed a fist into his palm in frustration. "If he dies, I will be to blame! Damn!"

Ignoring his profanity, the Abbess continued, "No one can take any blame except the man who drove the weapon through his shoulder."

"But surely he will not perish from so clean a wound?" Brianna questioned, her heart aching for Roland as well as his brother.

It was early evening and they were in Roland's room. Brianna sat on the edge of the bed, as if she would prevent Roland from jumping to his feet and returning to Ranulf's side. The Abbess was seated on a straight-backed chair nearby.

"The wound is clean, that much is true, but he has lost a great deal of blood. And there is always the danger of putrefaction. He is so weak that I do not know how well his body would be able to fight it off."

Roland closed his eyes in frustration. Only the hiss of the torches broke the heavy silence that seemed to press down on the three people. "If only I knew who betrayed us! What snake in the grass do we harbor, I wonder."

"If you can apprehend Rob, mayhap you will discover who the traitor is," Brianna offered, wondering if she were condoning the punishment of Hilde or Walter, for surely they would be implicated.

"Perhaps," Roland agreed. "I will tear him from limb to limb, the sniveling coward! To fight and retreat to safety like an ignorant peasant!"

Brianna put a hand over his, but it was the Abbess who spoke. "You will do naught until you are healed, Lord Roland. First you must recover yourself and then help us bring your brother through this alive. Now I must return to Lord Ranulf. I suggest you try to sleep—" Roland threw her a disbelieving look. "You will do your brother more good by recovering quickly yourself."

When she had gone, Roland pulled Brianna against his chest tightly. "Stay with me, my love—I need you so."

Brianna settled within the circle of his arms, enjoying the soothing sound of his steady heartbeat.

"We cannot be married tomorrow, Brianna, you know that."

Her muffled "aye" assured him she understood.

They sat in silence for long moments, reveling in the feel of one another. Brianna raised her face to see his expression and encountered warm, firm lips. A tingle went down her spine, and as he caressed her mouth with his, all else seemed to fade into obscurity.

When at last he drew away, Brianna sought to reassure him. "Reverend Mother and I will do everything humanly possible, Roland. Please believe that and have faith."

He stroked her hair and let his hand wander down to her back. "Oh, but I do have faith, sweet Brianna. You have restored my faith in many things, and I am the most blessed of men. But most of all, I have faith in *you*—in all you are to me and to everyone around you. And in your love. I would be a shell of a man without you, my Brianna, my woman of strength. Love me always, or I shall surely cease to be."

Brianna rose reluctantly, and he did not try to stop her. "You look so tired, Roland. Why don't you take Reverend Mother's advice and sleep? I give you my word that I will wake you if there is any change in Ranulf."

He nodded soberly in agreement. "Be sure you do, Brianna, for he is very dear to me."

Ranulf looked pale; his shoulder and half of his chest were swathed in bandages. He had regained consciousness once, but had refused the watered wine Abbess Marie had offered. Brianna brushed back his hair from his forehead, noting the warmth of his skin.

The Abbess said, in a hushed voice, "I did not speak of this in Lord Roland's presence, but had the spear been a hairsbreadth to the right, it would have pierced his lung."

Brianna glanced up, her hand still on Ranulf's forehead. "I am glad you said nothing. He is worried enough as it is."

The Abbess nodded and checked the pad of linen immediately over the wound. "His skin feels fevered, but I suspect 'tis only from loss of fluid." She glanced at Brianna. "Why don't you go down and eat something? There is nothing more to do for now."

Brianna shook her head. "Oh, Reverend Mother, he cannot die." Her words were a mere whisper of sound.

"That . . . that is unlikely, as . . . I am not prepared to leave this world yet." Ranulf's words were soft and said with an effort, but both women heard them clearly. His eyes fluttered open, and Brianna could have wept with relief.

"Oh, Ranulf, you must not speak. Try to save your strength," she begged with tears in her eyes.

He tried to smile but could do little more than grimace. "For what must I save it?" he asked, ignoring her plea. "Unless you mean for the trip . . . to Wexton, for I intend to return—" He fell silent, exhausted, before he could finish. Soon he was asleep again.

"He has not lost his sense of humor," the Abbess observed, and Brianna smiled through her tears.

Lightning lit the sky, and a peal of thunder shook the hall hard on its heels. Brianna shivered as she stared at Roland's twin. She prayed the ominous play of the elements did not portend disaster.

The Abbess had persuaded her to get something to eat, so Brianna had left the good nun with Ranulf. Passing Roland's room, she was drawn to it as if by a magnet. Quietly approaching the bed, Brianna found he had given in to his exhausted body's need for rest.

How she loved him! The past days and nights were etched upon her memory forever, and her love for him was an indelible part of her now. She longed to take him in her arms and soothe away the lines of tension that had not eased in slumber—to tell him that Ranulf would be well soon, that Rob would trouble him no more, that everything would be fine. Only she would be lying, for Ranulf was far from out of danger, Rob was still as dangerous a threat as ever and nothing had been resolved. And she, Brianna, had lied to him on more than one occasion.

She pulled a light cover over his sleeping form and turned away. Closing the door quietly so he would not be disturbed, she made her way down the stairs.

She had to tell Roland about her involvement with Rob, and soon, for the longer she kept silent the more enmeshed she became in her own deceit. Could she convince him she had not been in contact with Rob since Gilbert's death? That she had never truly done anything but talk to the man? It seemed unlikely, for despite Dane's words she found it difficult to believe Roland could forgive her for *this*.

A brief interlude of stillness interrupted the approaching summer storm, and the hot, heavy air seemed more relentless than ever. Ranulf moved slightly, and Brianna was out of her chair and at his side.

"What is it, Brianna?"

Brianna chewed her lip thoughtfully in answer to the nun's question as she stared at Roland's twin. Why not tell her now?

"It is not like you to keep things from me. I sense there is something else bothering you."

Brianna walked around the bed and sat down at the Abbess' feet, much as she had done as a child at Walshire when she wanted to pour her heart out to the woman she regarded as a mother.

"Oh, Reverend Mother. Nothing is simple anymore—like things were at Walshire." She hugged her knees and rested her chin upon them.

"No, indeed, Brianna. You are no longer a child, and you must deal with the harsh realities outside the convent walls."

Brianna sighed resignedly and glanced around at Ranulf.

"He is asleep, sweet. Unburden yourself to me."

Brianna's troubled blue-green eyes met the older woman's dark gaze. "I have been in contact with . . . with the man known as Rob."

If she had expected a reaction from the nun, she was rewarded only with a complacent nod. "You may not seem surprised because we are both Anglo-Saxon, but do you know what it would do to Roland if he knew?"

"But you are to marry him. Surely you have ceased your activities."

She nodded dully. "Aye, but I fear he will not forgive me this. I lied to him once, so how will he be able to believe me when I claim my innocence in this latest act of treachery? Roland believes Rob was alerted by someone here in the manor—and with good reason."

A low, distant rumbling once more heralded the approach of the storm.

"Roland knows you are honest and well intentioned, Brianna. And you are certainly not given to such perfidious behavior under normal circumstances. How can he blame you for doing what you thought was right at the time?"

Brianna shook her head, her glistening tears betraying her inner turmoil. "But I saw and spoke to Rob! I even sought him out on one occasion to offer my services! Would that not make me a traitress in Roland's eyes?''

The Abbess was silent, as if she were weighing her next words. And into the brief silence brutally condemning words fell like heavy stones. ''And if my brother dies, that will make you a *murderess* as well.''

Brianna's heart caught in her mouth. Her eyes went to the partly open door and froze. Roland stood in the doorway, his countenance a terrible mask of disbelief and wrath. Just then, nature, with her capricious sense of timing, sent a silver tracing of lightning across the heavens that starkly illuminated the torchlit room, giving his features a demonic cast.

Never had Brianna seen such black rage, and never had such a cold dread seized her heart in its frigid clutches.

Abbess Marie spoke first. ''Lord Roland, when you hear her out, you will discover—''

''That she played me for the biggest fool in England.''

The Abbess stood and faced him, a protective shield between Brianna and his cold fury. ''I suggest you calm down before you speak to her further. I know Brianna better than you, my lord, and she is no murderess, nor has she played you false.''

''Wa-water . . .''

Ranulf's groan cut through the tension like a sword blade, and Brianna was the first to react. Jumping to her feet, she reached for the pitcher of water on the table beside the bed.

''Don't touch him!''

Brianna started so violently she dropped the vessel with a clatter. She turned to Roland in astonishment. ''But he asked for water!''

''I will do it, child. Go talk to him,'' the Abbess said under her breath.

Brianna moved away from the bed in a daze and turned toward Roland. She recoiled from the look in his eyes as he stared at her in undisguised contempt. Her cheeks flamed in confusion, which sealed her fate in the eyes of her accuser.

"What . . . what shall I do?" she asked uncertainly.

"Tear yourself from my heart and my mind, witch, for you have played the game too well."

Brianna looked back at Abbess Marie bending over Ranulf and turned to Roland in appeal. "I wish . . . I wish to speak to you alone, Roland—"

How could he regard her so . . . so coldly? As if he were someone she had never seen before? Had he locked their shared intimacies in the vault of his memory forever? No—!

"Roland?"

"I must see to Ranulf." He limped forward, blood staining the wrapping on his thigh. "We have naught to say. Go to your chamber—anywhere!—but do not foul this room with your presence any longer."

Brianna stared out into the inky blackness that was punctuated by the crashing thunder, the shrieking wind and pelting rain and jagged streaks of lightning. The cacophony echoed her turbulent thoughts.

She had anticipated the worst, and it had come to pass. The look on Roland's face confirmed it. How was she ever to justify her actions before his cold, derisive anger? Everyone had subtly attempted to point out the wisdom of cooperation— the increasingly obvious fact that Roland de Beaufort was not an unfeeling mercenary come to milk Derford and its inhabitants of their meager resources.

But no. She had fought him to the point of betrayal—until the truth regarding Gilbert's death revealed the folly of her actions. And now both Roland and Ranulf had been injured— Ranulf possibly fatally—by a man whose methods were desperate and dishonorable. Where a wise leader would have been seeking peaceful methods to ensure the survival of his people in spite of the Norman yoke, Rob had been sacrificing English lives in vain. And she had been—for a brief time—his eager accomplice.

* * *

The wind blew cool droplets of rain onto Brianna's flushed face—a refreshing change from the hot stuffiness in Roland's chamber. She was awaiting his return, despite the unwelcome reception she knew she would receive. *Do not ever regret your desire to free England from the Normans,* her conscience whispered, *for only a fool would relinquish his heritage without a qualm.*

The sound of heavy footsteps in the hallway brought Brianna out of her troubled preoccupation. Roland was lithe as a cat—whose approach could this weighted tread herald? she wondered fleetingly as she turned from the window.

Leaning against the doorframe was none other than Roland. Brianna was shocked by the drawn, defeated cast of his countenance. He seemed to have aged a score of years.

Forgetting her trepidation, Brianna automatically started toward him. "Roland!" she exclaimed softly.

At the sound of her voice, his head jerked up sharply, revealing a revulsion in his eyes that made Brianna's blood run cold. "By what right do you invade the privacy of my bedchamber, woman?"

"By . . . by the rights possessed of your betrothed!" she retorted in self-defense.

He pushed away from the door and limped toward his bed. "I release you from the betrothal, Brianna. Hell will freeze over before I will ever grant you any rights again." He reached for a flask of wine and poured some into a cup on the side of the table.

Brianna bristled at the harsh, rude tone of his words, her fear and despair momentarily pushed aside. She moved toward him purposefully, determined he should hear her out.

"Stay away from me!" He slammed the tumbler down after a long draught and looked at her through eyes heavy-lidded and red-rimmed from fatigue. "So, 'twas *you!*" he exclaimed softly, bitterness threading his words.

Brianna had halted a few paces from him at his terse command. "It was not I!" she countered. "I swear before God I did not betray you!"

His eyes narrowed dangerously. "Are you not done with lying, Brianna? Or do words of deception come as easily to you as your wantonness in bed?"

She was stung by the calculated cruelty of his words, not knowing it was his only defense against the fact she still aroused him, despite his anger and disillusionment. Her face turned scarlet. "I . . . I have not lied to you since Gilbert's death," she protested.

His voice turned deceptively soft. "Then why did you insist on seeing the man we had captured? You acted as if you didn't know him. If you hadn't lied to me since Gilbert's murder, why were you so eager to see him? To obtain his release? Why were you so concerned about a stranger?"

Brianna suddenly recognized the horrible web of deceit she had unwittingly woven around herself. Not only had she failed to reveal her acquaintance with Ian, but she had declared that her belief in Roland's innocence had stemmed from conversations with Dane and Lord William—even from her own growing love for Roland. And try as she might, she could only succeed in tightening the web in her efforts to explain her actions. Dear God!

"I knew Ian," she whispered, "and he was the one who revealed Rob's part in Gilbert's death."

Blind fury clouding his reasoning, Roland never stopped to think that Brianna would have had little reason to continue supporting the man responsible for her husband's death. He was on his feet in a blur of motion, ignoring the dull throbbing in his thigh. He grabbed her upper arm in a viselike grip. "I ought to kill you for your duplicity, wench, do you know that?" he grated. She nodded miserably, thinking he referred to her deception involving Ian. Her soft sobs were barely audible against the increasing fury of the storm outside. "Look at me!" he snarled.

Brianna forced her chin up and her eyes met his. Roland

felt his control slip as he gazed into those luminous blue-green
pools. He flung her away before he could succumb to the
traitorous yearning within him and moved to the table to retrieve the cup of wine with trembling hands. "You even have
my poor brother beguiled until he seeks one just like you in
Wexton, throwing his lifelong desire to serve God to the
winds! He thinks you are an angel!" He remained with his
back to her and threw back his head and laughed sardonically.
"And Dane— What fools you must think us Normans! All of
us down to my pages are besotted with you! Surely you are
proud of your accomplishments, my fine, convent-bred sor-
ceress! And I—I am the *king* of lovestruck imbeciles! I could
not tear my eyes from you at Hastings, even with death and
destruction all around me. You cast your spell upon fertile
ground when you sought to captivate Roland de Beaufort with
your clever combination of meekness and defiance. Even William of Normandy saw my attraction to you and used it to get
me to remain in England despite my reluctance."

Brianna glanced up at him warily. He was in a dangerous
mood, and the more he spoke, the more volatile he became.

"Aye, Brianna—I was maneuvered into ruling the lands
taken from the man who saved my life. And *you* were the
bait. You with your incredible eyes and inviting lips, your
beckoning blue-black hair. Nothing else on this earth could
have succeeded in luring me here, and William sensed that."
He paused and emptied the cup, his back still to her as he
continued to speak with bitter eloquence. "And I followed
you to Wessex, exactly as William hoped. Finding you once
again, defending that poor crippled shell of a boy in the mud-
slick road, I knew I would have no peace until you were
mine."

"Roland—Roland, despite what you think, I did not
seek to—" Brianna began earnestly.

He whirled around to face her, his white face evidence of
the agony the movement cost him. "Spare me, witch. I have
had enough of your falsehoods. Whatever your reasons, you

succeeded admirably in making an idiot of me. But that pales in importance compared to what happens to Ranulf. If Ranulf dies, you will wish you had died with him, Brianna. Do you hear me? *You will wish you had died also!*''

Brianna moved toward the door like a wooden puppet and disappeared through it without another word.

Roland stared at the heavy oaken portal for long moments, tears wetting his cheeks. Tears of exhaustion, anger, bitter disillusionment. Tears for his brother. Tears for the part of him that had died with Brianna's admission of guilt.

CHAPTER 22

Sheets of rain cascaded from leaden-gray skies. Dane's long strides took him through the steady downpour to the tiny stone church across the compound. Instinctively he knew Brianna would be there.

She was kneeling before the simple altar, her head covered and bowed. She was alone and Dane slowly approached her, hesitant to disturb her prayers. He stopped a few paces behind her, and she raised her head, sensing another's presence.

"Brianna?" he queried softly.

She rose to her feet at the sound of his voice, whirled around and threw herself into his arms. "Dane! Oh, Dane, I am so glad you have come! Ranulf is sorely wounded and Roland—" She began to cry softly, her head against his chest.

"Hush, *ma petite*. It is not so bad as that yet." He held her to him protectively, as if he would shield her from further unhappiness.

Brianna was hard put to push away from him; she felt as if she had found something solid to grasp in a quagmire of troubles. When she did look up at him, she could only barely make out his darkly handsome features in the dim surroundings. "Did you just arrive, Dane? Where is Lord William?"

He wiped a tear from her smooth cheek. "Father is in the north with the King. I was asked to remain in London in their absence, but nothing could prevent me from attending your marriage to Roland, sweet."

"There will be no wedding," she said dully.

"There will be no wedding this day, Brianna, but in time my proud friend will realize his mistake."

"You spoke to him?"

"Aye, I've been with him this past hour, and I do not believe for a moment that you betrayed them."

"Oh, Dane," she sighed despairingly. "Never have I seen him like this. Not even when he has been angered in the past."

He put an arm around her shoulders and steered her in the direction of the door. "Roland is under the burden of thinking that the woman he worships is responsible for his brother's brush with death. Tell me what happened, Brianna."

They stood looking out at the dull, wet morning from the shelter of the cool stone sanctuary. "It was my habit to dress as a lad, as you know, when you first came to Derford."

A hint of a smile threatened his sober expression. "I remember it well."

Brianna stared unseeingly into the rain as she continued. "I came across Rob himself one day when I was attired thusly. He explained his purpose, thinking I was a lad from the village. I offered my services and he accepted, but I never really told him anything. Since Gilbert's death I have had no contact with him."

"But Roland does not believe this."

She shook her dark head slowly. "Nay. I told him I knew the man you had captured—Ian. The night before you left for London I spoke to Ian. He disclosed that Rob had told him to murder Gilbert to turn me more solidly against Roland." She turned to Dane in appeal. "How could I ever have cooperated with Rob after discovering what he had done? I swear, Dane, I told no one of their intentions to go to Wexton!"

Dane nodded thoughtfully, his expression grave. "We must get Ranulf through this, Brianna. That will be one less thing Roland can hold against you." He tucked the fold of her mantle more securely about her head to protect her from the rain. "Roland told me you are to help Abbess Marie tend Ranulf, for his wound festers. We can do nothing more than see to Ranulf for now, Brianna.''

She nodded, her eyes clinging hopefully to his.

"Come." He led her out into the persistent drizzle.

"What do you here?"

Brianna straightened her shoulders in an unconscious effort to pull herself together. "I came to change the wrap on your thigh."

Roland glanced down at the badly stained bandage for the first time since he had awakened. He shrugged her offer aside. "I will survive."

Brianna moved toward him where he sat alone in the hall, the remnants of a late breakfast before him. She determinedly ignored the look in his cold gray eyes. "I do not have time to dispute your wisdom, Roland. Reverend Mother awaits me to relieve her, and I am to do this small task for her as well." She began to roll up the leg of his braies with deft movements.

Roland tightened a fist in response to his thoughts. "I would rather bleed to death than suffer your touch," he said harshly in an effort to suppress his awareness of her.

The intentional cruelty of his words had the desired effect. Brianna's cheeks colored softly and she bit her lip to control its treacherous quivering. "You surely will bleed to death if this bandage is not replaced—or the wound could fester."

"You will have to remove the breeches if you want to see the wound, Brianna," he said softly.

Too late, Brianna realized her mistake in coming to him impulsively instead of preparing herself. She had nothing with which to cover his midsection or even to replace his dressing.

To her dismay, he stood and unfastened the shielding garment. When he sat down again, the breeches were draped across his groin.

"Where is Dane?"

"He went up to see Ranulf."

Roland flicked a glance toward the stairs, hoping either

Dane or the Abbess would appear and rescue him. "Did you plead your innocence to him as you did me, Brianna? I'll wager he was much more eager to believe you, for he and Ranulf still belong to that group of unfortunates who are convinced you can do no wrong."

Brianna raised her eyes to his granite profile, lips parted to speak.

"Roland, may I speak to you?" It was Guy de Montrain.

Roland turned his head. "Of course, *mon ami*. What is it?"

"I would speak to you alone—"

"There is naught I would hide from my betrothed. There have never been two people closer to one another—no two people freer from subterfuge and pretense, is that not true, sweet?"

Brianna's movements ceased in midmotion. The bleak look in her eyes as they met his failed to induce him to halt his cruel game. "I . . . I will fetch clean linen, and you and Guy may have a few moments in privacy."

"*No.* You will remain here with me." He turned to the knight waiting before him. "Speak your mind, de Montrain."

Guy looked uncomfortable, but the moment the words were out of his mouth, his tense features visibly relaxed with relief. "I . . . I believe I know who may have betrayed you and Ranulf."

Roland nodded thoughtfully. "Then, 'tis no longer a secret, for I have known since last eve. I thank you for your concern, my friend, but Brianna has made a clean breast of it, however unwillingly."

Her humiliation was complete. Now everyone would know.

"Brianna?" Guy repeated in bewilderment.

"Indeed."

Both men stared down at her, and Brianna wanted the floor to open up and swallow her in the ensuing silence. She flushed to the roots of her hair and the tears spilled forth.

"I . . . I am sorry, Roland," the *chevalier* muttered and

turned away, puzzled but nonetheless looking as if a great burden had been taken from his shoulders.

Brianna stood slowly. "You do me the gravest injustice, my lord," she managed.

His next words were so savage they could have come from a complete stranger. "And *you* did *me* the gravest injustice every time you donned your filthy, makeshift disguise to run squealing to that den of vipers! Perhaps you would partially atone for your sin and lead me to them?"

"I do not know where they are, Roland," she denied miserably. "I was unconscious when they took me to see Rob."

Roland stood up before her, heedless of his uncovered wound and his state of dishabille. His fingers gripped her chin firmly as he forced her gaze to meet his. "I could overlook much if you would tell me this one thing, Brianna. Do not add to your crimes by lying now."

Something inside her suddenly came to life. She jerked her chin from his grip. "Add to my crimes? Forgive me, Norman, but I have committed no crimes worth mentioning, except to fall in love with one who is quick to condemn when the answer to his dilemma eludes him! How convenient for you to be able blame me for what happened yesterday. God knows I am sorry for Ranulf—for he is very dear to me—but perhaps you have taken advantage of me all along. Perhaps you had planned to lay the blame for some horrible act at my feet in order to get out of marrying me. You took my virture—isn't that what you set out to do from the beginning?—and then—"

The room exploded with a thousand lights as Roland's open palm made contact with her unprotected cheek. For the briefest instant something like regret flitted across his features and then was gone. "Do not turn the tables on me, my treacherous witch!" he grated. "Your reasoning is absurd! *You* made a travesty of my love for you. *You* trafficked with a traitor behind my back—when I would have trusted you with my life. *You* betrayed us to Rob, Brianna—*you!*" A muscle twitched in his cheek, and he looked as if he wanted to choke the life from her.

"I will finish here, Brianna," interrupted the curt yet infinitely welcome voice of the Abbess. "Go to Lord Ranulf. He is sleeping quietly for the moment, but that can quickly change." She turned to Roland. "Be seated, my lord. Let us be quick about this."

Brianna threw her a grateful look and walked away, her head high but feeling utterly defeated inside.

What had Guy meant when he said he knew who betrayed them? She knew he hadn't meant herself. But whom? she wondered a short while later as she sponged a restless Ranulf, who was muttering deliriously.

"Guy! Ask him . . . de Montrain—"

She struggled to raise his head and shoulders enough to put a cup of cool watered wine to his parched lips. He swallowed a few drops, and she felt hope surge through her. He needed liquid badly, and she was encouraged that he managed to get even a little down. Then he slept again.

What could Ranulf have meant? she mused as she watched over him. Perhaps there was some connection between Ranulf's ravings and Guy de Montrain's words. She had the distinct feeling that Guy had really believed he knew who had been the informant. But, she thought in despair, even if Guy told her what he knew, Roland would never accept it. And Ranulf was delirious. Even if his semiconscious ramblings were of any importance, he was in no condition to confirm anything.

She kept seeing the hatred and contempt in Roland's eyes, and a despondency worse than anything she had ever felt settled over her like a smothering shroud. Nothing would ever be right again, she thought as she stared at the brother of the man she loved.

Damn her to hell!

Like a magnet to metal, Roland's eyes were drawn again

and again to the raven-haired beauty across the room. The fury coursing through his veins like fire left no room for anything but disgust with himself. He, Roland de Beaufort, who had always managed to avoid cloying entanglements with the ease born of experience, had been caught and was held fast by a mere slip of a girl as if he were a moonstruck youth.

He closed his eyes against her image. Never in his adult years had he felt such conflicting feelings—such extremes of emotion. *Forgive me, Ranulf,* he whispered to the brother who lay gravely ill upstairs. *She is a poison in my blood, my heart, my soul, and I cannot stop loving her.*

"My lord?" Kerwick's voice broke into Roland's tempestuous thoughts.

He looked up at the grizzled old man with the brightly intelligent blue eyes. A glowering Walter was behind him, jaw jutting out stubbornly. "Aye, Kerwick. What brings you here at this hour?" he queried. Kerwick's answer, however, whipped his attention into focus.

"My son has something to say, Lord Roland."

Roland's keen gaze moved to the young man. "And what might that be, Walter?"

Walter looked as if the last thing in the world he wanted to do was speak to Roland, but speak he did. "I know where Rob abides."

Roland's heart skipped a beat, but his expression remained unreadable. "I see. And how do you know this?" he asked with seeming casualness.

Walter reddened uncomfortably, but one glance at his father's menacing expression gave him the impetus he needed. "I have been there."

Roland nodded slightly; his gaze swept the hall, and he noted that Dane had returned from escorting Brianna upstairs and was heading toward them. "And how long have you worked for this devil known as Rob?" His eyes returned with frightening speed to knife into Walter's.

The young man clenched his fists in anger. "That title suits *you* far better, de Beaufort."

Kerwick elbowed his son with rib-cracking force. "Tell him, you young whelp, before I thrash you right here!"

Walter's expression turned sullen. "Naught my father had done would have made me speak up except that Lord Ranulf saved my life when the keep was fired. He—"

"Never mind your reasons, Kerwickson. Were you the one who alerted the Anglo-Saxon?"

Walter nodded.

Dane had quietly joined them, an enigmatic look on his face, but Roland was too intent on the story unfolding before him to acknowledge his presence with more than a glance. He leaned forward and held Walter's gaze implacably. "And how did Brianna tell you of our plans, Walter?"

A slow, infuriating grin split Walter's face. "You think your precious Brianna betrayed you?"

Roland's eyes narrowed, glittering dangerously. "Do not play cat and mouse with me, boy. You had better tell me all, or things will go very badly for you."

"Do not put words in his mouth, Roland. He did not say 'twas Brianna," Dane cautioned.

Roland's eyes remained upon Walter. "Keep out of this, Dane. Now, Walter, answer my question."

"You do not know Brianna very well, Norman. She would not betray you."

Roland did not believe his words. He had always known Walter cared for Brianna, and despite the youth's jealousy and the bad feelings between him and the girl since he had brought her to live in the manor, Roland sensed the boy would protect her at any cost. Therefore, he was prepared not to believe him. "You are lying, Kerwickson. But no matter, this has already been settled. Tell me instead where I can find Rob."

Brianna changed the dressing on Ranulf's shoulder. She winced as she exposed the ugly, half-closed hole. Blood still oozed from the torn flesh, but it had diminshed enough to offer hope that the wound would soon heal completely. She gently sponged it clean, which caused the sleeping Ranulf to stir in acute discomfort. She quickly wrapped the shoulder tightly once more, perspiring from her efforts in the stifling warmth of the room.

"*Wa-water—*" Ranulf's eyes opened and, the silver-gray gaze momentarily unclouded by delirium, regarded her in silent communication.

"Ranulf!" she dared to breathe, afraid he would slip away again. Bracing his broad shoulders with her slender arm was no mean feat, but the joy of seeing him lucid and requesting drink gave her added strength. "Here, Ranulf, drink your fill."

His eyes closed wearily as he sank back on the bed. " 'Twould have been less of a chore . . . for you if it had been Roland."

Tears blurred her vision as she reached out to push back the sandy hair that lay across his brow. " 'Tis no chore, Ranulf, you can be sure. I love you as—"

"Ranulf—how do you feel?" A strong, sun-bronzed hand closed over Ranulf's, and Brianna looked up to see Roland standing across from her.

Ranulf grinned with an effort. "Like . . . like a wooden stake in yonder stockade, brother," he said softly. "And someone is pounding me into the earth . . ." His eyes closed again. Then, "*Look to your left, Roland!*" he cried hoarsely; his eyes opened suddenly, and he stared unseeingly. "*He is a clever . . . clever devil, my brother.*" And then, "*Ask him . . . ask de Montrain—*"

Brianna sponged his brow and then the rest of his face, carefully avoiding looking at the man across from her. But Roland was frowning, perplexed by his brother's mention of Guy de Montrain. He stood up in agitation, fingers plowing through his fair hair, and he moved to stand before the cold hearth.

"We ride on the morrow to rid ourselves of your cohort once and for all."

Brianna's breath caught in her throat at his words. "But . . . but you are not yet well yourself! To go riding off into the weald in search of Rob with a wound not yet healed—to search blindly for one so cunning and well acquainted with the woodlands—"

"Are you concerned for me or for Rob, Brianna?" He turned toward her, the shutter lifting from the gray eyes for a brief instant, and Brianna glimpsed his anguish. She wanted to reach out to him, to assure him that she loved him above all else, but she didn't dare. He would only reject her, and she couldn't bear his outright repudiation again.

"Once you would have known the answer to that, Roland," she answered quietly.

For a moment his expression seemed to soften and Brianna thought he would move toward her, but then his look turned harsh and unyielding. "Things have changed, Brianna." He moved to the bed and looked down at Ranulf. "Sleep well, my brother," he murmured, "so you may rise from this bed soon."

Brianna watched him leave the room. "God go with you, Roland," she whispered.

He stopped at the door, his hand on the latch. Without turning, he said, "If you harbor any ideas of warning your leader, disabuse yourself of the notion. A man-at-arms will be posted in this corridor until we return."

CHAPTER 23

Brianna tossed uneasily on her feather mattress. Visions of Dane returning with a lifeless Roland over his saddle haunted her dreams and prevented her from obtaining the deep, undisturbed slumber she needed. Then her eyes opened drowsily and she rubbed the sleep from them uncertainly. Had she overslept? The sun was low in the trees—it was early evening.

She sat up abruptly, swinging her bare legs over the side of the bed. Why had she slept so long? Reverend Mother would be expecting her to—

And then she remembered. The Abbess had taken over tending Ranulf at dawn.

She hastily rinsed her face, pulled a comb through her tousled mane, dressed and was about to see how Ranulf was faring when the thunderous staccato of horses' hooves announced the return of Roland and his men. She bit her lip in an effort to control the sudden apprehension that seized her and went straight downstairs rather than looking in on Ranulf.

The men who had not gone with their lord crowded around their returning comrades, their shouts of excitement piercing the air. Brianna stood poised on the threshold of the door, uncertain of the wisdom of joining the exhausted but jubilant party. She had counted fourteen leaving that morning, plus Walter Kerwickson. Praise God they had all returned.

As Brianna waited impatiently, she overheard remarks made by the Normans as they led their horses away.

". . . really that Saxon swine himself?"

"Aye. In the flesh," answered a rich-timbred voice that could only be Roland's.

"Where are the others? Did the cowards flee?"

Dane was the one to answer this time. "Cowards they were not, but no doubt they had been instructed to save their own hides should their leader be taken."

"How did they fight out in the open—against adversaries they had to face man to man?"

Roland's answer once again could be heard above the undercurrent of excited voices. "They put up a brave enough struggle before they saw it was hopeless. Most of them were not very skilled—remnants of the untrained fyrd, I would guess."

Brianna's pulse quickened in dread anticipation of coming face to face with Rob. But the first one to emerge from the group of men was Walter, looking pale and shaken. "Walter!" she exclaimed sharply, concern creasing her brow.

As he neared her his expression turned sour. "I am a bigger fool than even you, Brianna. I betrayed him because my father convinced me I owed it Lord Ranulf. He will probably die anyway, and I will have made the biggest mistake of my miserable life."

Brianna's eyes widened. *"You?"*

"Aye." His hazel eyes were dark with self-loathing and disgust. "I am every bit as contemptible as you."

Before she could say another word, a movement directly behind him caught her eye and silver-gray eyes bored into hers as Roland came up behind Walter, leaving the others to mill about the new captive. "Good eventide, *madame*. How is my brother?"

Brianna's whirling thoughts became even more confused as he strode relentlessly toward her until he was so close his breath brushed her cheek as he looked down into her upturned face. Pale from loss of blood from his reopened wound, disheveled and smelling of blood and sweat, he nonetheless still possessed the power to tongue-tie her and make her weak for want of him. Every inch the conquering Norman *chevalier* despite his appearance, Roland de Beaufort was bloodied yet unbowed in the wake of his recent encounter.

She forgot Walter, Rob, Dane—everything but the man before her. *Can you not see, Roland? Do you not know, in your heart of hearts, that I could never betray you? Oh, Roland, Roland—*

"Well?"

The reality of the moment came crashing down around her. "He . . . he is the same. At least he was when I left him last night."

His features took on a grim cast and he limped past her toward the stairs. "You might want to greet our *guest,*" he directed her over his shoulder, the mockery in his voice unnerving her already tautened senses.

Slowly, woodenly, Brianna turned to look toward the approaching men. Dane led the way, followed by Beorn and Vachel, who flanked Rob on either side. Dane spoke to Brianna, but she never heard what he said as she watched the long-haired Saxon leader stumble toward her as the two men-at-arms shoved him roughly.

Roland's cold, accusatory looks were mild compared to the burning hatred and the fervid denunciation in Rob's dark eyes.

She moved aside to make way for the three men, and as they passed, the captive's lips drew back. "Robert of Wessex *spits* on you." His eyes quickly went to Walter, standing at a table pouring mead with a trembling hand. "And on you, you puling Judas!"

Robert of Wessex? *Robert of Wessex?*

The room began to spin crazily and there was a roaring in

her ears as Brianna began to slip into oblivion. *Robert of Wessex—her father!*

"Brianna!" Dane's face floated before her and it was the last thing she remembered. She never saw Roland glance back from halfway up the stairs to witness Rob's vituperative attack. She never knew that although it was Dane who called her name, Roland was the one who, gritting his teeth against the stabbing pain his leg, bounded down the steps with lightning speed to catch her in his arms before she hit the floor.

Brianna came to in her own bed. As she remembered what had caused her to faint, she threw back the light blanket someone had thoughtfully placed over her, determined to speak to Robert of Wessex. She returned the cool wet cloth that covered her forehead to the washbasin and, standing up on fairly steady legs, she reluctantly went below to the hall.

She had mixed feelings about speaking to this man who was her father. Part of her wanted to speak to him at length—to discover what he was like and why he had given her into the care of strangers when she was a small child. Yet another part of her could not reconcile his actions concerning Gilbert and his brave and tenacious resistance to Norman rule. That same part of her felt an uncharacteristic hatred and disillusionment which she found difficult to put aside.

Dane was at the bottom of the stairs, and Brianna was relieved that Roland was evidently still with Ranulf. "Dane, I must speak to Rob—"

"Wait just a moment, Brianna. How do you feel now?"

A wave of a slim hand dismissed this question as unimportant. "I *must* see him alone before Roland can stop me. You see, he is Robert of Wessex, Dane. My father."

Dane sucked in his breath at her admission. "Your . . . your *father?*"

"Aye, but I swear before God that I did not know it until this eve. *Please*, Dane—let me go to him now."

He hesitated only a moment, his topaz eyes searching her face as if seeking an answer to some unspoken question. "Very well, Brianna. God knows how this all came to pass, but do it quickly, before Roland discovers what you are about. Should he learn that the man is your sire, it will only serve to strengthen his belief that you played him false."

She nodded blindly, the events of the last two days bearing down on her at last with a crushing weight.

It all seemed unreal—a dream, a recurring nightmare. Nightfall, the same vacated granary, pitch torches at either side of the rough doorway casting flickering shadows across the features of the guards. Only this time there were two men— Vachel and Roger—and they were awake and alert as Dane approached with Brianna in his wake.

"Why did Roland remove him from the hall?" Brianna whispered.

"There are gyves in the wall here. Wulfric must have used the hut to hold wrongdoers, as there are none to be found in the hall."

"Why do you bring the lady Brianna here, my lord?" asked Roger, a trifle put out at seeing Brianna so near a dangerous captive.

"Mind your tongue, boy!" growled Vachel. "Do you question his authority?"

Roger flushed at the rebuke in Brianna's presence, but the darkness hid his embarrassment.

"Brianna has my permission to speak with the man inside— in private. If he is well secured there is no need for concern, as he cannot harm her while he is shackled. Do not hesitate, however, to go in after her should you hear anything untoward. Do you understand?"

"Aye, my lord," answered Vachel, but even he looked skeptical in light of this strange visit by his lord's betrothed.

Brianna looked up at Dane, trepidation and determination warring inside her. "Thank you, Dane. I will not forget this."

"Have a care in there, Brianna. Roland will have my head for this."

There was no need for a torch of her own, for there were two inside, in brackets set in the crude walls. Brianna drew a deep breath before she allowed her gaze to settle on the man known as Rob. That he had actually been taken alive and made a prisoner was still hard to believe. When she met his cold regard head-on, however, there was no denying it. The dark shoulder-length hair, lightly threaded with silver, was tied with a thong around his high forehead. The well-cut features were the same as she remembered, and he had not been beaten as had Ian. His dark, icy eyes were riveted to her face unnervingly. Like a snake watching its prey, Brianna thought with a light shudder.

Rob did not miss her frisson of unease, and he drew up his knees to brace himself against the wall. "So you fear me, Brianna? You shouldn't, you know." But the menace in his voice belied his words.

Brianna found her tongue. "Why? Because you are Robert of Wessex—my *father?*"

He frowned at her question. "Who told you that?"

"Abbess Marie—"

"Gave her word that she would not reveal your parentage," he interrupted sharply.

"Things were so . . . uncertain after Hastings. Reverend Mother wrote me words of comfort after my husband was disabled and, not knowing what would become of Walshire Abbey or herself, she disclosed the secret lest she die with it."

"Better it had happened thus. I did not need a whining female as a millstone about my neck."

In the face of his dark annoyance, however, her own anger grew until the questions came hurtling out like swift, well-aimed arrows. "Why did you give me into the care of Abbess Marie? Why did you not reveal yourself to me when first we met in the forest? *Why?*"

The hiss of the torches, the faint clinking of the chains as he shifted slightly, the smell of burning pitch and sweat—all were imprinted upon her memory forever as his answer hit home. "I had as good a reason as any man could ever need. You were not of my loins. Your mother tried to foist you off on me as her life drained away after giving birth, but I would have none of it. Do you hear me? None of it!" Burning hatred suddenly twisted his features frighteningly as at last he allowed years of bitterness to destroy his iron control. "You are a bastard born, Brianna. And the final irony of it is that your sire was probably Norman."

Brianna stared at him uncomprehendingly for a moment, and then his words echoed through her mind. Not her father? The offspring of a Norman? Her hand went to cover her mouth lest she scream in rage at the trick the fates had played upon her. Half Norman? Kin to those who had brought England to its knees? Nay! She shook her head in mute denial.

"Aye, Brianna! You were willing to betray your own kind—until you went soft on me." He smiled grimly, once more in control.

"You used me," she managed through bloodless lips as her anger grew, replacing dismay and disbelief.

"And why not? Your mother used *me*. She never truly cared, or she would have overlooked my harmless indiscretions." He leaned forward as far as the gyves would allow to give emphasis to his next words. "I was only to love *her*, she said. Gullible and naïve as a child she was, to ever have believed a man could remain constant forever. So she took her disillusionment to Edward's court and there found solace in the waiting arms of some all-too-willing Norman slime!" He leaned back once more to better gauge her reaction.

"But . . . but how unfeeling you were to take it out on an innocent child! I can still remember the hurt your leaving caused me, even though I had not been with you long and knew little of love or simple affection at your hand. But you were my father, or so I believed, and you left me with strangers!''

"Only a rare pang of conscience made me retrieve you from the care of old Sven and Gytha after several years. In a matter of months the mere sight of you reminded me so strongly of your mother's duplicity that I could no longer bear to even look upon you.''

"But . . . but who is my true sire?'' She sank weakly to her knees, her eyes glued to his face as she awaited his answer.

He laughed harshly—an ugly, grating sound. "I have not the slightest idea, girl. Your slut of a mother could have bedded anyone with her looks and childish naïveté. Perhaps you could go to the Bastard himself and ask him to help you discover which one of his conquering horde spawned you.''

Brianna's fists clenched against her thighs as she knelt before him, her face pale with anger at his intentional slurs. "You are heartless, Robert of Wessex!'' she whispered fiercely.

"And *you* could have redeemed yourself, Brianna—do you know that? You could have raised yourself out of your shameful bastardy by proving your worth to me in my efforts to chase the Normans from our shores!''

"What makes you think yourself so noble as to pass judgment upon others who do not live up to your twisted expectations? You, who murder harmless innocents incapable of defending themselves!''

The rattle of the gyves indicated the force of his reaction to her verbal attack as he forgot himself and tried to lunge toward her. Vachel's head appeared in the doorway, squinting into the brightly illuminated interior. "Is aught amiss, Lady Brianna?'' he asked suspiciously.

Brianna glanced back at him. "Nay, Vachel. I am fine.''

Satisfied, he withdrew, shaking his head.

Her gaze returned to Robert of Wessex. "I have heard of you, Robert of Wessex, and your staunch loyalty and faithful service to the Godwins. What a pity you could not find enough compassion in your heart to accept an innocent child, born of the wife you must have once loved. You have much to learn of life, Thane Robert."

His eyes were two burning coals in their sockets, the venomous hatred in them all-consuming. "Do not lecture me about life, girl, when I have lived for more than twice your years! Did you mewl to Ian of such drivel? Did you even bother to speak to him? Or were you too busy spreading your legs for de Beaufort?"

"Enough!" she cried, struggling to get to her feet in the wake of his onslaught. But her legs were shaking and she stumbled toward him, completely losing her balance and pitching forward. Too late she realized her mistake in being alone with Robert of Wessex as he managed to throw out an ankle and clamp it to her windpipe, applying enough pressure to effectively cut off her air.

"And now you will pay for your sins, Alicia!"

Alicia. The name whirled round and round in the back of her memory as her fingers pulled desperately at his leg and she fought for air. *Alicia—Alicia—* Someone else had spoken of Alicia.

Her vision began to dim and her strength, already hampered by her awkward position, began to fail her. It came to Brianna in a blinding revelation in this moment so close to death that William d'Avranches was her natural sire. *William d'Avranches, not Robert of Wessex.* But it was too late— *I am going to die,* she thought with an odd detachment as Rob's heavily muscled leg relentlessly pressed her fragile throat. *Lord William will never know and Roland will always believe me guilty—*

Suddenly the pressure on her air passage was gone and Brianna inhaled a sweet rush of air. Rob grunted in pain as a fist knocked his head against the wall with a dull thud, stunning him for a moment. "Are you much hurt, Brianna?" Dane's voice questioned as he helped her to her feet. Vachel and Roger stood behind him, ready to lend a hand.

"I am all right, Dane," Brianna answered as she gingerly fingered her bruised throat.

She looked at Robert of Wessex one last time. He was staring at her, his eyes going to Dane and back to her face again. "What is your surname, Norman?" he demanded softly.

"What can it matter to the likes of you?"

But Brianna felt strangely compelled to reply. "D'Avranches," she answered for Dane before turning to him and allowing him to take her by the elbow. A low rumble of sardonic laughter filled the small structure as they reached the door, and the hair on Brianna's neck stood up at the sound of it.

"What happened in there?" he asked abruptly, his annoyance with himself for letting her have her way evident in the sharpness of his words.

"I . . . I lost my footing as I tried to leave. I landed practically in his lap and—well, you saw how quick he was to take advantage."

They stopped outside the entrance, and Dane pulled her around to face him in the dancing light from several mounted flambeaux. "You are not so clumsy as that, Brianna. Or did he say something to cause you such distress that you were less than surefooted?"

She looked past him in an attempt to avoid his probing regard. "He said much to me, Dane, and I was shaken, but only I can reconcile his revelations within myself." Her eyes returned to his. "I think he is mad. He called me by my mother's name as he tried to strangle the life from me."

"That does not surprise me. He has become obsessed with his hopeless cause, and no doubt it drove all else from his mind till he lost his grip on reality." He sighed and lifted her chin, turning her head to inspect the slim column of her neck.

"You know Roland will be told." She turned her face to him in alarm. "Aye. Vachel and Roger serve him directly, and I do not have the authority to demand they keep this from him. You were so intent on speaking to him I would not allow myself to dwell upon the consequences, but we must face them now."

Hard pressed to prevent herself from revealing to him what she had guessed until she spoke to Lord William, Brianna straightened her shoulders resolutely. "Whatever happens, I will not let you take the blame. It has happened too many times already, and I have been the source of enough discord between you and Roland." She turned to enter the hall before she said in a voice full of quiet despair, "Why should he care anyway, Dane, when he despises me so?"

The heavy oaken door was pushed open and Roland entered Ranulf's room to find Ranulf resting quietly enough and Brianna sleeping in the chair beside the bed. Upon seeing the faint shadows under her eyes, he couldn't bring himself to awaken her, although he was tempted to confront her with the fact that she had spoken to Rob.

For the second night in a row he had slept fitfully, the strain of the last several days lying upon him like a pall and robbing him of an undisturbed night's rest. Inevitably he was drawn to the room that held the two people who meant the most to him. He winced inwardly at that thought, for it seemed akin to blasphemy—Ranulf, who was so upright, so honorable, and Brianna, who was—

Roland allowed his gaze to settle upon her sleeping countenance. How achingly lovely she was! Yet how wicked— A knife twisted in his heart each time he thought of what she had done. He would have given his sword arm to know that she was innocent. Nay, he would have given everything in this world, save Ranulf's life, in return for the assurance that she was free of blame.

Common sense told him to turn away, but logic did not enter where love was concerned.

Her head was turned slightly in his direction, and from his vantage point above her, he could see every detail of her small, piquant face. With a will of its own, his hand reached out ever so carefully to caress her cheek, the powerful fingers accustomed to wielding a heavy sword in battle brushing the smooth skin as fleetingly as a butterfly's wing. She stirred slightly and Roland froze, dreading the moment those mesmerizing sea-blue eyes would open and see him standing beside her, totally enthralled. But the opalescent lids remained closed and she merely shifted her head to face away from him, exposing her slender neck to his gaze.

Relaxing visibly, he let his hand slowly drop to his side before the ugly purple bruise on her throat caught his eye. It was an obscenity against the creamy, silken expanse of her neck, and outrage coursed through him. It would have been so simple to kill the Saxon rabble imprisoned within the granary—

Vachel had told him everything when he reported before retiring. Roland had also been sorely tempted to wring Brianna's lovely neck, but he wisely curbed the urge, thinking to confront her on the morrow. And Dane. Once again he had interfered on Brianna's behalf, almost getting her killed in the process. Heads would roll in the morning, to be sure.

His expression turned hard at the thought of Brianna's bold action right under his nose. It was like a splash of cold water, thoroughly arousing him from his rapt contemplation of her features. He had to get hold of himself. It was no concern of his if she tangled with that treacherous miscreant now. They were two of a kind—scheming, desperate, lethal. It *must* not matter that she had been hurt by her leader. Somehow he had to eradicate the all-encompassing love and need he felt for her, but how? It had taken nearly a full year for his feelings to reach such tremendous proportions. God help him if it

should take a like number of months to recover from her devastating hold on him.

He turned and moved wearily from the room. As he glanced
up at the door of the chamber across the passage where the
Abbess was sleeping, the answer suddenly came to him. Why
hadn't he thought of it before? he wondered as he made his
way to his room. Well, no matter. The solution to his dilemma
was very clear to him now.

He would send her back to Walshire Abbey.

CHAPTER 24

Roland stood before the completed castle in the cool morning mist, studying it through narrowed eyes. The stockaded wooden keep sat sturdily atop the mound of well-trampled earth, a result of the diligent stamping of many of Derford's inhabitants. A ditch encircled the earthen moat and its court, or bailey, which had yet to be filled with water. This would be the first line of defense in the event of an attack. Roland's critical eye roved over the lesser structures contained within the palisaded bailey—a stable, lodgings for his men, two small barns, a smithy and several workshops and storehouses for grain and wine. The stockade surrounding the bailey was the second line of defense.

I pray I never have to use it, he thought soberly, and with a quick glance at Odo standing quietly behind him, he crossed the wooden bridge spanning the empty moat to inspect the keep firsthand.

As he moved toward the structure the dull ache in his thigh reminded him how far from recovered he still was. He rubbed the side of his leg unconsciously and awkwardly started up the ladder to the door above him. At last he stood on the threshold of the keep itself which was both a watchtower and an arsenal and was the last stronghold of defense. He was even with the middle level, a fair-sized eating room with several long tables and benches and a sideboard. Below was the storage area, and below that, the well. Above were the sleeping quarters.

He eased himself down onto a bench directly before the entrance and gazed out at the verdant English countryside. How peaceful it was here, he mused, and allowed the surrounding silence to lull him as he lost all track of time.

All too soon Dane's tall form filled the doorway, a wary smile of good humor on his face. "I thought I might find you here."

"Did you seek to confront me with an explanation for your behavior last eve before I could take you to task?" Roland inquired grimly, his gaze brushing over Dane's features and then returning to the fields and forests before him.

Dane sighed resignedly and leaned against the wall, arms crossed over his powerful chest. "I did seek you out with the intention of explaining my actions—"

"Your irresponsible, reprehensible actions!" Roland's eyes met those of his friend, anger evident in their stormy gray depths. "How could you have exposed Brianna to such danger? I shudder to think how easily she could have been killed."

"You sound like a man still in love."

"And are you such an authority on the subject? I would have been just as concerned had it been the Abbess or—"

"Hilde?" Dane supplied quietly.

Roland's mouth tightened. "No, of course not, but—"

"And neither would you have reacted similarly if it had been Abbess Marie."

"My feelings for Brianna are not under discussion here, Dane. I want to know why she wanted to see him—although I suspect I know the reason—and why you even consented to help her when you knew I would never have permitted it!" He leaned his hand on his wounded thigh in his agitation and grimaced.

"Robert of Wessex—or *Rob,* if you will—is her father," Dane said unexpectedly.

Roland threw him a dubious look. "Surely you have a better excuse than that."

Dane spread his hands and shrugged his shoulders in denial. " 'Tis the truth, Roland."

Incredulity tracked across his brow. "Her *father?* Robert of Wessex?"

"So she said. She knew you would never allow her an audience with him, so she enlisted my aid while you were occupied elsewhere."

Roland stared unseeingly out the door once more, struggling to collect his thoughts. "Then she was aiding her sire all along . . . That explains many things."

"Nay, Roland. She did not know it until last eve."

Roland furrowed a hand through his hair, seeking to right his whirling thoughts. "Well, then how did she find out last night? I tell you, Dane, she lied in order to get your help. You are as big a fool as I." He rose and limped to the door. "I will get to the bottom of this, Dane, for I am weary of deceit and secrecy. Come, let us break our fast; God knows I will need my strength."

As they rode back to the manor Roland told Dane of his intention to send Brianna back to Walshire.

"Back to Walshire? Are you mad?" The dark-haired Norman gestured impatiently at his friend. "Of course you are mad—mad in love. Do you honestly think you will be able to forget her if she is out of your sight?"

But Roland refused to be baited. "As soon as Ranulf is out of danger, she can return with Abbess Marie," he said with finality.

Dane shook his head in exasperation. "You are a fool, Roland."

"That I already know. My brother's condition is proof of it."

Brianna freshened up with slow, unenthusiastic movements. A glance in the polished metal mirror revealed faint hollows beneath her cheekbones, and she knew her despair was beginning to show. Living without the warmth and security of Roland's love was having a devastating effect upon her.

With a heavy heart and dragging steps, she went down to the hall. She should have known Roland would be at the board, for his usual activities were curtailed because of his injury.

Some of the other men were scattered at several other tables, talking in undertones. The completion of the keep and the capture of Rob had relieved them of the most pressing tasks, but Ranulf's condition had cast a dark cloud over all. The hall was strangely silent for the number of people in it.

Brianna kept her eyes downcast as she sat beside Dane. "Good morningtide, Dane," she greeted softly.

"Good morningtide, *petite*. How fares Ranulf?"

"The same, I am afraid. Reverend Mother says that it is not all bad, though." She toyed with a piece of cheese on the hard bread trencher set before her, what little appetite she had gone now with Roland sitting so close to her, quiet and aloof.

"Pray God his fever breaks," Dane said gravely, his eyes on the stairway for a brief moment. He stood up and stepped over the bench as if on cue. "I believe I will look in on Ranulf, Roland." With an encouraging pat on Brianna's shoulder, he moved away.

Brianna hazarded a glance at Roland. His profile was set as he picked up a goblet to wash down his food. Before she could look away, his head came around and she was caught in that steel-gray stare—a stranger's stare. "Who is with my brother now?"

"Reverend Mother."

Without another word he stood up and took her by the arm. "Come. We have some unfinished business."

In a daze, Brianna allowed him to steer her toward the great door. Then, in sudden alarm, she pulled back. "Where . . . where are you taking me?"

He did not slow his pace; his fingers firmly around her

upper arm pushed her forward. "Do not try to pull away, Brianna, if you do not want a scene in front of my men."

She looked at his granite features but found no help there. And he was right. There was no way she could have escaped his grip of iron. But he could not control her tongue. "This is absurd, Roland," she began with much more bravado than she felt.

"I think it makes perfect sense!" he snapped, revealing a crack in the barrier of indifference he had erected between them. "You insisted on sneaking around behind my back to work your treachery. Now we will see how well you do before Robert of Wessex himself." And ignoring the surprised looks of the two guards stationed at the door of the tiny hut, he all but pulled her through it.

At the sound of their entrance, Rob's head snapped up, and he smiled malignantly at the sight of Brianna and the angry Roland. "Well, well. What have we here?"

Ignoring him, Roland turned to Brianna, the torchlight emphasizing the rage in his eyes. "Why did you come here last eve?"

Brianna took a deep breath. "I had learned that he . . . that he was my father, and I wanted to speak with him." She tried to hold his eyes but looked down all too soon before the hostility in them.

Rob spoke again before she could answer, his dark eyes shining with perverse humor as he quickly assessed the situation. "An admirable effort, Brianna, but you must tell your liege lord the truth. I am not your sire, and well you know it."

Brianna closed her eyes for a moment. *Give me strength to fight him,* she prayed, for in the wink of an eye she saw that Robert of Wessex would do his utmost to undermine her credibility before Roland. "He is not my *natural* father, but in name I am his."

Roland's eyes narrowed dangerously. "I did not bring you here to play games," he said with menace. "You came here to plot with him—as if what you did to Ranulf wasn't enough!''

"Nay, Roland. Please believe me—you *must* believe me! I came only to determine why he had not revealed his identity to me prior to this—''

"God knows, he had many opportunities, did he not, Brianna?''

"Ample opportunities, de Beaufort, I can assure you,'' Rob supplied.

"Roland," Brianna began desperately, "I had naught to do with him after Gilbert's death. How could I after he had Ian kill my husband?'' She grabbed his arm. *"Think*, Roland! Ian told me Rob ordered him to kill Gilbert, thinking to turn me even further against you. How could he ever command my loyalty after that?''

Rob feigned perplexity at her words and then deliberately changed his expression as Roland caught his eye.

Fooled by the Anglo-Saxon's attitude, Roland shook her hand off his arm like some bothersome insect. Brianna's eyes filled with tears of frustration. "I did not betray you!'' she cried furiously. "He would discredit me, Roland, can you not see?''

Roland shook his head in denial. "And why would someone to whom you rendered loyal service do that, Brianna? Why would any man possessed of the least bit of fair play seek to seal the doom of one of his own followers?''

How could she ever explain? How could she tell him of this man's suppurating animosity when she herself could not comprehend the depth of his grudge? Brianna jerked her head toward one of the low-burning wall torches, exposing her bruised throat to Roland. "Then why did he do *this* to me?''

In the silence that followed, for so brief a moment that it could have been imagined, she thought she saw doubt flicker in Roland's eyes. But, to her dismay, it disappeared before she could press her advantage. "That I do not know, Brianna. Perhaps he desired to spare you the slow death I might have planned for you had Dane not fortuitously come to your rescue.''

Brianna's mouth fell open in consternation, but then Roland was addressing Rob. ''Robert of Wessex you may be, but you shall die on the morrow. And,'' he added stonily, ''if my brother should perish before your execution, you may count on dying a slow and painful death.''

Brianna tried to get some rest during the afternoon, but her turmoil pervaded her dreams. It seemed to her that nothing would ever be right again. Even if Ranulf recovered, it would not change how Roland felt. And she was sure Ranulf would never believe or forgive her either. Or would he? She desperately needed someone else on her side besides Dane. Even the other men had been avoiding her. Whether they believed her guilty, she could not be certain, but it was obvious they did not wish to displease their lord by openly sympathizing with her.

Unable to sleep, she went to look in on Ranulf. The Abbess welcomed her with a fond smile that tugged at Brianna's heart.

She stopped at the bedside and looked down at the sleeping man. ''Has there been no change?'' she asked, sounding defeated.

''He woke not long ago and was lucid enough to accept some warm broth. That is a good sign.''

Brianna touched his hand and felt the fevered skin beneath her fingers. ''Oh, when will we *know,* Reverend Mother? I cannot bear this . . . this waiting, this not knowing!''

''You will bear it because you must, Brianna. You know these things can take days and even weeks. I believe he will recover because he has not grown any weaker. His wound has stopped leaking blood, which means he is healing. And since he has been taking in some nourishment, he is better able to reserve the little strength he has.''

Hope surged through her at the nun's words. "Reverend Mother?"

"Aye, child."

"I spoke with Robert of Wessex last eve."

The Abbess looked from Ranulf to Brianna. "I am glad. You should make peace with your father no matter what happens."

Brianna walked over to the single window in the room and gazed out at the sunny afternoon. It was a day for laughter and love—not misery and hatred. She turned to face the Abbess with her next words. "Robert of Wessex was responsible for Gilbert's death."

A look of stunned surprise crossed the Abbess' face before she could gain control of her expression.

"And he is not my natural father."

After a few moments of silence, the nun walked over to her and, putting her hands firmly on Brianna's shoulders, turned her around. When their eyes met, Abbess Marie read unhappiness and confusion in Brianna's. "That means naught, Brianna. A child cannot help who his parents are—or are not. You must not let that weigh upon your mind."

"You do not seem surprised."

The Abbess shook her head slowly. "No, that does not surprise me, for what real father could give his only child into the care of others from birth? A childless couple—Sven and Gytha—came to me shortly after Thane Robert brought you to Walshire. At one time Sven was one of your father's retainers until he lost a leg. They inquired after you, for they had cared for you for the first years of your life."

Brianna shook her head in disbelief at the thought of being given away at birth.

"Only an angry and bitter man could have done that," the Abbess continued. "A man who knows without a doubt the child is another's."

Brianna said slowly, "I believe William d'Avranches is my natural father."

The dark eyes lit momentarily. "Indeed, child. I am glad if you have reason to believe 'tis he."

Brianna turned toward the window again and took a deep breath of fresh air. "But no proof," she added sadly. And no way of bringing her suspicion to William's attention, after Roland's rejection. Truly, she had lost everything.

The Abbess was at a loss to find words to comfort her. She returned to her station at the bedside, stopping in midstride as her glance fell upon Roland standing in the doorway, his eyes fixed on Brianna where she still stood at the window. For an unguarded moment, the nun recognized longing in his expression. "Come in, Lord Roland. Your brother seems determined to recover."

Brianna whirled around. She felt pinned to the spot under his cold, hard scrutiny and wished she were anywhere but in this room with him.

In the face of her silence, he came forward. "He will live?" he asked with sudden, unexpected emotion tingeing his words.

"I do not wish to raise your hopes unduly, but by all indications he is holding his own. We will not know for certain until his fever breaks."

Roland took his brother's hand in his. "Come, Ranulf," he chided softly, "do not die and leave me alone to deal with these stubborn English. Take of my strength, my brother. You can, you *must*," he finished with gentle urgency, his expression warm and tender as his love for his twin overshadowed everything else in that moment.

Brianna's eyes were luminous with tears at the heartfelt entreaty. And with sadness for that warmth and tenderness that had also been hers, and now was withdrawn from her forever. She quietly walked toward the door, feeling a sudden need to escape from Roland and the reminder of what she had lost.

"Do not leave yet," his deep voice commanded, all tenderness gone. "I have come to a decision which I wish to tell you both."

Brianna went to stand beside the Abbess, dread taking hold of her at his foreboding words. The older woman took her hand reassuringly. "What is it you have decided, my lord?"

Roland let go Ranulf's hand and turned to regard them implacably. "When Ranulf is out of danger, you may return to Walshire, Reverend Mother." She nodded slightly in acknowledgment. "And you"—his chill gray eyes went to Brianna's pale face—"will accompany her."

Despite the fact that she had expected some sort of punishment, Brianna had not been prepared for this. She bit her lip until she drew blood in an effort to hide the effect of his declaration.

" . . . will be better for all concerned. Dane will accompany you with several of my men. He will then return to London to join Lord William and the others will come back here. I release you from your oath of fealty and our betrothal."

Abbess Marie was the first to speak. "And what will you do when you discover you have made a dreadful mistake, Lord Roland?"

"There will be no such discovery, *madame.* I assure you I have not made this decision lightly. Tomorrow Robert of Wessex will be executed. Walter Kerwickson and Brianna will be beside me to witness his death as part of their punishment."

"That is barbaric!" the nun exclaimed in outrage.

"It is just! Kerwickson will also die if Ranulf does not recover from his injury. Were I not still so bewitched by her I would mete out the same punishment to Brianna." His voice shook very slightly from the raging emotion he felt.

Walter? Put to death? Mother of God! Brianna swayed forward, but the Abbess' arm swiftly snaked around her waist and held her firmly. "Do what you must, my lord, but you will one day answer to God for your actions," the Abbess said through stiff lips, once more in control.

Roland turned his head to look at his brother's flushed face before answering. "If God condemns me for avenging the senseless death of Ranulf, then so be it. But''—his eyes returned to the two women standing before him—''until that time, I am the arbiter of justice in all my holdings, and I have given you my decree.''

Both women were silent in the wake of his exit from the room. Then the Abbess gently disengaged her arm from Brianna's waist and poured her a cup of wine.

Numbly, Brianna swallowed the wine. It warmed her from within enough for her to collect her wits. " 'Tis for the best, you know. There is nothing for me here with Gilbert gone and Roland's love destroyed. At least I can return to friends and dedicate my life to God.''

The Abbess fingered the gold crucifix at her breast thoughtfully. ''It will be as he wishes, then. You must pray to God for the strength to see you through this abominable execution on the morrow. We will then endeavor to pull Lord Ranulf through this so we can leave for Walshire.'' She guided Brianna to the door and paused, her dark eyes full of purpose and determination. ''You have been gravely misjudged, my Brianna, and your wound runs deep, I know. But you must have faith. From all that I know of Lord Roland, he will seek to right this terrible wrong when his grievous error comes to light. I only hope that when the time comes, you will find it in your heart to forgive him.'' She touched Brianna's cheek gently, reassuringly. ''Go, child, and seek direction through our Lord.''

Brianna's steps, however, did not take her to the tiny sanctuary, but rather down the road to the homestead that had belonged to Gilbert. Oddly, it was still empty, and compelled by some invisible force, she went inside.

After her eyes adjusted to the dimness of the interior, she found everything was just as she remembered. The central hearth, now cold and silent, where she had done their cooking and soiled her face when the Normans came; the settle and the few chairs scattered about, a thick layer of dust coating their surfaces.

Then her eyes fell upon the charred remains of a garment lying abandoned in a corner, perhaps the same tunic Roland had tossed into the hearth in such a rage when—

She sat down then and put her head into her crossed arms on the table where they had taken their meals. And she wept for her devastating loss, until great, racking sobs shook her slender body and she purged her anguished mind of pain and guilt, easing the intolerable thought of a cold and empty life to a dull, deep-seated ache.

Her head turned slightly to the side as she took a great gulp of air, her face wet with tears. Her warm, flushed cheek encountered something hard and refreshingly cool. She sat up and looked down, her gaze falling upon William d'Avranches' heavy gold ring as it dropped down the length of chain to which it was attached with a soft clink. Brianna stared at the glimmer of gold for a moment as it bounced against the valley between her breasts with a muted thud and stilled. Her fingers closed around it. What had Lord William said to her? *Send this and we will come to you.*

She opened her palm and studied the soaring hawk whose garnet eyes winked up at her. She closed her eyes, willing her pounding heart to still. Could she go to Lord William? Her excitement abruptly diminished.

She had forgotten Roland. Always Roland at the center of everything. Rising to her feet reluctantly, Brianna wiped the remaining traces of tears from her cheeks. Somehow, some way, she would deal with Roland, convince him of her innocence. Just the thought that she might be able go to William lifted her shattered spirits enough to give her hope where Roland was concerned. And Ranulf—surely he would recover. Had not Reverend Mother said as much?

It was late and the manor was quiet. Brianna was kneeling beside Ranulf's bed, praying.

A few moments more and she raised her eyes to Ranulf's face. *Please get well,* she implored silently, and then she rested her cheek against his hand. *You are Roland's brother and I love you. Please get well—you must* . . . Her entreaties died away as she slowly sank down on the rush-covered floor, the side of her face just touching Ranulf's limp fingers, and drifted off to sleep.

But her slumber was interrupted by one dream chasing after another. And always Roland's angry, accusing face appeared before her. *Traitress! Witch —Nay Roland,* she denied. *I did not betray you! —You were the bait; nothing on earth would have succeeded as well. If Ranulf dies—if Ranulf dies—* She shook her head. *Nay! Ranulf will not die, he will not—*

Brianna—Brianna! 'Tis Ranulf! Wake up, Brianna— The dreams faded and Brianna awoke from her light sleep, but her eyelids were heavy. She snuggled her cheek against the bed-clothes, the warm, damp bedclothes—

She opened her eyes abruptly. Damp?

''Brianna?'' It was a whisper.

Please God—nay! Roland was here, whispering to her—Whispering?

''Brianna?'' came the faint query again. ''Is this any . . . any way to greet a man who—''

Ranulf!

Her head snapped up and her eyes met his, clear gray and rational. ''Ranulf! Oh, Ranulf, thank God!'' She kissed his hand and held it to her breast, the great blue-green eyes moist with tears.

''If I did not know better, I would say my brother had fooled us all merely to receive the attentions of a beautiful woman,'' Roland drawled from behind Brianna. Ranulf's eyes met his brother's, and he smiled wanly.

''From what I can recall, she has . . . been with me faith-fully.''

''Oh, Roland, he is restored to us!'' Brianna's face shone with joy, and her incredible loveliness as she gazed up at Roland for one magical moment would have melted the hardest of hearts.

"Aye, that he is," he answered, and Brianna thought she saw a flash of warmth—and something more—in the pewter-gray eyes.

Recovering herself quickly as Roland's gaze settled upon his twin's countenance, Brianna stood and looked down at the hand she was holding. The forearm was covered with a fine sheen of perspiration. "Roland, the linens! We must change the linens; they are wet."

"Now?" he inquired with mild impatience.

"Aye. We do not want him to catch a chill." And she motioned for Roland to hold Ranulf's upper torso while she stripped the bed beneath him.

"Can I not even rest?" Ranulf grumbled softly with feigned annoyance.

"You have been resting nigh on a sennight, lout." Roland laughed, and Brianna thought how boyishly carefree it sounded.

They finished changing the bedding, and Brianna took the kettle of broth down to the kitchen to be warmed over the cooking fire she knew would be burning. It seemed to take forever for the liquid to heat through and Brianna's fingers lightly tapped the table beside her impatiently. Ranulf was going to live and Roland—Roland had actually smiled at her! Her heart sang.

But when she returned to the bedchamber, she was disappointed to find that Ranulf was asleep once more and Roland's eyes were dark, the expression once again chillingly indifferent.

"Now that he is out of danger, I will send for Hilde to sit with him till morn. You will need your sleep in view of what is to come on the morrow." He turned toward Ranulf in what was most decidedly a gesture of dismissal.

Brianna's heart sank to her feet. *What is to come?* Surely that could only mean the execution of Robert of Wessex. Numbly she walked to her room, her thoughts awhirl. Nothing had changed. What a fool she was to think that Ranulf's impending recovery would make Roland forget everything and love her again. Reality homed in with crushing force, and she threw herself onto the bed weeping bitterly.

CHAPTER 25

Snow-white tufted clouds cavorted across the early September sky on a breeze that hinted at the cooler autumn weather to come. It was a far cry from the heavy, humid atmosphere of the past week, Brianna thought with some detachment as she leaned on her elbows at the window ledge, her chin cupped in her hands. It certainly was not a day for dying, came the unbidden thought, which pushed her more deeply into the melancholy that had settled over her.

Several of Roland's men rode in through the palisade gate. As they dismounted, Roland strode out to meet them, his stride light and swift, as if a great burden had been lifted from his shoulders. He was once again every inch the self-assured Norman knight now that he knew his beloved brother would be restored to him.

Brianna drew a shaky breath, watching his every movement, every gesture, as he stood in the bright sunlight talking to his men. She bit her quivering lip, ashamed of wanting him so. This was the Roland she had known and loved before everything had come crumbling down about her ears. And what hurt more than anything else was the fact that he now seemed unaffected by the situation between them—as if all the anguish he had suffered in the belief of her betrayal had faded into insignificance in the face of his latest victories. She only knew that she still remained hopelessly in love with the beautiful Norman knight in the yard below, and she ached for him until she felt she would die of it.

Roland, Roland! her heart cried out to him, and he slowly turned around. For one maddening moment Brianna thought he would look up at her, for it was an easy thing to see her from where he stood. But he deliberately refrained from raising his gaze.

Fool, she thought in misery, *you would have to fling yourself down at his feet to gain his attention!* A hysterical bubble of laughter rose in her throat at the thought. A dramatic but fitting end, no doubt. Her shoulders suddenly sagged and she leaned her warm forehead against the cool wooden shutter, utterly defeated.

Roland motioned to someone in the doorway below, and then one of the squires led Odo to him, and Brianna watched as Roland mounted and rode off with half a dozen men and a trussed-up Robert of Wessex following him. *Where will I find the strength to get through the beheading of Robert of Wessex?* she wondered dully, and found she didn't have the will to care anymore.

Suddenly strong arms slid around her, pulling her against a broad, solid chest comfortingly. "Brianna, *petite*," Dane spoke into her hair. "Come, come, *mon ange,* do not let him do this to you." He held her close, letting his strength communicate itself to her. "Come, little sister," he soothed. "You will show him your mettle, or my name is not d'Avranches! What say you, eh? Show him what he lost when he foolishly cast you aside." He held her away from him, and Brianna looked deeply into his golden-brown eyes, her heart constricted with the pain of her secret.

A wan smile curved her lips in answer to the determined expression on his darkly handsome features. "Aye, Dane. For you I will be strong."

"Nay, Brianna. Be strong for *yourself*—be strong for your innocence, your convictions, your honor, for surely you have all of these to equal any man." His fierce words fired something inside Brianna, and that indomitable spirit that had sustained her in the past year came to the fore. "That's my girl," he said encouragingly as her look of defeat changed before his eyes into something strong and resilient. He winked conspiratorially at her. "Now you are ready to face the lion."

Roland had chosen his site well, Brianna thought as she and Dane approached the new keep. From here, with the forbidding-looking fortress as a backdrop, Roland could impress upon the people of Derford that he was lord of the surrounding area, with might and men to back him if need be. And the people had come, all of them, to witness Rob's death, either out of curiosity or at Roland's command.

As Dane helped her dismount she noted Rob standing upon a small platform, obviously erected for the execution. Vachel and a white-faced Walter stood to his right, Roland to his left, his glance encountering hers and then flicking away to the Saxons standing around them uneasily. Brianna knew intuitively that she would be expected to take the place beside Roland, and a shiver of mingled excitement and apprehension went through her at the thought of being so close to him. How much could she endure? she wondered briefly before Dane's gaze met hers and he nodded reassuringly. Squaring her shoulders, Brianna let him escort her to the two crude steps leading up to the square platform. As she mounted them, her head held proudly, her eyes met Rob's, burning and hate-filled. Strangely, she felt only pity for him.

At a signal from Roland, Vachel, his gleaming, razor-honed sword in hand, commanded, "Kneel!"

Slowly Rob complied, stepping forward to drop down before the crowd of English and Normans.

"So, good people of Derford," Roland's clear, rich voice rang out, "be advised that while 'tis noble to fight in defense of one's lands in the face of an invader, 'tis also deplorable to create havoc within the new order of things as decreed by God. This man, Robert of Wessex, has done just that, killing Norman and Saxon alike in his attempts to incite rebellion against King William."

The breeze ruffled the shoulder-length chestnut hair of Robert of Wessex; Brianna could not help but admire his composure. She looked through the crowd for Hilde but could not find her. Had the girl fled the village to avoid sharing Rob's fate should Roland decide Walter spoke the truth?

" . . . was discovered within our midst," Roland went on implacably. "Unfortunately, 'twas Brianna of Derford who betrayed Ranulf and myself."

A murmur of disbelief rippled through the crowd, and Brianna's cheeks burned in spite of her determination to keep a tight rein on her emotions.

"Ranulf will recover from his injury, thank God, and therefore neither Walter Kerwickson nor Brianna will be put to death for their collusion with the man known as Rob. Rather, their punishment will be to witness his execution firsthand for their part in the troubles we have endured because of their treachery."

Brianna looked at Walter and was surprised to see that his eyes were glued to her face. Misery and regret were etched across his youthful features, and the sullenness was completely gone. He seemed to be reaching out to her in silent supplication.

"Because of Kerwickson's revelation regarding the outlaw's whereabouts, I sentence him to one year of hard labor on my demesne. Brianna, however, will return to Walshire Abbey to pray eternally for God to forgive her transgressions."

Brianna's fists clenched in outrage at her undeserved humiliation before all of Derford, but before she could react further, Walter stepped before Roland and went down on one knee. "I beg you, my lord, to reconsider your decision to punish her. I swear on King Harold's soul 'twas not Brianna who betrayed you." He raised a tear-streaked face and looked at the startled Brianna, remorse shining in the hazel depths of his eyes.

Roland frowned at the interruption. "Who was it then, Kerwickson?"

" 'Twas . . . another, but I cannot reveal her identity—"

"So you would let an innocent suffer for one who is guilty?"

Walter shook his head miserably. "All right, then—'twas Hilde."

Brianna was not surprised at the admission, and neither was Roland; he did not believe the distraught youth. The crowd was growing restless, for they sensed something of importance was happening. There were murmurs of anger and dissent among those who knew and loved Brianna as one of their own.

"An admirable effort, Walter, but I am not so easily gulled. I know of the love you bear Brianna, and it clouds your judgment—"

" 'Tis obviously more steadfast than that which *you* supposedly bore her!" the agitated youth snapped unthinkingly.

Roland's mouth tightened, the only indication Walter's rash words had affected him. "Get back to your place."

Walter complied after a last quick glance at Brianna, and Roland stepped forward beside the condemned Anglo-Saxon. "Before your sentence is carried out, have you aught to say?"

Roland blocked her view and Brianna could not see Rob's face, but his impassioned words were indication enough of his sentiments as he addressed his people. "Our cause is not yet lost, my fellow Anglo-Saxons! Even now they riot in the northern shires against the Norman tyrant. We do not ever have to submit, as long as there are those who have the will to resist!"

Roland spoke up then. "Know you that rebels will be meted out harsh but fair justice in return for their opposition to King William. Therefore, you are condemned to die, Robert of Wessex."

Roland stepped back beside Brianna, and out of the corner of her eye she could see Rob place his head on the crude wooden block. An unexpected burst of demonic laughter floated on the cool breeze and echoed throughout the buildings standing in the bailey.

Vachel raised the sword with both hands and paused, awaiting Roland's signal.

Down came the weapon of death, and in the instant before it struck its terrible blow, Brianna glanced at Dane, drawing strength from his very presence. *Be strong for yourself,* his look said to her, and then the dull thud of metal meeting flesh and cartilage sounded in the tension-filled stillness. Blood spurted everywhere from pulsing arteries, and the crowd cried out in horror and backed away.

Try as she might, Brianna could not control the roaring sound in her ears. *Do not swoon before him,* her pride screamed, but nature's buffers against harsh reality are not so easily controlled. Her knees gave way and she began to sink down, down—

An iron hand seized her by the elbow, and Roland's touch abruptly brought her to her senses as her pride could never have done. Storm-gray eyes bored into hers as her world began to right itself once more, and in response to the cold accusation in their icy depths, Brianna lashed out at him in the only way she could. "You deign to touch a traitress?"

"Traitress you may be, wicked Brianna," he answered grimly, "but I wonder if perhaps I shouldn't wed you after all."

Her strength returning, she tried to wrest her arm from his grip, but to no avail. "I will *never* marry you, Norman," she gritted through clenched teeth, "'no matter what you decide!"

He smiled slowly, a chilling smile that did not reach his eyes. "Oh, but think on it, Brianna. Would it not be an even more fitting punishment than living within the cold walls of Walshire? Your everlasting penance would be to wed me and live with my contempt after having known my love."

Stunned, she could only stare up at him, wondering belatedly if the stranger before her had ever really been the tender, compassionate Roland de Beaufort who had wooed her so patiently yet so ardently throughout the long months since she had first met him on a bloody battlefield.

"I'll escort you home, Brianna." Dane's voice broke the spell.

Brianna turned to him gratefully and felt Roland's fingers slip from her arm. Dane guided her to her mare, avoiding conversation with the milling onlookers. "Are you fit to ride, Brianna? You looked stunned a moment ago—what did he say to you?"

"Oh, Dane, he said he is considering marriage!"

Dane's forehead creased in bemusement. "What do you mean? He just told all of Derford that you were to be sent to Walshire." He shook his head and glanced over his shoulder in perplexity, only to see Roland standing just as they had left him, watching them with an enigmatic expression on his face.

"He thinks 'twould be an apt punishment, for he would make life with him a living hell, or so he said," she explained bitterly.

"I swear he is addled! He is a bigger fool than I thought if he thinks he can wed you and have the upper hand, and he is still too much in love with you to succeed in making you miserable for long. I thought Ranulf's recovery had taken much of the hostility from him, but it seems I was wrong." He raised his eyes to stare at the wooden keep, his face a study in vexation. "He is different since that incident on the way to Wexton. I know him almost as well as a brother, and I swear to you, Brianna"—his eyes returned to her face—"that I have never seen him like this. So bitter and vengeful . . ."

"He cannot truly force me to exchange vows with him, can he, Dane?" Brianna asked anxiously, a hand on his arm. Before he could answer, Nedra came up to them, Edythe and Aleen in tow.

"I beg your pardon, my lord," she said to Dane apologetically, "but I wondered if I might speak to Brianna before she leaves."

"Nedra!" exclaimed Brianna, eager to speak to someone

from outside the manor. "Of course Dane does not begrudge you a word with me." She hugged the older woman and found Nedra's embrace comforting and freely given.

"I will await you yonder," Dane informed her, and nodded to the newcomers before leading his destrier away.

"Oh, Brianna, how could he be so cruel?" blurted Aleen, her face still wan from the gruesome scene she had just witnessed.

"Hush, girl," warned Nedra. "He is lord here and he must punish wrongdoers."

Edythe touched Brianna's arm. "He believes you betrayed him, Brianna, and of a certainty that has added to his burden as liege lord. Give him time to sort things out."

But that was little comfort to Brianna.

"Why don't you come and spend the afternoon with us, child?"

Brianna's face brightened at Nedra's suggestion. Oh, to be away from the manor and all the troubles and bad feelings contained within its walls! She nodded with the first enthusiasm she had shown in days. "I would love to."

"Why, you can sup with us," put in Aleen, her mind temporarily distracted from her disillusionment with Roland. "Then you can stay even longer."

Longer? The entire afternoon and into the evening hours? Brianna looked up at the cloud-dotted sky. It was only just afternoon. Her mind began to work as she led her mare across the empty moat to where Dane stood talking to René de Falaise. She had a good horse in her possession, and Nedra and Kerwick could provide her with food and water. And she had Lord William's ring still nestled between her breasts.

Suddenly she felt strangely at peace within herself for the first time since Roland had overheard her confession to Abbess Marie. She had come to a decision. She only had to implement it, and it appeared that the opportunity was at hand.

"Are you *mad*, girl?" demanded Kerwick disbelievingly.

"Nay, Kerwick, but I *shall* go mad if I am forced into this travesty of a marriage."

"But . . . but that it is dangerous is only one of many considerations, Brianna!" he sputtered, unexpectedly feeling as helpless before her determination as he had a year before when she had insisted on traveling to Hastings.

"My horse is fresh, you can give me food to see me through and I have many hours before dark. How can I ignore the chance?" she insisted.

"Let me go with you, Brianna," Walter pleaded earnestly, already accepting the fact that she would go.

Kerwick rounded on his son angrily. "You have stirred up enough trouble, boy, and you are fortunate to have escaped with your life. Surely Lord Roland would have your head if you had any part in this lackwitted scheme!"

Nedra contemplated Brianna thoughtfully, calm as always in the eye of the storm. "What if William d'Avranches is not your sire, Brianna?"

Unperturbed, the girl shrugged in dismissal. "Then, at the least, he will help me return to Walshire. He has pledged his protection if ever I should need it, and I do not doubt his word. Perhaps King William himself will take my side if I must enlist his aid against Roland as well." Excited at the opportunity provided by chance, Brianna did not stop to envision what could go awry.

"It will be dark before Lord Roland inquires after you," Brand added exuberantly. "You could be halfway to London by then!"

Brianna smiled indulgently at him. "Aye, so I can—if your father will give his approval." She looked at Kerwick and Nedra, sudden concern marring the alabaster brow. "I do not believe Roland will harm any of you in reprisal. Only his pride will be damaged when he discovers he has lost the pawn in his cruel game. He truly does not love me." Her voice trembled with emotion at her admission. "He merely seeks to hurt me in retribution for what he considers my misdeeds."

Nedra shook her graying head in disagreement. "You are wrong, child, but even Lord Roland does not yet realize how much he still loves you."

Brianna bit her lip to stop the tears that threatened. "May I borrow breeches and a tunic of Brand's? It will be safer for me to ride as a lad."

Kerwick paced the room in agitation, knowing he would not be able to prevent her, yet unwilling to give in. "And how will you get past the manor with a horse, lass? You cannot drag the mare through the thick weald."

Edwin answered for her, much to his father's annoyance. "There is a path in the forest, to the south. It eventually goes past the castle. I can lead Brianna to it, and once we are safely by the manor and keep, I can accompany her to the Roman road, which leads straightaway to London."

Kerwick looked helplessly at Nedra, the question hanging in the air. She decided for him. "If Edwin guides her safely past Lord Roland's lands, by nightfall she will be well on her way to London. She will be more secure on the Roman road at night dressed as a lad. But she needs a weapon."

"I have a dagger," Walter offered, and reached into his tunic to produce a small but wicked-looking knife. He handed it to Brianna, a grave look on his face. "It was given to me by Rob."

At Brianna's hesitation in the wake of his words, he placed the weapon in her hands, holding one of his own over hers. " 'Tis little enough after the way I have wronged you, Brianna. God go with you, and remember that I will love you always." Before she could respond, he kissed her chastely on the cheek and left the hall, obviously disturbed by what she was about to do.

Kerwick cleared his throat to break the awkward silence. "Go quickly and fetch her some clothing," he gruffly ordered Brand. "We dare not tarry."

He eyed Brianna doubtfully, a frown revealing his concern. "For what 'tis worth, you have my blessing, Brianna. You will need every bit of luck and divine intervention you can muster.'' Brianna nodded solemnly, but her eyes shone with the excitement of the challenge. ''Have a care, child, for I have most serious reservations about this hare-brained scheme. In fact''—he looked at the other members of his family, noting the same excitement on the other youthful countenances—''I do not like this—I do not like this at all.''

Roland sat on the settle before a small fire built to hold the threatening chill at bay in the great hall. Supper was over, and some of the men were playing dice or chess to pass the evening. Roland sat alone, staring into the dancing, leaping flames, a jeweled goblet of wine in one hand.

To his vexation, Brianna's image kept appearing in the orange-red glow. Perhaps he was fooling himself, he thought dully. If he couldn't get her out of his mind when she was not present, to what degree would his thoughts torture him should they become man and wife?

He frowned and drained the goblet, stretching his long legs out before him carelessly. He would speak to Father Simon; they could be wed in the morning. Abbess Marie would remain, no doubt, until after the ceremony. And then what? He shook his head in exasperation. *You will carry on with your life as usual!* he thought in irritation. But he knew that wouldn't happen. There would be new troubles aplenty. And Brianna would not countenance his indifference forever—*if* he could remain indifferent. No matter how betrayed he felt, he could not live with Brianna as husband in name only. And after that his lovemaking would reveal what his words would not. That he loved her still, damn her scheming soul to hell.

Perhaps he should forget this travesty and send her packing to Walshire. No doubt she would prefer it. But he could not bring himself to let her go. The thought of life without her left him cold and empty, and seeing her poise and courage before the people of Derford this morning had brought him to the realization that no matter what she had done, he could not bear to lose her.

He stood abruptly, unable to contend with his musings any longer, and started for the stairs. Twilight was falling and Brianna would be returning soon. He wanted to spend some time with Ranulf before he dealt with her.

He strode down the upstairs corridor, slowing his steps as he entered his brother's room. Abbess Marie was clearing a cup and a bowl off the beside table. Ranulf was smiling up at her, still pale but looking better than he had in days.

At Roland's entrance, Ranulf's head turned, and his eyes lit up at the sight of his brother. "You think to sneak up on the invalid, eh, Roland? Well, I am not so disabled as that."

The lighthearted words were music to Roland's ears. He grinned and moved forward. "So you think you are ready for battle because you've had some watered wine and sopped bread."

The Abbess threw him a disapproving look. "He is hardly ready for aught, Lord Roland, having only just come back from death's door."

Instantly contrite, Roland sobered. "Of course, Reverend Mother. I was merely jesting."

"Well, jest all you like then, my lord, only do not tire him overmuch." She took the tray and left the two brothers alone.

Roland sat down beside the bed, placing a hand over one of Ranulf's. "So you have finally decided to waken and learn what you have been missing."

Ranulf smiled again. "By all means, you must enlighten me."

Roland's expression turned serious. "Robert of Wessex, also known as Rob, was beheaded this morn."

Ranulf looked surprised for a moment and then toyed with the linen sheet beneath his fingertips. " 'Tis a pity to have put such a valiant man to death—"

"*Pity?*" Roland broke in, the good humor vanishing from

his face. "The man almost kills you and you mourn his death? I think the fever left you addled."

Ranulf closed his eyes for a moment, and Roland feared he would sleep again. "Of course he did not fight in the accepted way—which would make him seem a coward in the eyes of a *chevalier*. But to him the only thing that mattered was winning, and he could not have won with his pitiful handful of men had he fought in the conventional manner."

Roland sighed. "I thought to keep good company when I sought you out. Instead you preach to me of an outlaw's virtues. Besides," he added darkly, "he tried to throttle Brianna."

Ranulf's eyes opened to show concern. "She is unhurt?"

"Aye. Dane went to her rescue—*after* having second thoughts about giving her an audience with the wily devil."

Ranulf frowned, puzzled. "Why in God's name would Brianna ever wish to speak to Rob?"

Roland's mouth tightened and his words were suddenly forced, clipped. "To conspire with him."

Ranulf started to laugh softly, and the movement jarred his upper torso. His breath caught at the pain in his shoulder. " 'Tis a poor jest, Roland. You must not make me laugh yet, for—" Then his eyes met Roland's, and the latter's expression told him Roland was serious. "You really *believe* that?"

"I do. She played us false, Ranulf. *She* was the one." His eyes communicated the anguish he felt. "I am sorry, Ranulf," he said bitterly, "for although she would have had you killed, I cannot get her out of my mind. . . ."

Ranulf returned his gaze for a long moment. Then he sighed and turned his head away, his eyelids drooping tiredly. "Roland, Roland! When will you cease your blundering where Brianna is concerned?" Roland's eyes narrowed, but he said nothing. "You have always dealt so skillfully with the women in your life, and I envied you that." He opened his eyes then, but his voice was even weaker from the effort of speaking at length. "But then you met Brianna, and when your experience was needed most, for some reason I cannot fathom you be-haved like a bumbling clod in your efforts to woo her. I marvel that she ever consented to wed you.''

''Just what are you trying to say, Ranulf?'' Roland asked softly, a tight rein on his exacerbated temper.

''Brianna was not responsible for what happened the morn-ing we rode to Wexton.''

Roland's expression did not change, for he would not per-mit himself to dare hope that Ranulf spoke the truth. ''Who was?'' he asked, his voice tinged with sarcasm.

''Hilde.''

In the stillness that ensued, Roland fought a silent battle to squelch the tiny flicker of hope that blazed to life within him. Ranulf was the second person to name the fair Hilde as the culprit. He stood up so abruptly the chair tilted precariously and then righted itself. ''That cannot be. Brianna admitted to her involvement with Rob.'' He walked to the window, his lean, well-shaped fingers gripping the back of his neck in ag-itation. The dusk revealed the last pinpoints of light on a glo-rious pink and violet horizon over the trees, but Roland was blind to the beauty before him.

''I . . . I do not know of her dealings with the Saxon, but . . .'' Ranulf's voice trailed off, and Roland spun around and strode to the bed, suddenly bent on hearing his brother's rea-son for thinking Brianna blameless. At first he thought Ranulf had fallen into exhausted slumber, but his fingers clenching the edge of the light coverlet told Roland he was still awake, and he leaned over the bed, his heart thumping in his chest.

''Tell me, Ranulf—how do you know 'twas Hilde?''

Ranulf tried to open his eyes but failed. ''The night before . . . we left, I saw her . . . saw her leave the hall and—''

''Aye, Ranulf, go on,'' he urged.

With a last effort, Ranulf's heavy lids lifted and his gaze met Roland's. ''She went to the bower—de Montrain's. I was talking to him while he awaited her.''

Roland straightened and, still not quite convinced, shook his head slowly. "But that proves nothing, Ranulf."

"Guy was . . . drinking heavily. You need only think back . . . to remember how loose-tongued he becomes when he is in his cups." He raised a hand toward his brother and Roland caught it. "I would wager the de Beaufort name . . . that he unwittingly let slip what he knew."

Roland raised his eyes, staring unseeingly. Remembering the morning that Guy had come to him. *I believe I know who betrayed you and Ranulf.* If de Montrain had thought it was Brianna, he would never have told Roland in her presence, no matter how Roland had insisted.

If Ranulf were right, Guy had been trying to voice the same suspicion that Hilde had relayed what she discovered to Walter, not Brianna.

Sweet Jesus, what had he done?

CHAPTER 26

"London?"

Kerwick nodded unhappily, his worst fears coming to fruition before his lord's disbelieving and then angry countenance.

"I tried to dissuade her, my lord, but my arguments were in vain—"

"And you denounced her before all of Derford, Lord Roland," Nedra broke in to remind him gravely. Keen gray eyes knifed into hers as she continued. "Why should you object when she means naught to you? You should consider yourself well rid of her if you believe she played you false."

A muscle twitched in Roland's jaw, betraying his fury. "Surely, woman, you know me better than that. Surely anyone who has ever loved would recognize the reason for my irrational behavior where Brianna is concerned. You dared much, both of you," came the soft, menacing reply.

"It is not too late to catch up with her, my lord," interjected Aleen timidly.

Roland's expression changed to one of wary bemusement. "But why in the name of all the saints would she go to *London?* There is no one there to whom she could turn for help."

"Lord William is there," answered Nedra, "and Brianna believes he is her natural father."

Roland looked at her as if she were undone. "Her father? What madness is this?"

"Rob told her that her real sire was a Norman, and it appears Lord William knew Brianna's mother."

Of course. Why hadn't he thought of it sooner? Hadn't there been a maddeningly elusive resemblance between Dane and Brianna which, until now, he had never pinpointed? And when Brianna had spoken of her natural father in Rob's presence, Roland had been too overwrought to pay any heed to the implications of her claim.

But he was wasting precious time. "When did she leave, Kerwick?"

"Shortly after we returned from the execution."

God help him, that was hours ago. "How did she go?"

"By the Roman road, my lord," volunteered Edwin. "We thought she would be safer traveling the road at night and dressed as a lad."

Roland turned to the young man bleakly. "There is no such thing as 'safe,' Edwin, as long as there are deserters from William's ranks and dispossessed Englishmen roaming the countryside." He faced Kerwick and Nedra once more. "I know you both love Brianna, and perhaps you feared for her at my hand. But even in my darkest hour of doubt I would never have harmed her. When I did not know if Ranulf would live or die because of what I perceived as her treachery, I still did nothing save hurl angry words at her."

He moved toward the door, his shoulders squared with sudden strength of purpose.

"Godspeed, Lord Roland," said Kerwick as he followed Roland outside.

"Aye, my lord," added Nedra, close behind Kerwick. "Brianna got to Hastings and back unscathed. She is a match for any renegade, Norman or otherwise."

Roland swung onto Odo's back, automatically adjusting his sword, his battle-honed senses taking over instinctively. "No woman alone is a match for cutthroats or undisciplined mercenaries. And you forget she has been out of the convent barely a year. I can only pray that I reach her before anyone else does.''

"Shall I send Edwin to alert Lord Dane, my lord?" Kerwick offered.

He shook his head. "I shall apprise my man standing watch at the gate and Dane can catch up." He stared down at them in the moonlight, their faces mirroring his own concern and misgivings. "I pray God I am not too late."

Brianna lifted her face to the kiss of the cool evening breeze. A lambent full moon and a host of coruscating points of light peeking through the trees on either side of the road lulled her, as did the rolling movement of the animal beneath her. Brianna's confidence soared as the distance from Derford increased without incident. She hoped to be in London by daybreak.

Silver-gray eyes invaded her thoughts. And despite her desperate attempts to conjure up hatred, and to convince herself that he had nothing but her contempt, she had only managed to erect a whisper-thin barrier between her own emotional vulnerability and the overwhelming attraction he still held for her.

She sighed, the spell cast by the clear, peaceful night spoiled by thoughts of a warm, tender love gone cold. Well, she thought in an effort to marshal her wits, perhaps she could travel to Normandy with Lord William. Or she could return to the abbey. In either case she would never have to see Roland de Beaufort again, and it would be infinitely less painful to carry on her life without his presence as a constant reminder of what she once had, and suffering the unending torture of wanting and needing him when he was close, yet so far away from her.

The mare pricked its ears forward alertly, but Brianna was too absorbed in her thoughts to notice. Then the horse threw back her head in alarm, but it was too late. A huge hand clamped over her mouth and a powerful arm snaked around her waist, roughly hauling her down off the horse and pinning her against a hard body.

"What's this?" asked a voice in heavily accented English. "What could a lad be doing alone on this lonely road at night?" She was turned around, the hand slipping from her mouth in the process, and Brianna found herself face to face with Hugh of Brittany.

Her heart thudded in her chest until it drowned out all other sounds, and she could only stare wide-eyed at the Breton before her in the moonlight.

"Well? How are you called, English whelp?" He gave her a hard shake and, to her horror, Brianna felt her carefully pinned tresses slipping down. One thick lock slid over her ear to nestle impudently along her fragile jawline

As she stared into the Breton's face, recognition dawned in his eyes. "Well, well," he said softly, "what do we have here?" His hand carelessly raked through her hair, forcing it to spill down to her shoulders like a curtain of ebony silk. "Brianna," he breathed huskily, obviously stuck by his unbelievably good fortune.

"Nay!" she denied in a spurt of angry bravado. To have escaped Roland only to fall victim to *this!* Hugh of Brittany put a hand under her chin to raise it to the moon's radiant glow.

Brianna slapped it away, but this was no Roland de Beaufort—no man to back off in the face of an affronted maiden. The steely fingers only returned with the swiftness of a striking serpent to cruelly clamp to her chin once more as the owner inspected the delicate features, the eyes misty with tears of frustration.

"What is it, Hugh?" asked a voice in French from behind him. The man appeared around Hugh's shoulder, and Brianna's eyes, ablaze with outrage, met his. " 'Tis *she*—the one de Beaufort snatched from beneath your nose!"

Hugh's fingers tightened convulsively around Brianna's jaw at the reminder, and she cried out softly in pain. The Breton brazenly pulled her up against the length of him until she could smell the ale on his breath. Her stomach turned and she bit her lip to hold back the bile.

"A wench?" growled the man who had seized the mare's reins to prevent the animal from bolting. "What do we need a wench for? We can have our fill when we get back to Normandy."

Hugh relaxed his hold slightly and Brianna was able to back away a few inches, her eyes straining in the darkness to see them better. There were six of them, counting Hugh of Brittany.

"She goes with us," Hugh declared, eyeing his men one by one in open challenge.

"But she'll only hinder us. William is surely on the lookout for us. What if—"

"Do you think me so lily-livered as that?" Hugh cut him off derisively. "I will leave this island when I damned well please! William is too busy dealing with rebellious Anglo-Saxons to pay us—or any other disillusioned followers—much heed." He looked down at Brianna. "We need some time to get reacquainted, little dove, do we not?" he crooned silkily.

"And what of de Beaufort?" asked the man who had recognized Brianna. "If he wants her too, what is to say that he will not come looking for her, eh?"

"Aye, Hugh!" exclaimed yet another. "Mayhap she ran away from him and it will only serve to whet his appetite for her. I would not care to have *him* breathing down my neck!"

Hugh gave the man a contemptuous look and then gazed down at the silent Brianna. "What exactly *did* happen, little dove? Did you tire of de Beaufort's pretty face?"

At Brianna's stubborn silence, a new thought crept into his mind, and his expression turned black. "Did he make you his, wench?"

Brianna had the strongest urge to fling the fact of their love in his craggy face, but the look that twisted his features gave her pause. "I was only recently widowed, Breton."

He studied her face for a moment. "That wouldn't stop someone like de Beaufort for long. Tell me, did he—"

"Not now, for God's sake!" exclaimed one of the Normans in exasperation. "We are sitting ducks out here in the open road and under a full moon. You can talk all you want—and anything else—" a few sniggers sounded from the others— "when we return to the safety of the forest."

"You are right, Edward. See to the mare," Hugh directed someone behind Brianna.

"What . . . what are you going to do?" Brianna asked, struggling valiantly to keep the alarm from her voice.

He grinned evilly at her, the light from the star-studded heavens playing about his features to give his face a malevolent cast. "Why, I am whisking you away to our lair, beautiful Brianna. Surely you cannot object to my devoted attentions if you were fleeing that mincing peacock de Beaufort."

"You have no right to lay even a hand on me!"

His fingers tightened brutally on her arm. "Oh, but I have *every* right, wench! De Beaufort spirited you away from me after a hard-fought battle. To the victor go the spoils, and you were mine to take until he interfered."

Rage surged through Brianna at his temerity. "I am no man's—" she began through gritted teeth, but he cut her off sharply.

"And that little ploy his idiotic brother staged has only added to the debt he owes me."

"What ploy?" Brianna asked in an effort to keep him talking. For deep within her heart there was a faint glimmer of hope that Roland would come after her. That any moment he would come thundering into view on his invincible white charger, sword in hand, to cut down the man beside her in fitting revenge before the Breton could pull her into the obscurity of the weald.

"You mean he did not tell you of Ranulf's trick?" At the negative shake of her head, he ran his free hand over her breasts in a lewd assault on her dignity. Brianna stiffened in revulsion, but her pride refused to give him the reaction he sought. "Perhaps de Beaufort was foolish enough to leave you to your crippled husband. He is more stupid than I thought if he failed to see your worth as a confidante as well as . . . other things." His lips twisted into a sneer. "But we can talk all night long, little one." And he jerked her arm viciously as he started toward the black forest that rose before them.

The two horsemen cantered along the cracked stone road. Once Roman troops had traveled the length of it when it had been smooth and easily traversed. Now Roland feared the noise they would make at full gallop.

Surely we should have overtaken her by now, he thought with increasing trepidation. He raised an arm to signal Dane, and they brought their horses to a halt.

"What is it?" Dane asked curtly, his eager mount pawing the ground impatiently.

Roland ran a forearm across his brow and glanced around, trying to penetrate the shadows to the side of the road. "Something is not right. We should have overtaken her by now. Unless . . ."

Dane stared at his friend thoughtfully. "Do not think the worst, Roland. She may have heard our approach and melted into the forest."

"Then how can we protect her from harm if we cannot find her?" Roland asked angrily. "I can face anything that I can see, but this . . . this not knowing! By all that is holy, where *is* she?"

"Does your conscience bother you, *mon ami?*" Dane inquired softly, a touch of irony in his voice.

Roland tightened his grip on the reins in reaction to Dane's bold question. Odo tossed his magnificent head in silent protest. "If you were not my closest friend I would challenge you for that!"

"I merely question your motives. Do you only seek to bring her back to a life of misery with you in payment for her alleged betrayal of the de Beauforts? Or have you decided to forgive her?''

"There is naught to forgive." Roland nudged the war-horse forward, and they walked the animals along side by side.

Dane shot his friend a look of exaggerated disbelief. "No! Have you finally come to your senses, Roland?''

Roland kept his face forward, giving Dane only his granite profile. "I have wronged her greatly." His voice was taut with emotion.

"Ah, I see. And just how did you come to this belated— but nonetheless momentous—decision?''

Roland swiftly turned his grief-ravaged countenance upon his companion. "Enough! Ranulf told me Hilde was with Guy de Montrain the night before we rode to Wexton. He believes Guy told the girl what he knew after overimbibing. Walter Kerwickson also told me this morn that Hilde was the informant, but I did not take his word seriously.''

Dane's mouth twisted wryly. "So you have succeeded in playing the lackwit with the one woman you should have believed in the face of all odds.''

Roland's silver-gray eyes glittered dangerously in the luminous moonlight. "Do not lecture me now, my friend, or I may be tempted to silence you." He urged Odo to a trot.

A long, steely arm shot out in the darkness to catch at Roland's tunic sleeve, jerking him around enough to meet Dane's look of hostility. "I will say anything I see fit," he ground out harshly, "for *I love her too!* Do you think we all doubted her and questioned our affection for her just because of your idiocy?''

Roland shook Dane's hand from his sleeve. "You are right," he said unexpectedly. "I take back my rash words.'' He paused, then said quietly, "Your love was more aptly directed than you could ever have known, Dane. I have learned she fled to London in search of your father.''

Something in his tone made Dane's brows come together

as he pondered Roland's meaning. "Well, he offered her his protection if ever—"

"Nay, you do not understand. She has reason to believe that Lord William is her natural father."

Dane looked askance at his friend, the thought crossing his mind that Roland had finally been undone by the events of the past senninght, when Roland's hand went silently, swiftly to his sword hilt, his body stiffening in readiness as his attention riveted on something ahead of them.

His own hand repeating Roland's move in the blink of an eye, Dane strained to make out who—or what—was moving out onto the road from the shelter of the forest.

"Who goes there?" Roland demanded tersely.

"Brianna?" whispered Dane hopefully, for as the figure emerged from the shadows it appeared to be a youth—or someone disguised as a youth—leading a small English pony.

Roland, too, waited tensely, sword at the ready, for who else could it be at this hour but—

" 'Tis I, Walter Kerwickson, my lord," answered the youth, stunning both knights, and as he led his shaggy pony toward them, the glow from the full moon revealed him to indeed be Kerwick's rash middle son.

Bitter disappointment washed over Roland, and he thrust his sword back into its scabbard with unnecessary force. "Back into the thick of clandestine activities, are you, Kerwickson?" he inquired scathingly. "It would seem I was too lenient with you."

"Nay, Lord Roland," he denied vigorously. "I followed Brianna from Derford."

Dane glanced at Roland, his expression registering surprise, but Roland's eyes were locked with those of the young man before him on the moonlit road. "Then where is she?"

"A man named Hugh abducted her."

Roland's blood froze in his veins. *Hugh of Brittany.* He could only think of the inherent cruelty of the man, and the greedy, lascivious manner in which he had devoured Brianna with his eyes when he had accosted her at Hastings. *You'll pay for that little trick, de Beaufort! I'll not soon forget it . . .* And indeed he had not forgotten it, for he jumped Roland one night as the latter returned alone to his tent. Only because of Dane's timely interference had the Breton's life been spared after he managed to slice Roland's jaw with his razor-sharp dagger. And then he had sought and found Brianna, ostensibly to discover what had become of one of his henchmen when they had raided Derford. And now—now Hugh had snatched the prize he had so diligently tracked. . . .

"William ordered him from England, the last I heard. Why would he still be here?" Dane asked, not quite convinced.

"Brianna."

Dane looked at Roland.

"You saw to what lengths he went to discover if I had found her—to boldly ride onto my lands after attacking me at Hastings! The man is not the most intelligent, but he is sly and unpredictable. And now he has Brianna while believing Ranulf and I have both wronged him." What he did not say was more eloquent than anything he could have added.

Dane looked over at Walter, suddenly accusing. "Then why did you not go after them instead of hiding in the trees like some frightened child?"

Walter bristled. "I may have been a fool in my estimation of Lord Roland, but I am not stupid, Norman."

"Easy, lad," soothed Roland. His glance flicked briefly to Dane. "Walter is no coward, my friend, and he also happens to love Brianna." His eyes returned to the youth. "What happened?"

"The scum dragged her off the mare, and five others came out of the weald behind him. He recognized Brianna and said something about a debt owed him by you and Lord Ranulf."

Roland's jaw clenched, the only outward indication of his black fury.

Dane snorted derisively. "You were that close to them and did nothing? Come, Roland. We've wasted enough time."

"You forget one thing, Norman. Only *I* know where they have taken Brianna. You could search the weald for a fortnight and have naught to show for your efforts."

Dane fought the urge to jump to the ground and throttle Walter on the spot. "Then where *is* she?"

Walter ignored him and moved to within an arm's length of Odo. "Lord Roland, they were six to my one. I would have had no chance to secure Brianna's release against them. I knew you would come in search of her despite your decree that she return to Walshire. You see," he added quietly, "I know 'tis impossible to stop loving her."

Under different circumstances, Roland would have been moved by this touching declaration, but there was no time for sentimentality. "Where did they take her, Walter?" he asked in a low, urgent voice.

"I can show you better than I can tell you, my lord. Let me go with you!" he entreated.

"You cannot be serious!" Dane exclaimed impatiently, and then turned to Roland. "What use can he possibly be against seasoned soldiers?"

Still ignoring Dane, Walter stared up at the silent, unmoving Roland. "I have trained with you in the shadow of your own hall, my lord. And have you forgotten so quickly that I was tutored by Rob as well? Mayhap I can help you when you surprise them, for you cannot go charging into their midst on your war-horses."

"Aye, so we cannot, Walter," Roland replied as he raised his eyes to study the living black wall of forest looming before them.

"Then you will let me go with you?"

Roland hesitated only a moment before answering. "Very well, Kerwickson. You shall go with us."

"You will not regret your decision, my lord, for three to six is better odds than two."

Roland nodded his head and fleetingly returned his gaze to the young Saxon before him. Walter shuddered inwardly at what he saw in his lord's eyes. He could almost feel pity for Hugh of Brittany, for in those glittering gray depths was death.

"Here, wipe that muck from your face. I wish to see the spoils for which I've waited so long."

Brianna looked up at the Breton, sea-blue eyes mirroring her defiance. "I am not the same untried maiden you pounced upon at Hastings, Breton."

The homely face turned ugly with anger. "You will do my bidding, girl, or every one of my men will have a go at you when I've finished!" He took a drink of wine from a battered flask on the table beside him, wiping his mouth with the back of his hand afterward.

They were in the crude, filthy dwelling of a woodcutter, well within the forest. A small clearing had been made before the hovel by the previous occupant, and there, around a small fire, rested four of the Normans. The fifth stood watch, and Hugh of Brittany was grudgingly granted the luxury of the one-room shelter to share with Brianna.

"Clean your face!"

Brianna started as his harsh command shattered the quiet of the room. Reluctantly she put the sour-smelling rag thrust at her to her cheek. She sensed it was better to humor him, for the more he drank, the uglier his disposition became.

She was seated on the foul, rotting remains of a straw pallet on the hard-packed earthen floor. Her adversary had turned a rickety, straight-backed chair around and straddled it, a container of wine in one hand, the other hand braced on one knee. His leering dark eyes studied her keenly in the wavering light from the fire in the tiny central hearth. His expression was difficult to read, as the light was behind him, but Brianna's slightest movement was exposed by the flickering illumination.

She desperately sought a means to keep him at bay, for she knew that he fully intended to have her. Not only would the act in itself be the ultimate debasement, but she anticipated cruel physical abuse at the hands of her antagonist as well. The longer she was in his company, the more she dreaded what would inevitably come.

"You are beautiful by any light, little dove," he murmured softly after she had cleaned her face of all traces of grime. "In the bright morning light at Hastings, in the soft glow of a full moon on a deserted road and now before the orange-red splendor of a humble hearth fire in a woodcutter's hut. No wonder de Beaufort took such pains to find you."

Brianna bit back a searing riposte in the face of his unexpected eloquence. The man's moods were mercurial. "Lord Roland did not seek me out, Breton; he was sent to Wessex by William of Normandy."

The Breton laughed aloud. "Is that what he told you, Brianna?"

Not quite, she thought, racking her brain for a safer topic, for he obviously wanted to direct the conversation toward her relationship with Roland, and that was dangerous ground. "What . . . what trick did Lord Ranulf play on you?"

Her question made his eyes narrow in annoyance. "That fair-haired coxcomb convinced me that he hated his twin— that Roland had always been the favored son, and that he longed for revenge. He overheard me making plans to raid Roland's grant in Wessex and persuaded me that he knew exactly where to go and how best to anger his brother."

Suddenly Brianna remembered Dane's explanation, at Ranulf's behest, for the latter's part in the raid on Derford. She was treading thin ice, she realized as she glanced up at Hugh of Brittany. Thickheaded he might have been, but he seemed to have read her thoughts.

"You knew all along, didn't you, Brianna?"

She shook her head emphatically, her shiny skein of hair dancing about her porcelainlike features. "Nay, I—"

She got no further, for he was beside her on the pallet in a trice. One hand tangled in her hair, yanking her head back brutally as he rasped, "I think you are an accomplished liar, beautiful Brianna. I think de Beaufort has had you for his pleasure since the beginning, and therefore he has taken that which was rightfully mine!''

Tears of pain sprang into her eyes. ''Nay, Breton, 'twas not the way of it!''

''Enough!'' he snarled, forcing her down upon the moldering pallet and pressing his sticky lips to hers.

Brianna twisted her head frantically to get away from his cloying kiss, her hands ineffectually pummeling his back. He was strong as an ox, his weight upon her slender body pinning her helplessly; her lungs labored to get air.

And then she remembered Walter's dagger at her waist. She had worn it under Brand's breeches, and so far it had not been discovered. Perhaps she could— No! She would not kill again. Her life was not yet in danger. There could be no justification for the use of a knife.

Hugh of Brittany's hand came up like a striking snake to rip her overtunic down the front. He removed his mouth from hers long enough to swear softly at encountering Brand's chainse as well. Another jerk of his mighty arm and that, too, gave way. To Brianna's mortification, he eagerly grabbed a tender coral nipple in his mouth, sucking greedily. Desperately she tried to push him away, but he clamped down harder on the soft bud, causing excruciating pain.

Blindly she groped for the dagger, her previous reservations disappearing before his rapacious assault. Relieved, she relaxed slightly as her hand encountered it, and in response his invading mouth eased its cruel plunder of her breast as he took the cessation of her struggles for capitulation.

Slowly she eased the weapon from the strip of leather around her waist, sick inside at the things Hugh of Brittany was doing with his hands. She tensed before she arced the dagger outward to prepare her swing, and like a sly predator, ever alert to its enemies, the Breton sensed the subtle change. With surprising speed, his arm swung outward to ward off the blow, the back of his hand inadvertently impaling itself on the glinting tip of the knife.

He sat up abruptly, his other hand still pinning hers to the pallet while blood from the injured member seeped between his fingers. "Bitch!" he raged. "You think to stop me from having you with a puny dagger?" He stood and hauled her to her feet by the tattered ends of her clothing. Bringing her face up to his till she could see the very pores in his skin and smell the fetid odor of wine in a mouth of decaying teeth, he stared into her widened eyes for what seemed like an eternity. Then he shoved her backward with such force that she stumbled over the chair and went tumbling toward the stone hearth as his raucous laughter filled the room. As her temple struck the raised hearth and a myriad of lights exploded inside her head, she could only think that she would be better off dead than violated by this man.

Moments, or hours, later—she knew not which—her eyes opened tentatively and she felt the heat from the fire searing the side of her face. She pushed herself up to a sitting position, every muscle protesting, and focused her attention with difficulty upon her abductor.

Hugh of Brittany sat before her, his injured hand haphazardly wrapped, contemplating her thoughtfully. His tunic had been removed, exposing his massive chest of black fur. "So, little dove, you've decided to awaken from your beauty sleep. Well, you will have to wipe your face again, for your little mishap bloodied the side of your head. Tsk, tsk," he clucked as his eyes sought the rag she had used earlier.

She raised one hand to her temple. It came away with a crimson stain.

"Well, we seem to have lost it in the scuffle, but I think"—he studied her with exaggerated care, his dark head cocked to one side—"that I rather fancy you this way, with your hair in disarray and your face as wild-looking as some cornered vixen's."

At last his words began to penetrate Brianna's daze. *Dear God, how long was this cat-and-mouse game to continue?*

"Come here."

The words were low and full of menace, and Brianna felt utterly, hopelessly trapped. She did not posses the strength at that point to thwart him. But neither could she picture herself the victim of his lecherous pawing again. Her delicate features grew pale with apprehension, but her words were bold, belying her inner fear. "Nay, Breton. I will suffer no more abuse at your hands."

"And just how will you manage that, wench? You will do exactly as I say, or die for your defiance. Do you hear me?"

Why not let him put her out of her misery? Roland would never find her even if he had decided to pursue her—and that was doubtful at best. She stared at the man before her, indecision giving her pause.

"Once again, I say come hither!" He rose to tower over her.

Something snapped inside Brianna and, propelled by a force she did not understand, she rose from beside the hearth and slowly, reluctantly moved toward him.

She stopped a pace from him, impaled by the savage light in his dark eyes. "Now you will do exactly as I say, or you will be fair game for those eager Normans outside—and then, if you are still alive, I will slit your pretty throat."

As Brianna stood frozen before him, Abbess Marie's words of long-ago, carefree days returned with stunning clarity: *Pride and honor are for fools, child. Life! That is to be valued above all things in this miserable world. . . .*

CHAPTER 27

Brianna tried to free her mind of the bruising, ravaging kiss, and the way her naked breasts were crushed against the shaggy, bearlike chest. Her head ached, her limbs were weak, and the only reason she didn't collapse was that the Breton's powerful arms were around her waist and shoulders. *Merciful God, help me endure this . . . survive this—*

An earsplitting roar shattered the silence of the tiny room as the crude wooden door came crashing down into the cottage, torn completely off its leather hinges. Hugh of Brittany spun toward it, releasing Brianna toward the pallet so abruptly that she staggered back a few steps and lifted her eyes to the doorway, still half dazed from the blow to her temple.

Roland!

In the instant he took to assess the situation, Brianna's heart leapt with joy. His eyes shone almost black in the dim interior of the hovel, his drawn sword already crimson, his whole body poised for battle. His face immediately contorted from calm, deadly impassiveness to savage fury as his eyes swiftly took in the blood on her face, her shredded tunic.

"Take hold of your sword, Breton, for this night you will learn what happens to any who dare what you have."

Brianna's blood curdled at the lethal sound of his voice. But Hugh of Brittany reached for his heavy sword, which was propped up in its scabbard against the chinked wall. "So you have finally decided to face me fairly in a contest of skill, eh?"

342

"Nay, Breton—I have decided 'tis time to put you out of your misery."

Hugh of Brittany circled around the room warily, sizing up his opponent, weighing his chances for victory in what could only be a fight to the death. "You took what was mine at Hastings."

"Brianna belonged to no one—least of all you."

Hugh of Brittany thrust skillfully toward Roland's midsection after a feint to the left. Roland, just as unerringly, dodged, bringing his weapon around to knock the Breton's sword aside.

It was then that Brianna noticed two things that caused her heart to sink. There were clanking, thudding sounds from beyond the open door, indicating that although Roland had not come alone, the fighting was not yet over outside. Who would come to his aid if he should need it?

There was already a bright red stain on his left sleeve. He must have been hurt before entering the cottage, and Brianna did not like the way he was favoring his injured limb.

"Your brother had no right to—"

"He had *every* right to divert you from your devious purpose, Breton." Roland lunged swiftly as a striking panther. Hugh of Brittany had to jump backward to avoid being gored. In the cramped quarters, he hit the wall, causing a loose peg to fall and skitter across the floor. But Roland was undeterred. His storm-gray eyes fastened upon the Breton intently. He thrust again, forcing his opponent to defend himself with his back to the wall. Sword to sword, man to man, they stood stalemated, both straining in the wavering firelight to overcome the other.

Only the crackle of the fire and the rasp of their breathing could be heard in the room. Brianna bit her fist to keep from crying out; the cloth over Roland's left thigh was turning dark with blood. His newly formed scar had split with the strain and swift movement of the struggle. How much longer could he continue before weakening from blood loss?

Hugh of Brittany ended the impasse with a mighty shove.

It sent Roland leaping over the low hearth to avoid being singed. Brianna could see beads of sweat glimmering on his forehead.

Dane suddenly appeared at the door, sword in hand, and Brianna silently implored him to help Roland. As he stepped into the room, Roland saw him out of the corner of his eye. "Leave him! He's *mine*."

Dane complied reluctantly but signaled for Brianna to move around the periphery of the room toward him. She shook her head emphatically, and Dane got the silent but impassioned message. She would not leave Roland, even though she was in imminent danger herself.

Hugh of Brittany, making the best of Roland's apparent weakening, launched himself from his position against the wall. He attacked furiously, sparks flying from the clashing steel weapons. Roland stood his ground parrying the Breton's thrusts and riposting with undeniable expertise. The last spectacular retreat across the cottage, however, had cost him dearly. His desperate efforts to put his adversary on the defensive was unsuccessful.

Sweat trickled down Roland's face. Brianna trembled with fear for him. *Please God*, she silently pleaded, *give him the strength he needs!* Her fists were clenched so tightly in her agitation that the fingernails punctured the skin and drew blood.

Without warning, Hugh of Brittany trod on the wooden peg lying on the floor and awkwardly skidded toward the fire. In an effort to avoid the hot flames he twisted to the side, providing Roland with an open shot at his chest.

Roland took advantage of the opportunity and managed to slice across the Breton's naked breast. The blade did not penetrate deeply enough to do much but enrage him. In a reckless attack he drove the debilitated knight toward the corner where Brianna was flattened against the wall.

"Now I shall skewer you before your precious Brianna!" he rasped. Disengaging Roland's sword from his own, he put all his skill and strength into a swift, horizontal slice aimed at Roland's neck, gripping the sword hilt firmly with both hands, forgetting his injury until it was too late. He grimaced slightly at the sharp pain, yet he continued the lethal swing, knowing he could not stop.

But Roland caught his split-second hesitation—the infinitesimal pause that threw off the lightninglike stroke. It was enough to allow the exhausted knight to duck in one last, swift spurt of energy and dodge the murderous blade. In the time it took the horrified Brianna to draw breath, Roland's own sword plunged upward. It pierced the Breton's massive chest, shattering the rib cage and penetrating his heart. A look of surprise froze across his features forever, and Hugh of Brittany slowly sank to the floor. Brianna stared at his unmoving body for long moments, unable to believe it was over so quickly. Then she looked toward Roland, relief washing over her in a wave.

He was leaning on his upended weapon, profound weariness slumping his shoulders.

"Are you much hurt, Brianna?" Dane's voice broke the sudden silence as he came to her side. Roland turned toward her, awaiting her answer, intense gray eyes on her pale countenance.

"Nay, Dane," she replied shakily. "Only a cut to the brow, no more."

He hugged her to him. "Thank God."

"He could have killed you." Roland's words were soft, thoughtful, tinged with self-reproach. Then he straightened. "We will see you to London. There will be no question of your going alone." And he limped from the room.

Brianna made to follow him, but Dane held her back. "But his wounds need tending!" she protested.

"He needs to think, Brianna, to pull himself together."

"But *why?*"

Dane walked her over to the chair Hugh of Brittany had recently occupied and gently pushed her into it. Clutching the remnants of Brand's tunic together, she stared up at him, the question still between them.

"Roland discovered who the informant was earlier this eve. Ranulf told him."

"And he is ashamed of his behavior toward me? Is that it, Dane?"

The dark-haired knight shook his head. "Only partly, Brianna. You must understand that Roland has always prided himself on his good judgment. But this error was rash and made with his heart, not his head."

"But I *love* him! I am willing to forgive him anything, Dane—anything!"

He smiled gently and pushed a tangled lock of hair back from her face. "I know you are, *petite,* but there is something else eating at him, I suspect, with which he must deal himself."

But Brianna was insistent. "What else could possibly affect him so?"

Dane pursed his lips thoughtfully. "Knowing Roland as I do, I would say he feels he has just let you down again." At Brianna's bemused expression, he continued. "Roland is highly skilled with a sword but gave a poor showing just now—for him."

"But he was losing blood from two wounds. He could hardly stand—you saw him leaning on his sword." Her exquisite mouth tightened in anger. "The important thing is that he did win, no matter how." She stood in sudden decision.

"Where are you going?"

"To tell Roland I care naught for his ridiculous pride and honor!"

Dane's hand firmly clamped onto her wrist. "Listen to me, Brianna," he entreated. "Roland was prepared to ask your forgiveness for doubting your word and treating you as a traitress. But now I think he feels he's added to his burden of guilt. He must forgive himself first for almost letting you down again. Give him some time, *petite.*"

In her frustration and confusion, Brianna's expression turned mutinous. "How long must I remain docile, awaiting his decisions? What of *my* feelings? *My* needs?" She sat down in agitation.

"Brianna?"

Brianna looked toward the door. "Walter!"

He came toward her hesitantly, sporting several bruises on his face and a torn tunic. "Did he . . . hurt you, Brianna?"

"Nay, Walter. But what do you here?" she asked quizzically, as if he were the last person she had expected to see.

His eyes went to her half-covered bosom and he reddened, looking hastily back to her face. "I followed you, Brianna, from Derford."

"He led us here, Brianna. If it weren't for Walter, we would never have found you." The approval and gratitude in Dane's voice more than made up for the disdainful manner in which he had treated the youth on the road.

Walter beamed under the warm praise, but just as quickly a frown crossed his features. " 'Twas the least I could do for Brianna, my lord. I had sorely wronged her."

"Speak of it no more, Walter. 'Tis over and done with." Her lips curved upward in a wan smile, but her eyes, bewilderment and pain in their sea-blue depths, were on the doorway.

Brianna stepped out into the night, her eyes squinting against the darkness. The same luminous moon that had guided her toward London hung in the velvet black tapestry of the heavens, aiding her in her search.

He sat propped against a decaying stump at the perimeter of the clearing, his face turned toward the sky in contemplation. The smell of death permeated the heavy night air, but he appeared oblivious to it.

Silently she wended her way toward him, sidestepping two of the bodies sprawled motionless on the ground. "Roland?"

The bright moonlight allowed her to see the instant tensing

of his body in acknowledgment of her query. Yet he remained motionless, with only his upturned profile meeting her searching gaze, a muscle twitching in the cheek turned to her hinting of the inner battle he was waging.

He needs time, Dane had told her.

She dropped to her knees beside him, a trace of renewed anger sifting through her at his withdrawal. Hadn't there been enough misunderstandings? She sighed and tried again, her voice husky with emotion as she decided to have done with begging. "Your wounds, Roland—let me see to them." And as she reached for the arm that lay limply across his lap, he turned his face to her.

"Dane can see to my hurts, Brianna." The shadowed hollows and ridges of his beautifully chiseled countenance were accented by the play of moonlight, but the expression in the eyes she loved so well was impossible to discern. Brianna unexpectedly thought of a bizarre mask with fathomless black holes where the eyes should have been.

She rose slowly, the sobering truth hitting her. Dane was mistaken. Whatever he had learned earlier that evening had done nothing to absolve her in Roland's eyes.

Bitter disappointment, frustration and despair gathered in a lump at the back of her throat, almost choking her. "So be it, Norman," she managed. "I will go to London to find the man I believe to be my real father, William D'Avranches. Then I will return with him to Normandy, if he will have me, and you can be damned!"

But when she swung around, tears burned the back of her eyes and gathered so swiftly that she stumbled, half blinded, over a grotesquely positioned dead Norman in her haste to get away from Roland. Off balance, she was pitched to her knees and caught herself with her palms against the hard earth. And as she drew a deep breath, the distinctively metallic stench of blood—and death—brought back memories of another time when she had fallen to the gore-saturated earth with the same unnerving presence of this man behind her, and her loss was all the more brutally brought home.

"Do not flee from me, *ma chère*."

The voice was husky, intense. The words floated through the stillness of the night to reach out and envelope her like a caress, to disarm and immobilize her as nothing else could. Brianna marshaled her wits enough to push herself away from the ground and to her feet.

She shook her head wildly. "Nay!" It was a whisper. "Go away!"

She started to run forward blindly, tears slipping down her flushed cheeks unchecked. But his hand on her arm stopped her. "Please, my own Brianna, hear me out—"

That voice. It had the power to make her blood sing through her veins, to send a thousand tingling sensations through her finely tuned body. Just as his flesh against hers could make her forget all her intentions . . .

He turned her around before him and dropped his hands from her shoulders. In the ghostly incandescence playing about the sculptured planes and angles of his face, it seemed to Brianna that his features bore a thin veneer of contrition, which poorly concealed his underlying confidence. "You cannot continue to play games with my feelings, Roland," she cried angrily. "What can you possibly have to say? I tried everything to restore your faith in me and I would have tried equally to soothe your pride, but 'twas all so flagrantly disregarded as if it never was of any import!"

The dark gray eyes clung to hers with a tenacity and a force of their own which would not allow hers to drop, and Brianna was helpless before his firm resolve as she had been so many times in the past.

"I implore you, Brianna, let me try to make amends for the unspeakable wrongs I've done you." His voice made love to her, tenderly, sweetly, yet the words held a vague note of uncertainty, as if for once the self-assured Norman knight were not in control of the circumstances, and that hint of doubt caught at her heart. But it was too late.

"You . . . you cannot do this to me!" His chiseled face became a blur in the moonlight as her tears once more gave vent to her sorrow and pain. "When I would have stanched the bleeding of your spirit as well as that from your physical wounds, you rejected me once again because of some . . . some absurd point of honor." She drew a ragged breath. "And now you try to lure me with your words of assurance? Nay!" She turned her back to him then, tearing her gaze from his countenance lest her resolve weaken.

But his hands caught her shoulders and he pulled her up against him, holding her firmly, his lips at her ear.

"You have no right," she cried softly. "Unhand me!"

"Never, Brianna! If you leave I will follow you wherever you go, do you understand? England be damned. I will have naught but my burning desire, my profound love for you. Lands, titles, wealth—they all mean nothing if I cannot have the treasure for which I was prepared to search the whole of England." He turned her around and stared down at her, his eyes brimming with emotion. "I will spend every waking moment of my life making it up to you, Brianna. You must believe that if you believe nothing else."

She pulled away from his grasp and gazed up at him, suddenly silent except for the soft sobs that punctuated her breathing. Her stillness gave him hope, spurred him on. "I was twice a fool where you were concerned, but no more. I had no right to accuse you of treachery, Brianna, and I had even less right to shut you out while I nursed my self-pity. It has never been my wont, and I swear by all that is holy that you will never witness such behavior in me again." He wiped away her tears, his touch so infinitely tender that Brianna felt a fresh wave threaten. "Do you think, my dearest love, that I pursued you so ardently, so desperately, only to lose you because of some misguided sense of betrayal? Do not condemn me to follow in your wake until I die, a pale shadow, an empty husk of a man.''

These last words were so eloquently impassioned, their underlying tremor revealing their profound effect upon their speaker, that Brianna felt her love for him flow forth like some warm, soothing balm to overwhelm and expunge every doubt, every fear, every hurt. ''Roland,'' she whispered brokenly.

He crushed her to him with his good arm, taking the very breath from her body. ''Surely no man has ever loved as I do,'' he murmured into her hair. ''Forgive me.'' And then his fingers lifted her chin, and his mouth descended to meet hers.

EPILOGUE

"My lord, the King is here!"

Roland turned toward Roger, an eyebrow arched in silent query. He had just finished dressing and was about to descend for the evening meal.

"Tell the servants to prepare accommodations for my lord and his retinue, Roger." Roger nodded and quickly disappeared down the corridor.

"What is amiss, Roland? Have they found Hilde?"

His eyes met Brianna's as she took Roger's place in the doorway of his bedchamber. "Not yet, *chérie*. 'Twould seem we have a visitor, and a royal one at that."

He moved forward, and Brianna noticed he wore the same scarlet overtunic he had worn on the day the people of Derford had sworn fealty to him. He had never looked more devastatingly handsome than now, despite the fact that he was a trifle pale. Wine and the warmth of the evening had done little to put color back into his face. "I would not doubt that William d'Avranches accompanies him, Brianna. If you remember, he was invited to our wedding."

Her eyes widened, and then she lifted her face to receive the warm touch of his lips. "You two have much to discuss," he added at last as he reluctantly withdrew his mouth from hers and guided her toward the stairway and the hall below.

Twilight was descending and the golden glow from the lowering sun encompassed the two figures standing in the doorway of the manor hall as William I of England rode through the palisade gate, his standard-bearer before him, a party of armed Normans surrounding him and a knight in full mail abreast of him.

The King dismounted and strode up to Roland, but William d'Avranches sat his horse a moment longer. He removed his helm and placed it under his arm, gazing at Brianna, a silent question—or was it a statement she had never noticed before?—in the golden-brown eyes.

Dane came up behind them and placed a hand on Brianna's shoulder. "Father!" he exclaimed as his gaze went beyond her, and Brianna's pulse quickened at the sound of that one word.

She gave William a brilliant smile, her eyes shimmering with tears of joy at the answer she found in his moving gaze. His lips silently formed her name, but William of England was speaking.

"We missed the wedding, I take it?"

Roland shook his head after greeting the King. "We are awaiting Ranulf's recovery, my lord King."

William raised a quizzical eyebrow as he eyed Roland's slightly pale countenance and the linen bandage bulging beneath his chainse sleeve. "And what of you, Roland? What befell *you?*"

Roland shrugged and looked down at the lovely girl beside him. "Hugh of Brittany."

William's dark, thick brows drew together in a frown. "He was to have left England a fortnight ago. You killed him?" At Roland's affirmative nod, his dark eyes went to Brianna.

"This is Brianna, my lord," interjected William d'Avranches.

"Ah, yes, Brianna. You came to Hastings in search of your husband." He glanced at the older knight and then back to Brianna, but Roland came to her rescue by turning to usher the King and his retinue into the hall and promptly issuing orders to the scurrying servants.

Despite the unexpectedness of the King's arrival, there was

plenty of food for William of England and his entourage. Joints of pork and mutton, juicy pheasants, grilled fish, vegetables, cheese and crusty bread filled trenchers up and down the length of the trestle tables. The tantalizing aroma of food permeated every corner of the cavernous hall and mingled with the smell of sweating bodies, and the noise of men enjoying the de Beaufort hospitality and one another's company.

At Ranulf's insistence—and against Abbess Marie's better judgment—he was carried downstairs on a pallet to join in the merrymaking.

Far into the night, Roland stood beside Brianna on the porch of the manor, staring out into the night, his hand over hers. William d'Avranches came up behind them. "May I have a moment alone with Brianna, Roland?"

"Of course, my lord." And he brushed a kiss across her sweet brow before leaving them.

The muted noise from the hall, the sounds of the night and the soft sibilance of the resinous flambeaux at either side of the entrance all melded into a soothing, intimate background for the knight's next words. "I never suspected I had a child by Alicia, my dearest Brianna." His voice was suddenly fraught with emotion. "Robert whisked her off to one of his manors in Wessex. I had truly given up hope, for, after all, Alicia was wed to Robert and I had no legitimate claim on her. If she did not come to me willingly, there was naught I could do.

"But when Dane told me about you and then I saw you for myself, I wanted—against all odds—to believe you were my daughter, but I could not presume to make so bold a declaration with no proof and in the face of your hatred of Normans."

"Oh, my lord—Father," she whispered as her eyes met his. "Dane and I have always felt a sense of . . . of kinship, and when I met you—" She paused, emotion freezing the words in her throat.

"I know," he said softly, taking her in his arms and resting his chin on her head as he stared out into the peaceful night.

Alicia was finally laid to rest.

"My lord—Brianna?" came Roland's voice, born on the benign evening breeze. Both figures turned toward his imposing form, limned by the light from the hall. "The King would like to hear Brianna sing. Would you so honor him, *chérie?*"

He moved aside as Brianna nodded her assent and stepped into the hall, one arm linked with her father's. A tremor of unease ran through her at the thought of what she must do for the man who had subjugated her people. But then Roland was walking beside her, drawing her free arm through his and smiling reassuringly down into her eyes. "After all, my love, we must show him we can equal anything Normandy has to offer, mustn't we?"

A slow, sweet movement of her lips lit her features with the animated perfection of her smile as, glancing from one man to the other, she took up the challenge. "Indeed, my lord, we must."

Authors of exceptional promise...

THE AVON ROMANCE

Historical novels of superior quality!

CROSSWINDS Nancy Moulton
89591-9/$2.95 US/$3.75Can

A tumultuous pre-Civil War saga of deceit, jealousy and passion.

Also by Nancy Moulton

DEFIANT DESTINY 81430-7/$2.95

CALL BACK THE DAWN
Diane Wicker Davis 89703-2/$2.95US/$3.95Can

To save her family's plantation from ruin, a beautiful young woman agrees to marry the mysterious gambler who had won her land...and now wants her heart.

MOONSPELL Linda Ladd
89639-7/$2.95US/$3.95Can

During the reign of King William, a pale Irish beauty hides behind a mask to play a clever game of deception.

Also by Linda Ladd

WILDSTAR 87171-8/$2.95US/$3.95Can

Each month enjoy the best...

THE AVON ROMANCE

in exceptional authors and unforgettable novels!

TYLER'S WOMAN   Linda P. Sandifer
89792-X/$3.50US/$4.50 Can

In Texas in the 1860s a beautiful heiress to a cattle fortune challenges a vengeance-driven man to regain his heart...and her happiness.

THE WILD ROSE   René J. Garrod
89784-9/$3.50US/$4.50 Can

Alone amid the ruthlessness of the California Gold Rush, a plucky English beauty is powerless to resist the one love she dares not take.

HEART OF THE STORM   Jillian Hunter
89956-6/$3.50US/$4.50 Can

Forced to marry, this tempestuous saga charts the course of two lovers consumed with conflicting desires.

SHADOW OF DESIRE   Fela Dawson Scott
89981-7/$3.50US/$4.50 Can

A beautiful renegade—driven by vengeance—vowed to trust no man...until she met the one nobleman that could tame her defiant heart.